TEATIME
for the
FIREFLY

TEATIME
for the
FIREFLY

SHONA PATEL

HARLEQUIN® MIRA®

Recycling programs
for this product may
not exist in your area.

ISBN-13: 978-0-7783-1547-6

TEATIME FOR THE FIREFLY

For questions and comments about the quality of this book, please contact us at CustomerService@Harlequin.com.

Printed in U.S.A.

First printing: October 2013
10 9 8 7 6 5 4 3 2 1

To the pioneer tea planters of Assam, "the iron men in wooden ships," who gave their lives to grow the finest tea in the world.

And to the memory of my parents, Leela and Paresh Nag.

"Early in the day it was whispered that we should set sail in a boat, only thou and I, and never a soul in the world would know of this our pilgrimage to no country and to no end."

Rabindranath Tagore
From *Gitanjali*

CHAPTER

1

My name is Layla and I was born under an unlucky star. The time and place of my birth makes me a *Manglik*. For a young girl growing up in India in the 1940s, this is bad news. The planet Mars is predominant in my Hindu horoscope and this angry red planet makes people rebellious and militant by nature. Everyone knows I am astrologically doomed and fated never to marry. Marriages in our society are arranged by astrology and nobody wants a warlike bride. Women are meant to be the needle that stitches families together, not the scissors that cut.

But everything began to change for me on April 7, 1943.

Three things happened that day: Boris Ivanov, the famous Russian novelist, slipped on a tuberose at the grand opening ceremony of a new school, fell and broke his leg; a baby crow fell out of its nest in the mango tree; and I, Layla Roy, aged seventeen, fell in love with Manik Deb.

The incidents may have remained unconnected, like three tiny droplets on a lily leaf. But the leaf tipped and the drops rolled into one. It was a tiny shift in the cosmos, I believe, that tipped us together—Boris Ivanov, the baby crow, Manik Deb and me.

It was the inauguration day of the new school: a rainy-sunshine day, I remember well, delicate and ephemeral—the kind locals here in Assam call "jackal wedding days." I am not sure where the saying comes from, or whether it means good luck or bad, or perhaps a little bit of both. It would seem as though the sky could not decide whether to bless or bemoan the occasion—quite ironic, if you think about it, because that is exactly how some people felt about the new English girls' school opening in our town.

The demonstrators, on the other hand, were pretty much set in their views. They gathered outside the school gates in their patriotic white clothes, carrying banners with misspelled English slogans like: INDIA FOR INDANS and STOP ENGLIS EDUCATON NOW.

Earlier that morning, my grandfather, Dadamoshai, the founder of the girls' school, had chased the demonstrators down the road with his large, formidable umbrella. They had scattered like cockroaches and sought refuge behind the holy banyan tree.

"Retarded donkeys! Imbeciles!" Dadamoshai yelled, shaking his umbrella at the sky. "Learn to spell before you go around demonstrating your nitwit ideas!"

Dadamoshai was an advocate of English education, and nothing irked him more than the massacre of the English language. The demonstrators knew better than to challenge him. They were just rabble-rousers anyway, stuffed with half-baked ideas by local politicians who knew what to rail against, but not what to fight for. Nobody wanted to butt heads with Dadamoshai. He had once been the most powerful District Judge in the state of Assam. With his mane of flowing hair, his long sure stride and deep oratorical voice, he was an imposing figure in our town, and people respectfully stepped aside when they saw him coming. To most people he was known simply as the Rai Bahadur, an honorary title bestowed on him by the British for his service to the crown. There was even a road named after him: the Rai Bahadur Road. It's a very famous road in our town and anybody can direct you there, yet it appears unnamed on municipal maps because it does not lead to any place and dead-ends in a river over which there is no bridge. The Rai Bahadur Road is just that: a beginning and an end unto itself.

When I arrived at the school that morning, the demonstrators were a sorry lot. It had rained some more and the cheap ink from their banners had run, staining their white clothes. What was even sadder was that somebody had tried to hand-correct the spellings with a blue fountain pen. Somewhere down the line, they had simply lost heart. They sat listlessly on their haunches and smoked cigarettes while their limp banners flopped against the wall.

One of them nudged the other when he saw me coming. I heard him say, "It's her, look—the Rai Bahadur's granddaughter!"

I must have rekindled their patriotism because they grabbed their banners and blocked my entrance to the school. "No English! India for Indians! No English!" they shouted.

I was wondering how to get past them when I remembered something Dadamoshai once told me: *Use your mind, Layla— it is the most powerful weapon you have.* I continued to walk toward them and pointed my mind like a sword. It worked: they parted to let me through. The gate shut behind me, and I continued down the graveled driveway to the new school building. It was an L-shaped structure, freshly whitewashed, with a large unpaved playground and three tamarind trees. Piles of construction debris lay pushed to one side.

The voices of young girls chirruped on the veranda. Students aged nine or ten sat cross-legged on the floor, stringing together garlands of marigold and tuberose to decorate the stage for the inauguration ceremony.

"Layla!" Miss Rose called out from a classroom as I walked past. I peeked through the door. Rose Cabral was sitting at the teacher's desk, sorting through a pile of printed programs. There was a large world map tacked to the back wall and the room smelled overwhelmingly of varnish. Miss Rose, as she was called, was a young Anglo-Indian teacher with chestnut brown hair and pink cat's-eye glasses with diamond accents. The small fry of the school swooned with adoration for her and wanted to lick her like a lollipop.

Miss Rose was about to say something when she sneezed daintily. "Oh dear," she said, wiping her nose on a pink handkerchief edged with tatting lace. "I don't know if it's the varnish or this fickle weather. Layla, oh my! How you have grown! What a lovely young woman you are. Are you still being privately tutored by Miss Thompson, dear?"

"No, not any longer, Miss Rose," I said. "I passed my matriculation last year."

"So you must be all ready to get married now, eh? Suitors will be lining up outside your door."

"Oh no—no, I don't plan to get married," I said quickly. "I want to become a teacher, actually." I did not tell Miss Rose that marriage was not in my cards. It would be hard to explain to her why being born under a certain ill-fated star could negate your chances of finding a husband.

A tiny, round-shouldered girl with thick braids appeared in the doorway, pigeon-toed and fidgeting.

"Yes, what is it, Malika?" Miss Rose said.

"Miss...miss..."

"Speak up, child."

"We have no more white flowers, Miss Rose."

"The tuberose? I thought we had plenty. All right, I am coming." Miss Rose sighed, bunching up her papers. "I better go and see what's going on. Oh, Layla, there's a packet of rice powder for you lying on the secretary's desk in the principal's office. I suppose you know what it is for?"

"It's for the *alpana* I am painting in the entryway," I said. Miss Rose looked blank, so I explained. "You know, the white designs—" I made curlicue shapes in the air "—the kind you see painted on the floor at Indian weddings and religious ceremonies?"

"Ah yes. They are so intricate. Boris Ivanov will like that. He loves Indian art. I hope you have brought your brushes or whatever you need, Layla. We don't have anything here, you know."

"I don't need any brushes," I said. "I just use my fingers and a cotton swab. I have that. Miss Rose, is my grandfather still here?"

"The Rai Bahadur left for the courthouse an hour ago. He said to tell you he will be home for lunch. Boris Ivanov's train is running three hours late. Let me know if you need anything, Layla. I am here all afternoon."

It was close to lunchtime when I got the *alpana* done, so instead of going to the library as I had planned, I went home. Dadamoshai's house was a fifteen-minute walk from the school. I passed the holy banyan tree and saw that the protestors had abandoned their wilted banners behind it. The tree was over two hundred years old, massive and gnarled, with thick roots that hung down from the branches like the dread-locks of demons. In its hollowed root base was a collection of faded gods surrounded by tired marigold garlands. I walked past the stench of the fish market, the idling rickshaws at the bus stand and the three crooked tea stalls that supported one another like drunken brothers, till I came to a four-way cross-ing where I turned right on to the Rai Bahadur Road.

It was an impressive road, man-made and purposeful: not like the fickle pathways in town, that changed directions with the rain and got bullied by groundcover. The road to my grandfather's house was wide and tree-lined, with *Gulmohor* Flame Trees planted at regular intervals: exactly thirty feet apart. Their leafy branches crisscrossed overhead to form a magnificent latticed archway. On summer days the road was flecked with gold, and spring breezes showered down a torrent of vermilion petals that swirled and trembled in the dust like wounded butterflies. Rice fields on either side intersected in quilted patches of green to fade into the shimmering haze of the bamboo grove. Up ahead, the river winked over the tall embankment where fishing nets lay drying on bamboo poles silhouetted against the noonday sun.

I adjusted my eyes. Was that a man standing under the mango tree by our front gate? It was indeed. Even at that dis-tance, I could tell he was a foreigner, just by his stance. His legs planted wide, shoulders thrown back, he had that ease of body some foreigners have. I was curious. What was he doing? His hands were folded together and he was gazing up at the branches with what appeared to be deep piety. Oddly enough, it looked as though the foreigner was praying to the mango tree!

The man heard me coming and glanced briefly in my di-rection. He must have expected me to walk on by, but when

I stopped at our gate, he looked at me curiously. He was a disconcertingly attractive man in a poetic kind of way, with long, finger-raked hair and dark and steady eyes behind black-framed glasses. A slow smile wavered and tugged at the corners of his mouth.

When I saw what he was holding in his cupped hands, I realized I had misjudged his piety. It was a baby crow.

"Do you live in the Rai Bahadur's house?" he asked pleasantly. He spoke impeccable Bengali, with no trace of a foreign accent. I figured he must be an Indian who probably lived abroad.

"Yes," I said.

The man was obviously unschooled in the nuances of our society, because he stared at me candidly with none of the calculated deference and awkwardness of Indian men. I could feel my ears burning.

The crow chick struggled feebly in his hand. It stretched out a scrawny neck and opened its yellow-rimmed beak, exposing a pink, diamond-shaped mouth. It was bald except for a light gray fuzz over the top of its head. Its blue eyelids stretched gossamer thin over yet unopened eyes.

"We have a displaced youngster," the man said, glancing at the chick. "Any idea what kind of bird this is?"

"It's a baby crow," I replied, marveling how gently he held the tiny creature. It had nodded off to sleep, resting its yellow beak against his thumb. He had nicely shaped fingernails, I noticed.

I pointed up at the branches. "There's a nest up that mango tree."

He was not looking at the tree, but at my hand. "What's that?" he asked suddenly.

"Where?" I jerked back my hand and saw I had traces of

the white rice paste still ringed around my fingernails. "Oh," I said, curling my fingers into a ball, "that's...that's just from the *alpana* decoration I was doing at the school."

"Are you related to the Rai Bahadur?"

"He is my grandfather."

"Is this the famous English girls' school everybody is talking about? What is the special occasion?"

"Today is the grand opening," I said. "A Russian dignitary is coming to cut the ribbon."

"Boris Ivanov?" he asked.

I stared at him. "How did you know?"

"There are not many Russians floating around this tiny town in Assam, are there? I happen to be well acquainted with Ivanov."

I wanted to ask more, but refrained.

He tilted his head, squinting up at the branches, then pushed his sliding glasses back up his nose with his arm. The chick woke up with a sharp cheep that startled us both. "Ah, I see the nest. Maybe I should try and put this little fellow back," he said.

"You are going to climb the mango tree?" I asked a little incredulously. The man looked too civilized to climb trees. His shirt was too white and he wore city shoes.

"It looks easy enough." He looked up and down the branches as though he was calculating his foothold. He grinned suddenly, a deep crease softening the side of his face. "If I fall, you can laugh and tell all your friends."

I had no friends, but I did not tell him that.

"There's not much point, really." I hesitated, wondering how I was going to say this without sounding too heartless. "You see, this is very common. Baby crows get pushed out of that nest every year by..." I moved closer to the tree, shaded my eyes and looked up, then gestured him over. "See that other chick? Stand right where I am standing. Can you see it?"

We were standing so close his shirtsleeve brushed my arm. I could smell the starch mingled with faint sweat and a hint of tobacco. My head reeled slightly.

He tilted his head. "Ah yes, I see the sibling," he said.

"That's not a sibling—it's a baby koel."

His face drew a blank.

"The Indian cuckoo. Don't you know anything about koels?"

"I am afraid not," he said, looking bemused. "But I beg to be educated. Before that, I need to put our friend down someplace. I am getting rather tired of holding him." He looked around, then walked over to the garden wall and set the baby crow down on the ground. It belly-waddled into a shady patch and stretched out its scrawny neck, cheeping plaintively.

I was about to speak when a cloud broke open and a sheet of golden rain shimmered down. We both hurried under the mango tree. There we were all huddled cozily together—the man, the chick and me.

A cycle rickshaw clattered down the road. It was fat Mrs. Ghosh, squeezed in among baskets and bundles, on her way home from the fish market. She looked at us curiously, her eyes bulging slightly, perhaps wondering to herself: *Am I seeing things? Is that the Rai Bahadur's granddaughter with a young man under the mango tree?* This was going to be big news, I could tell, because everybody in town knew that the Rai Bahadur's granddaughter avoided the opposite sex like a Hindu avoids beef.

The cloud passed and the sun winked back and I hurried out from under the tree. To cover up my embarrassment, I launched into an involved lecture on the nesting habits of koels and crows.

"The koel, or Indian cuckoo, is a brood parasite," I said. "A bird that lays its egg in the nest of another. Like that crow's nest up there." I pointed upward with my right hand and then, remembering my dirty fingernails, switched to my left hand. "See how sturdy the nest is? Crows are really clever engineers. They pick the perfect intersections of branches and build the nest with strong twigs. They live in that same nest for years and years."

"Are their marriages as stable as their nests?" The man winked, teasing me. "Do they last as long?"

"That...that I don't know," I said, twisting the end of my sari. I wished he would not look at me like that.

"I am only teasing you. Oh, please go on."

I took a deep breath and tried to collect myself. "The koel is a genetically aggressive bird. When it hatches, it pushes the baby crows out from the nest, eats voraciously and becomes big and strong. Then it flies off singing into the trees. The poor crows are so baffled."

The man smiled as he pushed around a pebble with the toe of his shoe. He wore nicely polished brown shoes of expensive leather with small, diamond-shaped, pinpricked patterns.

"And what do the koels do, having shamelessly foisted their offspring onto another?" he asked, quirking an eyebrow.

"Ah, koels are very romantic birds," I said. "They sing and flirt in flowering branches all summer long, with not a care in the world."

"How irresponsible!"

"Well, it depends how you look at it," I said, watching him carefully. "Koels sing and bring joy to the whole world. In some ways they serve a greater good, don't you think? And getting the crows to raise their chicks is actually quite brilliant."

"How is that?" he asked, looking at me curiously.

"Well, not all creatures are cut out for domesticity. Some make better parents than others. The chick grows up to be healthy and independent. In many ways, the koels are giving their offspring the best shot at life."

"That's an interesting theory," he said thoughtfully.

He sighed and turned his attention to the baby crow. It lay completely still, breathing laboriously, its flaccid belly distended to one side, beak slightly open. He squatted down and nudged it gently with his forefinger. The chick struggled feebly, opened its mouth and uttered a tiny cheep.

"It's still alive," he said dispassionately. "So what do you suggest we do? We can't just leave it here to die, can we?"

I shrugged. "It's the cat's lunch."

He looked at me in a playful sort of way. "Please don't say you are always so cruel," he said softly.

I turned and looked out at the distant rice fields, where a flock of white cranes was circling to land. "I used to try and save baby crows all the time when I was a child," I said. "But Dadamoshai said I was interfering with nature. He thinks we need more songbirds and fewer scavengers."

The man stood up and dusted his hands, and then smiled broadly. "I just realized we've had a long and involved discussion and I don't even know your name!"

"Layla."

"Lay-la," he repeated softly, stretching out my name like a caress. "I'm Manik Deb. Big admirer of the Rai Bahadur. Actually, I just dropped by the house and left him a note on the coffee table. Will you please see he gets it?"

"I will do that."

"Goodbye, Layla," Manik said. "And thank you for the lesson on ornithology. It was most enlightening."

With that, he turned and walked off down the road toward

the river. A thin sheet of golden rain followed Manik Deb, but
he did not turn around to see it chasing behind him.

On the veranda coffee table there was a crushed cigarette
stub and a used matchstick in the turtle-shaped brass ashtray.
Tucked under the ashtray was a note folded in half, written on
the bottom portion of a letterhead that Manik Deb had borrowed from Dadamoshai's desk. The note was addressed to my
grandfather, penned in an elegant, slanted hand:

7th April 1943
Dear Rai Bahadur,
*I took a chance and dropped by. I am trying to contact Boris
Ivanov and I understand that he is staying with you. Could you
please tell him that I would like to meet with him? He knows
where to get in touch with me.*
Sincerely,
Manik Deb

I took the folded note and placed it on my grandfather's desk
on top of his daily mail. That way he would see it first thing
when he got home.

Later that day, at lunch, I watched my grandfather carefully as he sat across from me. Had he read the note? Who
was Manik Deb?

Dadamoshai took his mealtimes very seriously. He always
sat very prim and straight at the dining table, as if he was a
distinguished guest at the Queen's formal banquet. Most days
he and I ate alone. We sat across from each other at the long,
mahogany dining table designed for twelve. All the formal
dining chairs were gone except four. The others lay scattered
about in the veranda, marked with tea stains, their rich bro-

cade fading in the sun. My grandfather had a constant stream of visitors whom he received mostly in the veranda, and it was often that we ran out of chairs.

Dadamoshai had just bathed and smelled of bittersweet neem soap. His usual flyaway hair was neatly combed back from his tall forehead, the comb marks visible like a rake pulled through snow. He was dressed in his home clothes: a crisp white kurta and checkered *lungi*, a pair of rustic clogs on his feet. His Gandhi-style glasses lay folded neatly by his plate. His bushy brows were furrowed as he deboned a piece of *hilsa* fish on his plate with the concentration of a microsurgeon. Unlike Indians who ate rice with their fingers, Dadamoshai always used a fork and spoon, a habit he had picked up from his England days. The dexterity with which he removed minuscule bones from Bengali curried fish without ever using his fingers was a feat worth watching.

"A man came by to see you this morning, Dadamoshai," I said nonchalantly, but I was overdoing it, I could tell. I helped myself to the rice and clattered noisily with the serving spoon.

Dadamoshai did not reply. I wondered if he had heard me.

"Ah yes," he said finally, "Manik Deb. Rhodes Scholar from Oxford and—" he paused to tap a hair-thin fish bone with his fork to the rim of his plate "—Bimal Sen's future son-in-law."

"He's Kona's…fiancé?" I was incredulous.

"Yes," said Dadamoshai, banging the saltshaker on the dining table. The salt had clumped with the humidity. He shook his head. "That Bimal Sen should think of educating his daughter instead of palming her off onto a husband. With money, you can buy an educated son-in-law, even a brilliant one like Manik Deb, but the fact remains, your daughter's head is going to remain empty as a green coconut."

I was feeling very disconcerted. Bimal Sen was the richest man in town. The family lived four houses down from us, in an ostentatious strawberry-pink mansion rumored to have three kitchens, four verandas with curving balustrades and a walled-in courtyard with half a dozen peacocks strutting in the yard. The Sens were a business family, very traditional and conservative. Kona was rarely seen alone in public. Her mother, Mrs. Sen, was built like a river barge and towed her daughter around like a tiny dinghy. I remembered Kona vaguely as a moonfaced girl with downcast eyes. I knew she had been engaged to be married since she was a child. It was an arranged match between the two families, but I had not expected her to marry the likes of Manik Deb. It was like pairing a stallion with a cow.

"Is he Bengali?" I finally asked. Had I known Manik Deb was Kona's fiancé, I would have avoided talking to him, let alone engaged in silly banter about koels and crows. My face flushed at the memory.

"Oh yes. He is a Sylheti like us," Dadamoshai said. "The Debs are a well-known family of Barisal. Landowners. I knew Manik's father from my Cambridge days. We passed our bar at the Lincoln's Inn together."

Barisal was Dadamoshai's ancestral village in Sylhet, East Bengal, across the big Padma River. The Sylhetis were evicted from their homeland in 1917. Once displaced, they became river people. Like the water hyacinth, their roots never touched the ground, but grew instead toward one another. Wherever they settled, they were a close-knit community. You could tell they were river people just by the way they called out to one another. It could be just across the fence in someone's backyard, but their voices carried that lonely sound that spanned vast waters. It was the voice of displacement and loss, the voice that sought to connect with a brother from a lost homeland—and the voice that led Dadamoshai to connect with Manik Deb's father in England.

"A most extraordinary young man, this Manik Deb," Dadamoshai was saying, helping himself to some rice.

"How so?" I asked. My appetite was gone, but my stomach gnawed with questions.

"What do you mean?"

"Well, what makes Manik Deb—like you say—so extraordinary?" I tried to feign noninterest, but my voice squeaked with curiosity. I absentmindedly shaped a hole in the mound of rice on my plate.

"He has an incisive, analytical mind, for one thing. Manik Deb has joined the civil service. His is the kind of brains we need for our new India."

Chaya, our housekeeper, had just entered the dining room with a bowl of curds. She was a slim woman with soft brown eyes and a disfiguring burn scar that fused the skin on the right side of her face like smooth molten wax. It was an acid burn. When Chaya was sixteen, she had fallen in love with a Muslim man. The Hindu villagers killed her lover, and then flung acid on her face to mark her as a social outcast. Dadamoshai had rescued Chaya from a violent mob and taken her into his custody. What followed was a lengthy and controversial court case. Several people went to jail.

Dadamoshai turned to address her. "Chaya, Boris Sahib will be having dinner with us tonight. Please remember to serve the good rice and prepare everything with less spice."

With that, Dadamoshai launched on a long discussion of menu items suitable for Boris Ivanov's meal, and Manik Deb was left floating, a bright pennant in the distant field of my memory.

CHAPTER

2

On the day of the school inauguration, Boris Ivanov donned a magnificent Indian kurta made of the finest Assamese *Mooga* silk, custom tailored to fit his six-foot-four, three-hundred-pound Bolshevik frame. He gave a rousing speech, and just as he was walking across the stage in his fancy mirror-work *nagra* slippers—which any Indian will tell you are notorious for their lack of traction—he inadvertently stepped on a fallen tuberose. His foot made a swiping arc up to the ceiling and the *nagra* took off like a flying duck. Boris Ivanov yelped out something that sounded suspiciously like "BLOOD!" I later understood he had yelled *"Blyad!"*—a Russian expletive—before landing with a thundering crash that sent quakes through the room. A horrified groan went up in the audience; small children shrieked, and in the middle of it all, I saw fat Mrs. Ghosh roll her eyes heavenward and whisper to her neighbor that this was *allokhi*—a very bad omen indeed. Just as well Dadamoshai did not hear her, because he would have flattened her out for good. My grandfather had very low tolerance for "village talk."

Boris Ivanov was forced to change his itinerary. He had planned to leave for Calcutta the next day to visit Rabindranath

Tagore's famous experimental school in Santineketan. Instead, with his leg cast in plaster, he moved into Dadamoshai's house as our guest and stayed with us for three whole weeks.

He accepted his fate cheerfully and slipped into our life with barely a ripple. He was a big, bushy man, bearded and baritone, who spent long hours reading and writing on the veranda with his plastered leg lying on the cane ottoman like a fallen tree trunk. Most afternoons he dozed in the plantation chair with the house cat draped over his stomach, his snores riffling the afternoon. He woke up to drink copious amounts of tea with four heaped spoons of sugar in each cup, blissfully unaware that it was wartime and sugar was in short supply. He spent the rest of the evening contemplating the universe.

The veranda was the most pleasant room in our house—open and airy, with soft filtered light creeping through the jasmine vines. Dadamoshai's big desk sat in one corner against the wall. On it were his piles of papers weighted down with river rocks and conch shells. His blue fountain pen sat snugly in its stand, right next to the chipped inkwell and a well-used blotter. There was a calendar with bird pictures on the wall, busy with notes and scribbles on the dated squares.

A door from the veranda led to Dadamoshai's study. It was packed from top to toe with books of all kinds: art, philosophy, religion, poetry and all the great works of literature. Here *The Communist Manifesto* leaned comfortably on Homer's *Odyssey*, and the *Bhagavad Gita* was wedged in by *Translations from the Koran*. Just as comfortably inside Dadamoshai's head lived his thoughts and ideas—separate skeins interwoven with the gentlest compassion and wisdom to form his rich philosophy and outlook on life.

Boris Ivanov was writing a treatise titled *Freedom and Responsibility*, a rather obtuse and philosophical work full of difficult arguments. He spent long hours debating ideas with Dada-moshai on the veranda. India was on the cusp of her independence after more than two hundred years of British rule. A great renaissance was sweeping through our nation and many social and educational reforms were under way.

Many people considered Dadamoshai a great scholar and independent thinker, but others saw him as a blatant anglophile and called him an English bootlicker. He was unabashedly Western in his dress and liberal in his thoughts. He lived frugally and thought deeply. He did not take siestas in the afternoon and cursed fluently in seven languages.

Dadamoshai believed that women were not given a fair chance in our society, largely due to their lack of education. Why were Indian boys sent to study at the finest universities abroad, he argued, while girls were treated like some flotsam washing in with the river tide?

Traditionalists accused Dadamoshai of rocking the social order and luring women away from their jobs as homemakers. What good would it do for women to bury their heads in math and science? Or, for that matter, to go around spouting Shakespeare? Pots and pans would grow cold in the kitchen and neglected children would run around the streets like pariah dogs.

In many ways, Dadamoshai saw me as the poster child for the modern Indian woman. He gave me the finest education and taught me to speak my mind. I was free to forge my own destiny. Sometimes I struggled to stay grounded like a lone river rock in a swirl of social pressures. But in truth, this was the only option I had.

Miss Thompson, my private English tutor, lived in a small primrose cottage behind the Sacred Heart Convent. A spry woman with animated eyes, she had about her a brisk energy that made you sit up and pull in your stomach. Her father, Reginald Thompson, the former District Magistrate of Assam, was Dadamoshai's predecessor and mentor. Dadamoshai had seen Miss Thompson grow up as a young girl.

I was Miss Thompson's first Indian student. Ever since I was seven, I took a rickshaw to her house three days a week. After my lessons, I would walk over to Dadamoshai's office in the old courthouse where I'd sit and do my homework, surrounded by the clatter of typewriters and the smell of carbon paper until it was time for us both to come home.

Miss Thompson was a stickler for pronunciation. She made sure I enunciated each word with bell-like clarity with the stress on the right syllable. I learned to say *what, where* and *why* accompanied by a small whoosh of breath I could feel on the palm of my hand held six inches from my face. It was Miss Thompson who instilled in me my love for literature. She encouraged me to plumb the depths of Greek tragedy, savor the fullness of Shakespeare, the lyrical beauty of Shelley. As I grew older, I saw less and less of her, until our meetings became just the occasional social visit. She had more Indian students now, she said, thanks to Dadamoshai's flourishing girls' school.

I decided to drop by and see her. She was usually home on Tuesday mornings, I knew. I arrived to find a rickshaw parked outside her gate and an elderly servant woman sitting on the porch. Miss Thompson must be with a student, I imagined. Young girls were never sent out unchaperoned in our society. Dadamoshai, on the other hand, always insisted I go everywhere alone. This raised a few eyebrows in our town. I was about to turn around and walk away when Martha, Miss Thompson's Anglo-Indian housekeeper of sixty years, called out to me from the kitchen window. She said Miss Thompson was indeed with a new student, but asked me to wait as the lesson was almost over.

I sat on the sofa in the drawing room. Through the slatted green shutters a guava tree waved its branch and somewhere a crow cawed mournfully. Nothing changed in Miss Thompson's house. Everything was exactly where it was the very first day I walked in ten years ago. The small upright piano with a tapestry-cushioned pivot stool, the glass-door walnut curio cabinet with its fine collection of Dresden figurines I knew so well, the scattering of peg tables topped with doilies of tatting lace. On the wall were faded sepia photographs of Reginald Thompson in his dark court robes, his pretty, fragile wife who'd died young and Miss Thompson and her sister as young girls riding ponies.

Voices trickled in through the closed door of the study. I heard a timid, female voice say something inaudible, followed by Miss Thompson.

"*Breeze.* Lengthen the *e* please and note the 'zee' sound. It is not *j*. It's *z. Zzzz.* Make a buzzing sound with your lips. Like a bee. Breezzzze. Breezzzze."

"Bre-eej," the girl repeated hesitantly.

I could just see Miss Thompson tapping the wooden ruler softly against her palm, a gesture she made to encourage her students, but it only intimidated her Indian girls, who saw the ruler as a symbol of corporal punishment.

"*Breeze,*" Miss Thompson said patiently. "Try it one more time."

"Brij," said the girl.

"That, dear child, is *j* like in *bridge*. You know a bridge, don't you? The letter *d* coupled with a *g* has a *j* sound. Bridge. Badge. Badger."

Badger! My heart went out to the poor girl. How many Indian children were familiar with a badger? A mongoose, yes, but a *badger*? I only happened to know what a badger was because, thanks to Miss Thompson, I had read *The Wind in the Willows* as a child. British pronunciation was completely illogical, I had concluded a long time ago. I remember arguing with Dadamoshai why were *schedule* and *school* pronounced differently. If *schedule* was pronounced *shedule* should not *school* be pronounced *shoole*? Dadamoshai said I had an intelligent argument there, but there was really no logic—besides, the British were not the most practical-minded people in the world. Americans were much more sensible that way: they said *skedule*.

There was silence in the next room, then a rustle of papers. I heard Miss Thompson say, "Never mind, dear. I think we've practiced enough for today. Now, no need to fret about this. It will come. Pronunciation is just practice. After all, your mother tongue is very different, isn't it? I understand the letter *z* doesn't even exist in your language, so how are you expected to say it?"

A chair scraped back. "Thank you, Miss Toomson," a high girlish voice replied.

There were footsteps, and Miss Thompson held the door open. "You are most welcome, Konica," she said. "I'll see you next Tuesday."

I had expected a small child to walk out of the study; instead it was a grown woman dressed in an expensive pink sari with gold bangles on her wrists, her hair oiled and fashioned into a formal bun. She looked strangely out of place in Miss Thompson's modest English home.

"Oh, Layla! What a lovely surprise," cried Miss Thompson, seeing me. The girl looked up and our eyes met. "I will be with you in just a minute, dear. Let me just see Konica to the door."

Konica? Kona Sen!

Kona's bangles chinked softly as she walked by with mincing steps. Her eyes stayed on the floor the entire time; she did
not glance up even once as she passed by me sitting on the sofa.

I must have looked pale and in need of fortification, because
Miss Thompson said, "You look exhausted, dear. Let's have a
cup of tea, shall we? Martha, some tea, please!" she called toward the kitchen then turned to me. "That was Konica Sen.
She lives on Rai Bahadur Road, same as you. You must know
each other?"

"I don't think we've actually been introduced," I said
vaguely. "I've seen her around of course."

"Her father came to see me. Mr. Sen is anxious Konica im-
proves her spoken English. She is getting married soon, you
know. The boy is Indian but has lived in England all his life.
He walks and talks just like an Englishman, Mr. Sen said. The
young man has joined the civil service in Calcutta. Konica
will live there after they are married. Her father is worried
she won't be able to mix in her husband's social circles if she
cannot speak English."

My brain was still unscrambling from the shock of seeing
Kona. Did she recognize me? It was hard to tell because Kona's
face was expressionless, like a boiled egg. It did not give out
much.

"To tell you the truth, I would have never taken on a new
student her age," Miss Thompson continued. "It's an uphill
task to teach spoken English to someone who comes from such
a traditional Indian family. Learning to speak a language, as
you know, calls for a lot of oral practice. Nobody in Konica's
family speaks English. Even her father can barely get by."

"Ah, here we are...thank you, Martha," she said as Martha,
old and bent, hobbled in to set the tea tray down. Turning to
me, Miss Thompson added, "I know Konica is having an ar-

ranged marriage, but I don't understand why Mr. Sen would get his daughter married to someone she can't even talk to."

"He does speak good Bengali, you know—"

"Her fiancé does? Oh, so you know this young man, Layla?"

"No, no," I said quickly. "I mean he *probably* speaks Bengali. If he is an Indian educated abroad, I am sure he is bilingual. Most of them are."

"I hope so for Konica's sake. The poor girl. Her father said to give her plenty of homework. 'Mastering a foreign language is not a matter of homework, Mr. Sen,' I told him. It's a matter of practice."

"She can practice her English with her fiancé, I suppose," I said. Just thinking about Manik and Kona cozying up together triggered a stab of jealousy.

"I suppose so, dear. I am not sure how often they meet or how much they talk to each other, really. It's all very formal, this arranged marriage. More between the two families, really." Miss Thompson paused thoughtfully. Suddenly her face lit up and she clapped her hands. "Why, I just got me a grand idea! Why don't you help her, Layla? She can practice speaking English with *you*. You are both the same age—I am sure you will find plenty to talk about. How very fortunate you are neighbors! May I suggest this to Konica's father, if you don't mind?"

"Yes, of course," I said numbly. What else could I say?

Miss Thompson looked very pleased. "So that settles it, then," she said. "Now tell me about yourself. The Rai Bahadur says you want to become a teacher? Marvelous! I am so proud of you, Layla. You were born to follow in your grandfather's footsteps. I know he is counting on you to take over his school someday. You will do a brilliant job."

"I hope so," I said absently. All I could think of was how

Kona had chinked past me with her musical bangles and the faint scent of jasmine that trailed softly behind her.

Of course, I knew I would never hear from Kona or her father, but how could I ever explain that to Miss Thompson? Although the Sens lived just a few doors down from us, our families always avoided each other. Dadamoshai was openly contemptuous of Mr. Sen's narrow-minded politics, and the Sens probably thought my grandfather a loose cannon and disapproved of how he was raising me. They were both ideologically different—in fact, polar opposites.

Dadamoshai had plenty of inherited wealth but gave it all away to charity and chose to live like a monk. Mr. Sen, on the other hand, came from a trader class and had risen from frugal means to become the richest man in town. The joke in town was that he had built an entire mansion with bricks he pilfered from a construction site during his constitutional walks. This, of course, was just a manner of speaking, but he was known to be an unscrupulous businessman who accumulated his wealth slyly and at the expense of others.

But at the very heart of the matter the fact remained that I was an inauspicious child. Bad luck was viewed as something contagious in our society. It was believed one person's luck rubbed off onto another. This was the reason why I was never invited to social functions like weddings and births. At funerals, on the other hand, I was always welcome.

Miss Thompson continued to puzzle over why her "grand idea" never took root. She mentioned that Kona's father said he would practice speaking English with his daughter if that was what was required. Miss Thompson did not have the heart to tell him it would do no good. Mr. Sen's own English was pretty dismal, she said, but she did not want to offend the poor man, so she let it pass.

Perhaps the best way I could have explained it to Miss Thompson was this way: Kona and I were like two separate rivers flowing side by side, but our geographies were so vastly different it was certain we would never meet. Hers was a course, smooth and predictable, leading straight to the ocean, while mine was uncharted and unknown, only to be determined by the invisible landscape of my destiny.

Sister Cecilia, the chinless nun with bristling whiskers and an ashen complexion to match her habit, was in charge of a small library of the Sacred Heart Convent. She beamed seeing me, hopeful perhaps, I was leaning toward the fold. Unmarried and educated, I was, after all, a perfect fit for the convent. Why else would I be at her library every Tuesday to immerse myself in Bible studies? Little did Sister Cecilia know I would have headed for the same bookshelf by the window had it contained books on amoebic dysentery. Besides, my aspirations were far from holy.

The Sacred Heart Convent stood opposite Miss Thompson's house. The shelf filled with books on Bible studies was by the window from where I could get a clear view of Miss Thompson's front gate and see Kona every week. I only caught a brief glimpse of her as she emerged from the house and stepped into the rickshaw. I noticed how she waited demurely for the rickshaw to be brought up to her. How she stepped up daintily on the floorboard, arranged her sari pleats nicely and sat with her hands folded primly on her lap. I tried to see her through Manik's eyes. She was very feminine and walked on delicate feet, I decided. I imagined she had beautiful, long hair, luxurious even, when left open. Maybe Manik liked demure women with long hair, delicate feet and gold bangles that chinked softly, and a soft voice that chinked softly, too. Not someone brisk and angular, full of inflamed opinions and sharp of speech. Which man liked an argumentative woman? It was grating and unfeminine. I began to steadily loathe myself.

I peeked over the top of The Book of Job I was holding. Sister Cecilia caught my eye and gave me an encouraging smile. I closed the book and slid it back into the empty slot on the shelf.

"Thank you," I said to Sister Cecilia as I walked toward the door.

"See you again soon," she called back in a cracked old voice. "God bless you, my child."

I wondered what Sister Cecilia would say if she found out my real reason for coming to the library? She would be terribly disillusioned, no doubt. Not only was I pretending to be holy, I was secretly coveting a man who was formally betrothed to another. But thankfully, Sister Cecelia would never find out, because I, Layla Roy, was the self-proclaimed mistress of deceit.

CHAPTER

3

I returned home one evening and from the garden path I could hear voices on the veranda. My heart took a tumble, for there he was—Manik Deb. I felt instant panic. For some reason, Manik Deb could trigger a flight response in me faster than a house fire.

Boris Ivanov, Dadamoshai and Manik were engaged in animated discussion. I tiptoed past the jasmine vines, crept into the house through the back door in the kitchen and went straight to my bedroom.

My bedroom window opened out onto the veranda, and I had a clear view of Manik Deb through a slit in the curtain. I fingered a small tear in the fabric as I watched him. I admired the contours of his face and the easy way he inhabited his body. It was a trait common in animals, I thought, that unconscious intimacy with self, an unconditional acceptance of gristle and bone. His thumb absently stroked his lower lip as he listened.

"What our patriotic brothers don't understand," Dadamoshai was saying, "is that I am advocating English as the official language simply because it is the most practical solution. India has twenty-one different languages and each of those has several dialects. We are a culturally diverse people—Indians are not of a feather and we are not going to flock together. It's like trying to get twenty-one different species of birds to talk to one another. Besides, who is to say which language is the best for our country? Some have proposed Hindi. The Bengalis are insulted because they believe their language is superior. The South Indians are ready to go to war. South Indian languages, as you know, are completely alien from all other Indian language. Can you teach a blue jay to coo like a mourning dove? You tell *me*."

Manik laughed softly. He leaned forward to tap the ash from his cigarette. Tap, tap. One, two. He paused deliberately between each tap, as though he was thinking. "So you suggest we all become parrots and learn a different foreign language altogether. English, in this case," he said.

Then Boris Ivanov's voice rumbled like water running down a deep gorge. "The esteemed Rai Bahadur believes that the English language will, how do you say this…" He shrugged expressively, before turning to Dadamoshai to break off into Russian.

"Put India on a global platform. Connect us with the bigger world," Dadamoshai said.

"Sounds sensible," said Manik Deb. "So who is opposing English education?"

"So-called patriots. Morons," said Dadamoshai. "It's easy to be a rabble-rouser instead of coming up with a concrete solution. Our donkey leaders have no clue what they want."

"Could be just bad timing," said Manik. "It's hard to advocate English when our country is hell-bent on throwing the British out."

"They are throwing the baby out with the dishwater, are they not?" Boris Ivanov said.

Boris Ivanov meant bathwater, but he was right. Zealots

seemed to forget that the British had done plenty of good for India. They built roads, railways and set up a solid administrative and judicial system. They exemplified discipline and accountability. But with the "Quit India" movement in full force and patriotic sentiments running high, anything and everything British was being rejected.

"Let's not mix politics with education," said Dadamoshai. "They are separate issues. I want India to be free just as much as anybody else, but I also want our country to survive as a democracy. I want India to have a sure footing in the world. I am proposing the English language as a conduit, not as an endorsement of British politics."

Teacups tinkled down the hallway. Chaya entered the veranda and set down the tea tray on the table.

"*Velikolepno!*" Boris Ivanov cried, rubbing his hands with gleeful anticipation. "I cannot get enough of this Indian tea."

"Think about it—none of us would be here, had it not been for Assam tea," said Dadamoshai.

"What do you mean?" Manik asked. "What does Assam tea have to do with anything we are talking about?"

"Ah! You know it was tea that put Assam on the world map, don't you?" said Dadamoshai, stirring his cup. "It's quite a remarkable story."

Not so long ago Silchar was just a small fishing village, with its slow, winding river, paddy fields and sleepy bamboo groves. It all changed, however, in 1905, when the British made it the seat of central government for three major counties in Assam. Before that, the British had hardly turned an eyeball for Assam.

"Assam is India's most neglected and backward state," said Dadamoshai. "It is disaster-prone and inaccessible. We have devastating floods every year. You can see why the houses are built on bamboo stilts and have boats stored on the roofs."

"It does rain an awful lot here. More than England, it seems," said Manik.

"Oh, much more—Assam gets *triple* the amount of rain compared to England," said Dadamoshai. "And *England* is considered a rainy country. Sometimes there seems to be more water than land in Assam. Rivers spring up overnight and change courses all the time."

"Also big earthquicks happening here," added Boris Ivanov, shaking his massive fists at the sky. "One time, so much—shake, shake, shake—I think the world is end today."

I smiled, remembering. Several years ago Boris Ivanov was on one of his visits when the tremors struck one sleepy afternoon. He got so disoriented he fell right out of the plantation chair and was jittery for days. Earthquakes were common in our state. Assam straddled a major seismic fault, and throughout the year mild tremors rocked Assamese babies to sleep in their bamboo cribs.

When I turned back to the conversation, Dadamoshai was talking about the Ahoms—the rice farmers who lived in the silt-rich valley of the Bhramaputra.

"They are a simple, pastoral people," said Dadamoshai, "of Sino-Burmese descent. All they want to do is chew their betel nut, drink rice wine and live life *lahe-lahe*."

"What's *lahe-lahe*?" Manik asked, tapping his unlit cigarette.

"Slowly-slowly," said Dadamoshai. "This lazy mentality of the Assamese has kept them in the dark ages while the rest of India has marched on. Of course opium has a lot to do with the *lahe-lahe*."

But it seemed the Ahoms were not left alone to enjoy their salubrious lives. They were constantly harassed by marauding tribes who thundered across the Burmese border to ransack and pillage their villages, carrying off every slant-eyed, honey-skinned woman they could lay their hands on. All they left behind were toothless widows.

"I am not surprised," said Manik. "Assamese women are delicate beauties. They remind me of orchids."

I felt a pinch of jealousy. *No wonder he likes Kona*, I thought. She was dainty and feminine—like an orchid.

"The Ahom kings tried their best to fight off the Burmese invaders but they did not have the might or the mettle," Dadamoshai continued. "Out of sheer desperation they appealed to the British for help."

"But you say before the English are having no interest in Assam—" Doris Ivanov began.

Dadamoshai held up his hand. "Aha! But now suddenly the British were interested—oh, *very* interested in Assam."

At any other given time the plea for help might have rolled right off the *sola topees* of our colonial leaders, but recent developments had piqued British interest in Assam. It was the discovery of tea. And this was not just any old tea—the most exquisite tea in the world had been found growing wild in the mist-laden hills of the Bhramaputra Valley. This accidental discovery smacked of commercial gain, so the British made a bargain with the Ahom kings: they offered protection against the Burmese invaders in return for developing a tea industry in Assam.

"I still don't see what you, the Rai Bahadur, have to do with the tea industry," Manik said.

"Let me explain," said Dadamoshai.

The British needed to set up a central government to manage its affairs in Assam. They picked Silchar, a town strategically located close to the tea-growing belt. But when they

looked to employ Indian staff to man their government offices, they discovered Assam had a surplus of rice farmers and
toothless widows but not a single educated Indian to be found
in the entire rain-drenched valley.

"But all was not lost," Dadamoshai said, "because just a
stone's throw across the Padma River there was a rich pool of
qualified Indians—the Sylhetis of East Pakistan, many of whom
were educated in universities abroad." He looked at Manik.
"People like your father and I. We were lured to Assam with
nice salaries and fancy titles to work for His Majesty's service.
So here we are in Silchar—all because of Assam tea."

Dadamoshai did not mention his real reason for accepting
the post as District Magistrate of Assam. He had shrewdly figured his dream to promote English as the medium of instruc-
tion in schools was in perfect alignment with colonial interests
in India. As the powerful District Magistrate he would have
the clout to make it all happen. But India's struggle for independence skewed everything the wrong way. Dadamoshai
had anticipated a shift in loyalties, but he had not counted on
the blinkered view of our politicians or their narrow personal
agendas. Before long he faced a tall embankment of opposition
and found himself separated by an ideological divide that no
amount of reason or common sense could ever hope to bridge.
And he was left on the sidelines, an angry old man shaking his
umbrella at the sky.

Darkness had fallen. Drums throbbed in the fishing village
across the river. Manik Deb stirred in his chair. "Fascinating,"
he said. "Funny how little I know about my own country. I
have been gone for too long."

"Did you do your earlier schooling in England, as well, before Oxford?" Dadamoshai asked.

"Yes. I went to Harrow. My father's younger brother paid for my education. He lives in England—married an English lady, my aunt Veronica. They practically raised me."

"I knew your father well in Cambridge," said Dadamoshai. "You may not know this, but at one time we were both in love with the same English girl, the beautiful red-haired Estelle Lovelace."

Manik laughed. "So what happened? Neither of you married her, obviously."

"We both came back to India to marry good Indian girls," Dadamoshai said. "Like you are doing."

Manik fidgeted in his chair. "So you had an arranged marriage?"

"No, I fell in love with my wife, Maya. She…she died very young."

Boris Ivanov came to life with a noisy harrumph. He had been listening quietly to the conversation.

"When I first saw the Rai Bahadur's wife—" Boris Ivanov gave a big flowery wave "—Maya was a famous beauty. Layla, the Rai Bahadur's granddaughter, looks just like her."

I straightened at hearing my name.

"So who arranged your marriage?" asked Dadamoshai, changing the subject. He still had a hard time talking about my grandmother, I could tell.

"My oldest brother," said Manik. His voice was taut. "He became the patriarchal head of our family after my father died. My marriage was arranged seven years ago. I was sixteen, too young to understand. I am committed now. If I break my engagement, my brother tells me I will ruin our family's name. Sometimes I feel like I am bound hand and foot by pygmies."

Manik ground his cigarette into the ashtray, sighed and

then got to his feet. "This has been a delightful evening, but I must take my leave."

"Wait," said Dadamoshai. He grabbed a small flashlight from the coffee table and shook it awake. "Here, take this. Battery is low but it's better than nothing. The road toward the river gets a little treacherous."

"Oh, I will be just fine," said Manik.

"No, no, I insist," said Dadamoshai, pushing the flashlight into Manik's hand. "I enjoyed talking to you. And please do drop by again."

I shifted my feet. I had been so engrossed in watching Manik Deb, I had fingered the small tear in the curtain to a walnut-size hole. But I was unable to pull myself away from the window. Just looking at him gave me immense pleasure. It was like watching a sunset: arresting, mesmerizing even, but distant and, ultimately, unattainable.

CHAPTER

4

Boris Ivanov left for Calcutta, and Manik Deb continued to come by to visit with Dadamoshai, often stopping on his way to the Sens' house. They seemed to resonate on many levels and enjoyed talking to each other. He always sat on the same cane chair, the one with the defective leg. He skewed it a little to one side, facing the jasmine trellis, and lounged deep in the cushions, stretching his long legs past the coffee table. He dominated the floor space easily, as if it was his to occupy and own. He smoked constantly, lighting cigarettes with quick, easy strikes of his match, tilting his head back sharply to inhale. I noticed he had changed brands, downgrading from the fine English Dunhill cigarettes to Simla, an Indian brand. He had been in India for six weeks now.

Once he showed up wearing Indian clothes—a long white kurta and loose slacks—looking elegant and princely. Was he becoming more Indian? I wondered. Whatever the reason, it suited him well. The starched cotton was creased around his sleeves and hung gracefully on his long frame. He did not wear an undershirt, and the dark hairs of his chest bled through the thin fabric. Wearing traditional Indian clothes defined him as a Thinking Indian. It was the dress code of the intelligentsia. Patriotism was at a fever pitch in our country and recent political events had sparked a heated debate among intellectuals.

All over India people were deeply caught up in the current events of the day. The world was at war, and Bengal was in the throes of a devastating famine, but what worsened the catastrophe was a heartless and diabolical British policy of war.

The Japanese had inflicted a crushing defeat on British forces in Singapore and were threatening to invade Burma, one of the strongholds of the British Empire, which bordered Assam in India. In a desperate and shocking attempt to stall the enemy, the British employed the merciless "scorched earth" policy. They destroyed crops, dwellings, infrastructure and communications— anything to inconvenience the enemy from encroaching into India. This was done with total disregard for human life. The effect was widespread, the horror unspeakable. Millions died of starvation.

Educated Indians like Manik and Dadamoshai, normally staunch supporters of the British, were outraged and disillusioned beyond belief. It brought to glaring light the self-interest of colonial rule in India. There were agitations and uprisings all over the country.

"We need our independence more than ever now," Manik said, "but there is so much divisiveness among our leaders. Their ideologies are poles apart. On one hand, we have the followers of Gandhi touting nonviolence. On the other hand, militant leaders like Netaji are brandishing guns and conspiring with Hitler to overthrow the British by force. As for the millions who are dying like flies as a result of this famine, do you think they care a fig for freedom? All they want is their next bowl of rice."

"Our leaders are like rushes and reeds," lamented Dadamoshai. "They will scatter to the winds if they cannot come together to be woven into something useful."

"That's Rumi, isn't it? What you just quoted?"

"Yes. Jelaluddin Rumi. Sixteenth-century Persian mystic. Very wise man."

Manik was exceptionally well-read, I discovered. I felt hopelessly conflicted when I thought of him. He seemed so intelligent and progressive, and yet he was not resisting a traditional old-fashioned arranged marriage. It had to be about the money, I concluded. Kona Sen would bring a substantial dowry, which made Manik Deb, for all his enlightened talk, a typical money-minded Indian male. I needed to find a reason to hate him, just so I would not feel so bad about him marrying Kona Sen.

My reverie was shattered when Dadamoshai called out to me from the veranda.

"Layla! Where are you?" he shouted in his booming voice.

I was so startled that my breath caught in my throat. I scrambled off the bed, straightened my sari, smoothed my hair and went out to the veranda.

Manik was sitting in his usual chair, about to light one of his perpetual cigarettes. He looked up at me as I came in, sat up a little straighter and smiled. My throat was dry, and I must have looked a little panicked, thanks to my guilty thoughts.

"Layla, there you are. Have a seat," Dadamoshai said amiably, pushing the newspaper off the sofa and patting the cushion with the blue elephants next to him. "We were just talking about you."

"Me?" I asked incredulously.

"Yes, Manik Deb wants to know your opinion. Manik, do you want to explain why we need Layla's input on this one?" Dadamoshai tented his fingers and waited with eager anticipation, as if he was about to enjoy the opera.

Manik leaned back in his chair and stretched his legs across the floor, leaving just three inches of space between his toe and mine. I quickly tucked away my feet and worried a piece of wicker on the armrest of the sofa.

"Layla, your grandfather and I were talking about the changing roles of women in society." Manik paused to see if I was listening. "Well, we were wondering if our society is ready for the change. Are we ahead of our time?"

"Why do you ask me?"

"Why not?" said Manik. "You are a bright young woman, well-read, well-bred and getting ready to conquer the world."

The roots of my hair felt hot and I could feel my ears redden.

Nothing intelligent came to my mind. I pulled a sliver of wicker from the ratty old armrest and curled it into a small ball between my fingers. I uncurled the ball and curled it again. I looked up.

He was watching me as he tapped his unlit cigarette on the arm of the chair. I realized both he and Dadamoshai were waiting for my pearls of wisdom. There were none forthcoming. My head was empty except for Manik Deb floating inside like a trapped balloon. Suddenly I felt uncontrollably crabby.

"What does Kona say?" I blurted out before I could stop myself. I immediately felt like biting my tongue off. Oh, God! What a faux pas. I was talking of his fiancée as though we were bosom buddies.

"Who? Oh, Konica." He looked startled, just for a moment. "Well, I never thought of asking her," he added, looking vaguely uncomfortable.

I don't know what got into me then—whether it was my nervousness, embarrassment, awkwardness or what—but once I got started, my tongue just took off. "Well, you should *ask* her, then. She is going to be your wife, you know." I sounded unflatteringly shrill. "Or maybe it does not matter. Kona must be delighted to marry a civil officer, and anxious to boss around servants and have lots of children." I staggered under the avalanche of my own words and felt sick to my stomach.

Manik's eyes popped slightly; his mouth fell open. He did not look very attractive, I noted with satisfaction. He recovered quickly enough, though.

"Well, Layla, don't you want to marry a civil officer, boss around servants and have lots of children, too? Is that not every woman's dream?" Did I detect a hint of sarcasm in his voice? I could not be sure.

I took a deep breath. I realized this conversation had gone seriously off track and wandered into a dingy and suspicious neighborhood. I felt disgusted with myself.

"You did not answer my question," Manik said softly.

"Which was?" I had lost the thread of the conversation. I recalled only my embarrassment at blurting out things I should not have.

"What *do* you want to do with your life, Layla?"

I watched a dragonfly settle on a dry twig on the jasmine trellis. Its wings quivered slightly, catching a small rainbow of light. What did I want to do with my life? Suddenly I was not so sure anymore.

"I want to do good for the world," I said, hoping to sound noble and intelligent, but sounding more like a charity nun. "I don't think I was ever *meant* to marry, or to have any children," I added a little hesitantly. To my dismay, my voice broke. I quickly gathered my emotions. "I would really like to help other women...to carry on Dadamoshai's work."

"You will be a great asset to the Rai Bahadur," Manik said. "Careful, though, some nice young man does not come along and make you change your mind. That would indeed be a serious loss to womankind." He smiled like an imp.

"Oh, Layla is a very determined young woman!" piped in Dadamoshai. He looked at me gently and reached out to push back a strand of hair from my face. "She has made up her mind. Where would one find a man good enough for her, anyway? Most young fellows these days are duffers."

Manik tapped open his matchbox, but then changed his mind. He put the cigarette back in the pack, pushed back his chair and stood up. He was suddenly very serious.

"Duty calls." He tilted his head toward Kona's house, looking resigned. "I am expected for dinner."

Dadamoshai and I walked with him to the porch. I hated to see him go.

"Wait!" I said. I lifted my hand to tug his shirtsleeve, and then jerked it back. I felt reckless and out of control.

"Yes?" Manik's hands were in his pockets. He leaned back, looking at me curiously, his eyebrows slightly arched.

"You never told me what *you* think about women's education, and how it might change society," I said.

I needed to hear it for myself. I had to know Manik Deb was a typical Indian man, a blatant hypocrite. That way I could put him away, once and for all, like a shoe that looked good but did not fit.

Manik leaned back on the balcony railing and tapped out a cigarette from his pack, lighting it in his cupped palm. He tilted his head back and blew a perfect smoke ring into the air. I noticed a small shaving nick on his chin. I wanted to touch it. He was so close. Again I was embarrassed by my thoughts. I watched the smoke curl from his nose.

His eyes tightened thoughtfully. "Every human being should

have the right to choose," he said. "I don't think women have a choice in our society."

I was stunned. Why, he sounded exactly like Dadamoshai!

"For that matter," Manik continued, "I don't think men have much of a choice, either. We are pigeonholed by social expectations, but society is more forgiving toward men. Think of it—an unmarried man is a bachelor, and he is eligible till his dying day, but an unmarried woman...well, she becomes a seed pumpkin."

A seed pumpkin: the only pumpkin left in the patch. That was what our society called spinsters. Was Manik Deb calling *me* a seed pumpkin? But I had no need to worry.

"Unless, of course, she is Layla," he said, smiling down at me. "You see, Layla, you can have anything you want in the world. You are no flotsam drifting with the tide. You are making choices for yourself and that is enviable. Not many of us have that luxury."

"It's funny," I said, feeling a burst of joy for no earthly reason at all. "And here I thought you were a very traditional man with stereotypical views."

"What made you think I was so typical?" Manik looked surprised and puzzled.

"You were educated abroad and are going into the civil service, for one. That's typical for most educated, upper-class Indians, and..." I paused, hesitating.

"And I am having an arranged marriage?" He took the words right out of my mouth. "I think I understand what you are saying."

I had not meant it to sound so crass.

Manik glanced at his watch and quickly stubbed out his cigarette. "Which reminds me it is getting awfully late. You have no idea how terrified I am of my future mother-in-law."

I stood there with Dadamoshai on the porch stairs and watched Manik Deb walk away. In my heart there was a small, sad feeling as though I was missing the last train going some-place mysterious and wonderful.

CHAPTER

5

That summer I got to know Manik Deb. Those premonsoon evenings are etched in my mind in the melancholy strokes of an aching heart. Knowing that he could never be mine was, in a way, my release. Gone was the need to impress him with my wit and intelligence. I was free to slip into a more natural version of myself. We became friends. But despite the pleasant evenings we spent together, I was always aware of a wistful sadness that floated softly in the dregs of my being.

Sometimes our talks on the veranda carried on late into the evening, and Dadamoshai would excuse himself and retire to his room. Left by ourselves, we often talked about books and authors: Tolstoy, Tagore and Dostoevsky. In all our times alone, never once did Manik overstep his boundaries as a guest in my grandfather's house. He made no untoward advances. He was always polite, interested and attentive—the impeccable guest.

On our last day together, Manik stayed almost until dinnertime. He would be leaving for Calcutta the next day. The monsoons were heavy in the air, the stillness of the evening hanging in dense folds around us. We sat in silence absorbing the faint sounds that penetrated the quiet: the small tinkling of a prayer bell, the bark of a faraway dog. A shaft of light fell sharply across Manik's face. It hid his eyes but illuminated his chin and mouth. He looked poetic and thoughtful. The tall areca palms rustled with the approaching storm. Lightning whipped the distant sky, and thunder pealed across the dark river.

The BBC news from my grandfather's radio wafted through the waving curtains of the living room. Winston Churchill's strident voice came on the air:

"Hitler knows that he will have to break us in this Island or lose the war…."

His voice faded out with the weak transmission, and then burst into clarity.

"Let us therefore brace ourselves to our duties, and so bear ourselves that if the British Empire and its Commonwealth last for a thousand years, men will still say, this was their finest hour."

The news ended with "God Save the King." Then the dulcet notes of a popular wartime song about the white cliffs of Dover trickled out to the veranda.

How strange, I thought to myself. This was the first time I was hearing popular English music play on my grandfather's radio. He usually switched the radio off after the news.

"Vera Lynn," murmured Manik softly. "What a magnificent voice. Do you listen to Western music, Layla?"

"I listen to Western classical mostly," I replied. "Dadamoshai has quite a collection of Russian and German composers."

"There is something I have wanted to ask you," said Manik. "How did both your parents die?"

I was not surprised he had heard about my parents. He must have thought it odd that I lived with Dadamoshai and not with my mother and father.

"My father was a freedom fighter. He died in the Cellular Jail."

"In the Andaman Islands? Is this the same notorious Cellular Jail where they hanged political prisoners?"

"Yes."

I did not tell him I had heard that political prisoners were not only hanged in the gallows there, they were sometimes tied to cannons and blown up. The British meted harsh punishments when it came to political dissenters.

"Have you heard about the Chittagong armory raid?" I asked.

"Oh yes. A famous guerrilla movement in the '30s, was it not? To overthrow the British? It was led by a schoolmaster, I believe."

"That's right. My father was a revolutionary in that movement. He was captured and hanged."

"And your mother? I know women fighters played a big role in that uprising."

"My mother..." I hesitated, because I had never shared this with anyone before. "My mother drowned. In a lily pond. She killed herself."

I have a photo of my parents and me, taken when I was about a year old, just before my father was captured and exiled to the Andaman Islands. The faded sepia image shows a thin man with fiery eyes seated on a straight-backed chair in what appears to be a courtyard, with a chicken pecking in the background. Next to him stands my mother, frail and taut. She is wearing a plain-bordered sari and old-fashioned blouse with sleeves up to the elbow. Her arms are crossed over her chest; her eyes are naked and staring, a quiet desperation lurking in their depths. By then she was already lost to the world.

Another song was playing on the radio now by the same

singer. It was a sentimental love song presented in a slow caressing style. The singer's voice trembled with heartbreak as
she expressed the unbearable sorrow of parting with her lover.
It got me right in the gut.

My face was hidden in the shadows, but Manik must have
sensed my tears because he reached into his kurta pocket and
fished out a clean white handkerchief, which he offered me
across the coffee table. He did not try to touch my hand or
say anything. In the dark, I tucked the handkerchief under the
cushion of the sofa. I never gave it back to him. We both sat
quietly till the song ended and the plaintive strains of the or-
chestra faded, followed by nine hollow strokes from the pen-
dulum clock that echoed in the hallway.

Manik leaned forward and stubbed out his cigarette. He
still had not said a word. I choked back a lump in my throat,
thinking: *This is our last time together. The next time I see him, he
will be a married man, belonging to another.*

"Let me go and find Dadamoshai," I said, dashing inside
the house. In the dark passageway, I hastily wiped off my tears.
Dadamoshai was nowhere to be found. Chaya said he had gone
to the neighbor's house to borrow a newspaper.

I returned to the veranda feeling more composed. "Dadamoshai's gone out, but he'll be back any minute. Do you want
to wait?" I said, hoping to buy a few extra minutes. "I am sure
he would like to say goodbye."

"I am running terribly late, Layla," Manik said, getting to
his feet. "Please thank the Rai Bahadur for all his kindness and
tell him I will write from Calcutta, will you?"

"Of course."

We stood together awkwardly under the porch as we said
our goodbyes. I watched a rain beetle dash itself on the naked
lightbulb with a tiny ting, then spin in dizzy circles on the

floor. I was about to turn and walk back into the house when Manik did something unexpected: he reached out and brushed his fingertips lightly across my cheek. It was a fleeting gesture, a butterfly's caress.

"Lay-*la*..." He breathed my name with such tenderness that it trembled in the air between us.

Then he simply turned around and walked away, while my heart quietly broke, the pieces scattering like petals on the gentle night breeze.

CHAPTER

6

Soon after I was born, my mother began to unravel. Her descent into madness was slow and surreptitious. It began with a slackening of the mind, a stray thread, a small tug in the wrong direction. She complained that the Small People in her head kept her awake at nights. She pulled at her lovely waist-length hair till her scalp bled. The Small People scrabbled in her eardrums and pulled her nose, turning it inside out like a foot sock, right into her brain. This drove her even more insane, because every time she sneezed she imagined that bits of her brain blew out into her handkerchief. By the time I was two years old, my mother had sneezed most of her brain out of her head. She became empty and hollow, a green coconut devoid of substance.

When I was three years old, my mother, on the advice of a Holy Man, decided to marry me off to a banana tree. This act was not the outcome of sheer lunacy alone, but a very antiquated ritual in our society: marrying off a bad-luck child to an object, traditionally a banana tree, was believed to "cancel out" one's negative horoscope.

One overcast morning in June, my mother dressed me like

a traditional Bengali bride in a red sari with a gold veil, put kohl around my eyes, dotted my forehead with sandalwood paste and lined my tiny feet with *alta,* the red paste worn by brides. She carried me to the grove by the lily pond and tied me by my veil to a banana tree. She blew a conch, broke open a coconut, chanted prayers and sprinkled holy water, and left me there. A slanted drizzle fell straight through the afternoon. I was bitten by red ants and caught a death of a cold. I was discovered in the early evening by a neighbor.

My mother was also found at dusk, floating in the lily pond, facedown in the water. Her skin was waxy and cold, her lips blue, and her eyes had turned dull as mud. Her delicate hands bobbed by her side like the wings of dead birds. She had been dead several hours.

After my mother died, I was cared for by my maternal grandparents for a while and then I moved in with my great-aunt, Mitra Mashi, whom I called Mima.

Mima was a great big woman who wore her sari a whole foot off the ground, the tail end tucked into her waistband like a sumo wrestler. She was an earthy woman who laughed easily and was given to manly backslapping that made the elders cringe.

Mima stories abound in the family. My favorite one is about the time she laughed so uproariously that she accidentally swallowed a stinkbug. Another time she thumped an old uncle enthusiastically on the back and made him swallow his dentures.

To Dadamoshai's great delight and approval, Mima earned a master's degree and fought her way up the teaching ladder to become the first female vice principal of the most prestigious *boys'* school in Sylhet.

Mima created a mild scandal when she fell in love and married the science teacher, Robi Das, a pigeon-toed young man with a nervous stutter, who was small enough to tuck under her armpit like an evening purse. She surprised everyone even further by giving birth to a healthy baby girl at the ripe old age of thirty-eight. Her daughter's name was Moon.

Although Moon was only six months older than me, she was technically my aunt, a fact she rubbed in with exasperating frequency. Moon and I existed in the same house like two prickly cacti in a pot, too close for comfort, our thorns occasionally poking each other.

Moon had a round face and corkscrew curls that stuck close to her head, a gap-toothed smile and coal-black, starry eyes with lashes so thick that they jammed back into her eyes when she tried to look through her binoculars.

Moon took her profession as an explorer very seriously. She carried her binoculars around like a doctor carries a stethoscope and viewed the whole world through them. She studied the grass, the clouds, the fence and even her own shadow.

People stared at us both because we were so different. I was an oddity in our town of brown-skinned, dark-eyed people. I had delicate bones; dark, straight hair; and enormous, smoky, gray-green eyes that reminded people of sad, impenetrable things like forest fires and river fog.

Mima, on the other hand, saw no difference. She hugged and spanked us both at the same time. Mima's policy was if one child was naughty, the other one got spanked, as well. It was a preemptive measure, a disciplinary vaccination, to ensure the misdeed did not reoccur in any shape or form. The same applied to hugs: always a double shot.

Mima's child rearing defied all logic, but she had no patience for logic. "*Everybody* mind your ways, otherwise there will be trouble for *all*," she would hiss fiercely, her eyes narrowed. Even my uncle Robi was terrified. He sat tucked into the sofa like a tiny brown cushion and looked at us sadly through his fat, foggy glasses. He was sympathetic, but of no help.

I fitted easily into Mima's boisterous household and all its bosomy comfort. My tragic childhood was all but forgotten. Bits of my past emerged at times, pieced together by gossip and a significant amount of embellishment thrown in by Moon. She was fed stories by their garrulous housemaid, Rekha, a wisp of a girl with gap teeth splayed out like the fingers of a hand, through which the gossip of the entire neighborhood flowed.

"Your mother was a madwoman and you are a Banana Bride," Moon declared. We were both around six years old and playing in the backyard. "I wish *I* could marry a banana tree," she added wistfully, and then with complete irrelevance, "but I have a doll that vomits and you *don't*."

I did not care about being a Banana Bride, but I badly wanted a vomiting doll.

"You can marry a banana tree anytime," I said. "Why don't you?"

Moon sniffed with scorn. "Don't talk like a donkey. *Azzifff* you can marry whomever you like. Your parents have to *propose* for you."

"Then *ask* your mother to propose for you." Nobody would dare turn down Mima's proposal, least of all a banana tree.

"I told her I wanted to marry a banana tree and she got *very* angry. She wanted to know who had told me things about you. I said, 'Rekha told me everything.' Then Ma went into the kitchen and screamed, 'If I ever hear you talking to the children about any of this, I will throw you out like a dirty rat and you can go back to your village.' Rekha was crying and begging. Then Ma turned and yelled at me, 'I will throw you out, too, like a dirty rat, if you tell Layla *anything*.'" Moon looked at me ruefully, absentmindedly pulling on a corkscrew curl. "I am not supposed to talk to you, about the banana wedding, your crazy mother, or anything."

Moon was so enthralled with my tragic childhood that our favorite pastime became to enact the macabre little drama in all its gory details. Our favorite character was my mother. We took turns playing her, tearing out our hair and sneezing our brains into a handkerchief. Nobody wanted to play Baby Layla the Banana Bride, because all she did was sit under the tree and cry. Instead we dressed up Moon's vomiting doll in a red dishcloth and stuck her under the banana tree while we concentrated on elaborate wedding rituals, throwing rice and pretending to make conch sounds by blowing on a rock. The doll was then made to switch roles and become my mother. We sneaked out the plastic bucket from the bathroom and floated the doll facedown in the water. Moon and I became the professional mourners, throwing ourselves on the ground, beating our chests and wailing.

Then one day we got caught like two stricken cockroaches under a flashlight. Mima came looking for the bucket and found us wailing and saw the doll floating in the water. She knew exactly what was going on and gave us both the spankings of our lives. She said she would throw us both out of the house like dirty rats if she caught us playing the game again.

Many years later, I realized that all that role-playing must have been cathartic at some level, because my real-life tragedy had become woven through with imagination, a colorful fable to be accepted, elaborated upon and embraced, until—to the wonderment of it all—I could let my past go and fly free.

Moon and I spent our holidays in Dadamoshai's house. Every summer, Mima's family packed up and took the ferryboat across the Padma River from Sylhet to Silchar. Here we stayed for two lazy, sun-dappled months in paradise.

We loved Dadamoshai's huge, dilapidated house with its creaky, lopsided gate leading into a big, rambling garden with its birdbath, sundial and sleepy snails that waved their feelers up and down the garden wall. It was a peaceful time. Mima became cuddly and warm and threw discipline to the winds. She got foot massages and snoozed on the veranda. Moon and I climbed the mango tree, demolished anthills, mothered baby crows and challenged Dadamoshai's brain with obtuse and difficult questions.

One year, two crow chicks fell out of the nest in the mango tree. Moon and I adopted one each. Two days later, Moon woke up to find her chick dead. She burst into tears, shoved me hard against the wall and ran howling through the house, looking for Dadamoshai. She found him writing peacefully at his desk on the veranda.

Dadamoshai was the appointed mediator of squabbles. Unlike Mima, who would have either smacked or hugged us, depending on her mood, Dadamoshai listened to both sides and was always judicious.

In between angry sobs, Moon told him that her baby crow had died because of my bad luck.

Dadamoshai pushed up the glasses on his forehead and rubbed his eyes wearily.

"What is bad luck?" he asked innocently.

"When somebody dies because of somebody else."

"Explain to me, please. I am too old to understand," said Dadamoshai, looking round-eyed and befuddled. I was incredulous. *Did he not know what bad luck was?* Why, he sounded like a numskull.

Moon puffed with importance. She stood stoutly with her hands on her waist, looking like a mini Mima herself. "See, Layla is bad luck—everybody knows that, right?"

"Really?" Dadamoshai looked astounded, as if she had just told him the chicken had laid a square egg.

"Yes, yes." Moon shook her curls. She was getting tired of our grandfather's feeblemindedness. "Layla is very bad luck. *Maximum* bad luck," she added for emphasis. Moon's new favorite word was *maximum*. "Her father died because of her, her mother died because of her—let me see...who else? Oh, and now the baby crow died because of her. So see?"

"Whose baby crow died because of whom?" Dadamoshai asked.

"Mine, because of her."

"But if *she* was the bad luck, would not *her* baby crow die instead of yours?"

Moon looked confused.

"Am I bad luck?" Dadamoshai asked her, looking timid and fearful, as though something was going to bite him.

"Ufff-ho! No, no, why should you be bad luck?" Moon retorted irritably. "Her! Her! *She!*" She pointed an accusing finger as I cowered behind Dadamoshai's chair, feeling like a lowly insect. But Dadamoshai did not turn around to look at me.

"Oh dear, oh dear," Dadamoshai lamented sadly, shaking his head, "I think I am very bad luck, too. My wife died, you know, very young, and my daughter. My father died, too, and my mother died...a cat, also, some chickens, and so many cockroaches I can't even count. But sometimes my clogs have a mind of their own and do very bad things."

"Oh-ho, Dadamoshai! You are confusing anything with everything! Making a big *kheechoori*. Don't worry—you are not bad luck. Layla is different."

"How? I don't understand."

Moon sighed noisily. "Dadamoshai, you are too old. You don't understand anything anymore," she said and stuck out her lower lip, glowering at the floor.

"Okay, come here, you two," Dadamoshai said, suddenly very alert and businesslike. He capped his pen with a smart click and closed his journal. He motioned us over to the sofa and scooped the sleeping cat off with the newspaper. "Sit down. I want to show you something." He was tossing around a heavy glass paperweight in his hand. It had blue swirls and glass bubbles suspended inside. "See this paperweight?" he said. He held it up to the light with his thumb and forefinger. We could see the palm trees and sky through it. He positioned his hand above the coffee table and looked as if he was about to drop the paperweight on the glass.

"If I drop this and break the glass, is it good luck or bad luck?"

"Bad luck," we said in unison.

"If I drop the paperweight, but catch it with the other hand before it breaks the glass, is it good luck or bad luck?" While he waited for our answer, Dadamoshai dropped the glass ball, which he caught expertly with his other hand, an inch before it hit the table. We gasped.

"Good luck or bad luck?" he repeated, looking at us both. His eyes were bright like a chipmunk as he tossed the orb around in his hand.

Moon and I looked at each other. "Good luck," we agreed. "Because nothing got broke, thank God," Moon added, crossing her heart. I followed suit. That was the new thing we had both learned watching a nun at the Sacred Heart Convent, where Dadamoshai had taken us for a charity sale. Crossing our hearts was high on our list of priorities. We crossed our hearts several times a day. Sometimes Moon substituted it for "touch wood" or "bless you" when a person sneezed, or "don't mention it" when someone said "thank you." She was a prolific heart-crosser.

"So tell me, who is making the luck happen?"

It was a trick question.

"You?" I ventured.

"Are you sure?" Dadamoshai pinned me with his magistrate's eye, sharp as a pickax.

Moon skipped gingerly from one bare foot to another. "Maybe yes, maybe no," she said ambiguously.

"Layla is right," Dadamoshai said. "I am in control here. I am making luck happen. Now listen carefully, you two. All of us can create our own luck, good and bad. We cannot make luck happen for anyone else, understand? This simple truth of life is called Karma. Now I want both of you to go and think seriously about what I just said."

We both walked off feeling slightly muddled.

The very next day, as if to prove Dadamoshai's luck theory right, my baby crow died, as well. By then we were too confused about luck to know who or what to blame.

Later that night, Moon was asleep and I was tiptoeing to the bathroom when I heard the adults talking on the veranda. Both Mima and Dadamoshai were smoking cigars and enjoying a brandy, while Uncle Robi voiced his displeasure with tiny coughs of disapproval.

"She will get a hiding for this," Mima said. "I have warned Moon. I can't believe she said Layla is bad luck."

"Don't blame your daughter, Mitra," Dadamoshai said. "Small towns do not let people forget their pasts. In Sylhet, Layla will always be the madwoman's daughter, the bad-luck child. She will hear it until, sadly, she starts believing it herself. How will she survive? That girl will grow up to be a beauty. Have you noticed how people stare at her? Do you think you can prevent men from taking advantage of her? They will only mislead her, abuse her trust and marry someone else. I know the double standards of men in our society only too well, Mitra. I cannot bear to see anything bad happen to Layla... that child has been through too much already."

A chair creaked as someone shifted their weight. My uncle coughed. He usually had nothing to add to conversations.

"Dada, what you say is true," said Mima softly. "It makes me sad, really." I heard her blow her nose. "I try my best to protect Layla, but I may not be doing enough. I don't know what else to do."

"I have been thinking about it," Dadamoshai said slowly. "Layla is better off here in Silchar than in Sylhet. No one knows of her past here. People will talk and eventually find out. But I have clout in this town, and nobody will dare take liberties with her. She is safe with me. At the very least, I can make sure Layla gets a good education and learns to stand on her own feet."

Mima laughed. "If anybody can give that child a future, it's you, Dada. But how will you manage? A young girl needs a mother...."

"I have Chaya. She is a good-hearted, nurturing woman, and she will take care of Layla's needs," said Dadamoshai. "And

I will be counting on you, Mitra. You have been a wonderful mother to Layla."

Then, to my surprise, my uncle piped up. He was always so quiet that it was strange to hear his voice. "It will be for the best, Mitra," he said, in his thin, raspy voice. "But I will miss Layla. She is like our own daughter."

Mima sniffed. "I can't imagine our family without her. And what about Moon? Those two fight like crickets, but they are good for each other." Her voice broke.

"Think about it, Mitra," Dadamoshai said softly. "Moon will marry someday and leave home, and what will become of Layla then?"

"Moon? Marry?" Mima gave a funny broken laugh. "I have no high hopes, Dada. As long as that child stands on her own feet and bulldozes her way through life, I am happy."

"I want to take over Layla's care—as soon as possible," said Dadamoshai. "These are impressionable years. It will only get harder as she gets older."

"But she is only seven years old, Dada!" Mima cried. "What am I going to tell Moon? She will be hysterical!"

"Tell her the truth."

"I can't do it, Dada."

"Well, then," said Dadamoshai, "I will tell her. There will be tantrums, no doubt."

I could hardly contain my excitement. I crept back to the bedroom. The dim light from the veranda fell over Moon as she lay sleeping. She was sprawled sideways across the bed, her limbs akimbo, round fists balled up as if for a fight. I pushed her to one side to make room for myself and whispered into her ear, "Move over, sister. This is going to be my house and my bed from now on. The next time you visit, you will be my guest."

She flailed her hands and swatted at me. I was suddenly overcome with love. I wrapped my arms and legs around her and kissed her cheek. For the first time, I realized how very much I loved Moon, and how terribly I would miss her once we were no longer together.

CHAPTER

7

Shortly after Manik left for Calcutta, the monsoon broke with a fury. It poured like the bottom had fallen from the sky. Rain splattered in buckets from rooftops, turning into turbulent streams that raked up mud and debris and furrowed down past our house. The river overflowed its banks. Small koi fish jumped in the paddy fields and ragged children vied with one another to catch them in broken bamboo baskets. The sky was a deep asphalt-gray. Clouds darkened after a pause, only to gather forces for another deluge. Occasionally a rainbow throbbed in the sky, and sometimes the evening ended with a poignant, cloud-filled sunset.

Dadamoshai's desk on the veranda was covered up with tarp, his papers moved inside. The blue elephant cushions on the chairs were wet and smelled of mold. Disheveled sparrows perched, puffed and glum, on the jasmine trellis, lulled by the downpour. Almost overnight, moss inched up the garden wall, and brilliant orange fungi sprouted in cracks. A chorus of cacophonous frogs ribetted through the evening.

When the rains paused, the air was so dense it was hard to breathe. Gone were the sparkling fireflies. Mosquitoes came out in angry droves. They attacked like suicide bombers, whining into ears, biting arms and legs, between toes and in the most unscratchable places.

I stayed home, nursing a monstrous cold, drinking ginger tea and staring at the calendar, watching the days tick by. Only five and a half months remained before Manik's wedding day.

After four days, the postman finally resumed his rounds. I saw him lean his bicycle on the front gate and walk up the garden path, sifting through the letters. There was a small package for me.

It was professionally wrapped in brown paper, tied neatly with white string and fastened with red lacquer seals. There was a return label that read *The Oxford Book Suppliers Ltd.* and a Calcutta address. I opened it quickly to find a slim volume of Tagore's poems, *Gitanjali.* It was a beautiful handmade book, bound in red silk with a gold-patterned border. It reminded me of a wedding sari. I flipped it open to a page that held a bookmark. The bookmark was cream-colored, die-cut of nubbly handmade paper with a block-printed gold paisley motif. The name and address of the bookstore was printed below it. I read the poem on the marked page, my heart beating wildly.

Pluck this little flower and take it, delay not! I fear lest it droop and drop into the dust.
I may not find a place in thy garland, but honor it with a touch of pain from thy hand and pluck it. I fear lest the day end before I am aware, and the time of offering go by.

Inside the cover of the book, Manik had inscribed *For you* in an elegant scrawl that ran right across the page. It was signed with an *M.* Mysteriously obtuse, no names mentioned anywhere. Inside was a folded note.

Dear Layla,
I came across this book of Tagore's poems and thought of you.
Please accept this small gift as a remembrance of our talks to-
gether.
Manik

I could envision him scrawling across the page, the nib of his fountain pen catching slightly on the rough fibers of the handmade paper. Was it a coincidence that the bookmark had been on that particular page? Of course not! I chided myself. He was just a friend, nothing more. Yet what if...? Tiny tendrils of hope pushed through my brain.

That night I slept with the book and Manik's handkerchief under my pillow. I had the strangest dream. Manik Deb was standing in a lily pond among the reeds and shaking out the pages of the silk-covered book. Hundreds of fireflies fell out into the water. They spun around in dizzy circles, sizzling like cumin seeds in hot oil before their lights extinguished one by one. At the far end of the pond, on the opposite bank I could see a small girl stretching out her thin arms toward him. "Look at me, Dada, I can fly!" she cried in a chirping voice. But Manik did not see or hear her. He just continued opening the pages of the book and releasing the fireflies.

It was then that I woke up.

It is hard to describe the emotional turmoil I went through in the weeks that followed. I felt hopelessly conflicted. There was so much I wanted to believe and so much I dared not. A streak of guilt coursed through my mind every time I thought about Manik Deb. Our society was bound by unwritten rules and I had overstepped an invisible line. Accepting a gift of love poems from another woman's fiancé was as illicit as being kissed. Yet it was deliciously arousing and I felt hopelessly drawn.

I could have brushed off Manik's gesture, put the book on my shelf and gone on with my life. Yet I clung to it like my last, slim, red-and-gold hope on earth. I caressed the silk cover, kissed the long pen strokes of his inscription. I savored every poem and swelled with the cadence of the lines and felt irresistibly connected to the heart where it was coming from. I knew it was the poet and not Manik who wrote the words but I wanted desperately to believe otherwise. Those were strangely melded days where I floated in limbo, an outsider to the world around me, a firefly baffled by daylight.

CHAPTER

8

Finally the rains abated. The sky gathered her dark, voluminous skirts and swept over the Himalayas into Tibet, leaving behind a drizzle like a sprinkling of fairy dust. Life returned to normal.

The ground was rich and moist. The earth turned a shrill and noisy green, vibrant as a parrot. The evenings felt lighter now, and on some days there was a lilt of autumn in the air. A river breeze flitted through the house, suffusing rooms with the scent of jasmine. Dadamoshai resumed his writing on the veranda.

It was late afternoon and I was reading in my room when I heard an unfamiliar voice calling out a greeting on the veranda. I parted the curtains a crack. My heart skipped a beat when I saw it was Mr. Sen, Kona's father. He was not a regular visitor to our house.

Mr. Sen was a portly, round-shouldered man, dressed traditionally in a white dhoti and a handwoven brown waistcoat over his long starched cotton shirt. His face was black and shiny as a plum. He had oily hair, bright, beady eyes and a neatly trimmed mustache over a small mouth that was

pulled tight as a purse string. His small plump hands were
weighted down with an array of auspicious gemstone rings—
coral, tigereye, topaz—each promising some aspect of health
or wealth to its wearer.

Dadamoshai was in the middle of his writing, and I could
see he was distracted with a thought half strung across his
brain. As usual, he looked like a preoccupied sage, surrounded
by his books and papers, his snow-white hair unkempt, his
glasses askew on his nose. He was barefoot, his worn wooden
clogs undoubtedly lost somewhere under his desk.

"My dear Rai Sahib, I have been meaning to pay you a
visit." Mr. Sen leaned his umbrella against the post and held
out his hands in an exaggerated gesture of effusiveness toward
my grandfather.

"A pleasant surprise, Sen Babu, a pleasant surprise indeed!"
Dadamoshai exclaimed, patting absentmindedly for the cap of
his fountain pen under his papers and shuffling his foot under
the desk to feel for his clogs. "Please, please, do have a seat."

Mr. Sen gathered the pleats of his dhoti with care and
perched on the edge of the sofa, like a plump sparrow on a
windowsill. He watched with a beatific smile as my grandfather
tried to get his bumbling act together. Despite all the cordial-
ity between him and my grandfather, their relationship bordered on distaste. Mr. Sen's visit was undoubtedly suspicious.

I strained my ears to listen to their conversation. Mr. Sen was
talking about the preparations for Kona's wedding. He dropped
numbers here and there, pretending to bemoan the costs of
things, but all the while seeking to impress Dadamoshai with
how much money he was spending.

"You have no idea how much it costs to get a girl married
these days. We are in the middle of wartime and every item

is either in short supply or priced to make your hands bleed," he lamented.

Dadamoshai was trying very hard to look engaged. "I must congratulate you, Sen Babu. You have indeed made a fine choice of a son-in-law in Manik Deb. He is an exceptional young man with a remarkable future ahead of him," he said conversationally.

Mr. Sen's eyes wandered off into the jasmine trellis. He suddenly looked morose and crestfallen. His mustache twitched, and he nibbled his lips nervously, looking amazingly like a rodent.

"Manik Deb..." He paused, as if recalling a painful toothache. "Manik Deb has let us all down badly. He has devastated his family name and mine. It is unforgivable what he has done."

Dadamoshai sat up, surprised, his eyes bright with curiosity. "Goodness gracious, is something wrong?"

"More than wrong, Rai Bahadur, sir, more than wrong! The biggest calamity has befallen our family." Mr. Sen wiped his brow with the tail end of his starched cotton dhoti. He leaned forward, took a grateful sip of tea from the cup Chaya had just set down and sighed deeply and sadly.

I pressed against the wall of my bedroom, almost fusing myself into the plaster, trying to get every word.

"Can you believe that this foolish fellow has given up his prestigious job in civil service and decided instead to become a tea planter!"

"A tea planter!" exclaimed Dadamoshai in wonderment, and with a twinge of awe.

"Yes, a tea planter." Mr. Sen spat out the words distastefully like small eggshells he had just found in his omelet. "Imagine that! Who goes through a fine Oxford education with honors and distinctions to become, of all things, a *tea planter*?"

I could see Dadamoshai was highly amused. He threw back his head, let out a belly laugh and thumped the sofa cushion. Mr. Sen stiffened.

"Why does this amuse you, sir? Please explain yourself. I do not see the joke in this."

Dadamoshai quickly composed himself. "Pardon me, Sen Babu. I did not mean to insult you," he said apologetically. "But I do think it is rather bold and adventurous of the young man to deviate from the beaten path. I have heard tea jobs are very prestigious. It is rare for an Indian to be employed by a British company. They only hire Europeans, I know. I think you should be proud of your future son-in-law. It is a great honor for an Indian to be selected, really."

"Honor? So that he can run around in the jungles with those debauched Englishmen? Rai Bahadur, sir, I have not been so deeply ashamed in my entire life! He has made a laughingstock of us all. Kona and her mother have not stopped crying since they got the news. All we received was one brief telegram, that's all. 'Change of career. Accepted job with Jardine Henley Co. as Assistant Manager in Aynakhal Tea Estate. Details to follow.' What details? There has not been another squeak from Manik Deb. He has not replied to any letters from his family for the past month. He has simply vanished like a coward into the jungle."

I could hardly believe what I was hearing. *A tea planter?* Why would Manik want to do that, of all things?

"And that is not the worst part," Mr. Sen was saying. "Manik Deb has signed a contract that does not allow him to marry for the first three years. It is the company rule. He did this without telling any of us. The shame of it all."

"This may not be a bad thing," Dadamoshai mused. "It

will give Kona some time to mature before she marries. It is always advisable."

"Mature, you say! Why, sir, my daughter will be a *seed pumpkin* by the time Manik Deb is ready to exchange garlands with her. How can I risk that?"

Mr. Sen nibbled his lips some more. Even from a distance, I saw glistening beads of sweat on his brow. "She has already waited seven years for this worthless fellow and spent all this time embroidering tablecloths! What is she to do for another three years? Embroider more tablecloths, you tell me?"

"Send her to school," Dadamoshai suggested brightly. "An educated girl will make a fine companion for Manik Deb. He seems to enjoy intellectual conversations."

"No, no, no, Rai Bahadur, sir, you are not getting the point!" Mr. Sen fanned himself furiously. "A girl of a marriageable age cannot be left on the shelf for too long. She will become like the suitcase left behind at a station where trains do not stop by anymore. Then I will have to pay even more money to get her married. I am beginning to doubt Manik Deb's sanity. His tea-garden job has no future. Life in the plantations is very—what shall I say—different. There are only Europeans. I don't know how my daughter will fit in. If only he could give us an explanation for his senseless decision. Which, my dear Rai Sahib, brings me to the reason why I have come to see you today. I need a favor from you."

"Ah," said Dadamoshai. He had probably suspected all along that his wily neighbor had an ulterior motive for dropping by.

"I know Manik Deb spent a lot of time in your company. He is a great admirer of your ideas, writings and such." He waved his hand dismissively. "Did he by any chance talk to you about applying for a tea-plantation job?" Mr. Sen eyed my grandfather suspiciously, as if he was a coconspirator in Manik's deceit.

"My goodness, he mentioned not a word of it to me," said Dadamoshai, his eyes round and innocent as a child. "I am sure Manik has his reasons for making a career change. Have you tried to contact him?"

"Oh yes, we called the Jardine Henley Head Office in Calcutta several times. I finally spoke to one senior director. He was most cordial. When I told him I was calling from Silchar, he asked me if I knew you. His name is James Lovelace."

"Oh yes, James Lovelace! Of course, I know him well." Dadamoshai smiled broadly. "He is the brother of a very dear friend of mine. I heard James was in India, but I had no idea he worked for a tea company."

"Well, James Lovelace is a big shot of Jardine Henley & Company. He is very impressed with your work in the field of education, and praised your intelligence, character, etcetera. And since you are such a dear friend of his brother's in England..."

"Sister, actually," Dadamoshai said a little dreamily.

Mr. Sen's piggy eyes were quick to catch on. Ha! He seemed to be thinking, the sister—no doubt one of the Rai Bahadur's sleazy English mistresses. But this was no time for moral judgments. He was on a crucial mission.

"Well, his sister, then...but maybe you could use your influence with James Lovelace to contact Manik Deb? We urgently need to speak to him. Manik's older brother, who arranged this marriage, is very disturbed. He thinks he can convince Manik to change his mind before it is too late, which is why we have not postponed the date for the wedding."

"That...I cannot promise," said Dadamoshai evasively. He did not believe in arm-twisting someone in his or her career choice. "Maybe we should trust the young man's decision. What I have seen of Manik tells me he is no run-of-the-mill fellow. The tea-plantation job may suit his adventurous spirit just fine."

"But what about my daughter? Who knows what goes on in those tea gardens? I don't know a single person who knows anything about the kind of life there, do you?"

"As a matter of fact, I do. I have an English friend who visited his brother in a tea plantation here in Assam. What he described to me was most interesting." Dadamoshai rubbed his chin thoughtfully. "I also read the most fascinating book on the history of Assam tea. It's a real eye-opener. You should read it, Sen Babu. It will give you a much better understanding."

Mr. Sen twirled the coral ring around his finger forlornly. He picked up his cup, but it was empty.

"Another cup of tea, Sen Babu?"

"Yes, thank you, I would like that very much," said Mr. Sen. He decided to change the subject. "So how is everything going with the English school project? James Lovelace was very keen to know the details, but unfortunately I did not have much information. I told him I would give you his telephone number and you would contact him."

"The school project is most challenging, Sen Babu. We have an acute shortage of funds as you can understand. Perhaps you would consider making a small donation? We have sixty students and only two classrooms. How can the poor girls concentrate on their studies when they are sitting four or five to a bench butting elbows, with no place to write?"

Mr. Sen waved his hands as if brushing off a gnat. "My dear Rai Bahadur, whose fault is that? Young girls were not meant to go through such hardships. They should stay at home and prepare for marriage. The importance of cooking and sewing for girls should not be undermined. Besides, what are the girls going to do with all this education? It is a cart with no horse!"

I could see Dadamoshai stiffening. "Mr. Sen, is not dignity and self-confidence in a young woman worth anything? Our society treats women like they came floating down the Ganges. Should they not be given a choice in their future?"

When Dadamoshai got riled up, his eyebrows bristled. He leaned forward, tapping the coffee table with his forefinger. "Tell me, Mr. Sen, how is a woman supposed to fend for herself if things go wrong? Young girls are married off to men twice their age! We have too many child brides and too many young widows in our society, Mr. Sen, *too many widows*! And you know how our society treats widows."

"Rai Bahadur, sir, I agree it is unfortunate if a young wife loses her husband, but at least she still has her in-laws. Who does a spinster have? No one. I still believe marriage is the best solution for girls. At least it grants them an honorable place in society." Then he waved a heavy ringed hand dismissively in the air. "But forget all that, getting my daughter married will put me in the poorhouse. I will not have even one anna to spare. You cannot imagine the exorbitant price of *rui* fish these days. I was speaking to the fishmonger only yesterday..."

But I was not listening anymore. Something told me unseen forces were shaping my future in mysterious ways. I was getting pulled into the flow, not exactly as flotsam, but a buoyant, eager participant, fully trusting the tide. And who knew? Maybe with the right "breeje" I would catch a current and float right into Manik Deb's life.

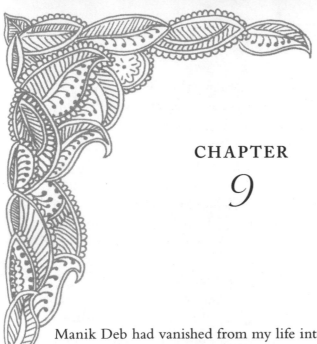

CHAPTER

9

Manik Deb had vanished from my life into a tea plantation, swallowed by the roiling, steamy jungles of Assam, a territory so remote and forbidden that it was deemed inaccessible to common man.

Nobody knew much about tea plantations. It was an esoteric, colonial world barricaded by a cultural divide, so far removed from the life in our teeming Indian subcontinent that it may as well have been several stratospheres away.

Now that one of our local boys had disappeared into this rarefied atmosphere, our small town tittered with gossip. The question on most people's mind was, *why*? Why would Manik Deb throw away a good job, jeopardize a marriage alliance of seven years and strain relations with his family to become a tea planter? To what end? A tea planter's job had little merit or security.

And what sort of life would his wife have? There were no temples, no cultural functions, no like-minded Indians to socialize with. Forget about the Europeans. They were a different ilk. They stuck to their own. With their promiscuous women in short skirts, shamelessly exposing their legs, their uncontrolled whiskey drinking and wild dancing in the clubs, how would an Indian boy fit into this society? But anybody could see, Manik Deb was hardly a typical Indian boy. In many ways he was more like them. Yet, cynics would argue, Manik Deb may have buffed his fur with fine English education and manners, but he could never change his spots. He was an Indian and would always be one. The Europeans looked down on the likes of him: he was coconut-brown on the outside and white on the inside. Manik Deb would never be accepted into a white man's world.

I, more than anybody else, itched to know the answers. I kept my ears pricked for news and clutched at motes of information floating in the air around me. I decided to look for the book Dadamoshai was talking about. And there it was, in his library—a slim green volume on the history of Assam. It was a 1917 research publication and it had a whole section detailing the tea industry in Assam.

I could hardly contain my excitement. I raced through lunch that day so that I could curl up on the veranda sofa to devour its contents. It was a mine full of information. I had always been an obsessive fact finder. Dadamoshai said I had a researcher's brain that allowed me to sift through mountains of material and distill information. This was true. I learned more about Assam tea in one rainy afternoon than all the heads of our entire town put together.

In the 1940s, an era of the fading Raj, tea plantations in India remained the last stronghold of the British Empire. Owned by Sterling companies, they produced the finest teas on earth. Assam tea was grown exclusively for export and shipped from the plantations directly to London to be sold at the Mincing Lane tea auction for exorbitant prices. From there it was distributed to the rest of Europe and the world.

I stopped my reading to think. People in India drank a lot of tea, too. It seemed pretty ordinary stuff. So where did *our* tea come from? Here we were right in the middle of Assam, so surely it was Assam tea?

I got up from the sofa and went to the kitchen. I took down the container of loose tea and poked around the contents with my finger. It looked like fine granules, almost a powder. It smelled like tea. Nothing exceptional.

I decided to make myself a cup. I filled the kettle with water and put it on the stove. I leaned against the counter to continue reading in the dim light of the kitchen as I waited for the water to boil.

The next section was an eye-opener. Little wonder why we poor Indians never got a whiff of quality Assam tea. All the fine tea grown in the plantations, 100 percent, was shipped overseas. What was sold in the Indian market was the lowest grade, or what was commonly known as tea dust.

I closed the book, marking my page with a teaspoon. As I poured the tea through a strainer, I noticed it had a nice strong color and good aroma, but my newfound knowledge now told me I was drinking bottom-of-the-barrel quality. I would never have known that.

I carried my tea back to the veranda. The rain had stopped. The cat, all stealth and muscle, was creeping along the garden wall, stalking a sparrow, which was busy fluffing its feathers. The sun peeked through the parting clouds, and raindrops hung from the jasmine trellis like translucent pearls.

I returned to the sofa and stirred my tea as I read on.

The tea-growing belt in Assam was cradled in the fertile, silt-rich valley between two mighty rivers—the Surma and the Bhramaputra. The picturesque Khasi and Jaintia hills cut a green swath in between. This region was remote and largely unexplored. Tea plantations were located in far-flung areas, across bridgeless rivers, beyond the boundaries of any trodden path and in the middle of dense, malaria-infested rain forests surrounded by wild game and hostile head-hunting Naga tribes.

In 1823 an intrepid Scottish adventurer who went by the name of Robert Bruce tramped through the leech-infested jungles along the Assam-Burmese border, encountering unexpected mishaps and every manner of blight and misery along the way. He had barely recovered from a potentially lethal snakebite when he found himself spending a night up a tree, bone-rattled by a rogue elephant he had unwittingly enraged by misfiring his gun. As if that wasn't enough, he was constantly being stalked by the hostile head-hunting Nagas, who lurked in the brush with their black-painted faces and poison-tipped spears.

Robert Bruce was beginning to regret this whole mission. He was harried and at the end of his tether when he spied a thin curl of blue smoke spiraling over the treetops. He approached warily, gun drawn, and came across a tribal settlement deep in the forest.

He'd feared his intrusion would provoke hostility, and was surprised to find the gnomelike natives were a cheerful and friendly lot. They were the Burmese Singpo tribe, undoubtedly the sweetest, most benign people on earth! The Singpos welcomed him and escorted him with the beating of tom-toms to their moonfaced, lotus-eyed chief, who went by the grand name of Bessagaum Ningrual.

Bruce was seated on an elevated platform, fanned by palm fronds and offered a swig of steaming brew from a bamboo cup. Not wanting to offend his host, he took a few hesitant sips of this strange concoction. To his amazement, he felt immediately

relaxed and all his cares and woes floated away. After down-
ing the last drop, Bruce was so invigorated that he wanted to
scale a tree and shout at the sky. What *was* this strange drink?
He was told it was *Cha*, a beverage made by steeping the tender leaves of an unknown plant in boiling water. The plant
grew wild in the forest, and when he was taken to see it, he
found it was the size of a poplar tree and had deep green serrated leaves and pale waxy flowers.

Robert Bruce could not get over the remarkable rejuvenat-
ing properties of *Cha*. As he bade farewell to his friendly hosts,
he carried the seeds of the plant in his pocket and turned them
over to the Botanical Society in Calcutta for research and de-
velopment. The plant was subsequently named the *Camellia
assamica*. Research showed that when this plant was pruned
tight like a privet hedge it flushed with a profusion of tender
leaf tips. These tips, handpicked and processed, yielded the
finest tea in the world.

I was familiar with the camellia bush. It was a common
flowering plant in Assam. Till then I had no idea it was the
same plant that yielded Assam tea. In fact, we had a camellia bush growing right by the garden wall. I wondered if the
leaves smelled anything like tea.

Outside in the garden, the air was fresh and moist after
the rains. The cat had nabbed the bird. It licked its paws and
rubbed its whiskers and looked at me with baleful yellow eyes.
All that remained of the poor sparrow were a few feathers and
a bit of bloodied wing.

The camellia bush in our garden was heavy with pink blossoms. The flower was larger than a primrose and similar in
shape, and just as delicate and pretty. I picked a leaf and crushed
it between my fingers. Strange, it hardly had any tea smell at all.

A beautiful mottled green-and-gold snail inched up the

mossy garden wall. It moved ponderously, pausing to sense its way with large striped feelers. *Not like our impetuous friend, Manik Deb,* I thought, *who plunges into the unknown and goes crashing off into the jungles.* A little snail-like caution might have done him good. I was beginning to agree with the townsfolk: he did sound like a lunatic.

I returned to the veranda and picked up the book again.

It seemed the discovery of Assam tea in India could not have come at a more crucial time. Tea drinking was the rage in Victorian England, and the demand for fine teas had spread like fire all across Europe. The fad was started by the fashionable Duchess of Bedford in England, who experienced what she described as a "sinking feeling" in the late afternoons. It was she who popularized the tradition of high tea as an afternoon pick-me-up, and tea parties developed into a dainty ritual and became a fashionable pastime among the ladies of the court.

The only tea available in England back then was imported from China. As demands for the beverage skyrocketed all over Europe, the Chinese raised their prices and arm-twisted the British, holding them hostage. To counter this, the British resorted to subterfuge. They stole Chinese tea seedlings and smuggled them across the border through Burma into India and tried to secretly grow Chinese tea in Assam. Although the climate and topography in Assam was almost identical to China, the plant did poorly and the experiment failed.

It was about this very time when Robert Bruce stumbled upon the *Camellia assamica* after being befriended by the Singpo Chief, Bessagaum Ningrual. One can only surmise how elated the British must have been with this momentous discovery. *To find the best tea growing wild and free in their own colonial backyard!* Better still, the indigenous *Camellia assamica* was far superior to the Chinese variety. Growing tea in India opened up immense lucrative possibilities for the colonial empire and promised to augment the royal coffers significantly.

But sobriety soon set in. Discovering the plant was one thing; setting up an organized tea industry in Assam was another.

Assam could be brutal and unforgiving. The climate was a curse, the food unpalatable and the natives baffling. Assam received an astounding one hundred inches of rain per annum. Roads got washed away and bridges rotted to their demise. The most grueling part of tea-plantation life was the isolation and loneliness. The only way to keep the young men there was to make them sign a company contract. Planters were not allowed to marry for three years so that they could concentrate on their job without distraction and, more specifically, female whining. It was believed that women were the root cause of men quitting their jobs.

Many young Europeans fell victim to accident and disease, never to see the shores of their homeland again. Some took their own lives in desperation. There are hundreds of moss-covered graves scattered across tea plantations in Assam, mostly in wooded areas, tangled in vegetation and overrun by creepers. Many are unmarked but some have carved inscriptions that speak of the short, precarious lives of these young men in Assam.

For mysterious reasons, Manik Deb had disappeared into this uncertain and little-known world. I was suddenly filled with despair. Would I ever see him again? He seemed to have faded into the ether, beyond reach. What if something happened to him?

I closed the book. All I wanted to know was—why? Why had he just upped and gone?

Little did I know, I would soon find out. And I would hear it straight from the horse's mouth.

The letter was addressed to me in a familiar slanted hand. Just the sight of it made my heart flutter. I went to my room and shut the door. I turned the letter over. No return address. The smudged stamp of the post office read MARIANI. It was from Manik.

Aynakhal T.E.
17th September 1943
Dear Layla,
I take the liberty of writing directly to you. I hope you forgive my audacity. You are the only person I feel will not judge me too harshly. Maybe you will take pity on a lonely tea planter and write back. I only dare to hope.

I have not written a single letter since I have been in Aynakhal, which is almost three months. I feel a strange sense of disconnect with the outside world.

Before this job, I had little idea of life in the tea plantations. I was aware tea gardens in Assam are located in remote areas, but Aynakhal Tea Estate seems to be in the godforsaken nowhere.

All hints of civilization disappear by the time we cross the Dargakona Bridge, which is sixty miles east of Silchar. We enter the forestland and it takes another two-hour drive over dirt roads (if they can be called such) to get to the outreaches of Aynakhal. The last stretch is little more than an overgrown jungle track. It is common to see elephants cross the road. Plenty of sambar, barking deer and wild pigs, too. Once, late at night on our way back from the Planters Club, we saw a leopard.

We have had a spate of heavy rain, rather untimely for this time of the year. Puddles all over the jungle roads. Mud but-

terflies congregate by the hundreds. You don't notice them until you come right up to them. Their wings are the most brilliant cerulean-blue you can imagine. The flock takes off like a shimmering silk scarf when we drive past. I have never seen anything quite so magical.

Jardine Henley (the British company that owns Aynakhal plus six other tea estates in the Mariani district) provides us with company jeeps to get around. They are used army vehicles, four-wheel drive. Without them we could get nowhere. Actually, there is no place to go except to the Planters Club on Monday nights and visits to other gardens. I am still trying to get used to the isolation here but I can't say I am unhappy.

Most evenings I go hunting with Alasdair Carruthers. He is a Scottish fellow and Assistant Manager at Chulsa Tea Estate, the neighboring garden just cross the Koilapani River. He is a crack shot and is teaching yours truly the rudiments of shikar. I must admit he has me hooked. We have an excellent selection of wild game and plenty of opportunity to practice. It's Greener Pigeon season. Good eating bird. I bought myself a blunderbuss (an old 12-bore Belgium shotgun), which, to my exasperation, seems to jam at the most inopportune moments. But this is the best that I can afford right now.

I hope you enjoy the small book of Tagore's poems I picked up for you in Calcutta. I have fond memories of our time together. Best wishes,
Manik Deb

I lay in bed imagining Manik tramping through a jungle armed with his blunderbuss—a rusty old musket, in my imagination. The thickets rustled with dangerous game and flocks of greener pigeons took to the skies. I felt his keen sense of excitement and heard the joy in his voice. Manik Deb did not sound like a coward hiding in the jungle: he sounded like a koel set free.

CHAPTER

10

That October I started training as an assistant teacher under Miss Rose in Dadamoshai's school. In the afternoons I gave private tuition to students at home. One day just as the girls were getting ready to leave, I saw an army type of jeep pull up and park under the mango tree outside our gate. A European gentleman unlatched the gate and held it open gallantly like a doorman as the three little girls giggled past him. He then closed the gate and walked toward the house.

He was a stocky man with a craggy weathered face and the kindest blue eyes.

"Is this number eight Rai Bahadur Road?" he asked with a shy smile. He spoke in a rich brogue.

"Yes," I said, wondering who he was.

"I have a letter for Layla Roy from Manik Deb in Aynakhal," said the man. "My name is Alasdair Carruthers."

Alasdair Carruthers, Manik's hunting partner!

The letter had a postage stamp. Alasdair explained that Manik had asked him to post the letter in Silchar, but it was quicker for him to drop it off. He saw Rai Bahadur Road on the address and realized it was the very same road he took to go to the village across the river—which was where he was headed.

The village across the river, how very odd, I thought. No white person ever went there. It was a rather desperate section of the town, inhabited by poor Muslim fishermen and accessible only by boat. I wondered if Alasdair knew that.

Apparently he did.

"Somebody will come by boat to meet me on this bank," he said. "This fine road looks like it was designed for a bridge, y'ken, but it stops abruptly at the river. I have always wondered about it."

"There were plans for a bridge. It just never got built," I said. "Would you care for a cup of tea, Mr. Carruthers?"

"Aye, that would be lovely, thank you." There was so much I wanted to ask him. *He had breathed the same air as Manik Deb!*

But Alasdair spoke in generalities when it came to Manik Deb, describing him in his brogue as a "guid chap" who had a keen nose for shikar and was shaping up to be a fine planter. Aynakhal, he said, was one of Jardine Henley's most profitable and premium tea gardens in the Mariani district.

"You will be the *Chotamemsahib* of Aynakhal," said Alasdair.

"What do you mean?" I asked.

"The assistant's wife is called the *Chotamemsahib*, y'ken. Manik is counting the days when he can be married to you."

"Well…" This was terribly awkward and I wondered how to put it. "I am not Manik's fiancée. We are just friends."

"But he told me he was engaged…?"

"He still is, as far as I know."

"I beg your pardon—I do apologize!" Alasdair exclaimed, flustered. "Manik never told me a thing. Of course he didn't expect me to meet you in person. He only asked me to drop off the letter at the post office."

"That's quite understandable," I said and decided to change the subject. "Please tell me more about the tea gardens."

The term *tea gardens*, I realized, was misleading. They were not small tea farms as I had fondly imagined, but large-scale, sophisticated plantations, averaging 600 to 3,000 acres, some with over 1,500 residents, most of whom were *coolies*, or tea pluckers. Besides the tea-growing area itself, each plantation was a fully self-contained entity. It had its own tea-processing factory, forestland, rice fields, water and power supply, brickworks, housing and medical facilities. They were like mini townships and run like autonomous entities under the helm of the General Manager. Assam, I learned, had over 700 tea gardens dotting the river valley and most of them were located far beyond the reaches of civilization.

"Strange why such a large-scale industry was set up in such inhospitable terrain," I mused.

"Aye," said Alasdair. "It is not quite so incomprehensible, if you think about it." He was stuffing sprigs of tobacco from a round, flat tin into the bowl of his curved Dunhill pipe. "You see, the tea plant, this particular variety, is very fussy. It will not grow anywhere else."

Alasdair explained that the shy and reclusive *Camellia assamica* grew where it wanted, not where it was planted. Any attempts to relocate the plant outside its natural habitat caused it to wilt and die. Even transporting the seeds affected germination. This plant simply refused to budge.

"So, if tea could not be brought to civilization, civilization had to be brought to tea. The mountain to Muhammad, so to speak, aye?" Alasdair said. There was something utterly likable about Alasdair: he had the well-worn solidity and comfort of aged mahogany. "We British want to shape everything in the world to fit us, don't we? Aye, but only a fool tries to tame Assam. The harder we try to change the land, the more it will change us. Assam has untamed the white man and made *junglees* out of us."

Did I detect a hint of cynicism? Alasdair Carruthers was a curious man. I had never heard anyone speak so disparagingly of his own kind.

"What made you become a tea planter?" I asked.

Alasdair shot me a glance. He flicked open a gold lighter and drew in the flame to his pipe. Then he clipped the lighter shut. I noticed a crested emblem of a *C* etched on top.

"It's a long story," he said, pulling thoughtfully on his pipe. "Some would say I ran away."

"From what?"

"Tyranny." Alasdair smiled deeply and his eyes crinkled. He did not elaborate.

The more Alasdair talked about tea planters, I got the impression that "running away" to join tea plantations was more the norm than the exception. Planters were an odd medley of characters, and many sounded as though they were absconding from something or the other: Brits ran away from the gloomy weather of their homeland, soldiers ran away to forget their war demons, Alasdair was running away from tyranny and Manik from his arranged marriage. Tea gardens were the perfect place to shut out the world, and ferreting somebody out of those malaria-ridden jungles was as difficult as extricating a flea from a warthog.

Manik Deb was a canny fellow. He knew what he was doing.

After Alasdair left I tore open Manik's letter.

Aynakhal T.E.
14th October 1943 6:15 a.m.
Dear Layla,
I must have read your letter a hundred times!

As you can see, our postal service is not the most reliable. It took your letter twenty-seven days to get here. I had given up all hope of hearing from you!

I am replying immediately as I want to send this letter through Alasdair Carruthers. He is going to Silchar today and will post it in town so you should get it tomorrow.

I am sitting on a log in Division 3 of our tea plantation writing to you. I am on kamjari *duty, which is the field inspection we assistants have to do every morning (we are expected to be at our designated sections by 5:45 a.m. come rain or shine). Today my job is to supervise the pruning of bushes of Division 3.*

We have a small crisis here. A cow got stuck in the cattle trap last night. (You may not know what a cattle trap is? They are railing separators over culverts at the entrance to the tea-growing areas, mostly to keep domestic cattle out.) The cow had fallen in and broken both front legs. It took eight laborers to haul it out with ropes. What a job! All that kicking and bellowing and people shouting! They managed to push it onto the grassy bank on the side of the road. The poor creature is not going to survive, and we need to put it out of its misery, but that is not as simple as it sounds.

The laborers won't kill the cow because they are Hindu. Willfully killing a holy animal according to their beliefs will bring bad luck. We management can't do it either because if we shoot it, we risk a labor riot. This is a typical example of the peculiar problems we management have to deal with almost on a daily basis. Never a dull moment in Aynakhal.

From where I write I can hear the poor creature bellowing nonstop. I am keeping an eye out for our General Manager, Mr. McIntyre, who may show up here anytime. He is our slave-driving boss. There will be hell to pay if he catches me sitting on a log writing letters to a girl when we have a half-dead cow on our hands. Section 3 is under my jurisdiction and I am expected to troubleshoot any petty problem without involving him, be it a labor brawl, a cow with broken legs, snakebite or what have you. I am hoping Larry Baker, the other assistant, shows up soon. He may have a better solution to this bovine problem. He is a smart fellow and has been longer in tea than I have.

Enough about tea. (Oops, a raindrop ran the ink on this page—wait a minute, I need to get to a shelter....) Okay, now I am in the seedbari*—which is the covered planting nursery. I am surrounded by hundreds of pots with tiny tea seedlings under a thatched roof. It has begun to drizzle slightly.*

I just saw a single-seater British fighter aircraft pass overhead. A Spitfire, I think it was. It flew precariously low, rattling the malibari*, and I could clearly see the face of pilot wearing his goggles. He was busy looking down at the cow. There have been quite a few plane crashes around here. Several years ago, I'm told, a wreckage was found in the thick jungle bordering Aynakhal and Chulsa. The Aynakhal assistant (Larry's predecessor) made the coolies drag out the massive propeller and load it onto a garden truck and bring it to his bungalow, where it still graces the front garden as a lawn ornament.*

I have to end for now, because I hear Larry's motorcycle. This cow problem is hanging over my head. Mr. McIntyre will be here in 10 minutes. He is always on the dot of time.
My very best to you.
Manik

Alasdair mentioned he would be passing by our house again later that evening and if I liked he could carry a letter back for Manik from me. I penned a quick reply and a week later there was another letter from Manik.

Aynakhal T.E.
18th October 1943
Dear Layla,
I am so pleased you chose to send a reply back with Alasdair.
Imagine my surprise when he told me he had met you! I must
have driven him crazy with my questions!

Jamina's father lives in the fishing village by the river, next
to your house. I had no idea Alasdair had gone to see him. He
said it made more sense to drop off the letter than to post it. He
was very surprised to find you at home. I had not told him about
you, so I am not surprised he thought you were my fiancée. I
understand that caused some awkwardness between you two. I
do apologize.

Now to answer your very valid questions. I am actually very
glad you asked. Most people are itching to know, but dread the
answers. It is as if I contracted some terrible disease and they
fear the prognosis.

To get back to the point, yes, I gave up the civil-service job.
Why? Because Layla Roy did not want to marry a government
officer! Of course I am joking! The simple reason is the gov-
ernment job looked bureaucratic and boring. In a single word:
soulless.

I actually applied to Jardine Henley on a whim, curious to
see what the tea job was all about. An English friend of mine
in Calcutta told me that Sterling Tea Companies were open-
ing up managerial positions for the first time to Indians. I went
for the interview and to my surprise I was offered the Assistant
Manager job in Aynakhal Tea Estate. The Assistant Manager
position is the lowliest rung of the managerial ladder.

They asked me some very strange questions at the interview.
The first one was, if I had plans to get married in the next
three years. I don't think I even batted an eye when I answered,

"No." Many people would call me a blatant liar. Suddenly it was clear as day—I was not ready to get married. I saw this job as my survival. I need to buy some time to think things through more clearly.

The rest of my interview was equally odd. The Directors showed little interest in my academic achievements. They were excited to learn I played tennis and rugby. They asked if I liked to hunt, fish or play bridge. It felt more like an interview for a country club. Then came two of the strangest questions of all: Do you drink, and are you a vegetarian?

I answered "occasionally" to the first and "no" to the second. I later found that drinking is high on their list of credentials and being a vegetarian, an immediate disqualification. I figure what they really want to know is if I have the Westernized mind-set to fit into the tea culture. Everything else about the job can be taught.

Now that I am here, I understand this much better. Tea life is still very colonial. Social clubs, hunting, sporting events, formal dinner parties and so on. It is a whole different lifestyle, and I can see why most Indians would have a hard time adjusting.

But I digress: I don't want to sound like I am avoiding your questions. So back to your very stern interrogation. (Your questions make me far more nervous than theirs....)

Yes, I gave up the government job. My family still acts like I committed murder. They are shocked and enraged beyond belief. I have not written to anyone or been home since I telegrammed them. I am waiting for the dust to settle before I face the firing squad—not something I am looking forward to.

Question number two, albeit a more delicate one regarding Kona. Yes, she is upset. Her family is upset. The whole world is upset. I have not written or seen them, either. Kona's father had not bargained for his daughter marrying a junior tea planter

and living in obscurity in the jungles. She was groomed for a
cushy life in the city.

Everyone thinks I am throwing my future away, but strangely
I have no regrets. I am happier now than I have ever been in
my life. I think it is the freedom to choose that I love the best.

I hope you will not think less of me for making what many
may consider a poor decision. Sometimes there are reasons only
the heart understands.

Yours truly,
Manik

Any sensible person would agree that throwing away the
civil-service job was nothing short of impaired judgment on
Manik's part. What was more disconcerting, Manik had accepted the tea job "on a whim" without having a clue of what
it entailed. As for signing the contract agreeing not to get married for three years...*three years!* Did he expect Kona to wait for
him? I could sympathize with Manik when he said he felt he
was being pressured into marriage and understand him need-
ing more time to think, but his whole handling of the situation with the families was nothing short of dishonorable. I
could never imagine Dadamoshai, for one, doing something
so cowardly. But I found myself dismissing his shortcomings
for my own selfish reason: receiving his letters made me so
deliriously happy, nothing else really mattered.

CHAPTER
11

Manik and I continued to exchange letters over the next several months. The weather ceased to matter and I had only two kinds of days. Good Days and Waiting Days. April arrived and a subdued *dhola* drumbeat pulsed through the bamboo grooves. It was Rangoli Bihu, the spring harvest festival—the most joyous time in Assam, typically celebrated with a whole week of reveling and feasting. But that year the festivities were low-key because a thread of tension was running through our town.

In a surprise move, the Japanese Imperial Army had infiltrated India through Assam. They inched past the sawtooth mountains into Manipur and headed straight for the small Naga town of Dimapur, just northeast of Silchar. The invasion came on the heels of Britain's crushing defeat in Singapore and its faltering hold on other colonies around the globe. It was a tactical move by the Japanese to overthrow the British in India. Dimapur was the hub of the Assam-Bengal railway, the only lifeline of food and military supplies for British troops stationed in Burma. If the Japanese captured Dimapur it would have devastating consequences for British troops and the British Empire and most likely tip the balance of power.

Suddenly Assam was no longer inviolable. The lights in Dadamoshai's house stayed on all night as community leaders gathered on our veranda to discuss the Japanese situation. It was 2:00 a.m. and cups of tea remained untouched, dark rings forming on the inside rim. I sat quietly hidden in the shadows of the jasmine trellis, listening to the elders talk.

"New regiments have been deployed from South India," said Amrat Singh, the Police Chief. He was an imposing man with a fine turban and beard, who still looked dapper at that unearthly hour. "The convoys are traveling night and day. But it will still take another ten days to reach Guahati. Meanwhile, the Japanese are advancing fast. Three divisions are marching toward Assam—over 80,000 Japanese soldiers, I am told."

"I hear they have already blocked off the road between Kohima and Dimapur—is that true?" asked Dadamoshai. The crease lines on his forehead had deepened. He suddenly looked very old.

"So I hear," Amrat Singh said. "We get news of the Japanese movements from a guerrilla force patrolling the Naga Hills. They keep the generals updated on the enemy's advance."

"The Naga Hills! That is the most treacherous jungle," exclaimed Dadamoshai. "I can't imagine British soldiers surviving those grueling conditions."

"They are being assisted by the Nagas," said the Forest Officer. "The Nagas, as you can imagine, are the only people capable of navigating that mountainous terrain. Also being a strong and hardy people, they run up and down as stretcher bearers. The soldiers are cutting their way through using machetes and taking extra doses of Benzedrine to stay awake. Grueling, as you say."

I sat in the dark trying to imagine the British soldiers holed up in the rainy jungles with the Naga headhunters. I hoped to

God they had ample food. The Nagas were known to be can-
nibals. They were a ferocious tribe who wore bushy loincloths
and embellished their shields and earrings with the hair and
bones of slain enemies. But the Nagas were also known to be
an intensely loyal and moral people and they hated the "Japani."

"Hundreds of Nagas have also joined the regular British
Army in Kohima. People are coming together from all walks
of life to stop the Japanese invasion. Even the tea planters—
many planters have left their gardens to join the regiments."

"Tea planters!" I exclaimed, unable to contain myself.

All heads turned toward the dark corner where I was sitting.

"Who was that?" asked Amrat Singh, squinting in my direction.

"Oh, just Layla," said my grandfather dryly, "listening quietly as usual. Of late, Layla has a growing interest in the tea
industry. I found one of my books in her room."

I squirmed. "It's a very interesting...history," I muttered
vaguely.

"I agree," said Amrat Singh. "It's fascinating. Many Assam
tea planters are ex-army men, you know, from the First World
War. So it is only natural that they rejoin British forces in this
hour of need. I dread to think what will happen if Assam falls
to the Japanese."

Was Manik going off to war? I wondered. It sounded risky
enough living with leopards and elephants in Aynakhal; then
to march off to fight the Japanese with a bunch of Naga headhunters and armed with a blunderbuss that misfired sounded
like suicide. I wanted to ask more about the tea planters and
their involvement in the Japanese invasion, but Dadamoshai
had smelled a rat and I did not want to draw any more attention
to myself. So I excused myself quietly and went to my room.

★ ★ ★

As it transpired, the British allied forces defeated the Japanese only miles before they reached Dimapur. It was a precarious win. The colonial power teetered dangerously, only to upright itself in the end. Crushed and depleted, the Japanese Army crawled back over the border through Burma, thousands of Japanese soldiers dropping like flies along the way.

The news of the British victory came on a glittering spring morning. It was a beautiful jackal wedding day. A visible sigh of relief went through our town. The farmers came out with their *dhola* drums and *pepa* flutes and Assamese youth danced with abandon in the rice fields. Storekeepers threw open their shutters, dusted shelves and played cinema songs on their radios. The fish market reopened and rickshaws honked bulb horns and plied the red dirt roads carrying fat ladies with their shopping baskets. The *Gulmohor* trees on Rai Bahadur Road showered down blossoms and even the koels sang sweetly among the branches.

Aynakhal T.E.
30th May, 1944 2:45 a.m.
Dear Layla,
I am up at an unearthly hour, as you can see. The dryer in the factory broke down and I have been up all night battling with the mechanics to get it working again. Production got backed up. The leaf plucked today (and we are talking about 200 kilos of our best leaf of the season) has to be processed within six hours to avoid spoilage, so there was major tension until we got it running again. I probably went through half a bottle of whiskey and two packs of cigarettes.

We are in the middle of the second flush plucking season, the premium crop yield of the year, and we cannot miss a single cycle. The bushes plucked today will be ready to be plucked again five days from now. The sections are rotated. Tea grows at a furious rate this time of the year and Larry and I are kept on our toes to make sure the plucking schedules tie in with the factory production. The factory runs round the clock this time of the year.

Mr. McIntyre, our boss, is a legendary tea planter. Army man, brutal disciplinarian. Tea is very much a hands-on job and a good General Manager can make all the difference. Much as I grumble I am lucky to be learning from the best. There is so much to learn about tea growing and tea processing—I am not sure if I will pick it all up in one lifetime.

It's difficult to sleep now, knowing I have to be up in a few hours, so here I am sitting on my veranda writing to you. I just got the night chowkidar *to make me a cup of tea. It is almost dawn.*

I just reread your letter. I guess I forgot to explain who Jamina is. She is Alasdair's "Old Party"—OP as they are called in tea circles. In other words, his concubine or "kept woman." Jamina used to be a common prostitute, till Alasdair took her under his wing. They seem to be quite compatible. She is a simple Bangladeshi woman, very shy. Unfortunately the tea crowd ostracizes her.

Alasdair is another story. He is quite an enigma. You will hardly believe this, but he is of royal blood. Alasdair is the direct descendant of Scottish nobility and the Earl of Carruthers. He is the only living heir to the Carruthers land and title. And here he is a tea planter hiding away in the jungles of Assam with Jamina. I suspect he is running away. His obligations make him claustrophobic. I can empathize with that.

I should try and get an hour of sleep at least. Tomorrow is another hellish day. I can't wait for club night, Monday. I am getting to be an excellent bridge player.

Yours,
Manik

Manik's letters came fast and furious. He wrote at least once a week, sometimes twice. His letters always arrived in a square, blue envelope, addressed to me in his elegant hand. The *y* of my name dipped flamboyantly as if doing a curtsy.

I devoured his letters from end to end, and then reread them slowly in private. I loved the flowing lines of his blue fountain pen. I dwelled on the curve of each stroke, the way he stretched his *T*'s across the word, the impatient dots of his *i*'s that flew in tiny bird shapes ahead of the letter. He had the most exquisite penmanship I had ever seen. Whenever his letter arrived, my stomach fluttered with butterflies and my mind floated like a brilliant scarf over my everyday reality.

Often his letters would smell faintly of tobacco. Once he enclosed a serrated tea leaf and another time the waxy petals of a camellia flower, satiny brown and smooth as a baby's skin.

I kept his letters hidden under my mattress, where they formed guilty bumps that disturbed my sleep. Chaya was my coconspirator. She intercepted Manik's letters before the mail got to Dadamoshai's desk and put them under my pillow. She never asked any questions.

I was not sure what Dadamoshai would have to say about our alliance. Manik was still formally engaged to another woman. There were dos and don'ts in our society. I was secretly writing to another woman's fiancé, and no matter how platonic our letters, there was something improper about the exchange. I was torn by the complicity of the act. Sometimes my guilt bled through the thin fabric of my deceit—a dark telltale stain, spreading for the whole world to see. But there was no turning back. I simply did not have the power or the will.

CHAPTER

12

News of Kona Sen's broken engagement sent a tremor through our small town. Rickshaws clogged the narrow roads as garrulous housewives stopped each other on the way to the fish market to exchange gossip. Their mustard greens wilted and their fish spoiled, but these were but small woes compared to the misfortunes of the Sen family.

An outrage, they said, shaking their heads. The *poor girl*, after waiting so many years for that worthless cad! What will happen to her now? She was getting past her prime. She could easily become a seed pumpkin.

Toothless dames sat on four-poster beds, suffused by the scent of cloves and mothballs. They rolled acacia nuts into betel leaves and clucked sadly about the waywardness of youth. The big mistake parents make, they reminded one another, is to send their boys to study abroad in the first place. So many temptations! Who is to blame when the boys make poor choices? Look what happened to the District Commissioner's son—untarnished ancestry, fine lineage and everything, and what does he do? Marry an English waitress—a common peasant girl with man-size hands and ankles thick as tree trunks!

The son is a qualified doctor. He should know better! Who will feel sorry for him when his wife runs off with one of her own kind?

Maybe Mr. Sen with all his money could still find someone for Kona. Marrying Manik Deb would have been a grave mistake. He had no sense of family honor. And who did he think he was, pretending to be an Englishman? He would expect his poor wife to wear small skirts, drink and behave in unbecoming ways. Oh yes, Kona Sen was better off without Manik Deb, that was for sure.

My tongue burned with the secret. From Manik's letters I did not once get the impression he was a misfit. Rather, he seemed to have slipped into the tea lifestyle easily and quickly, without a wrinkle. As for Kona's problems, I'm ashamed to say, it was hard for me to feel sorry for her. When I heard of their broken engagement the first thing I felt was a tiny shoot of joy followed by zero qualms. Kona's plight was the last thing on my mind. I was now dwelling on the fragile possibility of my future with Manik Deb.

Just as well I did not waste my guilt because fortune soon smiled on Kona Sen. Through an obscure but lucky family connection, Kona's father found a rich landlord's son as a replacement groom and—oh, miracles—the horses were switched smoothly in midstream. Even luckier, the wedding date did not have to be changed; the caterer's order did not have to be canceled. Even the print shop agreed to reprint the cards at half price. They waived the extra charge for a rush order and in a fit of generosity threw in some glitter for free.

Mr. Sen was a happy man. Manik Deb may have taken the starch out of him temporarily, but now he was back to his old form. He smiled broadly as he went door to door, personally delivering the wedding cards. He expounded the merits of his new son-in-law and left behind a trail of gold dust that glittered as brightly as his optimism.

Rumors floated in the fish market that Kona's wedding was going to be the grandest occasion the town had ever seen. Despite the wartime rationing and shortages, nothing would be compromised. The *shenai* maestro—no less than the grand Ustad Palit himself—would be arriving from Calcutta with his entourage of musicians. An elevated two-story platform was being constructed for their performance. A twelve-course feast was planned. The very best *rui* fish, famous for its size and flavor, was being shipped in from across the Padma River. Guests would have their own silver finger bowls with scented rose water to wash their fingers. As for the mouth-freshening *paan* served at the end of the meal, it would be coated in real gold leaf.

Nobody talked about Manik Deb. He was the fallen son, the tainted seed. He had gone from being the most eligible bachelor in town to a nonentity. For the townsfolk, Manik Deb had ceased to exist.

Shortly after the broken engagement, I received a letter from Manik Deb. I expected it to be filled with his thoughts on what had happened, or more wistfully, his declarations of love for me. It was neither. It was all about a leopard hunt.

How odd. Surely he knew his own marriage had been called off? Why was there no mention of it in his letter? I decided to bring it up.

Aynakhal T.E.
10th October 1944
Dear Layla,
You make me laugh! Of course I know my own wedding has

been called off! As for how I received the news, it was a telegram. Short and sweet.

You offered me your condolences. All I can say is that you are a terrible liar! In all honesty, I am happy, and I suspect you are, too. Don't deny it! My biggest relief comes from knowing that Kona has found a more deserving husband. In all sincerity I wish her well. If my decision to take up this job had negatively affected her future, I can't say I could have lived the rest of my life guilt free.

The only people who have not reconciled themselves to these events are my family. I got a telegram from them, as well. Two telegrams in one week. A record! I have been officially disowned. I guess it was expected. There is little I can do to make good on that front. Their views are not aligned with mine.

Mr. Eastwood's visit went off without a hitch. To answer your question, a VA is a Visiting Agent. They are company directors from London who visit the gardens annually. It is a nerve-racking affair for us because we have to impress them. The plantation (especially the sections he will inspect) is spruced up. The factory looks spotless, the machinery running in impeccable order. Mr. McIntyre has been on edge and running us assistants ragged for weeks. He can be impossibly demanding. Not a single hair can be out of place.

The VA's visit was topped off with a dinner thrown by the McIntyres for all the planters in the district. A very formal affair, it was. I realized to my dismay a mouse had chewed a hole in my only dinner jacket, so I had to borrow one from Alasdair. I have placed an order for a new suit from Calcutta.

You also asked about a gentleman by the name of James Lovelace, an acquaintance of the Rai Bahadur's. I have heard of him. He is a director, I believe, at the head office at Jardines. I have never personally met him.

All else is well. I miss you.
With warm wishes,
Manik

Manik slipped as easily into his writing as he did his own skin. His letters were genuine and unhurried, never pretentious or seeking to impress. His life unfurled before my eyes. It was almost like sitting on the veranda talking to him. I watched for the faintest signs of interest buried in his words: a telltale giveaway to show his heart was leaning toward mine. Only once did he begin his letter with "My dear Layla" instead of just "Dear Layla." Another time he ended with "fondly" instead of "yours." Nothing besides that, from what I could tell.

Aynakhal T.E.
12th May 1945
My dear Layla,
I am still recovering from VE Day celebrations at the Mariani Club. It was a jolly if somewhat confusing affair. We planters are happy to celebrate anything at the drop of a hat. We sometimes celebrate when there is nothing to celebrate—in other words, we are a bunch of hopeless drunks. However, VE Day seemed a legitimate reason until we invited four British RAF servicemen to tag along. One of them is a fellow named Eddie. He is Flint White-stone's cousin. Flint is the Assistant Manager of Kootalgoorie, and my bridge partner.
The soldiers were hardly in a celebratory mood as they are being deployed to Burma. The victory in Europe seems unreal, they say, a farce, really. Hitler's war may have ended but the war with Japan is far from over. Fresh troops are arriving in India and Burma every day to fight the Japanese. While the rest of the world celebrates VE Day with buntings and banners and

dancing on the streets, it does not feel like the end of the war for these lads. Eddie said the soldiers of the British Liberation Army interpret the initials BLA as "Burma Looms Ahead." As you can imagine, our hearts broke for these poor fellows, and planters being the sympathetic and hospitable bunch we are, we invited them to drown their sorrows at the club—all on the house, of course. We gave them a grand and sentimental send-off. Now all four of them want to become tea planters when the war is over.

On a more sober note, talking to the airmen made me realize how shielded we planters have been from the austerities of war. We have remained relatively untouched because tea gardens are so remotely located and cut off from the mainstream and we don't depend on outside resources for our survival. The lads envied our big bungalows and lavish lifestyle. They were surprised to learn that we never had to deal with war rationing and shortages while the rest of the world suffered with five inches of bathwater, no heating and no bananas. I never realized how lucky I am, until I met those poor sods who are being shipped off to Burma.

I wish the war was over for all of us. It seems unfair that some celebrate, while others see no end in sight.

Yours truly,

Manik

Love survives in a bubble. It diffuses outer reality and reflects only what the heart wants to see. Looking back, I remember little of the grimness of war and the tumultuous events that were reshaping our world. I lived only for Manik's letters and a single sweep of his pen could set me sailing on a daydream. The fateful day the A-bomb dropped on Japan was a rude wake-up call. It made me aware of how myopic my world had become and how far I had strayed from my own moral compass and it shook me to my core.

20th September 1945

Dear Manik,

We are still reeling from the news of Hiroshima and Nagasaki. These are surely the darkest of times and I believe morally mankind has regressed back to the dark ages. Japan may be thousands of miles away but how can any human being with a conscience remain unaffected by this horrific tragedy? Dadamoshai says he wishes he had never lived to see this day. He and I spend hours trying to understand how the barbaric act of dropping an A-bomb can even remotely justify winning the war and we come up with no answers.

We held a special session at the school today to answer the many questions the students have about it all. Dadamoshai, as you know, does not believe in shielding children from the truth. He thinks it is essential they understand the mindless cruelty of war and the importance of peace. As a show of solidarity the children are making origami paper cranes to hang in the school hallways. I am enclosing one for you.

Yours,

Layla

I don't know when exactly Manik's letters became love letters. His emotions were so carefully woven into his writing, they were hard to detect. They were like the subtle creeping of dawn that imperceptibly transforms night into day.

If I spread out his letters in chronological order, across my bed, on the floor, along the windowsill and over my desk—because yes, that is how much space they were occupying in my life at that time—I can distinctly see the emotional tilt: a nuanced word here, a small heart tug there and occasionally a tiny but unmistakable flicker of passion.

It took Manik a whole suitcase of letters and two and a half

years to declare his love for me. This was the letter I received
from him dated November 12, 1945. It was the first time he
addressed me as "dearest."

Aynakhal T.E.
12th November 1945
Dearest Layla,
I stayed up all night thinking of you. Sometimes I long for you
so much, it hurts.

I don't know when I will see you again. I wish there was an
easy way. I could meet you in secret someplace. I choose not to.
It would be disrespectful to Rai Bahadur—not something I am
prepared to do, now or ever. I have decided therefore to play this
game by the rules.

Enough water has passed under the bridge and I think it is
safe for me to make my next move. Before that, I need to know
how you feel about me. I am keeping my fingers crossed.

I have nothing much to offer you, Layla. Only myself and
my rather unconventional life here in Aynakhal. If there is any
woman I would love to share this adventure with, it's you. I
promise to take care of you with every inch of my being, my life
and everything I have.
With all my love,
Manik
PS: How very absurd—I forgot my main reason for writing this
letter. WILL YOU MARRY ME, LAYLA?

I thought a hundred times of what to write back. I needed
to reply immediately. All I wanted to say was "yes" so I wrote
YES in the middle of the page. Was it too big? Too small? Did
it look hurried, overeager? Wobbly, unsure? I went over and

over the three letters, *Y-E-S*, with my pen so many times that the ink cracked through the paper to the other side. I wondered what else I should add.

What do you say when you are given everything you have ever wished for, handed to you on a silver platter? So I wrote in pip-squeak letters, small enough to blind an ant, "That makes me very happy."

There is thunder in the distance; the sky is a thick slate-gray. The lily pond reflects a broken moon, like cracked eggshells on dark waters. A thousand fireflies spiral down from the sky. They hit the water with a pop and spin in dizzying ripples of electric light. Manik is standing by the edge of the pond. He reaches down to catch the fireflies in his cupped hands but they spin out of reach. He takes a step forward, stumbles and falls. He clutches at the reeds but they give way. I see the long ropelike stems of the lilies unwinding from the muddy depths of the pond. They are muscular and strong. They twist around Manik's ankles. They pull him down. There is something floating up from the murky depths of the pond. It's a face: round, pale and placid as the moon. It's my dead mother. Her eyes are open and staring. She stretches out her pale, white hands. Her fingers are curled like chrysanthemums. She grabs Manik. He kicks and splashes before disappearing in a dark swirl of thick water. Ripples of neon wrinkle at the reedy shore. The waters recompose and the moon rocks like a cradle.

It was an ominous dream and I was overcome with panic. With an aching heart, I wrote Manik a letter.

Dear Manik,
Please do not forget that I am born under an unlucky horoscope. My fate could adversely affect yours. I do not want to jeopar-

dize your life. If you want to reconsider your proposal, I will
understand.
Fondly,
L.

Manik shot back a reply so fast that the ink smeared across
the page.

Absurdly and completely out of the question, dearest. If you think
I am being heedless, ask the Japanese why do they eat fugu? Be-
cause it is irresistible and worth dying for.
Yours,
M.

I was reminded of a Japanese *rakugo* I once read in a collection from Dadamoshai's library. The pithy stories were printed
in beautiful calligraphy on delicate rice paper. This particular
one, about the poison fugu fish, had an illustration of a beggar
holding a soup bowl with chopsticks while three men peeped
at him from behind a doorway.

Three men prepared a fugu stew but they were afraid to eat
it, unsure as to whether it was safe.

"Let's give some to this poor beggar," one of them suggested. "If he eats it and lives we will know it is not poison."

And so they gave a bowl of fugu stew to the beggar. Later
that day they encountered the beggar again and were delighted
to see he was still in good health. The three friends then hurried home to enjoy the rest of the stew.

The canny beggar, who had in fact not eaten the stew but
hidden it, now knew it was safe to eat.

Thus the three men were fooled by the wise beggar.

CHAPTER

13

As was the custom, Manik decided to formally ask Dadamoshai for my hand in marriage. What had only been a crack of hope was now becoming full-blown reality. I was not sure I was equipped to deal with it.

My biggest dilemma was Dadamoshai. How would he take the news? He had no inkling about our relationship. All those letters, over all those years. The way I had involved Chaya in my deceit. Surely he would feel hideously betrayed?

It was understood I would take over Dadamoshai's work someday. All along he had been grooming me to run the school. He was getting old. If I got married and left, what would happen to him? I was sickened with guilt.

Manik outlined his plans. He would write asking to meet Dadamoshai in private. He would explain everything, he said.

The postman delivered Manik's letter in the familiar blue envelope. It was addressed to my grandfather. His handwriting was confident, precise, without any trace of hesitation.

At dinner Dadamoshai said, "Finally our mystery man has resurfaced. I got a letter from Manik Deb. He wants to see me on a private matter. Some legal consultation, no doubt."

I did not say anything. Dadamoshai was looking down at his plate. He hummed softly. If I had any shred of integrity, I would have seized this opportunity and blurted it all out. That way I could prepare my grandfather for Manik's visit. But all I did was push the rice around on my plate. Choked by cowardliness, I was unable to utter a single word.

The next two weeks I worked myself into a nervous wreck. I lost sleep and ate little. My scalp itched, my skin broke out in angry hives and dark half-moons appeared under my eyes. When I saw myself in the mirror, I looked like scrap fit to be tossed to the crows.

The day of the meeting was the most unbearable of all. Manik was expected to arrive in the early afternoon. It took forever for dawn to break that day and for the sun to crawl across the sky.

Dadamoshai had taken the day off from court and was working in his study. I paced up and down my room, chewing on a hangnail. Random thoughts banged around in my head like bumblebees in a jar. I had not seen Manik in two and a half years. A lifetime, it seemed. I now recalled him only as distilled moments, blurred and sweet. I had turned these memories over a million times in my mind, till they were tumbled smooth like pieces of sea glass that ebbed and flowed in my memory.

A little after two o'clock, a mud-splashed jeep pulled up under the mango tree. It was identical to the one that Alasdair Carruthers had shown up in. I heard the gate clang shut and saw a man stride up the garden path. Was that Manik?

The man walking toward the house was deeply tanned and handsome in a formidable kind of way. His hair was cut short, closely molded to his skull. He wore a tweed jacket and a diagonally striped tie, which he straightened as he walked. On the porch steps, he hesitated and glanced down at his shoes. He wiped the dust off them on the back of his trouser legs and then bent and dusted his trousers off. This small gesture of humanness was oddly reassuring. It was Manik.

Chaya showed him into my grandfather's study. I heard them greet each other. Dadamoshai said something and Manik laughed. Their voices then muffled and became a hum as the door closed behind them.

Through the crack in my bedroom door, I saw Chaya walk by with two cups of tea. The murmur grew louder as the study door opened and closed. The clock ticked, my scalp itched and a horrible panic rumbled across the vast lonely plains of my stomach. An hour passed. The door opened, I held my breath, but it was only my grandfather calling for another round of tea. Another thirty-five minutes. Ticktock. Ticktock. What on earth were they talking about? Manik and Dadamoshai had been locked together for over an hour and a half.

Finally the door opened and my grandfather called, "Layla!"

I jumped to my feet so fast that my head went into a spin. I sat down again and took a deep breath to steady myself. I had not eaten any solid food all day.

I walked into my grandfather's office. Manik was sitting in the client's seat. He scraped his chair back with an awfully loud screech and stood up. He seemed incredibly tall. Taller than I remembered. He had taken his jacket off, and it was slung on the back of his chair. His skin was sharply tanned against the white of his shirt.

I could not meet his gaze. It burned through my skin.

Dadamoshai got straight to the point. "Layla, Manik Deb here has asked for your hand in marriage. He tells me you have been writing to each other, and he has communicated his intentions. Is that correct?"

I nodded, looking at the floor.

"Well, what is your decision?"

"My…decision?" I repeated, a little foolishly. I had expected a preamble, a lecture maybe, not a question shot at me like a dart.

"Yes, yours—whose else?" Dadamoshai's eyes twinkled. "Manik Deb has not asked *me* to marry him, has he?"

"Oh," I said dumbly. I had not looked up the entire time.

"Well, I take that as a yes. That settles it, then, young man," Dadamoshai said, rapping the desk with his knuckles. "Congratulations. I think you two need to talk. Come here, *maiyya*—sit in my chair." It was not often that Dadamoshai called me *maiyya*, little girl. He led me to his enormous high-backed chair, sat me down and planted a small kiss on the top of my head. He patted Manik on the shoulder and left the room, shutting the door behind him.

So that was it. Over in a flash.

Manik was looking at me in that disconcerting way of his that made me want to crawl down and disappear into my toes.

A thick silence floated around the room.

Contrary to popular expectations we did not fly into each other's arms; if anything at all we were awkward. A new layer of formality had just been added to our relationship. Getting married was serious business. It called for protocol. Decorum.

So there we were, freshly betrothed. I sat like a midget lawyer swallowed by the giant leather chair, fiddling with a yellow pencil, while my fiancé floated like an island across an ocean-size desk bobbing with pens, paper, blotters and paperweights. He stared at me and I stared at the giant globe on the floor stand. A slat of sunlight fell on Africa, a continent I suddenly found myself deeply interested in. I thought of Zulus, giraffes, acacia trees and grassland—anything but my newly acquired fiancé, sitting in front of me.

Now what? My stomach responded with a small squeal of terror.

"So?" said Manik softly. "Do you still want to marry me, Layla?" I peeked at him. He smiled his old slow smile and made my heart skip.

I nodded yes, but truthfully, I was not so sure. I didn't recognize this stranger before me.

"So what did he say?" I asked finally. My mouth was dry and my voice came out wavery like an old crone.

"The Rai Bahadur? Why, he was relentless!" Manik pretended to flick imaginary sweat from his brow. "He interrogated me like a criminal. He wanted to know all about my job, my life in tea and my future prospects. He wanted to make sure I was good enough for his precious granddaughter."

"And...?"

"I passed the inspection test, I suppose."

"What else did he say?"

"Among other things, he said if there was one person in the world he thought you would be happy with, it was me."

I flushed with joy.

"You are so beautiful," he said simply.

I covered up my embarrassment by drawing elaborate doodles all over the notepad. Some looked suspiciously like hearts so I scratched them out. Manik was watching me, his thumb stroking his lower lip.

"So when do you say we get married? Sometime early February?" he said suddenly.

I dropped the pencil and stared at him. "But that's...that's only six weeks away?"

"I wish it was today."

"But isn't February...too soon?"

"Not for me. I have to still give a thirty-day notice to Head Office. My three-year compulsory bachelorhood is up on January 7th. According to my company contract I can get married anytime after February 6th. You pick a date, then."

"Right now? Don't we have to ask Dadamoshai?"

"He said to decide a date between ourselves. I mentioned February and he did not seem to have any objections. You don't believe in getting married on a particular auspicious wedding date or anything, do you?"

"Of course not."

"I thought as much. If we decide on a date today I can go ahead and put in my application for leave with Jardines tomorrow."

My head was spinning. It was all happening so fast. Typically elders in the family made all the decisions. Whom to marry, when to marry, how to marry. The bride and groom were treated like sheep. How typical of Dadamoshai to put the onus on us.

"Well, how about...?" I fiddled with the pencil as I tried to think clearly.

"February 7th?" ventured Manik, winking. Then he waved it off. "I am only joking. No pressure."

Then I thought to myself, why wait? Manik might change his mind, there could be an earthquake, the whole world might collapse—who knows what else.

"All right—the seventh, then. February! Dear God, this is so unreal."

There was a small knock on the door.

"I am off to the court," Dadamoshai called from outside.

Manik jumped to his feet and opened the door. I stood up, as well. "Can I give you a lift, sir?" he said.

"No, no, no, you two carry on. You have much to talk about. I just wanted to tell you I am leaving."

Manik looked at his watch and winced. "Oh! I have to be back at Aynakhal by seven." He looked at my grandfather. "I will be driving through town, so I can drop you off. It's no problem. Seriously."

"All right, if you insist," said Dadamoshai. "But I didn't want to break up your tête-à-tête. Are you sure you have to leave now?"

"Positively," said Manik. "Mr. McIntyre, my General Manager, is throwing a dinner party for the Superintendent tonight. It is imperative I attend. Otherwise..." Manik aimed his finger like a gun to his head.

"Well, I had planned to walk, but if you are going to give me a lift, we still have another twenty minutes," said Dadamoshai. "You two can talk some more." He closed the door behind him with a soft click.

"Layla?" Manik turned back to me, his voice soft. "God knows I have waited forever to hold you."

I stood there trembling, looking at the floor. Manik walked over and pulled me toward him, and then...the stupidest, most absurd thing happened. The books on the shelves began to weave; I tried to grab hold of the desk, and instead collapsed in a dead faint into Manik's arms.

The next thing I knew the study was crowded—everybody hovering over me and chattering like monkeys. Even the cat was in there, tail in the air, meowing with alarm. Manik looked horrified. Dadamoshai fanned me with the *Court Reporter*, while Chaya dabbed my forehead with a damp towel and held a glass of water to my lips.

"I have not eaten all day," I said feebly, trying to explain.

I did not want Dadamoshai to think Manik had pounced on me. He almost had.

Dadamoshai's face was inscrutable, but I glimpsed tiny winks of mirth glimmering in the stony depths. "Enough of your foolishness, Layla," he said sternly. "Put her to bed, Chaya, and see she drinks some milk and eats something." He turned to Manik. "Layla is a hopeless eater."

"Are you all right, Layla?" Manik looked worried, his eyes full of concern.

"*Tcha!* Of course I am," I said impatiently. "I have been tense for weeks. I just collapsed from nerves, that's all."

My explanation must have satisfied them both, because they relaxed.

"You just get rested now," said Manik, gently. "Don't worry about anything. I will come again soon and we'll work out the details, okay?"

I nodded, feeling a little miserable for having missed my first kiss. I knew Manik would never be openly demonstrative in front of my grandfather. It would not be respectful or proper.

So just like that, my brand-new fiancé took off down the garden path with Dadamoshai, his jacket slung over his shoulder. He turned around before he opened the car door and gave me a brief sort of wave. The jeep coughed to life, and he drove off in a cloud of red dust, leaving me standing on the porch. It was all over so soon; so short, so sweet, so much and so little.

I turned to go back into the house when I noticed the small wooden chest on the coffee table. It had a stencil stamp:

PREMIUM ASSAM TEA

PRODUCT OF AYNAKHAL TEA ESTATE

"Chaya!" I yelled. "Forget the milk. Quick, make me a cup of this tea, please."

I sat on the sofa feeling warmly, sweetly and deeply overwhelmed.

The cat crawled out from under the coffee table and jumped
up on my lap. He rubbed his head on my shoulder and flicked
his furry tail under my nose.

"Guess what, kitty?" I said, scratching his ears. "I am getting married."

The cat purred with approval. He jumped on the coffee
table, sniffed the tea chest and proceeded to rub his whiskers
on the metal edge.

"He is a tea planter," I added, stroking the cat's belly with
my big toe. "And he lives in the jungles with cats much bigger than you. So the next time he comes, show him a little
respect, will you?"

The cat blinked his big yellow eyes and then narrowed them
down to slits. He was thinking deeply, I could tell.

CHAPTER
14

After my grandmother died, Dadamoshai never again slept in the master bedroom of the house. He moved out into a small room adjoining his study. It was narrow and sparsely furnished like a monk's cell with a single bed against the wall, a small side table and reading lamp and not much else.

The main bedroom remained dark and shuttered, largely unused. It had become a storeroom of sorts, filled with miscellaneous furniture and bric-a-brac. There were folding chairs, dusty files and old court manuscripts under the bed and a sitar in a cloth case in one corner.

The morning after Manik's proposal, Dadamoshai called me into his study. He was writing at his desk, his glasses askew and that preoccupied, faraway look he often had in his eyes. He opened a drawer absentmindedly and handed me a small silk pouch. It jangled. Inside was an old-fashioned bejeweled silver key chain, the kind traditional brides wore looped into the waistband of their saris.

"In the old bedroom you will find a trunk," Dadamoshai said. "One of these keys should fit. Inside are some of your grandmother's things. You may need them for your wedding."

Tears pricked my eyes. I sat down on the cane ottoman and buried my face in my hands.

"*Hai Khuddah*, now what's the matter?" said Dadamoshai, looking at me anxiously. "Why the tears?"

"What will happen…?" I began then choked up. "Who will take care of you, Dadamoshai? Who will do your work?"

Dadamoshai sighed deeply. He removed his spectacles and squeezed the inside corners of his eyes with his thumb and forefinger. "My goodness, *maiyya*, is that what is worrying you? Did you for a moment think I would put such a burden on your tender shoulders?"

I said nothing.

"Layla, the work I do is not dependent on you or me. We are only conduits for the bigger forces, don't you understand?"

The cat emerged from behind the bookcase and yawned, extending its forepaws in a long, luxurious stretch. He then rubbed his head on the cane ottoman and proceeded to sharpen his claws on the sides, making a sharp, rasping noise.

"Nobody is indispensable in this world," Dadamoshai continued slowly. "When I am dead and gone, the universe will find replacements. I let the old man upstairs worry about these things. For all I know, there may be people more capable than I am. My job is to do what I can during my small sojourn and move on."

"I thought you were counting on me to take over your school," I said.

"You were inclined to follow in my footsteps, *maiyya*, so I let you. But remember, child, this work is bigger and goes beyond you or me."

He studied me tenderly, a velvety softness coming into his

eyes. "Your life is with your husband now, *maiyya*. You were loaned to me for a little while. The time has come for me to let you go."

The master bedroom smelled damp and musty. I cracked open the shutters and sharp sunlight sliced into the room. Dust motes floated in the air. A cockroach scurried across the floor dragging a broken leg. The old trunk sat in the corner under a faded green tablecloth with a pile of old files sitting on top.

It was a solid bottle-green trunk, the old-fashioned kind, made of hammered metal, with brass rivets running along the seams. I tried the keys one by one in the rusty lock. It clicked open on the third try. The heavy lid swung open, and the air was suffused with the heady smell of cloves, sandalwood and mothballs.

Inside, individually wrapped in soft *mulmul* cotton, were the most exquisite saris I had ever seen. They were rare heirloom silks, each a collector's piece, breathtaking in their beauty. There were heavy brocaded *Tanchois* in aqua and mauve that captured light in faceted tones like mother-of-pearl. *Benarasi* silks flamed in vermilion, saffron and rich peacock-blue, interwoven with threads of pure gold. There were *Dhakais* delicate as gossamer and royal *Baluchoris* flamboyantly hand-embroidered with hunting scenes from the great *Ramayana*. Every sari had a perfectly tailored matching blouse and silk petticoat.

At the bottom of the trunk I found a Kashmiri sandalwood box. Inside was a photo of my grandparents on their wedding day. Dadamoshai looked tall and stately in his crisp white dhoti and *nagra* slippers, their upturned toes curled like the prow of a ship. His face was tilted slightly toward his new bride. They both wore tuberose garlands, thick as pythons around their necks. My grandmother wore a shimmering silk of a dark color and a gold embroidered veil. She was a tall, slim woman. The top of her veiled head reached just below my grandfather's chin.

Beneath the photo was a small brass container in the shape of a teardrop, with a thin applicator stick. It was a *sindoor* jar containing the vermilion powder worn by married Hindu women in the part of their hair. There was also a set of traditional white and red wedding bangles.

Later that evening I asked Dadamoshai why my own mother had not inherited the saris.

"Your mother was very different," Dadamoshai said. "She went the other extreme. She had very radical views and shunned material things. She became a communist when she eloped with your father."

"So why did you not sell the saris? They must be worth a fortune."

"I kept them for you," he said simply. "You look exactly like your grandmother. I imagined you would make a beautiful bride someday."

Guahati
5th January 1946
My dear sister,
I read your letter with great excitement. I can't believe you are getting married to a tea planter! As you can imagine I am just bursting with questions. I must say you kept your secret very well. But now coming to think of it, Manik only proposed recently, didn't he? Before that you had to be very discreet, I suppose.

It makes me sad to think how out of touch we have been all these years. Getting married and moving to Guahati took my life in a different direction altogether. The children came along, first Anik then Aesha. In between, my father-in-law suffered a

*heart attack. Living in a big joint family can be overwhelming.
I can't seem to find time for myself anymore.*

*I must say I am looking forward to your wedding. Unfortu-
nately Jojo will not be able to attend. He just got a new job with
a petrochemical company here in Guahati and he doesn't get any
leave. I am thinking of coming with Anik alone this time and
leaving Aesha with my in-laws. She is crawling now and doesn't
sit still for a single minute. I don't think I can manage both of
them on the train by myself.*

*I am sending you a photo of Aesha dressed up in a red sari
taken on the day of her rice-eating ceremony. What she is chewing on is a gold bangle! As you can see, Jojo has a very big extended family.*

*I am looking forward to seeing you soon, dear sister, and
catching up on our chats.*

Yours,

Moon

Despite our best attempts to keep things low-key, the an-
nouncement of my engagement to Manik Deb still created a
small furor in my hometown. It set tongues wagging up and
down the neighborhood, all around the coconut grove and
all the way past the *bamboobari* to the fish market by the river.

Most people thought it was an ill-conceived but oddly suitable match, like the marriage of two hunchbacks. Manik and
I were both discards of society: misfits, two of the same shoe,
hence not much use to anyone else.

After all, who would marry a man who had been disowned
by his family? Manik Deb had no future and no money to his
name. He was a dubious character, wayward and reckless. And
I, at the ripe old age of twenty, was almost a seed pumpkin. I
was the bad-luck child. I was overeducated. I had no parents.

I did not know how to embroider tablecloths or play the harmonium. I had no skills to raise a family or run a household. And the most unforgivable of all: I had no dowry to make up for my pathetic shortfalls.

But by and large folks wished us well. It was the charitable thing to do. Still, a dark cloud of foreboding loomed over our marriage. We were ignoring the rules of society. The fortune-teller had not been consulted, our horoscopes had not been matched and no auspicious wedding date had been selected. These were but small, preemptive measures against the enormity of fate. One did not take chances. Manik and I were openly inviting the wrath of the gods. Such heedlessness could only have harsh repercussions.

CHAPTER

15

I had envisioned my wedding as a simple affair, with a few close relatives and minimum fuss, but this was not to be.

One week before my wedding day, a huge flock of relatives descended upon us like noisy cranes from the sky. Many came from Dadamoshai's hometown in Sylhet, from across the river in East Bengal. These were the kith and kin I never knew I had. Cousins, aunts, grandmothers, great-aunts, and so-and-so related to so-and-so, twice removed from places unheard of in some village tucked in some bamboo grove somewhere.

First came the womenfolk with children in tow. They took over Dadamoshai's house, camping out like squatters on every inch of space they could find. Overnight our peaceful house turned into a raucous fish market. Every room except Dadamoshai's was invaded and filled with miscellaneous lumpy bags belonging to miscellaneous people. Small children tore through the rooms like mini typhoons. They romped and squealed and dragged quilts off unmade beds onto the floor. Every now and then an ear-piercing howl erupted when some irritable adult smacked one. The din was unholy, the chaos unbelievable.

Dadamoshai beat a hasty retreat to the town courthouse,

where he stayed for long hours, coming home only for dinner. I, on the other hand, was expected to mingle with the womenfolk and partake in the wedding preparations, which truthfully there was not much of.

Manik and I had opted for a secular *Bhramo Samaj* wedding ceremony, which many relatives considered drastically abbreviated and radically modern. It had none of the elaborate rituals and fanfare that went with the three-day, traditional Hindu wedding. For our wedding, there would be a simple exchange of vows and garlands followed by a blessing ceremony and a wedding luncheon.

The trimming down of festivities dismayed many of our relatives, but it hardly stopped them from using the occasion to have a party of their own. The *Biyebari*, or wedding house, traditionally the bride's home, was the place where relatives gathered to catch up with one another. Women came minus their husbands—husbands showed up later, usually on the day of the wedding itself—so they were free to gossip, joke and curse with glee.

The mobile kitchen arrived in an impressive convoy of rickshaws. There were the traditional wedding cooks sitting atop sacks of potatoes and onions, followed by helpers bearing big-eared brass cauldrons and ladles long as boating oars. The cooking crew dug a coal fire pit, strung a tarp for shade and set up a makeshift kitchen beneath the mango tree by the front gate. All day long, the ghee spluttered and spices sizzled while fragrant spirals of smoke wafted through the tree branches. Gigantic meals were served piping hot on fresh banana leaves to relatives and any neighbors or friends who cared to stop by. There was always plenty for all.

Mima swept in, bossy, energetic and bristling with excitement. Getting "the girls nicely settled" had been her top priority all along. Moon was already happily married with two children, and I was on my way. Mima dusted her palms, as though she had just put the last bun in the oven.

"Very good, very good," she kept muttering, beaming at all. "Now even Layla will be nicely settled." What "nicely settled" meant was anyone's guess.

Mima appointed herself as the event manager. She hitched her sari higher and pointed a fat finger and ordered everyone around, left and right. The skinny relatives scurried like cockroaches. The chubby ones grumbled behind her back. More often than not, things went hopelessly awry, and everyone blamed everyone else.

Mima took charge of my bridal wardrobe, as well. She summoned the town tailor, who arrived wheeling a bicycle heaped with bales of cloth, followed by a young lad carrying a sewing machine on his head. The tailor parked himself on one corner of the veranda. He tucked a pencil behind his ear and clenched sewing pins in his teeth as he rolled out bales of cloth across the floor, which he cut with a loud crunching noise of his mammoth scissors. The sewing machine clattered and stopped, clattered and stopped right through the sleepy afternoon amidst the chirping of sparrows, while his skinny helper boy hemmed and ironed.

With amazing speed and on Mima's bossy instructions, he turned out nighties, petticoats and blouses and, of all things, a frilly apron. Since nobody quite knew the functions of an apron or what it actually looked like, the tailor had to devise a design from an illustration in the *Woman's Journal Cookbook*. It pictured only the front, so he used his imagination to design the back. The end result was a frilly frocklike creation worthy of Goldilocks.

"If Layla is going to live with the English people, an apron is most essential," Mima declared.

"But when does one wear such a dress?" Spinster Aunt asked in her thin, reedy voice.

"When she is serving her guests tea and cakes of course," said Mima authoritatively. "I know these English people. It is very proper to wear an apron." She glared around, daring anyone to challenge her wisdom.

Mima's big concern was that I be decked in full regalia like a proper Indian bride, including copious amounts of wedding jewelry. For me that was an odious thought.

"Please, Mima," I begged, "the wedding sari is gorgeous enough. I don't need jewelry. It's too much!"

"What? What?" Mima's eyebrows knotted like two angry snakes ready to fight. "Do you want to look like a widow on your wedding day? Do you want everyone to think your Dada-moshai is a pauper? The whole town will call him a stingy cat."

"Dadamoshai does not care what the neighbors say," I retorted. "Besides, he *is* poor and not ashamed of it."

But there was no butting heads with Mima.

She wagged a fat finger at me. "Now, don't make big, big eyes at me, Layla. You will listen to your elders. I have decided you will wear all of Moon's wedding jewelry. Nobody needs to know it is not yours. I don't want to hear any arguments—understand? I have asked Moon to bring everything. You must dress like a proper bride."

"But, Mima, Moon is coming alone by train. Why are you making her carry her jewelry? She will get robbed!" I cried.

"Moon will throw chili powder if someone attacks her," Mima said confidently. "I have told her what to do."

I sighed. But despite my worry, I could hardly wait for Moon to get here. There was a personal matter I wanted to discuss with her. It was something I could not talk to anyone else about.

Three days later, I spotted Moon paying off the rickshaw man at the gate. A small boy clung to her sari and drummed his feet, throwing up small clouds of dust as he howled loudly. Big tears rolled down his cheeks; his mouth was a big open O. He was oddly dressed from top to toe in a motley brown.

"Who on EARTH are all these people?" Moon cried, seeing me. "My goodness, what a circus! I was wondering if I had come to the right house!"

The culinary feast was in full swing under the mango tree. The cook's helper, a frail lad, sat on his haunches chopping a mountain of eggplant. A cauldron of tea bubbled on the coals, and a transistor radio wedged between the branches blared out soulful cinema songs.

Moon was as pretty as ever. Despite the long journey and her slightly disheveled appearance, her honey skin glowed, and her curly hair, carelessly bunched up in a handkerchief, was coming undone all around her lovely face.

"Oh, Moon, thank God you are here!" I cried, hugging her. "The whole world has descended for my wedding. It is intolerable."

I peeked at the small boy clinging to her sari. He was staring at me wide-eyed through tear-clumped lashes. He was a cute little fellow, with coal-black eyes and a tumble of curly hair.

"Hey, who is this, Mr. Chocolate, all dressed in brown?" I asked.

"*Aye*, Anik," said Moon, giving him a little prod. "This is your Layla *didi*, who is getting married. You were asking all about her in the train, remember?"

As soon she mentioned the train, his face crumpled and he erupted into another howl.

"Enough, Anik!" said Moon sternly. She handed me her bag. "His toy engine fell down the train toilet. That's what the big fuss is about. Just as well I left the baby with my in-laws. There was no way I could have managed them both."

The cook's boy wiped his hands and came over to help unload Moon's suitcase from the rickshaw.

"I can't wait to see baby Aesha," I said. "She looks just like a little doll in the photo you sent."

"Everybody adores her. She crawls around everywhere and puts everything in her mouth." Moon swiveled around. "Oh-hoh! Let go, please!" she said irritably, flapping her sari, trying to shake off Anik, who was clinging tightly to her. She rolled her eyes and mouthed silently, *very jealous*. "And Aesha has a big brother who does not listen to his mother and wants to wear brown all the time."

"I like brown," piped up Anik defiantly.

Moon glared at him. "That is talking like a VERY SILLY boy," she said sternly. "Brown is not a flattering color for you. I have told you that a HUNDRED times, but you don't listen. Your complexion is brown and if you wear brown, you look like...like...MUD. If you fell down on the road, a rickshaw would drive right over your head because nobody can see you." She turned to me. "Brown, brown, brown. I can't make him wear any other color. He fights me like a wildcat. I have given up."

"I think he looks very delicious, like chocolate," I said, winking at Anik. He gave me a dimpled smile. He was warming up, I could tell.

Then looking past me, he caught sight of Mima on the veranda. *"Dida! Dida!"* he shrieked excitedly, and took off like a fruit bat toward the house, his arms flailing wildly.

"God, Layla, what a nightmare journey I had," Moon said wearily. "The tension of carrying all that jewelry. I hardly dared to sleep a wink."

"So needless. I don't know why Mima made you do this."

"Then that silly Anik opens my purse when I am not looking and gets chili powder all over his eyes. His stupid train falls down the toilet and he howls nonstop all the way to Silchar. God!" Moon threw up her hand. "I have two clingy men in my life. I tell you, Layla, you should have seen his dad at the station. In *tears*! Oh-hoh, I am only gone for four days."

Moon's husband, Jojo, adored her. He had seen Moon at the local *Durga Puja* function and fallen so desperately in love that he had gone on a hunger strike—"Just like Gandhi, imagine?" Moon said—until his parents came running to Mima to propose on his behalf. Moon had agreed to marry Jojo simply because she could not believe that someone would go on a hunger strike for her. The guy seemed like a decent bloke anyway.

"My God! Who are all those people on the veranda?" Moon cried. "And here I thought nobody was going to show up for your wedding."

"I wish nobody had," I said. "I had no idea we had so many relatives—did you? All I wanted was a quiet wedding, and look what happened."

"I can't imagine Dadamoshai putting up with this madness."

"He doesn't. He keeps running off to the courthouse on some pretext or the other." I slipped my arm around Moon's waist as we walked toward the house. "I am so happy to see you, Moon. There is so much I want to talk to you about."

"And I want to hear all about this mysterious Manik Deb. My, you are a dark horse, Layla, secret romance and all." She punched my arm. "You should have seen Ma, jumping up and down when she heard about your engagement. 'That Layla has some sense after all!' she said."

It was just after lunch. Siesta time. Moon and I were lying on my bed with Anik sprawled out between us, fast asleep. Moon grinned, staring at Manik's photograph. It was the only one I had of him. Manik and Alasdair Carruthers standing in a forest with their guns.

"Why are his shorts so flappy?" she asked.

"They call them Bombay bloomers." I laughed, propping up on my elbow to take a peek. Manik's shorts were like two open parachutes, his legs two skinny sticks below them. Alasdair was dressed just as oddly. "The garden tailor stitches them. One size fits all. Seems to be the dress code for tea planters on *kamjari* duty. Bombay bloomers, bush shirt, canvas shoes."

"What's *kamjari* duty?"

"Field inspection. Tramping around the tea plantation. It's full of snakes and whatnot."

"Anyone who looks good in bloomers has got to be seriously handsome," said Moon, squinting a little.

I sat up in bed. "Moon, do you want to go for a walk down to the river, or are you too tired?"

"No, no, let's go," said Moon. She swung her feet to the floor and twisted her hair into a bun. "I'd like that. It will be like old times when we were kids, remember? If Anik wakes up, his *dida* can take care of him."

We changed out of our rubber slippers into open-toed sandals and crept out of the house. It was a warm afternoon, and the whole household was in deep slumber. Even the cook was snoring on a mat under the mango tree, his round belly rising

and falling like a small mountain. His helper sat on his haunches
cleaning his ears with a matchstick and smoking a bidi.

We took our usual shortcut, crisscrossing over the rice fields,
past the sun-freckled bamboo grove, the holy banyan tree and
an empty tea shack. Our footsteps woke up a small pariah dog
from its nap. It gave a little yip and followed us, sniffing at
our heels.

"Jah! Shoo!" Moon stamped her feet and tried to wave him
off. She picked up a pebble and pretended to throw it. The
dog shied away but continued to follow us, keeping a wary
distance. We came to the tall mud embankment of the river,
where we ran up the side and then slithered and slid over the
crushed shells and debris down to the water's edge.

Everything smelled pungent and seaweedy. Fishing nets lay
drying on bamboo poles and upturned boats lined the bank,
their wood cracked and bleached a pale ash-gray in the sun.
We sat on a log and gazed at the vast stretch of water before
us. A small crab ran out from under us and scuttled sideways
to the shore. The water level was low, great clumps of vegetation floating lazily past. A long-legged heron with a tufted
head eyed us suspiciously as it stepped with finicky feet in the
shallows.

"So peaceful," Moon sighed. "I miss this. You have no idea
what a big, dirty city Guahati is. It's full of trucks and diesel
smoke."

"Are you happy, Moon? Married with children and all?" I
asked, examining my palm. I had a small splinter lodged in
my thumb from the log we were sitting on.

A small goat wandered on the opposite bank, bleating sadly.
In the distance, I could see the thatched rooftops of the fishing
village amidst clumps of trees and straight areca palms pointing up like arrows to the sky.

"Oh yes." Moon sighed with contentment. "Ma was very upset when you could not come for my wedding because of your exams. We could not push back the date—the next auspicious date was six months down the road and Jojo's parents feared he would go on another hunger strike if we waited too long. That man worships me! It's embarrassing. My in-laws live with us, as you know. They are the sweetest people in the world."

Moon hugged her knees and rocked, staring dreamily at the water. "Tell me, sister, do you plan to have children right away? Please don't. That's my one regret. Anik arrived on the dot, nine months to the day. Thank God, we planned it the second time around and Aesha came four years later."

"Moon..."

"What?"

"There is something I want to talk to you about." I faltered and stopped. Then I blurted it out. "I am so scared of...my wedding night."

She jerked her head and looked at me squarely. "What's there to be afraid about? You love him, don't you?"

"Yes, but I don't know what to expect. And living with Dadamoshai, you have no idea how little I know about... about these things."

"You've kissed him, haven't you?"

"The first time I fainted..."

"You *what*?"

"Well, I fainted when he tried to kiss me. It was ridiculous. So no, we did not kiss."

"But didn't he visit again?"

"He came twice. Both times it was very formal. Dadamoshai was there. Well, one evening he touched my cheek."

"Touched your cheek!" Moon squealed with laughter and

drummed her feet on the broken shells. "My God, Layla, I don't even know what to say to you!"

"Did you kiss before you were married?"

"Yes, yes. We were engaged for a whole year, remember? Most of the time we could only meet formally and all—" she rolled her eyes "—but we sneaked out a lot together. And before Jojo, there was another fellow..."

I looked at her, shocked. *"Who?"*

"Our neighbor's son," Moon said with a wink. "My God, Layla, you've known Manik Deb for two and a half years. What have you been doing all this time?"

"Writing letters, exchanging news. Next thing I know he wants to marry me, and I say yes."

"I bet he can't wait to do it."

"I am really scared."

"What's there to be scared about? He has a bat, you have a ball. You both play. Simple."

"Does it hurt?"

"What—*that*?"

I nodded, looking down. I pushed a coconut frond around with my toe in the dirt.

"It's not like giving birth or anything. It's more awkward than painful the first time." She gave me a little prod and giggled. "Relax, will you? Try not to faint. Don't yell and scream, for God's sake."

"I don't think I can even bear to take my clothes off," I said miserably.

"Don't worry—he'll do it for you, and everything will happen so fast, you won't even know it. After a few practice rounds you will get the hang of the bat-ball thing and then you both will have a whole lot of fun, believe me."

I sighed deeply. I hoped she was right.

CHAPTER
16

I awoke at 4:15 a.m. on my wedding day. A thin gray light filtered through the curtain in my bedroom. The house was stirring awake. There were soft voices on the veranda; somebody coughed. I lay in bed, my hand tucked under the pillow, thinking. From this day onward, everything would change. I would be unmoored from my familiar surroundings, set afloat in the world, my fate forever entwined with the life of another.

I thought of Manik Deb. How well did I really know the man I was about to marry? He had held out his hand, and I was ready to forsake the familiar and follow him into the unknown. But had he not done the same? Walked blindly into the unknown world of British tea plantations? There was something heady about taking chances, and I had signed up for the ride.

We would be getting married in Dadamoshai's school. The wedding ceremony was scheduled for two in the afternoon. As per the plan, Manik would be arriving at eleven. After the wedding he would stay for one night before heading back to Aynakhal. He would come to get me a week later, bag, baggage and all.

Many thought it was strange that he would be arriving

alone. There would be no *Borjatri*, the traditional groom's entourage: a band of laughing men, friends and relatives who buoyed the groom along to his wedding, teasing, cajoling and making silly demands on the bride's family. This was the custom. Manik's family had disowned him and refused to come. Alasdair was in Scotland, and Manik's Calcutta friends had not been able to get away at such short notice. Manik would arrive, not in a flower-bedecked car accompanied by the beating of drums, as was the tradition, but rather in his mud-splattered company jeep. Moon had been put in charge of him. She would take him to Dadamoshai's school, where Manik's wedding attire would be kept ready for him. He would freshen up and get changed in one of the classrooms, before meeting the rest of the wedding party in front of the school for the ceremony.

These paltry arrangements were not befitting the status of any groom, rich or poor. The bride's family treated the bridegroom like royalty. But ours was not a traditional wedding, and Manik was no traditional groom. Everything was a little off-kilter and nothing was according to the norm.

I had another argument with Mima. This time it was over the bridal makeup. Mima insisted I look like a traditional bride, which meant putting on a pancake foundation, doing up my eyes with kohl and having curlicues painted on my forehead with sandalwood paste.

"Please, Mima, I don't want to look like a clown," I wailed.

Moon came to my support. "Leave her alone, Ma," she said. "Layla does not need makeup. She is pretty enough."

"Clown! *Clown!*" Mima's voice rose to a crescendo. "Is marriage a laughing matter? You two STOP your foolish talk now. How will people know Layla is the bride if she does not have that finished look?"

To "finish" my look I was turned over to Spinster Aunt, a

birdlike woman, with fluttering hands and a thin, reedy voice. She was the bridal-makeup expert in the family and a familiar face at all weddings. Spinster Aunt arrived armed with an arsenal of powder puffs, paint jars, pencils and brushes, and took great pride in transforming every bride into a clown.

"Don't worry," Moon whispered in my ear. "She made me look absolutely ghastly at my wedding."

There was no escape. I sat in my blouse and petticoat, a towel wrapped around my shoulders, and tried not to look at the mirror while Spinster Aunt wreaked her havoc. The foundation made my skin itch.

Spinster Aunt got so carried away with her own artistry that she extended the sandalwood curlicues down my cheeks and even painted a little floral bouquet on my chin.

"*Bah. Bah,*" said Spinster Aunt, tilting my chin to admire her handiwork. She clucked appreciatively. "You look deeeevine. Realllly deeevine."

"Hopefully Manik Deb will recognize you," Moon said, looking slightly concerned.

Moon was ready and dressed in a beautiful peach *Tanchoi* sari with a heavy gold border embroidered with peacocks. She hardly wore any makeup, just a little kohl in her eyes and a simple *bindi*. A fresh garland of jasmine was twisted casually around her bun. I envied how fresh and lovely she looked.

"I better go see if everything is ready at the school," she said. "Your Manik Deb will be here in an hour."

Then she turned and smacked Anik's hand, snatching away the powder puff he was applying to his face. "SILLY BOY! What are you doing? You have gone and got powder all over your clothes." Anik's face was ghostly. He stared back at her balefully through white lashes. He was wearing his customary brown, now liberally dusted with powder. Earlier that morn-

ing the whole house had been entertained by the mother-
son tirade over Anik's attire. He had refused to wear the blue
kurta-pajama suit Moon had got him for the wedding. Trying to force even one leg into the pajamas had been too much.
She had given up in disgust. "Go away from here!" Moon had
yelled, flinging his clothes on the floor, while Anik stood
stoutly in his underwear, a small but immovable mountain.
Soon he was back in his customary brown shirt and pants and
buzzing happily around the house. Moon had given him the
cold shoulder all morning.

"Come here, *babu-shuna*," said Spinster Aunt in a sickly en-
dearing voice, "let me at least smooth the powder on your face.
Eh maa, chee-chee—look what you have done. Powder all over
your clothes. No wonder your ma is angry."

Moon sighed. "Somebody please give this child to the garbage man. I don't want him."

"Can I come with you, Ma?" Anik tugged the tail of Moon's
sari.

"You are NOT coming with me. You are NOT going anywhere dressed like a SILLY BOY! Besides, I am NOT talking
to you. So BE QUIET!"

She stormed off, with Anik mewing behind her like a dusty
kitten. I turned back to the mirror to study my fearful appearance. The face that stared back was not one I remotely recognized. I looked white and painted like a geisha. My hair had
been stuffed into a bun of mammoth proportions and held together by a hundred pins that poked into my scalp. My grandmother's heavy red-and-gold tissue sari had been laid out on
the bed with a hideous pile of jewelry I was supposed to wear.
It was all quite intolerable.

"My, my," said Mima, bustling into my room. "Layla-ma,
you are looking GOR-GEEE-OUS! Now she looks like a

proper bride, don't you think?" she said, turning to Spinster Aunt. "Shudha, you have not lost your magic touch. You are indeed the true artist in the family."

Spinster Aunt gave a toothy smile and batted her eyes demurely. "I am rather pleased, if I may say so myself. The sandalwood designs have come out rather fine."

Mima turned to me. "Layla, you must eat something. I have asked Chaya to make you some banana milk. You can drink it without spoiling your makeup. Remember, it will be a long time before you eat."

"Thanks, Mima," I said, giving her hand a little squeeze. *Better to be sensible*, I thought. *We don't want Fainting Fatima passing out on her wedding day.*

I sat on my bed weighted down by my two-ton sari and jewelry, feeling like a lonely chandelier in an empty mansion. I had only Spinster Aunt for company. Everybody had already gone to the school. Spinster Aunt regaled me with tedious accounts of all the weddings she had attended, what the brides had worn and all the nice things people had said about her artistry. Many relatives had urged her to become a professional beautician. She could charge a hefty fee and do the makeup of theater actresses, they said. Of course she had demurred, claiming she was nothing but an amateur. Her thin voice was beginning to grate on my nerves.

Meanwhile, time was ticking on. Something was wrong. I felt a knot in my stomach; my hives were beginning to act up. The whole house was deathly quiet. I looked at the alarm clock by my bed. It was already one o'clock. I was supposed to be at the school at twelve-thirty. Half an hour late. Why had not someone come to fetch me? The guests must have ar-

rived. I was filled with panic. Did Manik get cold feet? Maybe
he had had a terrible accident?

I told Spinster Aunt I needed some quiet time to pray. Being
the holy sort, she nodded understandingly and left the room. I
closed the door and sat on the edge of my bed, now engulfed
by full-blown panic. It was nudging one-fifteen. The school
was only a short distance away. I could have easily walked or
taken a rickshaw. But I could do nothing dressed the way I
was except wait for the car. Besides, the bride was supposed to
make a grand entrance. I had been asked to stay put.

The car arrived at one-fifty. I saw Moon sprinting up the
path, her sari hitched high, the garland in her hair coming
undone.

"Layla! Layla!" she yelled. "Quick!"

"What happened—did he have an accident?"

"Who? Manik? Don't be an idiot. Quick, hurry up. We are
running horribly late."

"Is he here?"

"Yes, yes, he's here. Let's go. Have you got everything?
Where is Auntie?"

"What happened?"

"Long story. I'll tell you later. Everything is fine, groom
has arrived, priest has arrived, guests have arrived. Come on,
come on. Auntie? AUNTIE! Where *is* that old bat?" Moon
ran off to look for her.

I slipped my red *alta*-rimmed feet into my bridal slippers
and jangled my way out to the veranda. It was hard to do anything with any semblance of mobility.

Auntie was nowhere to be found.

"I thought she was out on the veranda," I said.

"We can't wait for her. Come on, come on, let's go," said

Moon, taking hold of my elbow. "Walk faster, will you? Hurry, Ma is throwing a fit."

"Why is everything so late?" I asked, shuffling along, my stiff sari crackling like a wafer.

"Your Manik was late, that's why."

"Is everything all right?"

"Yes, yes. Just as well you are not getting married at the exact auspicious hour. You would have missed your timing and the wedding would be canceled." The car engine was running, and the driver held the passenger door open. "Here, let me help you get inside. I will lift your sari for you. Are you okay?" She ran and got in from the other side.

"Jaldi! Jaldi," she urged the driver in Hindi. *Drive fast!*

I breathed a sigh of relief. I was going to get married after all.

Everything after that was a blur. My arrival was heralded with the blowing of conch horns, ululation and the ringing of bells. I dimly remembered the flower-bedecked school porch, strung with garlands of tuberoses and marigold. Somebody had painted *alpana* designs on the floor, and there were rows of guests seated in folded chairs. I caught a glimpse of some familiar faces: the District Commissioner, the Forest Officer and Amrat Singh, the Police Chief, wearing a bright red turban sitting next to his fair, plump wife. There were also other well-known poets, artists and dignitaries—Dadamoshai's acquaintances, mostly.

I noticed Anik was actually wearing the blue pajama suit that had been picked out by his mother. He had obviously been bribed, evidenced by the brown smear of chocolate all over his face. Then I saw Manik. I hardly recognized him in his flowing silk shirt and pleated dhoti. Manik looked equally surprised to see me—even mildly suspicious, as if maybe the bride had been switched on him.

A small ceremonial area had been set up under the jacaranda tree. The path leading up to it was strewn with rose petals. I approached the small canopied platform accompanied by Moon. I could feel Manik looking at me. When I looked up and caught a glimpse of his face, I was taken aback to see there were several shaving nicks on his chin. What on earth had he shaved himself with on his wedding day? A dagger? I was also slightly disturbed to see his glasses were broken. They were held together with what looked like a piece of tape.

A small hush fell over the congregation as the minister, a Bhramo scholar, read out a Tagore poem, and a gust of wind sent a shower of purple blossoms from the jacaranda tree swirling at our feet. Manik and I exchanged garlands. Our hands were tied together with a string of jasmine. Ladies blew conch shells and threw puffed rice and rose petals.

The rather solemn and eloquent ceremony was momentarily interrupted when a ripple of laughter pulsed through the audience. Anik had got into a kicking fight with a small girl. When his mother shushed him, he pulled down his royal-blue pajamas and exposed himself brazenly to all the dignitaries in the front row. Mima clutched her heart and almost fainted. Anik was hauled off by Moon, kicking and screaming, undoubtedly to some dark dungeon to be spanked soundly. The ceremony then continued without further interruption.

I was constantly aware of Manik's presence by my side. I felt the warmth of his hand over mine, the brush of his shirtsleeve against my arm. The resonance of his deep voice vibrated through my body as he said his vows.

Finally it was all over. We were led to the flower-bedecked chairs to receive our guests. We touched the feet of our elders, who blessed us with sandalwood, rice husk and *darba* grass. I went through the motions like a sleepwalker, completely devoid of emotions. The long day had begun to take its toll. I barely remembered the wedding lunch.

"Hello, wife," Manik whispered conspiratorially, halfway through the first course. His breath was warm, and his lips buzzed against my ear. "I can't wait to be alone with you."

I felt a tremor of excitement followed by panic. The fatigue of the day was making my head swim. *Please, dear God,* I prayed, *please don't let me faint—that's all I ask.*

Dadamoshai's old bedroom was turned into the nuptial chamber. It had been cleared and aired, the double bed canopied with long tuberose and jasmine garlands that trailed down to the floor. The cream-colored bedspread was strewn with red rose petals. On a table there was an engraved brass bowl with white lotus flowers floating within it and a peacock-shaped incense burner in the middle. The air was heavy with the scent of sandalwood and flowers.

The door closed behind us, shutting off the sounds of teasing and revelry. Some kids banged on the door, hooting, then ran off laughing down the hallway. Suddenly we were alone. Manik and I. Married. Husband and wife.

I could hear my heart thudding. Every sound seemed amplified. The folds of my heavy sari crackled; a single movement of my wrist set off a noisy clamor of bangles. I stood in the center of the room feeling gold-laden and weighted down.

Unlike me, Manik looked happier and more relaxed than he had all day. Without a single word, he lifted me off my feet and twirled me round, toppling us both through the floral curtain onto the bed. I lay on top of him, pinned against his chest, my bangle caught in a silk thread of his kurta as he tried to kiss me through my veil.

I was trembling uncontrollably. The tension that had been

running through me for weeks amplified into what I can only describe as full-blown virginal terror. My hands clenched, my throat parched up and then to my horror, a tear rolled help-lessly down my cheek and plopped onto my husband's nose. Manik was taken aback.

"What's wrong, Layla?" he asked, frowning.

Two more tears plopped down. *Oh, God, oh, God, I am going to die*, I thought. I buried my face and sobbed right into his beautiful silk wedding shirt, leaving big damp patches of ugly makeup on his chest. I was past caring.

"Layla, look at me...please!" Manik was really worried. Shedding a nuptial tear or two was one thing, but weeping like an open faucet was another.

I sat up. My bangle was still threaded to his kurta so I cov-ered my face with my free hand. Manik peered down his nose. He squinted as he unpinned the bangle. He sat up, pushed his glasses up his nose and put his arms around me, but I was a small stony mountain surrounded by chilly winds.

"Layla, what is the matter? You must talk to me."

I wiped my face with the end of my sari. The gold brocade scratched my skin like wire wool.

"I am scared," I said finally.

"Of what? Of me?"

I didn't say anything.

"I see," said Manik quietly.

He slumped back down on the bed and lay there with his hands behind his head. I could see from the corner of my eye that he was thinking. "Layla, please," he said finally. "We won't do anything until you are ready. I promise. I give you my word."

I began to relax somewhat. I started to take off my heavy gold bangles.

"Here, let me help you," Manik said, sitting up.

He kissed my fingers as he squeezed the gold bangles from my wrists one by one and laid them on the bed.

"I'll leave the room while you undress. I can change in the bathroom."

I did not say anything. Manik walked over to his small overnight bag on the floor. He unzipped it and pulled out a few items.

"Don't run off on me now," he said, giving me a wink. Then he went into the bathroom and pulled the door shut behind him.

I took a deep breath. What a relief it was to get out of my wedding sari and undo the ten thousand pins that held up my bun. I opened the small bag that had been packed for me and saw with dismay the new, baby-pink, granny-looking night-gown Mima had selected for my wedding night. It had a silly lace biblike thing in front, a drool catcher of sorts. Romantic hearts were appliquéd in a merry-go-round on the breast. Mima's idea of enticing nuptial attire, no doubt.

I sat on the bed in my granny nightgown and waited, comb-ing out my hair and trying not to think squeamish thoughts. Manik was taking an awfully long time in the bathroom.

Finally he opened the door. He had on white pajama bot-toms and, to my embarrassment, not a scrap of cloth on top. Manik was more muscled and slim-hipped than I had imag-ined him to be. I was so rattled seeing his tanned skin and the million hairs on his chest, I could hardly bear to look at him.

"Are you done?" I asked, shuffling to my feet.

He held the door open and bowed me gallantly into the bathroom. I closed the door and leaned against it, my heart beating wildly.

I scrubbed my face with neem soap to get all the war paint

off. I looked in the mirror. My skin looked pale and my eyes were small and tired. But at least the person who looked back was someone I knew. I smoothed some sandalwood lotion on my face, combed out my hair, then stood by the door and counted to ten, trying to calm myself, before I reentered the bedroom. My heart was thumping all over again.

Manik was lying on the far side of the bed, ankles crossed, his hands behind his head, looking as if he was relaxing in a sunny meadow. He must have noticed my granny nightgown for the first time because he looked mildly shocked, but he made no comment.

"Just so that you know," I blurted, "this is not the kind of thing I normally wear to bed. This is my aunt's idea of a romantic nightdress."

He laughed. "I don't care," he quipped, "as long as it comes off."

I tensed. I am not sure he noticed.

"I could kill for a smoke just now. I am having a nuptial anxiety attack," Manik grumbled. "Giving up smoking just before the wedding was a bad idea. Now that I am married, I better spend my money wisely. Otherwise my wife will give me a bamboo-beating."

I was perched on the edge of the bed like a sparrow on a windowsill.

"Lie down and relax, will you," he said, patting the mattress. "I won't pounce on you, I promise."

The bed creaked as I lay down. My toes were pointed primly together; my hands were straight by my sides. I must have looked like an embalmed mummy. I was so dangerously close to the edge of the bed that if Manik so much as sneezed I would blow right off.

"Stop treating me like a leper, will you? Come over here,"

Manik said, patting the bed. "What kind of treatment is this? I have waited three lonely years and I am expected to abstain on my wedding night. Just who do you think I am—Gandhi?"

I inched over and he curled his arm around my shoulders. My cheek lay against the bare skin of his chest. I could hear the soft beating of his heart. He smelled really nice, too.

"It feels so good to hold you, Layla," he murmured into my hair.

"What are all these cuts?" I asked, touching his face. "What did you do—get into a catfight?" My hand grazed his lips and he chewed on my finger, sending a small shiver down my spine.

He laughed. "Why, didn't Moon tell you anything?"

"No, what happened?" I sat up and looked at him.

"Kiss me first, wife. Otherwise I won't tell you."

I hesitated then gave him a small peck on the chin. He crushed me to him.

"Don't blame me if things get out of hand now. You started it."

He must have seen the anxiety in my eyes because he said softly, sadly, "My God, you are really afraid, aren't you? I had no idea how unworldly you really are, Layla."

"So, what happened," I repeated, trying to change the subject, "on your way to the wedding? Did you have an accident?"

Manik laughed softly. "I was a wreck when I got here. The lads threw a party last night for me in Aynakhal. They got me completely plastered, dunked me in the bathtub and then shoved me in the jeep and sent me off with Alam, the driver. I slept all the way to Silchar. I was lucky I made it to the wedding at all."

I was shocked.

"So you can imagine the state I arrived in," Manik continued. "I did not have any time to shave, bathe or anything.

Moon was horrified. She took one look at me and pronounced me unacceptable. She gave me a big lecture and said I would disgrace the Rai Bahadur. I have a dubious reputation as it is, then to show up looking like a beggar at my wedding would only confirm everyone's suspicion that I was a gone case. My glasses were broken. Moon worried I would go and garland the wrong girl and create an even bigger scandal."

Manik twirled a strand of my hair. "The poor girl ran around to find tape to fix my glasses. She borrowed some relative's razor so I could shave. There was no shaving soap, and the blade was a hundred years old." He touched his chin gingerly. "So here I am all patched up and married to you."

I was thinking about the bachelor party. It must have been full of debauchery, I imagined. I did not dare to ask.

He must have read my mind because he suddenly asked, "Do you know what the *Kama-sutra* says?"

I had one foot on the floor and was ready to bolt out the door.

Manik hoisted himself on his elbows. He looked at me, his glasses askew. "My God, you didn't wait for me to finish, did you? So what do you think the *Kama-sutra* is all about?"

"I have a general idea…"

"I don't think you do. You may want to know it has some serious counsel for lovers and newlyweds. But listen, wife, I am not going to share anything with you, unless you start treating me in a more civil manner."

I lay back down with my head on his chest.

"That's better. The *Kama-sutra* says the first step to a happy and lasting marriage is for the husband to win a wife's trust before initiating sex. It is a delicate process and can take time. Women are typically less experienced than men. They bruise emotionally when roughly handled and this can create an

unhealthy power balance between man and wife. Eventually
it leads to distance between couples. Only once the wife has
overcome her shyness can the couple fully engage in the other
business you were thinking about."

Just imagining the "other business" created a mini avalanche.
The din in my head grew louder. We lay in bed, skin to skin,
our breaths intermingled, and *nothing happened*. I was dimly
aware that although we did not have a traditional wedding, we
were abiding by a time-honored rule. In a Bengali marriage the
couple was not supposed to engage in sex on their first night
together but use that time to get acquainted instead. What
"getting acquainted" meant was anybody's guess. I wonder if
Manik knew about this tradition. I did not broach the subject in case the conversation trotted off toward naughty ideas.

"Tell me about Aynakhal," I said.

"Aynakhal," Manik sighed happily. The timbre in his voice
deepened. "Aynakhal means 'Mirror Lake,' you know?"

Manik described the Koilapani River that flowed through
the tea plantation as a webbed waterway that widened into
the Aynakhal Lake before vanishing into a giant marshland
on the Kaziranga border. The Aynakhal Lake was a pristine
jade-green and resplendent with dazzling lilies—white, pink
and mauve, with centers of glowing butter-gold. There was
no easy access to the lake from the tea garden; the only way
to get there was on elephant back or by taking a boat through
the long meandering waterway. But Manik had discovered
a secret trail from behind his bungalow that led right down
to the water's edge. He often went there for a swim. It was
the most peaceful place on earth, he said. River otters played
among the lilies, and turtles sunned on fallen logs. The only
sounds you ever heard were the whisper of the reeds and the
gentle lap of water on the shore.

Manik's soft voice describing the peaceful lake made me deliciously sleepy. My breathing slowed and my whole being began to unfurl—like kelp in flowing water.

A small boat bobbed along the waterway. The lilies parted and the water crumpled like silk against the shore. I could see ahead the vapors from the marsh rising to meet a wind-torn sky. The boat caught an eddy and swirled in a graceful waltz to turn me around.

The boatman laughed. "Look," he said, holding up his empty hands, "I have no oars."

I shielded my eyes, trying to see his face, but his features were blurred.

"How do we know where we are going?" I cried.

"We don't," the boatman replied, "and we won't know till we get there."

I opened my eyes in the morning to find I was still in my granny nightgown. I had not been deflowered in my sleep, as I had secretly hoped, which was a pity because the whole thing would have been over and done with. Losing one's virginity, I naively imagined, could happen in a careless moment, like dropping a handkerchief.

My brand-new husband, sweetly tousled, his eyes soft from sleep, was propped on an elbow six inches from my nose, look- ing at me. Without his glasses he looked disarmingly boy- ish. He had a blue-gray stubble on his chin, and his nicks had turned a pinkish-purple. He stared at me in wonder as if I was some moon rock fallen from the sky. I looked back at him feel- ing a little astonished myself.

"What's the time?" I asked, rubbing my eyes.

"Hmm, time?" Manik murmured dreamily. Then he leaned over and kissed my mouth.

Not that I had expected to shake hands first thing in the

morning, but I must admit I was taken aback by the sweetness of his kiss. When I did not resist, he kissed me some more, but something happened to me halfway: a circuit tripped and my body shut down.

I hoped he would not notice, but to my dismay he stopped. After that, no matter how many times he tried, it was the same thing. It was hopeless.

By now I was desperate. "Please," I begged, shutting my eyes, "I want this to be over."

"Making love is not exactly a onetime tooth extraction, darling."

"Just take me."

"That's called rape," he said quietly

"I don't care," I said miserably.

"Your body cares," he said softly, stroking my cheek. "It is not going to work this way, love. We'll have to work at it a little longer."

"Promise me, you won't run away?"

"I don't think I can, and I am not sure I want to." He traced my lips with his thumb. "Right now, I don't know what I want more desperately, you or a cigarette. Probably you. Consider yourself flattered, my darling."

"Wish I could light up and offer myself."

He smiled his slow, beautiful smile. "You will, in time, like a very fine and exotic cigar."

"How can you be so sure?" I asked, looking at him curiously.

"Kisses don't lie."

I closed my eyes. "Please, then kiss me," I begged him, "for a little while. Till—"

I did not finish because his lips had found mine. Manik kissed me softly, sweetly, till the fear dissolved and the anxiety ebbed away. I thought if this was the kind of trust and hon-esty we had in our relationship, what could go possibly wrong? Little did I know I still had a lot to learn.

CHAPTER

17

Manik returned the following Saturday in the company jeep with Alam, the driver. Manik looked rested, clean-cut and handsome, although he was still in his workday clothes—white Bombay bloomers and a short-sleeved shirt. His canvas boots were caked with mud. He had brought along a change of clothing.

Dadamoshai's house overflowed with visitors. The entire neighborhood had turned up to give me a grand send-off. Tea-cups littered the veranda. They sat precariously on the railing, got pushed under the sofa and left smudged rings on the newspapers on the coffee table. My bags were lined up on the veranda. I was taking most of my books, my grandmother's old trunk and, at Dadamoshai's insistence, my grandmother's dressing table.

It was an elaborate Victorian contraption, of solid mahogany with intricate carved legs and a three-panel mirror that could be angled. The polished top looked as though it should be lined with powder puffs, potions and exotic perfume. For someone who used only sandalwood lotion and no makeup, it was overkill. I was not the powder-puff kind.

"It's too big, Dadamoshai," I said, hoping to talk him out of it. "This will never fit in the jeep."

"Then I will rent a truck and get it delivered to Aynakhal," Dadamoshai said. He was not the most practical man. "Manik said he had not thought of getting you a ladies' dressing table. You will need one, Layla, now that you are a married lady."

What were married ladies supposed to do? Preen all day?

But I knew my Dadamoshai. The dressing table was the last remaining relic that belonged to the woman he had loved. He was finally letting go.

I watched Manik as he leaned against the veranda railing. He was listening to Mima, his head tilted, his thumb thoughtfully stroking his chin. He shook his head and laughed. Then his eye caught mine, and an invisible string tightened between us.

Two men from the fishing village had come to give a hand with the loading. The big debate was how to fit the dressing table into the jeep. A carpenter was summoned. He took apart the dressing table in sections. The mirror panels were covered with burlap, and the whole thing was piled in the back and bound tightly with ropes.

Relatives and neighbors stood around with teacups and shouted advice, most of it random, contradictory and illogical. The jeep was beginning to look like a very tired and overburdened camel. Dadamoshai had been edgy and high-strung all morning. During the complicated loading operation, he lost his head, and called Senior Uncle "a half-witted donkey." Senior Uncle, a pompous and belligerent man—whose razor it was, incidentally, Moon had stolen—well-known for his epic fits of rage, got bug-eyed and speechless while his dentures clattered uncontrollably. Dadamoshai stomped off in his wooden clogs, and a chair was hurriedly brought out for Senior Uncle to collapse into. The loading operation came to an awkward halt, and a shouting match erupted between two warring parties of relatives. Parrots flew screeching from the mango tree while the workers sat calmly on their haunches and took a bidi break.

Manik was a model of diplomacy. He sauntered off with his hands in his pockets to observe the canna lilies. I wondered what he would think of my uncouth relatives. But when I caught his attention, I saw mirth in his eyes.

Then came the part I had been dreading the most. The bride's final leave-taking, which is typically marked by a tidal wave of tears. There were not many people present whom I cared about, except Mima, who wiped away mostly happy tears, and Dadamoshai, who had disappeared. But I knew him well: he had used the showdown with Senior Uncle as an excuse to be alone.

I went looking for him. Dadamoshai was nowhere to be found. He was not in his study, the dining room, garden or even the kitchen. The last place I thought of looking was the old master bedroom where Manik and I had spent our wedding night. The door was slightly ajar and Dadamoshai was sitting on the bed.

"Dadamoshai?"

He started. "Please, *maiyya*, go. It's time for you to leave. You are getting late."

I sat beside him on the bed and took his hand. The old bedcover was back on the bed and the mishmash furniture moved in but the room still smelled of the incense from our wedding night.

"I am thinking of moving back into this room," mused Dadamoshai. "I had forgotten how pleasant it is."

"It's the best room in the house," I agreed. I pointed to the empty space where my grandmother's dressing table used to be. "You even have space for a writing desk by the window with the beautiful neem tree outside."

"I was just thinking about that," said Dadamoshai.

We sat quietly looking at the waving branches. It dawned on me that by taking away the last physical reminders of my grandmother—her dressing table and her saris—I was setting Dadamoshai free from his past. We were both starting new journeys of our own. The same thought must have crossed his mind because he said, "This is a new chapter in your life, *maiyya*. You will be happy with Manik Deb. I could not have wished for a better life partner for you."

"You really think so, Dadamoshai?"

He nodded. "I would not have let go of you so lightly, *maiyya*. Not for anyone else. You are…" His voice broke, and his eyes misted behind his glasses.

I buried my face in his shoulder. "I hate to leave you alone, Dadamoshai."

Dadamoshai sat up. "Quickly now, you must not keep your husband waiting. I have plenty of things to do today." He waved his hand around the room. "I want to get this room organized and move in today. Might as well use those two fellows from the village to move the furniture while they are here." He touched my cheek lightly. "I won't come to see you off to the car, if you don't mind, *maiyya*. All that wailing and breast-beating will irritate me. Besides, I fear if I see your senior uncle, that donkey, one more time, I will give him a kick on his backside."

I smiled and put my arms around him. This is what I loved about Dadamoshai: even though he lost his temper, he rarely lost his sense of humor.

"Go now, *maiyya*," he said quietly, kissing the top of my head. He gazed at my face tenderly and pressed a thumb to wipe back a tear from my eye. "May God be with you, and know that all good things in the world are yours."

I stood up and walked toward the door.

"Send in those two fellows, will you?" Dadamoshai called after me. "Make sure they don't run back to the village. I want to get this room cleaned out now."

I nodded. Just hearing his parting words lifted my heart.

As I was getting into the car, a bunch of dubious neighbors and relatives set up a howling chorus. Their wails and shrieks echoed all the way down to the river. I stood there dry-eyed and silent while Manik awkwardly held open the car door. It was unheard of for a bride not to cry during her leave-taking. I was sure the entire town would hear about my coldheartedness.

Finally I got into the car and we were off. Manik drove and I sat in front with him, his Manchester rifle on the floorboard between us. As for the driver, Alam, the poor fellow was crushed in the back, sandwiched between suitcases and boxes with the burlap-covered legs of the dressing table two inches from his nose.

Manik blotted the sweat from his forehead on his shirtsleeve. He was a little taken aback with the unexpected drama, I could tell.

"I hardly know these people," I said irritably. "All they ever did was gossip behind my back, and now they cry as if I just died. So hypocritical."

We pulled out into the main road. Manik flicked his eyes at the rearview mirror and saw that the driver was buried out of sight. He pulled me over and kissed me. The car careened and sprayed gravel, and everything skidded around in the back, including poor Alam.

"Layla, I am so happy. Are you?"

"Yes," I said, trying to catch my breath. Nothing had begun to sink in quite yet.

In his last letter Manik had asked me to make a detailed list of every single item I might need. Even basic toiletries like soap, shampoo, cream, everything I could think of. Feminine items. There was not much available around Aynakhal, he said.

The nearest shops were in Mariani, which was little more than a fishing village, fifteen miles from the tea garden. There was also a club store at the Mariani Planters Club that stocked mostly imported provisions. Everything in the store was hideously expensive. Planters normally ordered exotic items from wholesale merchants in Calcutta. Common provisions and toiletries were purchased from Paul & Company in Silchar and picked up when planters came into town.

We bumped over a pothole and something rattled overhead.

"Careful," I said, "don't break a mirror. It's bad luck."

Manik grinned, took his hand off the gearshift and held his palm open on my lap. My hand slipped easily into his.

"You don't believe in things like that, do you?" he said softly, kissing my fingers. "Please say you don't."

I did not answer. I was balancing a fragile new world on the tip of my destiny.

"What are you thinking?" he said.

"Nothing."

"'Nothing' is not a valid answer."

"I worry sometimes about bad luck," I said. "You know I…"

"Please don't," he said, his lips grazing the back of my hand, his breath soft on my skin. "Think of all the incredible luck we have had so far. What were the chances of you and me getting married, you tell me? I feel like the luckiest chap in the world."

★ ★ ★

Paul & Company were general merchants with an all-European clientele. It was a family-owned business run by three Bengali brothers, triplets. They were impossible to tell apart, each one being as pudgy and soft-spoken as the other. Their original surname, Pal, had been anglicized to Paul for cultural congeniality. The Paul brothers were astute businessmen and spoke excellent English with roundy-poundy Bengali accents, as if they had plums in their mouths. The store had earned the loyalty of the tea crowd by carrying the right mix of provisions and extending generous credit to tea planters. They maintained a ledger with elaborate accounts for all the tea gardens in the Mariani district.

It was a big, musty store, high-beamed like a warehouse. Pigeons cooed in the dim rafters. The store stocked many imported grocery items dear to expatriates: Marmite, Polson's Butter, tinned sardines, Bournvita and Bird's Custard Mix, among others.

I easily found the things on my list. Manik quirked an eyebrow to see my rather meager requirements. I guess he had expected more expensive and complicated wifely maintenance items.

"Sure you're not forgetting anything?" he asked. He threw in some items of his own: torch batteries, Lifebuoy soap and razor blades.

An athletic-looking young European man had entered the store. He wore white tennis shorts, a white shirt and a cream ribbed sweater tossed carelessly over his shoulder. His straight, blond hair fell over his eyes like a sheet of pale sunshine, and his eyes when he looked up were the most startling blue.

"Ash!" cried Manik. "Fancy meeting you at Paulies."

"I have a match at the Gymkhana today, old chap," said the

man. He spoke with a singsong Irish lilt. "Just popped by to pick up the tennis balls I ordered."

"My wife, Layla," said Manik, introducing us. "Layla, this is Rob Ashton, champion tennis player, pride of Jardine Henley and Assistant Manager of Dega Tea Estate."

Rob's blue eyes admired me candidly. "Why hello," he said, sticking out his hand.

"Pleased to meet you," I replied.

"You speak impeccable English," Rob said wonderingly. "Did you go to school in England, Layla?"

"Oh no, just here in Silchar," I said. "I was privately tutored by English teachers."

"Fascinating," said Rob. "Debbie will be so excited to meet you. She is dying to make an Indian friend and learn how to wear a sari."

"Debbie is Rob's wife," Manik explained. "She's a lovely girl."

"I saw your loaded-up jeep parked outside, Manny. Looked like there was not an inch of room inside. I thought you brought your driver along?"

"I did indeed," said Manik. "Poor Alam has to squeeze in with all the furniture. He's going to be terribly uncomfortable on the journey back, I'm afraid."

"Well, here's an idea, old sport," said Rob, flicking back his blond hair. "I'll be heading home after the game. I can drop Alam off at Aynakhal, if you like." He winked at Manik. "I am sure you two newlyweds will want some private time on your romantic drive back to Aynakhal."

Mr. Paul, the triplet with the mole, who was tallying up our bill behind the counter, looked embarrassed. He twitched his nose and sniffed.

"Brilliant idea!" cried Manik, clapping Rob on the back.

"That settles it, then," said Rob. He turned to me. "We'll be seeing you plenty, Layla. Manik and I play tennis on Mondays. He thrashes me."

"Oh, stuff and nonsense," said Manik affably. "This guy is a champ. I am grateful he stoops to play with me at all." He turned to me. "Ash is representing Mariani in the district championship at the Silchar Gymkhana Club today. I'm not joking when I say he's a champ."

Manik signed the register and picked up our carton. "I'm afraid we have to run, old chap. We'll see you on Monday."

"S'long," said Rob. "Ask Alam to wait by my jeep, will you? I've parked behind the cantonment."

Manik glanced at my feet as we got into the car. "I hope you have sensible shoes," he said.

"These are sensible," I replied. I had on a pair of flat slippers.

"No, I mean *seriously* sensible footwear—like boots."

"Boots? What do you mean? I can't wear boots with a sari."

"Believe me, darling, you are going to need them. With all the leeches and snakes, slippers and sandals won't do."

"I don't have any closed shoes, if that's what you mean."

"Then we might as well swing by the Bata shoe store," said Manik. "It's on the way."

Our jeep inched along the clogged road. A convoy of military trucks thundered by on the way to the cantonment. Rickshaws honked, and cows wandered around aimlessly, chewing banana peels. We pulled up in front of the Bata shoe store.

The store was dim and shuttered and smelled of new leather and shoe polish. A radio blared out soulful film music. We spied a shiny baldpate behind a pile of shoe boxes on the counter. The salesman was napping. No customers came at siesta time. He lay with his head on his hands, a small drool

of spittle strung from his open mouth down to the counter-
top. The pages of his receipt book rippled gently with his soft
snoring.

Manik rapped the counter with his knuckles, causing the
poor man to scramble to his feet in such a terrible hurry that
he upset the shoe boxes, sending them clattering to the floor.

"Oh—*sir!*" he said, pop-eyed, wiping his mouth and patting his hair, which sat like an oily horseshoe around his head.

Manik walked over, tapped the display glass and pointed to
a hefty pair of canvas boots in the showroom window. "For
madam," he said.

The salesman babbled. "Most certainly, sir—what size?"

"What's your shoe size?" Manik said, turning to me.

"Five and a half, I think," I replied, wondering what was
going on.

The salesman beamed sweetly, giving me the full tilt of his
oily charm. "Excellent choice, madam," he said and picked
up a dainty white ladies' slipper from the display case next to
the canvas boot. "This is our very latest *Manjula* design." He
reverently held up the slipper in both hands for us to admire.
It looked like a dove about to take flight.

"No, no," said Manik, tapping the glass, "I am talking about
the boot. That khaki one with laces."

"For you, sir?" said the salesman, looking a little puzzled.

"For madam. Please hurry. We don't have all day."

Surely Manik was joking. He was pointing at a canvas boot
that looked belligerent and battleworthy. It was ankle-high
with an industrious sole and laces sturdy enough to hitch a
cow to a fencepost.

The salesman was still muttering in confusion as he came
around to measure my foot. The smallest size the boot came
in was still two sizes too large.

"We'll take it," Manik said.

"Manik, this is crazy!" I exclaimed. "How can I wear *these*? Besides, they don't even fit me."

"Layla, trust me, you won't regret it. Please, for my sake. You don't have to wear them if you don't want to. At least they are there if you need them."

"Need them for what? Where are we going? To war?"

"Yes, comrade," said Manik.

"O-ho-ho!" laughed the oily salesman.

I glared at him. I did not want to create a scene arguing with Manik, so I let it go.

That completed the purchase. A pair of combat boots, two sizes too big, plus two pairs of army socks. One to wear and one to stuff inside the toe. I was beginning to think my husband was a lunatic. But Manik looked pleased.

"All done," he said cheerfully. "Now I am going to take my lovely bride home to Aynakhal."

Manik drove rakishly, his body tilted, one elbow out the window with just three fingers on the steering wheel. His eyes flitted over the landscape, and the wind ripped through his hair. His foot never eased off the pedal as he dodged potholes with the grace and aplomb of a bullfighter. The farther we drove, the more relaxed he became. He breathed deeply; he hummed and turned occasionally to gaze at me with wonderment and joy, like a small boy admiring his prized marble.

We drove into the open countryside on narrow *bandh* roads, built on embankments that sloped down to rice fields. We passed through a small Assamese village, a small huddle of green surrounded by the striped expanse of plowed rice fields. Each village had a cluster of sleepy mud houses with low-fringed thatched roofs hemmed in by lopsided fences. Pendulous gourds clung to the thatched roofs. Creepers and elephant-eared taro, banana and areca palms grew abundantly in handkerchief-size plots. Tiny ponds winked gold and emerald-green in the flitting sun where ducks wagged their bottoms among purple water hyacinths. Slim-waisted Assamese women dressed in the traditional three-piece *mekhela-sador*, with orchids in their hair, swayed down narrow paths with mud pitchers balanced on tilted hips.

Manik leaned on his horn to overtake an unweildy vehicle that rattled and coughed diesel fumes. It looked like a ramshackle army truck converted into a village bus with sides of flattened tin all patched up together. As we passed I got a glimpse of its motley occupants: toothless old men, snot-nosed babies and village women with baskets of cauliflower and papaya. The sides of the bus were streaked with red *paan* spit.

"*Bustee* bus," Manik said. "It's the only means of transport for villagers. Mariani is the last stop, then the bus turns around and heads back to Silchar."

"So how do people get from Mariani to Aynakhal?" I asked. "It's still ten, fifteen miles from Mariani, isn't it?"

"Local people don't have any need to go to the tea gardens," Manik said. "Or if they do, they use private transport. Or they cycle or walk. And that, too, through some pretty treacherous and unpredictable jungle roads." He gave me a mock-stern look. "It's not very easy to run off, if that's what you are thinking."

The rice fields were thinning and we drove through a tall teak forest humming with cicadas. Dense forested hills loomed ahead, gray-green and mysterious. We were entering tea country, Manik said.

A large truck approached us, billowing a cloud of red dust. The driver pulled over and waited for us to pass. He lifted his hand in a salaam. The truck had CHULSA T.E. stenciled on its side.

"Chulsa Tea Estate is Alasdair's garden," Manik said. "It is owned by McNeil & Smith, a big tea company like Jardines."

"How did you know you'd like being a tea planter?" I asked. "Did you know much about the tea job or the lifestyle before you joined?"

Manik smiled wryly. "I had not a clue. I decided to find out."

"You gave up the civil-service job without knowing anything? Wasn't that a risk?"

"I don't see how else I could have married you."

"What do you mean?" I said.

His thumb caressed my cheek. "Surely you know, Layla, I did it for you?" he said softly.

I was baffled. "Did what for me? Take up the tea job?"

"I made up my mind to marry you the first time I saw you, Layla. How could I forget? Beautiful Layla in that golden rain." His eyes lingered on my face. "I had to derail my engagement to Kona to get to you. The big question was, would you choose to live in the tea gardens with me. It was a calculated risk."

"You broke up your engagement deliberately...for me?"

"A brilliant move, if I may say so myself. The strategic plan was to shunt one bogie off the rails and get the other bogie on. Some careful track manipulation was required. It would have been a tragedy if the Layla bogie derailed, as well."

It was not flattering to be viewed as a railway bogie to be shunted on and off a track. I felt a small wave of resentment.

"Your grandfather would not have approved if I openly broke off my engagement to Kona to marry you. The Rai Bahadur may be broad-minded but he is also an honorable man. I had to make it look like a natural turn of events. The tea job

came along. This was my chance. I had to bide my time and
hope Kona ran off and you didn't. A little risky, but it worked
out, didn't it?"

I sat there feeling a little stunned. Was it deceit or ingenuity?
I wondered. Manik had diabolically engineered his fate and
mine. It was a bold and risky move, and nobody had caught
on, including me. But the stealth and cunning with which he
had pulled it off made me uncomfortable. I wondered what
else would he engineer to his advantage without me knowing? I tried not to think about it, but the old knot began to
appear in my stomach. There was a comfort in not knowing
too much, I decided. I almost wished Manik had not told me
everything. It made me think differently about him, somehow.

CHAPTER
18

How can I ever forget my first sight of a tea plantation?

It came upon me like a breathless surprise. The tangled beauty of the Assam countryside parted to reveal waves upon waves of undulating green. So pristine, so serenely beautiful my senses were shaken.

Tea gardens stretched finger to finger across the bounteous plains of Assam. Quaint names sprang up on billboards like musical chimes, mysterious and evocative. *Bogapani* (White Water), *Hatigarh* (Elephant House), *Kothalgoori* (Jackfruit Root), *Rangamati* (Red Earth). Some tea gardens looked spruced and prosperous, others a little derelict.

"Such curious names," I said, mouthing them softly.

"Tea-garden names are enigmatic," Manik agreed. "They sound vague and random but they have some grounding in the local geography or history of the place. They are very similar to English village names that way." He laughed. "There's a tea garden called *Bandookmara*, which means 'shot by the gun,' and the one next to Aynakhal is *Negriting*—'slave girl hill.' Who knows how those names originated? I am sure there are interesting stories behind them."

I thought Aynakhal was the prettiest name of all. *Mirror Lake.*

In some areas, the tea plantation tumbled down to the very edge of the road. Each tea bush was pruned to a wineglass shape. Sunlight played with the young leaf tips, igniting them in dazzling shades of chartreuse and gold, and the top of the plantation glowed like splintered glass.

Manik slowed to a tortoise crawl and meandered across the road, steering with his elbows.

"Lovely, isn't it?" he murmured softly.

I could only nod.

"That's how I felt when I first saw you, Layla," he said in a caressing voice that made me flush.

"Why are the bushes planted in triangles instead of rows?" I said a little too abruptly.

"Elephants," said Manik. "See how the triangular sections create a zigzag path? It's designed to protect the tea pluckers so they can run away from wild elephants. Elephants can't run through a zigzag path. Humans can."

"You mean to say wild elephants come into the tea plantation?"

"It's very common," said Manik. He pointed to the coconut-size droppings on the road. "That's fresh dung. This is the exact spot where the herd crosses to go to the river on the other side. You often see them at dawn or dusk."

He pulled over to the side of the road. The brakes squeaked as the jeep rolled to a stop. Manik draped his arms over the steering wheel, and gazed at me. All I could hear was the tick-tick of the dying engine.

"Don't you think we've made enough small talk, Layla?" he said softly. A smile played on his lips, but his eyes were serious. "We are married now."

He got out of the car, walked over to the passenger's side,

opened the door and pulled me into his arms. His warm lips found the hollow between my collarbones, traveled up my neck, my ears and sought my lips. My head began to reel. All the colors collided around me, in torrents of green and shards of sun.

I became dimly aware of the sound of approaching voices. I pulled away. "Manik, someone is coming," I said, trying to gather together my sari.

"Dammit," Manik muttered, pushing back his glasses. He crossed his arms and leaned back against the jeep looking glum. We watched a group of women approach, walking down the road in a single file. They balanced piles of firewood on their heads and turned their heads to stare at us like a pack of gazelles as they passed. They were ebony-skinned, bony people, with tattooed arms, flat noses and high cheekbones: tribal looking. Their colorful saris were worn knee-length, wrapped as a single cloth around their bosoms. The younger ones had their hair oiled and pulled tightly into conical buns to the sides of their heads. On their hands and feet they wore thick pewter bangles shaped like cauldron handles. Small infants strapped to their mothers' backs bounced along.

"Who are they?" I asked.

"Tea pluckers," said Manik, still sulking.

I stared after them. They were primitive and rawboned women with wide-planted feet and the swaying gait of people used to carrying heavy loads. I had never seen people like them.

"They are Adivasi tribals from Bihar and Orissa," Manik explained. "They belong to the untouchable caste. Tea gardens employ them as contract labor. Tea pluckers are only women. Notice the height of the tea bushes? The plucking table is pruned exactly to three feet for their convenience."

Another line of women came into view, followed by another. It seemed a whole convoy of romance-wreckers were headed our way.

"I don't suppose we will be left alone here," Manik grumbled. He helped me back into the car then walked around, climbed into the driver's seat and started the jeep.

"How many tea pluckers does Aynakhal employ?" I asked as we pulled back onto the road. Judging by the average size of a tea garden, there sure seemed a lot of tea to be plucked.

"We have around twelve hundred tea pluckers," said Manik. "Aynakhal is one of the bigger gardens. We make top-grade premium Orthodox Assam tea." The pride in his voice was palpable.

I remembered the tea Manik had left on the veranda table the day he had come to propose. The tea was robust, full-bodied and aromatic. Like my husband, I thought, and trembled, remembering his lips on mine.

"What are you thinking?"

"I was thinking—" I hesitated "—that you are, well, quite an attractive man."

"Thank God," said Manik, with an exaggerated sigh of relief. "After all my repeated brush-offs, I was getting seriously worried."

A single-gauge railway track appeared out of nowhere and ran parallel to the road. We passed tiny tea stalls. Bunches of finger-size bananas hung from ropes, and jars of colorful biscuits sat on shelves. Men leaned on bicycles or sat on benches under a mango tree, smoking bidis and drinking out of foggy glasses. Mangy pariah dogs scratched and snapped halfheartedly at flies. More houses started popping up, followed by sidings, sheds and small factories. We passed trucks and bullock carts laden with market produce: banana, pineapple and sugarcane. A stench of dried fish hung in the air.

"We are getting close to Mariani," Manik said.

"Is it a small town?"

"It's more like a fishing village, really. But Mariani is a very important railway junction for the tea district. The rails bring in the coal to fire our generators to run the factory and also carry back our tea to Guahati, from where it goes by steamer to Calcutta."

The train signal turned red and a bell clanged as we approached a railway crossing. A boom gate dropped slowly in front of us. It had a big, round painted STOP sign with skull and crossbones and DANGER printed across it, but people continued to saunter across the railway track. A shrill whistle sounded, and a steam locomotive came gushing around the corner with a fierce clanking of pistons and big whooshes of smoke. The driver in the cab had a thin, careworn face and wore a khaki cap. He had a red rag around his neck. Several long, open trolleys piled high with coal and covered bogies all painted a deep rusty-brown clanked rhythmically past us. BENGAL-ASSAM RAILWAY was stenciled on the sides.

"Are there any passenger trains?" I asked.

"Only once a week," Manik said. "The passenger service is not very reliable."

The bell clanged again and the boom gate lifted. There was a tidal clash of humanity as people tried to cross over from both sides at the same time. Cyclists shrilled, bullock carts ambled and a whole melee of people with baskets on their heads or slung across their shoulders pushed, shoved and yelled. Truck and car horns blared loudly, adding to the din.

There was just one arterial road running through Mariani, with lopsided shops on both sides leaning on one another. One

shop was exactly like the next, selling anything and everything
from balls of twine to mounds of dried chilies, lumps of tamarind, small toys, rubber slippers and handmade soap shaped
like cannonballs. Shopkeepers sat cross-legged on gunnysacks,
jiggled their legs, chewed *paan* and swatted flies.

Driving through Mariani was like driving through a bubble of humanity. It was there suddenly and, just as suddenly,
gone. We passed through the smell of rotting timber; a large
plywood factory, with ASSAM WOODWORKS painted on
the roof, loomed up ahead. A tractor pulled into the gated entrance with a long trailer piled with logs.

"Assam Woodworks supplies plywood for the tea gardens,"
Manik said. "Our garden carpenters make the tea chests."

He was suddenly distracted by a black Morris Minor parked
near a small whitewashed house. The hood was up. It appeared
to have had a breakdown.

We pulled up alongside.

"Hussain!" Manik yelled, and a man in a khaki uniform,
presumably the driver of the car, scrambled out of a tea hut
and, seeing Manik, gave a brisk salaam.

"*Kitna deree?*" How long? Manik asked in Hindi.

"*Dus minut, saab.*" Ten minutes.

I was puzzled. "Is he having engine trouble?"

"No, no," said Manik, giving me a small lopsided smile.
"There is nothing wrong with the car. The driver is waiting
for Larry. Larry is visiting Auntie's."

"Larry Baker's aunt lives *here*?" I asked incredulously. The
white house looked very modest.

"Larry is visiting the Sisters of Mercy."

"This is a church?"

"Depends how you define a place of worship."

I listened in stunned silence as Manik explained that Larry

Baker was in some sort of house of ill repute doing his business while the driver pretended to have a breakdown waiting for him. Manik made it sound as if it was all very normal. I could not believe my ears.

I learned Auntie was an Anglo-Indian madam, who kept tea planters supplied with an assortment of whores. What was even more shocking was this indiscretion was condoned, even encouraged by the tea companies who believed the "Sisters of Mercy" played a vital role in helping young assistants survive their forced bachelorhood.

The question choked in my throat but I had to ask. "Do you...? Have you...?" Words failed me.

"Yes," said Manik carefully, before I could even complete my sentence. "My colleagues initiated me into the planter's life—with, well, all its perks."

I was not prepared to hear what I'd just heard. Yet, what did I expect? Judging from his kissing expertise, Manik Deb was no blushing virgin—that much I could tell. Besides, he had lived on his own for a long time in England, and I doubt whether he spent all that time drinking tea and playing croquet. I still found it unbearable to imagine him with another woman. Let alone a *whore*.

"But why?" I asked, feeling hurt and baffled. I sounded childish, but I could not help it.

Manik glanced at me. He was silent for a moment. "For the same reason people play cards," he said slowly. "To pass the time. To stay sane. What can I say, Layla? There's not much to do around here. Planters are starved for amusement. If not for the Sisters of Mercy, we would have gone mad and shot ourselves. One thing is for sure—you won't find a sex-starved bachelor in the tea gardens."

I could not believe his casual tone. So, I thought bitterly, for Manik Deb I was just another card to shuffle into his deck.

He must have read my thoughts.

"Don't worry, darling," he said. "I don't take my commitments lightly."

"How do I know that?"

"Sweetheart," he said gently, "nobody smokes a bidi when they have a fine cigar. Now I have you…"

But I no longer felt like a fine cigar. I was not even sure if I could light up for Manik Deb after hearing all this. What alarmed me was the inequality of our sexual experience. Here was my husband, who had batted balls with champions, and I had not even figured out my own equipment. The old knot appeared in my stomach.

"Do all tea planters go to Auntie's?" Surely there were a few honorable men who pined in celibacy for their one true love.

"Or they have OPs…their concubines."

"Like Jamina?"

"Yes. As a matter of fact, Alasdair got Jamina from Auntie's."

Got Jamina from Auntie's! Why, Jamina sounded like a puppy.

That made Alasdair one more rotten pea in the pod, I thought bitterly. So much for royalty and fine breeding. I was beginning to feel hopelessly depressed.

"Here is something you must understand, Layla. Planters have to stay sane under the most trying situations. It is lonely in the tea garden—the work is grueling—there are very few diversions. Assistants are forced to remain bachelors for three years. Then even when they are officially allowed to get married, it is hard to find a wife who will agree to come and live in the jungle."

"What made you think I was different?"

"I know you are."

"You hardly know me," I retorted archly.

"I would like to, if you let me." Manik held out his up-turned palm. I did not realize I had pulled my hand away and clenched my fists in my lap.

We drove in silence. I looked out my window hoping Manik would not notice the tears that brimmed in my eyes. *Stare into the wind, Layla,* I told myself. *Hopefully your tears will fly off like little birds, and he won't see them.*

The Koilapani River cut a gash a quarter mile wide across the road. A narrow suspension bridge straddled the two banks like a giant centipede. The bridge creaked on its girders and swung from side to side as the jeep lumbered across. The sluggish streams below meandered around mammoth rocks that stuck out like elephants' feet in the parched riverbed, cracked and pitted like a wasteland.

"You should see this river in the monsoons," said Manik, breaking the silence. "It swells and sometimes rips that bridge in two. Then Aynakhal is completely cut off. We'd be lost without Rupali, I tell you."

I thought for a moment he was talking about a Sister of Mercy. But Rupali, thankfully, turned out to be the resident elephant of Aynakhal. There were three elephants: Rupali, Moti and Tara, Manik said. All females. Tara was now retired. Rupali and Moti were indispensable as tractors. They hauled lumber, chased game with shikaris on their backs and served as a mobile bridge for emergencies during the floods.

"Larry's wife, Janice, once dropped her high-heeled slipper in the river when she was crossing on elephant back," said Manik, chatty as you please.

Talking of Larry reminded me of Auntie's and made me peevish. But I was curious. "Was there a medical emergency?" I asked. High-heeled slippers seemed impractical for an elephant ride. I realized this was the first time I was hearing Larry even had a wife. Why was he not at home, then, enjoying his fine cigar instead of smoking low-grade bidis at Auntie's?

"No, there was no medical emergency—she was just trying to get to the Mariani Club," said Manik airily. Getting to the Mariani Club on club night was apparently deemed important enough to cross a flooded river on elephant back, high-heeled slippers and all.

"She left Larry and went back to England after that," Manik continued. "Had enough of jungle adventures."

Ah, that explained why Larry was at Auntie's. At least Janice got away. A slow claustrophobia was beginning to seep into me. One thing was certain: getting in and out of Aynakhal was not easy.

We were now in serious jungle country. Tall trees crowded out the sky. They grew close together, knit by dense creepers that snarled over branches and dropped ropelike stems with giant leaves to the ground. The dense undercover was furrowed with labyrinthine tracks that disappeared into the dark interior. Pale lilac orchids sprouted from mossy armpits in branches. The road was rutted and bumpy, more a jungle track than a road. We turned down a fork with a banged-up and lopsided wooden marker with AYNAKHAL T.E. painted on it.

"This can't be the only road into Aynakhal?" I asked, feeling a little alarmed as we continued on our bone-rattling journey. *Where was he taking me?* I held on to the dashboard tightly as the jeep heaved and groaned over potholes, tipping precariously from side to side.

Manik hummed, unfazed. "There is a decent road from the

Chulsa end but that's twenty miles farther down the highway. I am taking you by the scenic route."

The bad road was probably only a five-mile stretch, but it seemed to go on and on.

Suddenly there were signs of civilization. The forests cleared, and we drove through rice fields lined by *bamboobaris* on either side. A large bird of the most brilliant plumage flew across the road, followed by three dusky mates.

"Jungle fowl," said Manik, slowing down to look. "Good eating bird."

We rumbled over an unmanned railway crossing to enter the tea estate. There was a boom gate across the road with a big red STOP painted on a circular piece of metal stuck in the middle.

Manik honked, and a sprightly man dressed in khaki shorts and shirt rushed out of a tiny guardhouse. He salaamed smartly before unwinding the rope and letting the boom gate ride up, then did a double salaam when he saw me riding in front.

A tractor lumbered down the opposite side of the road. It idled with its engine throbbing. As we passed, the driver lifted his left hand in another salaam. I noticed he was missing his right hand. Handless or no, people here seemed to salaam left, right and center.

We drove through neat sections of tea plantation and past the gated entrance of a long whitewashed building with big airy open sheds with AYNAKHAL T.E. painted in large blue letters on the silver roof. A deep malty smell of Assam tea filled my senses. Just then a high-pitched siren screamed through the air, making me jump.

"What's that?" I said, startled out of my wits.

"Factory shift change," Manik said. "Must be four-thirty. Oh, here is my office," he said, slowing down as we drove by a long building with several rooms connected by a veranda. There were a couple of bicycles leaning against the wall. The office looked rather unimpressive and rudimentary. I had expected tea-garden offices to be imposing and majestic, maybe because I had Dadamoshai's court office in mind.

The road curved to the right and wound up at a small forest-covered hill.

"That's my bungalow up there. Look, you can see the roof." Manik ducked his head, peering over the windscreen and pointing through the trees. A group of golden langur monkeys scampered across the road. We pulled up to a white-painted gate with overgrown hedges on either side. Manik blew the horn with his elbow. A small man with bandy legs ran out, bobbing and salaaming and getting all tangled with courtesy. He swung open the gates.

"Potloo. *Chowkidar.* Night watchman," Manik said, by way of introduction.

The driveway was edged with white-painted bricks buried diagonally in the ground and pots of marigold that looked freshly watered. The bungalow was built in a traditional *Chung* style and stood eight feet off the ground supported by tall wooden pillars. The heavy thatched roof looked like a head of overgrown hair; under it, small windows peeped out like bleary eyes. A small flight of wooden stairs led up to a spacious wraparound veranda. A profusion of bougainvillea showered down from the railings in heavy splashes of magenta.

Manik pulled up, and I saw a small and motley entourage lined up on the portico.

"Who are these people?" I said, astonished.

"Bungalow servants," said Manik. "To welcome the new *Chotamemsahib.*"

As I got out of the jeep a cacophonous chorus of "salaam

memsahib" went up. They were all males, four in all, not counting Potloo, the watchman, who was scurrying behind the jeep trying to catch up. A gnome-size man was dressed in a stiff white tunic so spanking new it still had the purple factory seal of the textile mill stamped on the chest. Gnome number two, who looked like his identical twin, was dressed in khaki shorts and shirt. The third was a skinny lad, cross-eyed with a large ringworm on his cheek, and the last an old man with bright brown eyes, his face wizened as a monkey.

Manik introduced us. The one in the spanking white uniform was Halua, the bearer. His twin in khaki, Kalua, the cook. The other two were nameless. The ringwormy lad was just called the *paniwalla*, kitchen boy, and the old monkey-eyed man was the *mali*, the gardener.

"You will meet the rest by and by," said Manik. So there were more of them, it seemed.

All the servants scurried around in confused circles, helping to unload, bumping into each other and falling all over themselves. I guess welcoming the new *Chotamemsahib* was a big event.

The wooden stairs creaked and groaned all the way up to the veranda. The view from the upper veranda was spectacular. The Aynakhal *chota* bungalow was set high up on a hillock. The grounds sloped down to a thick wooded area, with no fencing or boundary wall from what I could see. Bushes and trees grew wantonly, spilling and tumbling over one another. The only manicured plant in the garden was a tall hibiscus hedge that defined the property line by the main gate. Otherwise the garden just blended lazily into its natural environment. In the far distance, through a filtered curtain of foliage, a sheet of water winked, catching the light of the dying sun.

"Is that the Aynakhal Lake?" I asked.

Manik looked up to where I was pointing. He was absentmindedly riffling through some mail on the coffee table. Ever since we'd arrived at the bungalow, I'd sensed a strange formality about him. "Yes," he said. "It's quite a way down. But there's a shortcut through the property. I'll take you there sometime."

The veranda was furnished with four cane chairs with worn-out cushions, a low solid teak coffee table and two mismatched peg tables. There was a hat stand against the wall with an umbrella, a walking stick and two *sola topees* on the hat hooks. Above it was a mounted head of a sambar deer with impressive curving antlers and peaceful eyes. In a corner, sitting on the floor, was an oversize dustbin, hollowed out of an elephant's foot, complete with cracked yellow nails and bristling hair on the skin.

Manik saw me looking at the elephant's foot.

"Rogue elephant," he said. "It was killed by Jameson, one of the Aynakhal assistants. Planters don't shoot elephants unless they have to. You need a special permit. This rogue wreaked havoc and killed several people in Aynakhal."

"Did you shoot the deer?"

"Not this one," Manik said, admiring the mounted head. "It was in the bungalow when I moved in. I've shot similar ones, but I never have the money to get the heads mounted."

Halua—or was it Kalua?—had arrived. He stood fidgeting. He whispered into Manik's ear.

"How about a cup of tea?" Manik asked. "I'll show you the bedroom. You can freshen up, if you like."

The master bedroom was enormous, big enough to play badminton in. The curtains in the windows were made from what looked like women's saris, leaf-green with a crimson border. My suitcases were piled up on the floor. In the center of the room was a regular double bed that looked tiny in the vast space. A mosquito net billowed down to the floor in elaborate folds. There were two identical teak wardrobes, side by side, against the wall. One looked brand-new.

The bathroom had a white enamel claw-foot tub with a white slatted wooden tray straddling the top. The tall white washbasin was spotlessly clean. Manik's shaving things sat neatly on a shelf: a soft shaving brush with its hair all smashed to one side, a slim razor and a bar of shaving soap. There was a new pink toothbrush, presumably for me, next to an orange one in a water glass and a very erratically squeezed toothpaste tube with the top missing. The towels were white and clean and smelled of starch and sunlight.

When I returned to the living room, I found Manik fiddling with the oversize knobs on a round-shouldered radio in a lacquered case. It emitted a gloomy green light. There was a tired-looking settee, two padded armchairs and a cane ottoman, over which lay an upturned and dog-eared copy of *War and Peace*. A gramophone sitting on the floor unfurled its horn like a giant morning glory. Next to it was a small pile of vinyl records. The shelves along the wall, I noted with satisfaction, were crammed with books.

"Hopeless reception," said Manik, banging the top of the radio with his fist. The radio suddenly woke up and sizzled momentarily. Then the plummy voice of the BBC announcer sliced through, crisp and clear, amidst terrible squeals of static.

Manik switched it off. "I just wanted to see if it works," he said. "Here, let me show you around the rest of the bungalow. It's rather basic, I'm afraid."

The square dining room had an adjoining *bottle-khanna*, or pantry. There was a kerosene fridge, shelves with cutlery and glassware and a larder with double netted doors. Dozens of beer

and soda bottles neatly lined the floor. A swing door led down
a flight of stairs from the *bottle-khanna* to the kitchen, which
was not part of the main house at all, but a separate building,
a short distance away down a flagstone path.

There were two guest bedrooms with attached baths. One
looked as though it had been turned into a junk room. Manik's
hunting gear was everywhere: a disassembled shotgun lay on a
small table, along with half-open boxes of shells and gun-clean-
ing pipes and rags all over the floor.

"The taps don't work in this bathroom," said Manik. "Also
very important..." He stopped in front of a two-foot square
on the floor outlined with chalk. There appeared to be a fist-
size hole smashed right through the floorboards. "Don't *ever*
step inside this square. You will fall right through. The floor
has rotted. White ants."

I tried to peer into the hole but there was only darkness beyond. It looked like the perfect hideout for snakes.

Manik must have read my mind.

"There are snakes down there, as well," he added.

"So, why don't you get the floor repaired?"

"Right now we have a shortage of funds. This bungalow is
over a hundred years old and needs a major overhaul." Bungalow repair and other upgrades came out of what was known
as Capital Expenditure Submissions, Manik explained. What
the company sanctioned depended on the profits the garden
made that year. Every year a list of requirements was submit-
ted to the head office in Calcutta. It could be anything from
replacing bathroom fixtures to installing a swimming pool.
Manik, it seemed, had pushed for a tennis court rather than
repairs in his own bungalow. But now that he had a wife, he
said, his living conditions would need to be more shipshape.

"More than anything, what this bungalow needs is a *jali*

kamra," Manik said, closing the door to the guest bedroom. A *jali kamra* was an enclosed netted outdoor room, usually an extension of the veranda. "It's impossible to sit out here in the evenings, especially as the weather gets warmer. All kinds of creatures fly around—moths, bats, beetles, grasshoppers. But this time of the year it's very pleasant. We may as well enjoy the veranda while we can."

Kalua had laid the tea-tray service out on the veranda. Darkness was falling. A pack of jackals howled in the hills, the trees rustled and the jungle was filled with soft scraping sounds. A handful of fireflies had descended from the sky and winked softly around us. I watched a firefly land on a teacup. It pulsed softly, lighting the translucent bone china with sharp flashes of ethereal light. Manik let the firefly crawl on his finger. He blew on it softly and watched it wink away.

"The only trouble with a *jali kamra*," Manik said, "is that it will keep out the fireflies. I love sharing my teatime with the fireflies."

A hot soak was just what I needed before dinner. Halua had run me a bath in the master bathroom. The water in the claw-foot tub was scalding, the bathroom clogged with steam. I smiled seeing the two bars of soap: a misshapen red Lifebuoy carbolic soap, presumably Manik's, and a new oval bar of Pears Soap for me. I sank into the tub and contemplated my rather confusing day. I could hear Manik whistling in the bedroom. The cupboard door opened and squealed shut. Then there was a soft tap on the bathroom door.

"Yes?" I called, my heart beating fast as water dripped down my face.

"Is everything okay? I am having my bath in the guest bathroom," he said.

"Yes, thanks." I sighed with relief.

I was about to sink back into the tub when a small movement up on the ceiling caught my eye. A tiny fruit bat had flown into the bathroom through the open skylight. I watched anxiously as it flew in dizzying circles, round and round the ceiling. Then to my alarm, the awful creature made a nosedive into the tub and skimmed so close I felt its furred wing tip brush past my ear. I ducked and splashed and let out my own batlike shriek, which only seemed to encourage the creature further.

"Layla, is something wrong?"

"There's a bat in here!"

"Wait, I'm coming in."

Manik twisted the doorknob then banged on the door. "Did you lock the door?"

I did. Don't ask me why.

"Can you open it, please?"

"I can't get out of the tub."

The bat was circling lower and lower. I grabbed the long-handled scrubbing brush and swiped the air.

"Listen!" Manik yelled. "Look by the side of the tub. There is an old tennis racket—"

"A wha—? Oooh!"

"TENNIS racket. By the tub. Do you see it?"

I peeked over the rim. Sure enough, there was a battered old tennis racket leaning against the laundry basket. How peculiar.

"Yes?" I said.

"Give the bat a whack with that," Manik yelled. "I forgot to tell you. Bats fly into the bathroom all the time."

The bat circled high up on the ceiling, and looked as if it was swooping in for another attack. I grabbed the tennis racket and swung at it. To my surprise and astonishment, I caught the bat in midair and sent it smacking into the wall with a sickly thud. I peered over the rim of the tub and watched with morbid fascination as the creature lay twitching under the basin.

"I hit it," I yelled back. The bat was feebly stretching out a wing and giving tiny shudders. "I think it's...fatally wounded."

"Good! Do you think you'll be all right now?"

"I think so."

I got out of the tub and toweled myself dry with one hand while holding the tennis racket in the other. The bat had righted itself and was giving tiny flutters. Not wanting to take chances, I upturned a tin mug over it. I changed into a fresh cotton sari, combed out my damp hair, put on some sandalwood lotion and got out of the bathroom as fast as I could.

Manik's cupboard door was ajar. I peeped in. There were mostly white cotton work clothes, Bombay bloomers and white bush shirts, starched stiff and neatly folded into separate piles. On the hangers were a few suits, dinner jackets and a metal tie rack full of ties. There was a drawer for his white underwear and another for his socks, the pairs all nicely matched, one foot curled into the other. Tucked in the back of the underwear drawer was an unopened packet of cigarettes.

I appraised myself critically in the full-length mirror inside the cupboard door. The handloom cotton sari I wore was a creamy buttermilk color with a cucumber-green border. It was my favorite sari but now I was full of self-doubt. This was going to be the first dinner with my new husband. Would Manik like the way I looked? I could only guess. I twisted my hair into a casual hand bun and took one last look in the mirror before walking out of the bedroom door.

Dinner was an oddly formal affair. The table was laid with a stiff white tablecloth with place settings at the two far ends and what looked like an excessive display of silver cutlery. Covered serving dishes were laid out in a straight line, right down the middle of the table. In the center was a vase with red zinnias, their heavy heads drooping sadly over the rim of the vase, as though they were weeping into the tablecloth. Manik and I sat like two lonely bookends while Halua came around and served us. Kalua, his twin, the cook, had fixed an impressive six-course dinner. An egg and chicken banquet.

"I am afraid that's all he knows how to cook," Manik said. "Egg and chicken. He wanted to impress you, so I guess he made everything in his repertoire."

Kalua had prepared an egg curry, egg *bhajia* and a masala omelet. Then there was a chicken curry, a whole roasted chicken and breaded chicken cutlets. And for dessert, guess what? Egg custard. At the end of the meal, I imagined Manik and I would be clucking like hens.

"Is this what you eat all the time?" I asked. "Egg and chicken?"

"Yes. A different dish each day. Unless I shoot something... then we have jungle fowl, duck, pheasant, snipe or whatever I can get."

Still, a winged creature, I thought. How different could that be from chicken?

"Sometimes venison or wild boar," he added. I noted Manik had the uncanny ability to read my thoughts.

"You don't eat any vegetables?" I asked, trying not to sound too severe.

"What's that?" Manik laughed. "Honestly, I have not bothered. Most people grow their own vegetables around here." He waved away the egg curry when Halua came around. "Which reminds me—Mrs. McIntyre, our manager's wife, has invited you for tea on Monday. She has an impressive *malibari*. Don't call her *Audrey*, by the way. Call her *Mrs. McIntyre*. Things are formal around here."

"I can see that," I said. There was indeed a prissy kind of formality about everything. After his bath, I was surprised to find Manik all spruced up in white dinner slacks and a starched shirt. They were not exactly home clothes. Was it to impress me? However, something told me otherwise.

"Is this how you dress for dinner every day, even if you are dining alone?" I asked.

"As a matter of fact, yes," said Manik. He looked at me and grinned. "There are many things you will find peculiar in tea culture, Layla. I did, too, at the beginning. The dress code, for example. The only time we planters wear casual clothes is for *kamjari* duty. Nobody cares what you wear for fieldwork as long as you do your job. At other times we are expected to dress formally even at home, and we are expected to maintain our distance with the servants at all times."

"That is rather strange," I remarked. "It's quite the opposite for Dadamoshai. He dresses formally to go to work and changes into his home clothes when he comes home."

"You see, we tea planters live such isolated lives," Manik continued. "It is easy to become unkempt, slovenly, 'go native,' as the English say. This is frowned upon, because if you ease up on yourself, you ease up on others. You lose the respect of your workers and eventually you forsake your authority. So we are expected to keep a tight rein on our appearance and conduct. And yours truly, as the first Indian native in a managerial post, has to be doubly pukka."

Manik glanced around and dropped his voice. "Darling, all I want to do now is to be alone with you, but I have to wait for the servants to leave, the *chowkidar* to report for night duty and the generator to be switched off at the factory." He winked at me. "I know you are excited. Hopefully you can hold out for another half an hour."

"Please speak for yourself," I shot back. But I felt a small thrill: *finally this was going to be our big night.* After that everything would be all right.

After dinner I sat on the living-room sofa and watched a pale house gecko flick its tail and inch toward a moth on the wall. There were house geckos everywhere. I counted six in the living room, pasty albino-looking creatures that hung around the lightbulbs. They seemed very much at home, inside the bungalow.

Halua went back and forth clearing the table. We could hear him clattering in the pantry.

Manik flipped through the record pile. He paused at one, slid out the record from its jacket and blew off the dust. A few moments later, the lilting strains of Vivaldi's "La Primavera" filled the room. He joined me on the sofa and put his arm around me. "You smell lovely," he said, kissing my hair. His lips brushed my neck. "Very lovely." He looked at his watch. "Half an hour before the lights go out. The factory generator shuts off at nine."

The mood was quiet, and light from the low-wattage bulbs floated around us in dim pools. Lulled by his voice, big waves of sleep crashed around me. My eyelids fluttered. I must have dozed off on his shoulder, because when I opened my eyes, I found myself snuggled into the crook of his arm, my bun loosened and my hair undone. With every tick of the clock the lightbulb was waning. The corners of the rooms started filling with deep shadows.

Halua emerged from the pantry with a matchbox and lit two candlesticks stuck in chipped saucers. His face lit up with a ghoulish, half-moon glow. He placed one candle on the coffee table and the other on the bookshelf.

Manik yawned, and stirred from the sofa. He got up and shut off the gramophone. "The generator has been switched off. Our bungalow is quite far from the factory. It takes a few minutes for the electricity to fade out over the power lines."

He turned, because Halua and Kalua were standing before us looking like a double vision. Kalua carried a kerosene lantern in his hand.

"You may go now," Manik said. "Salaam."

"Salaam sahib, salaam memsahib," they chanted in unison. Then they ducked and bowed in that peculiar way of theirs before exiting the room.

Manik blew out the candle on the bookshelf and picked up the one on the coffee table. He held out his hand to me. Then he tensed, listening. I sat up, as well. What was that? Voices. Several voices, all talking excitedly in a local tongue. A flashlight swung up the stairs. I recognized Potloo, the *chowkidar*, and there was a tall man with him. The man had a checkered blanket draped over his shoulders and carried a kerosene lantern.

"Sahib?" Potloo called urgently.

Manik was already out on the veranda. The man in the blanket talked excitedly and gesticulated with his hands while the flashlight swung in arcs. Manik spoke in a low voice. Then all three of them went quickly down the stairs.

I crept out to the dark veranda and looked over the railing. Several men were gathered at the foot of the stairs. As soon as they saw Manik, they all started talking at once. Kerosene lamps threw crescent patterns of light on the ground. Most of the men were barefoot. I caught a glimpse of their faces. They had flat tribal features. Laborers. I caught a word here and there: *baag* (tiger), *khedao* (chase), *chokra* (boy), *khoon* (blood). Something was wrong.

Then Manik spoke at length to the man in the checkered blanket. He addressed him as "Jugal." He appeared to be some kind of leader. The men salaamed and shuffled off in groups of twos and threes, their lamps becoming small dots of yellow along the dark driveway.

Manik dashed back up the stairs. He almost bumped into me in the dark.

"Oh! Layla! What are you doing out here?"

"What's wrong, Manik?"

Manik threw up his hands. "There's a leopard in the labor lines. It's a man-eater creating havoc. It grabbed a child."

"What are you going to do?" I asked in alarm, following him into the bedroom.

"I need to go and see what's going on. These animals can become very bold. The leopard is hiding in a cowshed. I'll take this one down if I can."

Halua had placed a kerosene lamp on the dresser in the bedroom. Manik swung open the cupboard door and threw an old suede hunting jacket on the bed. He picked up his canvas boots from the shoe stand, sat on the bed, opened the bedside-table drawer and took out a flashlight. He shook it violently. It blinked a dim yellow. "Dammit," he muttered, and fumbled at the back of the drawer, pulling out three batteries.

"Please don't go, Manik," I pleaded. "It sounds so dangerous."

"It's not really," Manik replied absently. He changed the batteries quickly, tested the flashlight, placed it on the bed and laced up his boots quickly. He turned to me with a sigh. I was clutching his arm.

"Of all nights, tonight," he said wearily. He pushed his

glasses up his nose. He saw my face and put his arms around me. "This is such bad timing, love, I don't even know what to say!"

"When will you be back?"

"I wish I knew."

"Oh, Manik! Please don't go."

"This is a crisis, darling. Please understand. It's my job."

I followed him into the guest room, feeling sick with fear.

"Here, hold this, will you. Point the beam," he said, handing me the flashlight. He cracked open his shotgun, popped out two orange shells from the chamber, then rummaged in a leather pouch and picked out two red ones, which he inserted in the empty chambers.

"Please try and get some sleep," he said, snapping the gun shut. He put two extra red shells in his pocket. "And try not to worry." He held me close for a while, kissed the top of my head, turned and strode out onto the veranda.

"Jugal!" he called, and a voice replied from under the portico. Manik and the man in the blanket hurried off into the night, swinging their flashlights. The gate latch creaked, and Potloo's silhouette was framed in the yellow glow of the kerosene lamp. Manik said something to him. Potloo shut the gate and stood there watching until the flashlights disappeared around the bend in the road. He went inside his hut, and I saw the small square of yellow light appear in his window.

All around me was the blackest, darkest night you can imagine. No moon in the sky. No sounds. Only the furtive rustle of the trees and a pack of lonely jackals howling in the distance. All the servants were gone. The rooms in the bungalow looked gaping and cavernous. The floorboard creaked as I walked back into the living room. I blew out the last remnant of the candle spluttering on the coffee table and made my way to the bedroom by the glow of the kerosene lamp coming through the open doorway.

I sat on the bed overcome with desolation. An owl hooted in the tree outside. A deep dread filled my being. What if something happened to Manik? I was the bad-luck wife, after all. My husband had walked off into a moonless night to fight a man-eating leopard before we had even consummated our marriage. He did not even take the jeep.

I wished Dadamoshai were here. Dadamoshai discouraged worrying about the unknown. "Worry is the most crippling emotion, Layla. It's an impediment," he'd said to me once. "It is an irrational fear of the unknown. Worry will impair your judgment. It will rob you of the ability to make things happen."

But I was completely powerless. The dark churning in my mind would not stop.

CHAPTER
19

I woke up in a panic. What was that noise? Birds. Hundreds of them. Sunlight slanted into the bedroom through the parted curtain. Manik's side of the bed had not been slept in. *Where was he?* I was still wearing the clothes of the night before, but someone had covered me with a blanket. There was a note on the bedside table.

6:10 a.m.
Dearest wife,
I did not want to wake you. You were sleeping so peacefully. I had a hellish night. The leopard got away. I have to be in the office early. Mr. McIntyre has called an emergency meeting. I will be home for breakfast at eight. You may see some people gathered outside the gate. They are laborers, to welcome you, their new memsahib. It is customary to greet them.
M.

Thank God he was alive! I sank back into the pillow, limp with relief. The time on my watch said six forty-five. I must have just missed him. I wish he had woken me up.

I freshened up and changed. Halua was hovering outside the bedroom door. He stood up stiffly and salaamed when he saw me.

"What time did *Chotasahib* get back?" I asked him in Assamese. The language spoken by the coolies was a peculiar mixture of several Indian languages, but mostly Assamese and Bengali. They seemed to understand both languages.

"Two hours ago," he replied. It was just after *murgi-daak*, the first rooster crow of early dawn. So that had to be around 4:30 a.m., he surmised.

It was still dark when *Chotasahib* had returned, Halua said. There were several people with him. The young boy had been taken to hospital. The leopard had torn his leg off and dragged him halfway into the jungle. His injuries were very serious. *Chotasahib* had stayed for a quick cup of tea and rushed off again. He had not slept all night. Halua had been given strict instructions not to disturb me, but stay close at hand, in case I woke up. So here he was at my service, and would I like some tea, memsahib?

Indeed, I would.

"On the veranda, memsahib?"

"Yes."

The sun had just begun to skirt the treetops. A blue-gray mist hung like a tattered veil over the hills covering the lake. The garden was bursting with birdcalls interspersed with the whoop of monkeys that crashed in the high branches in the forest beyond. Blue jays skimmed the eucalyptus branches in streaks of startling blue.

A throng of people milled around outside the gates. Small children swung on the gate, peering into the bungalow, women sat on their haunches with their baskets on the ground and old men stood leaning on walking sticks.

Halua arrived with the tea tray. The teapot was tucked inside a faded but clean tea cozy. There were two cups, a milk server, small sugar bowl and a tiny tea strainer sitting in its cradle. There were also four round Marie tea biscuits fanned out decoratively on a small floral plate.

"Who are all those people?" I asked him.

Halua looked surprised. "To see you, memsahib."

"Oh," I said, remembering Manik's note. This was quite a crowd. I felt nervous just looking at them. "Well, ask them to come in."

"No, no, no, memsahib." Halua clicked his tongue sharply. "Coolie people don't enter bungalow."

I was expected to receive them at the gate, it seemed.

With some trepidation, I got up. *The tea can wait*, I thought. *Let's get this over with.*

I walked toward them. A small cheer went up in the crowd. Elders stood solemnly in the front lines; small children and riffraff were pushed to the side. As I came closer, I saw they were all dirt-poor. Most of them had bare feet or wore sole-bare sandals with missing straps, improvised by bits and pieces of rubber and rope. There were lots of missing teeth. They all seemed to be of the same ethnicity, ebony-skinned, flat-nosed with high tribal cheekbones and various tattoos on their arms and faces. The women had horizontal V shapes tattooed in the corners of their eyes that gave them a long-lashed look. They wore prominent nose studs, their ear tips clustered with a succession of tiny rings all the way down to the earlobe. Their hair was oiled, flattened and twisted into tight conical topknots that stuck out like anthills on the sides of their heads. Small children with round, tight bellies stared with big eyes. They wore amulets and magic charms and not much else. Even the sick and the maimed had shown up. There was a one-legged man and an old woman with a goiter the size of a grapefruit. A couple of mangy pariah dogs sat around scratching and yawning. It was quite a menagerie.

Halua swung open the gates, and the crowd started babbling in a language I could not understand. Finally, a wizened old man with dim watery eyes and only two bottom teeth but a great deal of authority held up his hand imperiously to silence the crowd. A young woman with heavy pewter bangles stepped out and put a garland of marigold around my neck. She was followed by another, and yet another. Soon I had four heavy marigold necklaces around my neck. I felt as if I might tip over.

The toothless old man launched off into an elaborate and long-winded speech. It was encouraged by appreciative nods and sounds of accord from the crowd. One curious word kept surfacing—*Mai-Baap*. Literally translated it meant *mother-father*. Halfway through his emotional speech, a small child began to squall and received a stern eye from the old man. The young mother, wearing a bright pink sari, clamped her hand down on the baby's mouth, and the elder waited impatiently for order to be restored before he continued in his monotonous, singsong voice. I had no idea what he was talking about. I caught an Assamese word here and there but that was all.

Halua translated for me. In effect what the elder was saying was that the honorable and highly respected *Chotasahib*, God be with him, on whose care and protection they all depended, whose bravery was unsurpassed and whose fairness and judgment was acknowledged by all, may the spirits bless and protect him, and may the new memsahib have good health, escape the evil eye and be spared from cholera, influenza, snakebite and malaria, not forgetting rabies, dengue fever and other causes of sickness and death, and may she bear the *Chotasahib* numerous healthy male children.

His speech was received with enthusiastic cheers, the equivalent of "bravo" and "encore," I imagined. The old man was so exhausted when he finished that he broke into a hacking cough, his face turned purple like an eggplant and he sat down abruptly in the dust. The crowd then turned eagerly toward me and waited for a befitting response.

I thanked them all, and did not know what else to say. Halua relayed back my words in what seemed like an illogically long speech. There were murmurs of approval and nods all around. Then people came forward and to my surprise started laying all kinds of things at my feet: four duck eggs, two guavas, a pumpkin, eggplants, a bunch of green beans, decorative baskets of assorted sizes, bananas, small bags of puffed rice and even a trussed-up, squawking chicken. The gifts kept piling up in lumps and bumps in ever-widening circles until I started feeling like a burdened goddess decked in marigold, rising from a sea of bundles, baskets, squawks and smells.

I told Halua to thank them all but I could not accept these gifts. I got no further because Halua shook his head and clicked his tongue again. It seemed as though I had almost made my second social blunder of the day.

"No, no, memsahib, you must take these gifts. It is the custom."

Manik had mentioned nothing about gifts in his note. So not knowing what else to do, I thanked them again, which Halua relayed back in yet another elaborate speech. Then I turned and walked back to the house.

I wearily took off the marigold necklaces and sat in the veranda feeling tired and overwhelmed. I poured myself a cup of tea, which thankfully was still hot. The crowd began to disperse. Two small boys got into a scuffle. A mangy dog yelped when it received a kick. The last person to leave was a very short woman who lurked behind the hibiscus hedge. She had a round face and wore a green sari, wrapped in the regular way like town people. Then she, too, finally turned and left.

Halua and Kalua went back and forth, ferrying all the gifts into the kitchen.

I was just pouring my second cup of tea when a man in a khaki uniform sailed up the driveway on a bicycle. He salaamed and handed me a note. It was from Manik.

Layla,
We will have a guest for breakfast.
Please inform kitchen staff.
I will be home at 8:30.
M.

My goodness! The curtness of the note! I was so irked, I just told the man to go without sending a reply. I sat there, fighting tiny ant bites of annoyance. Anyone would think a new husband who had been up all night chasing a man-eating leopard would be running home to spend some private time with his new bride. But oh no. Not Manik Deb. I was obviously not high on his list of priorities.

Our guest turned out to be an oily Indian government officer wearing a tan-colored safari suit. He had shifty eyes and terrible body odor. Manik introduced him as Mr. Sircar, the District Forest Officer in Mariani.

Manik's eyes were bloodshot; he was filthy and unshaved, and looked as if he had spent the night in the bushes, which was probably close to the truth. He excused himself and went inside to clean up while I kept Mr. Sircar company on the veranda. He was the most obnoxious man I had ever met. Mr. Sircar gave me a mind-numbing account of all the important forest-conservation programs he was managing in the state of Assam. He spoke in an imperious, oratorical voice, his eyes glazed over with self-adoration.

Manik returned looking more human. Breakfast was a tedious affair. Mr. Sircar, having dumped on me his accolades, proceeded to treat me like a sack of potatoes, engaging only Manik in conversation. Why on earth were we entertaining such an odious character? I wondered. I soon found out.

"So, Mr. Sircar, when do you think I can expect the permit?" Manik asked, spreading marmalade on his toast.

Mr. Sircar was wolfing down a monstrous omelet, shoveling it into his mouth with two teaspoons.

"Oh, the permit, you ask, Mr. Deb?" he said, chewing with his mouth open. "I have to use my considerable influence in this matter, you see? Getting a *hukum* from the government to shoot a leopard is no easy matter these days."

"We are talking about a man-eater, Mr. Sircar, not just any leopard. Two attacks in one month. You saw the state of that child in hospital today. We must put this animal down or we will have a labor riot on our hands."

"You are talking to a forest expert, Mr. Deb. Wild animals, as you know, will attack when threatened and confronted. One has to prove that this animal is a man-eater first."

"So, Mr. Sircar, are you saying this eight-year-old boy threatened and confronted the leopard to provoke the attack?" Manik chewed slowly, his eyes veiled.

"The permit is difficult to get is all I am saying. If your English people had not gone around shooting animals randomly and recklessly for sport, this would not have been the case. The government has now become very strict. Very strict. Nowadays they want to see proof that the animal is actually a man-eater before they issue the *hukum*."

"So I suppose we should just wait for someone to get killed and eaten, then." Manik was losing his patience, I could tell.

"Let me see what I can do for you," Mr. Sircar said, getting up from the table. He shot Manik a sly look. "Also please see what *you* can do for me, Mr. Deb, and thank you for the breakfast." He burped loudly and patted his belly. "I am now *fully* fed up."

Manik gave me a wink behind Mr. Sircar's back. "So am I, Mr. Sircar, so am I."

"Bastard!" Manik yelled, slapping down his breakfast napkin on the table. "I hate that scumbag. Always playing hard to get. He is not going to budge an inch till we give him a bottle of Scotch."

"Why don't you just kill the leopard? Why do you need a permit?" I asked.

"You can kill an animal and claim self-defense, like I was planning to do yesterday. But to track it down in the jungle you need a permit."

I was suddenly tired of it all. Manik's ranting and raving, the oily Mr. Sircar and the whole confusing welcome jamboree. And it was not yet midmorning. And here I was all chaste and waiting with my virginity on a silver platter.

But Manik had other things on his mind.

"Mr. McIntyre will *kill* me if I don't get that permit," he muttered. "That leopard will be back in the lines and create havoc all over again."

"And you, Manik Deb, as the brave protector of mankind, will leave your wife and run off toting your gun," I added tartly.

He quirked an eyebrow. "Oh, we are sizzling a little, are we?"

"What is this *Mai-Baap* thing those folks were talking about this morning? Manik, you did not warn me there would be such a big crowd. There must have been close to a hundred people."

Manik looked mildly interested. "So, how did the greeting ceremony go?"

"What is *Mai Baap*?"

He sighed. "Means mother-father. It's the parental role management has traditionally played in tea administration. The laborers are simple people, trusting like little children. They expect to be taken care of. Fed, clothed, protected from harm. Managers are made to feel omnipotent, invincible. It's a tall order. But we try not to fail them."

"How about playing *Mai-Baap* to your wife for a change? Did you for a moment think I might have been frightened all alone here in this big bungalow?"

"You didn't lose much sleep from what I can tell. You look refreshed and very lovely. I don't feel too lovely myself, I tell you." Manik sighed again. He pushed up his glasses on his forehead and rubbed his eyes. "Layla, please try to understand. We have a crisis. If the laborers start a riot because of the damn leopard, the whole tea garden will come to a standstill. I am expected to take care of this because it's my job. There is not much I can do about that, can I? As my wife, I expect you to be a little understanding. Besides, it's not like this all the time, you know." Then he grinned widely. "Hell, I will now have to bribe my own wife to get *my* permit!"

I knew what he was talking about, and I did not think it was funny.

He pushed back his chair. "I will have to go to the Forest Office in Mariani to get this permit business sorted out. But I will see you at lunchtime." He wagged a finger.

"Promise you won't run off on me now."

After Manik went back to work, I spent the rest of the
morning unpacking my suitcases and putting away my clothes
in the new cupboard.

A skinny man arrived carrying a small cloth sack of tools.
He introduced himself as the factory carpenter. Manik had
sent him to assemble my grandmother's dressing table, which
was still lying in its dismantled state, sewn up in burlap, in
one corner of the portico. When it was unwrapped, I noticed
with relief none of the mirrors had broken. I figured I had
had enough bad luck so far. In one of the drawers, I found a
small safety pin that must have belonged to my grandmother. I
opened and closed it, thinking she, too, had been a new bride
once, a stranger in her husband's home.

There was a knock on the door. It was Halua come to take
the lunch orders. He rattled off the selections. We had a choice
of egg curry, chicken curry, chicken cutlet, egg…

I stopped him halfway. I was quite familiar with the items.
They were identical to the night before.

"Any vegetables?" I asked. "Why don't you cook the pumpkin and green beans the coolies bought this morning?"

Halua's eyes wandered. *Chotasahib*, he said, detested vegetables. He would not touch them.

Hmm, I thought grimly to myself. I would need to have a
small talk with the *Chotasahib* about that. Back to the lunch
menu—it seemed as if I was stuck with only the cluckable
items, so egg curry it was.

Manik was forty-five minutes late for lunch. When he
showed up there was a big ink blotch on his shirt pocket. He
threw his mail down on the coffee table. A few envelopes slid
off the edge onto the floor.

"That bloody Sircar!" Manik exploded. "He's demanding to
see the paw prints of the damn leopard. He says he can't issue

the permit otherwise. *Paw prints!* Like you can tell a man-eater
from its paw prints! Then he makes me sign all these government forms—he can't even explain what they are for. He only
gave me the permit after I parted with my one and only bottle of Black Label. *Black Label!* Talk about casting pearls before swine. That was a wedding gift from Mr. McIntyre. But
I didn't have anything else."

I pointed to his chest. "What happened?"

Manik stared down his shirtfront. "Bloody hell! I was in
such a damn hurry to get out of the place, I forgot my pen cap.
Anyway, how's your day going?" he added flatly. He was faraway, and sounded as if he was talking to a hill. Then, seeing
Halua at the door, he said, "Ah, I see lunch is served."

So there we were again, Mr. and Mrs. Cluck sitting stiffly at
two ends of the dining table. This was not at all how I imagined it would be. I wondered what Moon would make of my
romantic, newly married life.

Halfway through lunch Manik said, "There's something I
have to tell you." He hesitated, studying my face. "You are
not going to like this, but I won't be home tomorrow night."

I stared at my plate. It was this other woman, I thought, my
heart beating wildly. He was going to tell me about the OP
he'd had all along.

"I have to take down this leopard," Manik continued. "We
can't waste any time because it will be back. We can't risk another attack. It's not going to be easy, so I've enlisted Alasdair's
help. He is a crack shot. Never misses. Our plan is to build
a *machan* up a tree. We will stay up on the *machan* tomorrow
night and hopefully shoot the leopard."

My relief was so great I actually smiled at my egg curry. Manik
could be up all night on a *machan*—whatever that was—with
Alasdair, just as long as he was not roosting with another bird.

"What's a *machan*?" I asked, conversationally.

"A bamboo platform built up on a tree. About two meters off the ground. We tie a goat to the base of the tree with a metal chain. Shikaris don't use rope because the leopard will just break it and drag the goat off into the jungle. Powerful, stealthy creatures, leopards are. If the goat is chained, the leopard is forced to eat it under the tree. Usually the animal gets sluggish after the meal and lies down. That's our best chance of shooting it."

"But the leopard could be anywhere in that jungle, and you could be waiting up the wrong tree?"

"We use trackers," Manik said. "They are jungle experts, who intimately know animal habits and can identify the path the creature takes through the forest. They study pugmarks along the riverbed, claw scratches on tree trunks and flattened areas of brush where the leopard rests after a meal. Our tracker tells us we are looking for a large male leopard with an injured foot."

A leopard became a man-eater only if it was injured or got too old to hunt, Manik explained. Humans were easy prey. Villagers and laborers often strayed near the edge of the forest to gather firewood, and this was when the leopard attacked. Sometimes the animal got very bold and came right into the labor lines to kill cattle or pick up a wandering child or dog. When this happened, the tea-garden management had a serious problem on its hands, like they did now.

"Our chances are better if we get a noisy goat that bleats loudly to attract the leopard. But the trouble is noisy goats don't always do their job when they are supposed to."

"Poor goat," I said.

"Or we could use you," Manik teased. "Chain you to the tree. Human bait works the best for man-eaters, you know.

You bleat loud enough as it is. But the chances are I might pounce on you before the leopard does."

That reminded me of our unfinished business. To cover up my nervousness I asked, "Are you going to use the old blunderbuss?"

Manik laughed. "Not a chance. Mr. McIntyre will lend me his .275 Winchester with five rounds. That's a good reliable gun." He studied my face. "Well?"

"Well, what?" I retorted. "You don't exactly need my permission for anything, do you?"

"Layla, I was so worried having to tell you this."

"What do you want me to say? I don't like the thought of you up on a tree all night in the middle of the jungle. What if you fall? This *machan* thing sounds awfully rickety."

"It's quite sturdy, really. We shikaris use them all the time. The only danger is of falling asleep. You have to keep quiet and remain supervigilant at all times. It can get terribly monotonous. We rely on lots of black coffee and fags. That reminds me—I'm out of fags. Dammit."

"There's a pack in your underwear drawer," I said absently.

He peeked around the vase of drooping zinnias and gave me a naughty look. "And what were you doing in my underwear drawer, pray? Next you'll be wanting to know what's inside my underwear."

I was shocked at his impertinence. My ears burned in my head.

Manik got up from the table. "Well, let's not keep you in suspense any longer, dear wife. Come, it's siesta time."

"What?" I exclaimed. "Don't you have to go back to work?"

He stretched and yawned. "I go back to work only at three, my darling. Planters sleep between one and three. Napping is the civilized thing to do."

"What about Mr. McIntyre?" Manik's taskmaster boss did not seem the type to nap, even less likely, to let others nap.

"What about him? Mr. McIntyre naps. You think I could take off siesta time if he was working? Of course he naps. Mr. McIntyre naps. Mrs. McIntyre naps. Mr. and Mrs. McIntyre nap—very nicely together, I presume. Are you coming?"

"I don't sleep in the afternoon," I said primly, feeling that familiar little coil in the pit of my stomach.

"Tsk, tsk. What a pity. What will you do, my darling, while your husband gets his beauty rest? Gaze at my underwear? I must say I am completely wiped out."

"I'll read."

"Suit yourself." He shrugged, sounding indifferent. I had expected him to cajole me, maybe even beg, but then without so much as a toodle-di-doo, he headed for the bedroom and shut the door behind him.

I sat there blinking back my tears. Something was going horribly wrong in my marriage. We were five-day-old newlyweds, on the verge of sexual intimacy, and we were behaving like the two wrong ends of a magnet.

Opportune moments came and slipped by. The perfect moment had to be seized. Like when you boil sugar to make taffy, there comes a time when the sugar is ready to congeal. The temperature is perfect, the consistency right. Hold off for too long and the taffy turns brittle. It was beginning to happen to our marriage: we were overcooking our emotions. What I was sensing in Manik was impatience, almost boredom. We were becoming strangers.

All I really had to do now was march into the bedroom, fling off my clothes, get deflowered and be done with it. How long would the whole business take? I wondered. Five minutes, ten minutes at the most? How painful could it be?

A tooth extraction without anesthesia. I could handle that. But Manik had not slept all night and had probably passed out by now. It would be awkward. Even hilarious. I could not risk that.

I sighed and went to the living room to find a book. I picked up *War and Peace*, still lying open on the ottoman, went back to the veranda and curled up on a chair. The afternoon was droopy and slumberous and the buzz of the bees dulled my mind. Then to my utter disgust, I fell fast asleep, right there, curled up on the chair.

I woke up to what sounded like a prayer bell in my ear. Manik was tinging the side of his empty teacup with a small silver spoon. He looked fresh and rested.

"'I don't sleep in the afternoon,'" he mocked. "You are a big fat liar. I sat here and drank my tea. You were snoring. *Snoring.* I could not believe my ears."

"What time is it?" I was stiff and grouchy. I uncurled my legs, and they splintered into a million pins and needles.

"Ouch," I grumbled. My head felt like a brick.

"Quarter to three. I'm off. I will be back six-thirtyish. Cheerio." With that he thundered down the stairs without even a kiss.

So there I was on my own again. I pulled on my slippers and floated around the garden staring at the dahlias, especially the droopy ones, seeing nothing but sadness. Maybe I would die a virgin, I thought. Maybe this cigar was destined to remain unlit, and Manik Deb would go back to Auntie's to smoke a bidi or two.

Back in the veranda, I made myself a cup of tea, picked up *War and Peace* and curled back on the chair again. But the page kept blurring with my tears, so I closed my eyes. I breathed in the scented afternoon to calm my mind. Wait, what was that?

The sleepy hum of the bees had turned into a sharp *zzzt zzzt* noise. I opened my eyes, and to my shock, I saw a monstrous black-and-yellow hornet heading straight at me. I shot out of the chair and flapped at it with my book. The hornet whipped around and came right back. It landed smack on my neck, and to my utter disbelief, it crawled down my blouse and stung me right between my breasts.

The pain was intense and I shrieked so loudly that both Halua and Kalua ran out from the pantry in their undershirts. They saw the new *Chotamemsahib* flinging off her sari and tearing madly at her blouse like a madwoman. Thankfully, without too much disrobing, the hornet fell out with a buzzing plop on the wooden floor. Kalua jumped up and crushed it with his bare foot. It made a sickening crunching noise and left a yellow splat, big as an egg yolk.

That was it. I threw up my egg-curry lunch all over the veranda floor. The pain was like a burning knife tearing through my chest, the agony so terrible I thought I would surely die.

Halua and Kalua were beside themselves. They flapped around like agitated ducks, fetching water, fanning me with a newspaper and shouting at one another.

Halua went scooting off to fetch Manik. I sat with my head in my hands, in a daze. The pain was fast spreading all over my body, shooting spasms. I staggered to the bathroom to take a look. There was a big angry welt in my cleavage and it was swelling fast. I found some Dettol in the small medicine cabinet and dabbed a little on a piece of toilet paper, applying it gingerly to the wound. It stung horribly. Then, not knowing what else to do, I just crawled into the bed and lay down. Nausea came over me in big sweeping waves.

Manik rushed in, hair flying, glasses askew. His hair was

tinged faintly blond with tea dust from the factory. He looked so horrified that I had to smile.

"Oh my God, Layla. What happened?"

"It's not too bad now. The pain is less," I said, lying through my teeth. Actually, the pain was worse.

"Let me take a look."

"No, no, I am okay, really," I said quickly.

"Layla, this could be serious. You could have an allergic re-action. If the stinger is still in there, you will need to take it out. That hornet is the most poisonous variety. I just saw it."

"I feel much better. I put some Dettol on it."

"Let me see."

"No, no, I'm fine."

"You are being ridiculous."

"*You* are being ridiculous. I'm fine, really. Stop worrying." The thought of my legally married husband seeing my bare breasts was worse than dying of a hornet bite.

"Dammit, Layla!" said Manik. He almost yelled. He sat on the edge of the bed and pushed up his glasses and rubbed his eyes. He looked very tired. "Please understand, I can't leave you here and go back to work without seeing how serious this is. If the hornet stinger is still inside, the pain will be ten times worse tomorrow."

"What is the worst that will happen? I will die."

"Most likely," he said dryly.

"You are joking?"

"Then stop asking idiotic questions," he snapped back. "What I am telling you is this could become septic and quite serious. It is better to take out the stinger before the area gets too swollen. It is much harder to locate it if the skin swells up."

"Then I will have bigger breasts," I quipped, trying to make him smile.

"I don't get to see those beauties anyway, so who gives a damn," Manik said irritably. He was not amused, that was for sure. "Bloody hell, Layla!" he yelled suddenly, his eyes flashing. "Grow up, for God's sake. I am getting fed up with your ridiculous, prudish behavior."

I sighed, unbuttoned my blouse and unhooked my brassiere. "Okay, go on, then, take a look." I shut my eyes tight with embarrassment.

Manik adjusted the glasses on his nose, leaned down and studied the bite. I peeked out of the corner of my eye. He looked very much like a doctor. Serious, intense and clinically detached. He smelled good, too. Tea dust, clean sweat and skin. He ran his finger lightly over the welt.

"There it is. I can feel the stinger. I can get it out. I know how to do this. Wait, I will be back."

Halua and Kalua must have been hovering outside the door, because I heard him tell them everything was all right and to go home.

Manik returned a few minutes later and my eyes almost fell out when I saw what he had in his hands. It was a butter knife and half an onion.

"My God! What are you going to do?" I exclaimed, sitting up in bed. Suddenly aware of my nakedness, I grabbed my sari to cover myself.

"Lie back down, Layla. It's a very simple procedure. I know how to do this."

"Do what? Kindly explain, doctor...."

"Trust me, darling."

"Not with a knife and an onion. Looks like you plan to make a stir-fry out of me."

"Maybe later," he said, "but first I must try and get the stinger out. Lie down, will you? You can usually locate the stinger with a blunt, flat surface. A butter knife works fine. I am going to run the blade lightly over the skin to find it. Then I will just pull it out. Simple. You will need to put some onion juice on the wound to bring down the swelling."

It sounded convincing, so I lay down.

Manik pushed his glasses up on his forehead. He ran the butter knife slowly over the area, first in one direction, then the other, while I tried to peer down my chin to see what he was doing.

He frowned. "Can't see the damn thing, but I can feel it, all right."

Then he looked me. "I have to do this the unconventional way, Layla. Bear with me." Without explaining any further he bent down and ran his tongue over the welt between my breasts very slowly. I could hardly breathe. He focused on a spot. Then, using his front teeth, he gripped something delicately and pulled it out. He transferred it from his tongue to his fingernails and held it up for me to see.

"There. It's out."

"Where?" I propped up on my elbows. I squinted, trying to see what he was holding between his fingernails, but I could see nothing.

"See that tiny curved, hairlike thing?"

"Where?"

Our faces were inches apart. Since he was such a handsome doctor, who had just saved my life, I had to thank him. So I leaned forward and kissed him on the mouth. Then, if that was not bold enough, before I could help it, I kissed him again. Slowly. Oh, it felt so good. I had the hardest time pulling away. Manik looked slightly cross-eyed.

"Layla?"

I did not answer. I just lay down and shut my eyes tightly, shocked by my own brazenness. My head was thundering, and I thought, *Oh my God, what am I doing? I think I am going to pass out.*

He bent down and brushed his lips gently over the welt, right between my breasts. Back and forth.

"Does it hurt much?"

I felt a deep warmth course through my body. The sensation was almost unbearable.

When I opened my eyes, he was looking at me. I realized his eyes were not black at all, but a very dark, rich, molten brown. He looked dead serious.

"So what will it be, Layla?" I felt his warm breath course down my neck. "Yes? No? Maybe?" he asked slowly, softly.

I barely heard his words. I waited for the familiar trip-up, the eventual shutdown. But nothing like that happened. All I felt was the most powerful longing, torrential and searing.

"Tell me." He breathed his words into my mouth. "I need to hear it from you."

"Yes," I whispered, and closed my eyes. This time I had not one iota of doubt.

Dear Mr. McIntyre,
My wife, Layla, has been stung by a hornet of the most venomous variety (Vespa Mandarinia or Giant Asian Hornet). She is doing poorly and needs my attention.

I would be grateful if I could be excused this afternoon. The water-pump estimate is not due till Wednesday, so I still have a few days to complete it.

Unfortunately Layla will have to decline Mrs. McIntyre's in-

vitation to tea tomorrow. She has asked that I convey her regrets.
She is looking forward to meeting her as soon as she is better.
Sincerely,
Manik Deb

Mr. McIntyre sent back a note excusing Manik for the rest of
the day. Audrey McIntyre sent us a delicious Dundee cake and
a sweet commiserating note via her driver. Kalua and Halua
were banished from the bungalow for the day. The chicken
cutlets prepared for our dinner were sent home with them.

We stayed in bed for the rest of the day. For Manik's en-
tertainment, I wore Mima's Goldilocks apron and served him
Dundee cake. We lopped off big pieces with the butter knife
and fed them to each other. The knife was discovered buried
in the covers, aimed straight at Manik's back.

"This could have been fatal, you know," Manik said, brandishing the knife. It flashed in the dark. He ran the blade softly
over his lips. "But I would have died a very happy man."

"I would surely have died a virgin if it had not been for
the hornet."

"Damn hornet—" Manik scowled fiercely. "It had no business getting inside my wife's blouse before I did. It deserved to
get squashed." He propped up on his elbows. "Here, pass me
that onion, will you? You need to rub some juice on the bite.
It will really help with the swelling, believe me."

"I'd rather swell than smell."

"Onion-flavored breasts would be an interesting variation
to my diet."

Manik sang "You Are My Sunshine" softly as he minis-
tered the onion. My husband could carry a tune and had a
nice singing voice, I discovered. I lay in bed feeling like the

one and only sunshine in Manik Deb's life. I knew I could make him happy, gray skies or blue, and nothing in the world would take me away.

CHAPTER

20

It was barely *murgi daak* when Halua marched right into our bedroom with the morning tea without so much as a teeny knock, making me desperately scramble for the cover sheet.

Manik took Halua outside to instruct him of his new protocol. Henceforth he was to knock on the door, remain outside and enter only when permission was granted. Halua looked bewildered. Nobody had ever asked him to knock before. He was used to barging into the bedroom. He looked at Manik with hurt eyes as though he was being scolded and nobody loved him anymore.

Ten minutes later, Manik was pulling on his clothes for *kamjari*. He laced his boots, and I sat next to him on the bed, my head leaning on his shoulder, my arms entwined under his shirt, enjoying the delicious warmth of his bare skin. My husband, I discovered, was a noisy morning whistler with a penchant for bouncy military tunes. Today it was Colonel Bogey's march.

"Why do you have to go so early?" I grumbled.

He buried his face in my stomach and blew Colonel Bogey into my navel like a trumpet.

"Stop!" I cried, squirming.

Suddenly he was serious. "How is that bite coming along? Here, let's take a look." He pulled off the sheet covering my body. He kissed the welt between my breasts with great tenderness. Then seeing me naked, he was hopelessly distracted.

"You naughty, naughty girl," he said, jumping to his feet. "I am going to report you to Mr. McIntyre for getting me late, wife."

"I'll see you at breakfast, then?"

"Yes, Mrs. Deb. Breakfast is called *chota hajri* around here. After that I can show you around Aynakhal if you are feeling up to it." He paused at the door. "We will stop by the hospital to see the boy."

"What boy?"

"The one who was attacked by the leopard. Poor fellow, they had to amputate his leg yesterday. We can also go and see the *machan* being built in the jungle. The laborers are working on it today. Wear your Bata boots, darling—you will need them. Big leeches and whatnot in the jungle. Snakes, too. Cheerio, lovely wife!"

With that he clomped off and thundered down the stairs. I heard the jeep start, then roar down the driveway. The front gates squealed open then clicked shut. Manik was gone.

I lay in bed. The small scrabble that started in my stomach was turning into a claustrophobic dread. I had forgotten all about the leopard hunt. Was Fate waiting to deal her final blow? The thought of Manik up on a bamboo platform in the dark jungle with a man-eating leopard on the loose had all the makings of a catastrophe. All I could imagine were guns misfiring, Manik falling off the *machan*, the leopard choosing him over the goat. Unchained and wounded, Manik would be the perfect meal served on a platter. The leopard would carry him off into the jungle to relish him at leisure, and I would be left lonely and forsaken in this old bungalow.

For all his charm, Manik had a reckless streak that worried me. But was it not that same free spirit that had attracted me to him in the first place? Closing my eyes, I crushed my face into his pillow, remembering the passion of the night before. His mouth had explored my body, arousing me gently as if from a deep slumber. We woke in the morning, our limbs still entwined. Manik was gone, yet he was everywhere. I could still smell him on my skin. He had ingrained himself in me forever.

Suddenly I was overcome with self-pity. A tear leaked out of the corner of my eye, and I watched it spread on the cotton pillowcase. What kind of husband was he? Running off and risking his life without a single thought for his new wife? Was I that unimportant? A devious thought crept into my mind. Maybe I could seduce him. Distract him; make him forget about the leopard hunt. But would he succumb? Something told me otherwise.

Manik was married to his job for three years before he was married to me. He had left his virgin bride on the brink of being deflowered to take care of his *Mai-Baap* duties. Talk about job commitment! How many men would do that? Tea companies were very clever, I decided. It took three years of intense brainwashing to make a tea planter, and the training was carried out in isolation without wifely distractions. It was almost like indoctrination into the priesthood. Cloistered. Intense. Focused. The difference was, with tea planters, celibacy was discouraged and marriage held at bay. They figured it took three years to cook the goose. Between the time I met and married Manik Deb, he was a fully cooked goose. It was just my luck, because this goose was now going to be fed to the leopard.

When Manik returned, I was sitting on the veranda with a boot on my lap wondering how to thread the laces through the complicated eyelets.

"Here, let me help you," he said, pulling up a chair. Just the nearness of him made me light-headed. Manik lifted my foot onto his knee and hummed happily as he pulled on the monstrous boot and laced it up with military efficiency.

"Hup, two, three, four!" He pulled me to my feet, drawing me into an intimate embrace, followed by a scandalized look. "Shame on you, Comrade!" he scolded sternly. "For your unprofessional behavior you will do double time." With that, he grabbed my hand and galloped me down the stairs.

Manik let me steer the jeep as we drove down the hill. A family of golden langurs with coal-black faces loped across the road with long swinging tails. One big fellow sat down in the middle scratching his head. I veered off the road to avoid him, almost landing us into the bushes. Manik grabbed the steering wheel out of my hands just in time.

"Never give way to monkeys," said Manik, straightening the wheel. "They are canny creatures and jump out of the way an inch before you think you are going to run them over. It's a game they play. Especially that one. That big male monkey."

He pulled over and we traded seats. The whole pack was back in the middle of the road watching us. "That one walks with a limp," I observed.

"I know. He probably got kicked by the wife. Or several wives."

"For good reason, too, no doubt."

Manik grinned as he turned toward a dirt road. He jerked his thumb in the opposite direction. "Factory, office, manager's bungalow, staff housing, that way. Hospital, tea plantation, river, this way."

We drove past a long *bamboobari* with paddy fields on the other side. The ground was being tilled for the new planting season and plow marks furrowed the earth. A young lad traipsed along the narrow dividers separating the fields. He wore a conical *japi* sombrero, his arms draped loosely around a bamboo pole slung across his shoulders. A small pariah dog with a curled-up tail ran ahead on dancing feet.

"Who owns these rice fields?" I asked.

"Our laborers do. They cultivate their own rice. They raise their own cattle. Besides the tea-growing areas, the *bamboobari*, forests, rivers, everything—" Manik waved his hands expansively "—belongs to Aynakhal. The tea garden covers over two hundred hectares."

The plantation area was divided into two out-gardens, Manik explained, manned by separate Assistant Managers. He was in charge of one, Larry Baker the other. The division under his jurisdiction bordered the thick forestland between Aynakhal and Chulsa Tea Estate.

"Aynakhal is so big. I had no idea."

"You had no idea your husband was such a big shot, either."

"That's true." I smiled. He sure talked like one.

Manik raked his fingers through his hair. His hand draped easily over the steering wheel; he hummed softly and tapped a beat. I smiled. Still Colonel Bogey. He was such a funny, handsome man.

"Koilapani River." Manik pointed to a slice of water between two embankments with a rope bridge slung across. We drove past what looked like a brick-making facility.

"The river clay makes good bricks," said Manik. "They are sun dried and pit fired in this plant. Mr. McIntyre set up this brick plant to build better housing for our laborers. He's very farsighted that way. Excellent manager. Not many tea gardens have their own brick-making facility. But theft is a problem. The laborers sell off bricks to Mariani locals for booze, so we have to keep an eye on them."

A parade of mud-caked water buffalo ambled ponderously down the middle of the road. They were massive beasts with short powerful legs, flat, wide foreheads and impressive forward-curving horns. A bare-bodied youth in ragged shorts clucked and yelled "Hoa! Hoa!" and swatted the buffalo with a bamboo stick to move them to the side of the road. As we inched through the sea of buffalo, the stench of putrid river mud filled the car. To my disgust, one buffalo stuck its ugly, wet nose into the car and snorted a big whoosh of snotty breath straight at me.

"*Eeesh!*" I cried, clutching Manik's arm.

Manik grinned. "Sorry, that was unexpected. Now you know why most wives run away from the tea gardens."

The jeep rattled over the rope bridge. I watched a fisherman standing in the river as he cast his net expertly in a graceful, sweeping arc across the water. The water shimmered with small diamond patterns as the net hit the surface. The fisherman gathered the folds and pulled the net toward him slowly, pausing with each draw.

On the other side of the bridge were long rows of huts with tiny yards and crooked cowsheds. They were the labor lines, Manik said, where the tea pluckers lived. Women sat on mud stoops tossing waves of rice on bamboo trays. Chickens pecked at husks on the ground and potbellied children, naked as baby birds, ran up to the dusty road to jump and wave.

"This is where I was the other night," said Manik.

I stared at him. "You walked all the way here from the bungalow?"

He turned to grin at me. "Don't be silly! I only walked to the factory to pick up the jeep from the workshop."

"Oh," I said. So he did take the jeep after all. Maybe Manik was not as reckless as I imagined.

"Here's the infirmary," said Manik, pulling into a small whitewashed building with a red-painted cross on its tin roof. A clump of sick laborers huddled around the veranda: men with bandaged limbs, bowlegged rickety children, gaunt women with infants drooping over their arms like half-empty sacks of rice. A round-faced man in a spotless white shirt was dispensing medicine over a counter through an open window.

"That's Baruah, our Compounder Babu," said Manik. "He runs this place. He takes care of broken bones, animal bites, gives shots, pulls out babies. He does whatever it takes to keep people alive. Running a hospital in a tea garden is rather like working in a combat zone. There is some calamity or the other, always."

Baruah ran out from behind the counter to greet us. "Good morning, sir!" he cried. "Madam..." Then, overcome with shyness, he stood there and fiddled with his stethoscope.

The sick laborers milled around us, hacking, coughing. Runny-nosed children reached out to touch my sari. A skinny nurse in a papery white uniform peeped at me from an open door. I was suddenly aware of the duffel-size canvas boots under my sari, but nobody seemed to care.

Baruah led the way to the dormitory. There were thirty beds in all, each one occupied. My heart sank when I saw the boy lying in the corner by the window: a small crumpled body, one leg a thick-bandaged stump that ended at the knee. His eyes were closed; his hands, clutched into tiny fists, rested on

his chest. A group of relatives squatted on the floor around
his bed. Seeing Manik, they rushed forward and threw themselves at his feet, wailing. I heard the words *bachao* and *baag*.
They were begging Manik to save them from the leopard.
One woman clutched my feet and wet my canvas boots with
her tears. Three children dead already, she wailed. The boy is
her only son. The patients in the other beds lifted their heads;
some held out imploring hands and others, deathly ill, turned
feeble, yellow eyes in our direction.

It finally dawned on me the monstrous responsibility that
lay in Manik's hands. The laborers entrusted him with their
lives. He was their *Mai-Baap*. They treated him like a god. I
watched Manik's face as he listened. I saw the solemn dignity
of his stance, the gentle compassion in his eyes. He reminded
me of Dadamoshai. Manik, I realized, was not only handsome
and smart. He had integrity, courage and leadership. He was
the kind of man I was proud to spend the rest of my life with.
Whether I would, only fate could tell.

Manik left for the leopard hunt at dusk, and I spent another
fitful night in Aynakhal. Only this time I did not sleep but sat
up in bed, all night, fully dressed. Halua, Kalua and Potloo
were camped out in the porch downstairs. I heard them talking softly in the night and caught whiffs of bidi smoke that
wafted up to my bedroom window. Manik had instructed the
servants to stay in the bungalow. He did not want me to feel
frightened and alone. But I was more lonely and frightened
than I had been in my entire life.

Murgi-daak was followed by a bleary dawn. Halua arrived
with my second pot of morning tea. I looked at the clock.
Seven o'clock! Surely the hunt was over? Was it possible the
leopard was still prowling around in the daytime?

I decided to consult Halua. Oh no, memsahib, Halua said. Leopard only came at night. Had *Chotasahib* ever been on this kind of *machan* hunt before? Yes, he replied, but mostly in Chulsa with Alasdair Sahib so he did not know when they got home.

I fretted. So where was Manik? I could feel a pounding headache coming on.

My only consolation was Alasdair was with Manik. Good old Alasdair. I hadn't seen him since arriving at Aynakhal, but I remembered his kind eyes and calm voice. There was something solid and trustworthy about the man.

A small crowd of laborers had gathered outside the gates. Squatting, chatting, smoking bidis, they looked suspiciously cheerful. Halua informed me they were there to celebrate because the hunt was going to be successful. *Chotasahib* had very prudently chosen a Thursday and the *machan* was built facing an easterly direction. It was all very auspicious.

Then I heard the sound of the beating drums and shouts of a crowd. The laborers outside the bungalow jumped to their feet and pelted down the hill. All the servants ran down from the porch and out of the gates, leaving it yawning open. The sound grew louder. Now I could hear the blaring of the jeep's horn keeping time with the drums. What a din! Then they came into view: Alasdair at the wheel of the jeep, Manik half-out of his seat brandishing his gun. They were both covered with marigold garlands and followed by a big cheering crowd, beating *dholas* with bamboo sticks and dancing on the road. The golden langurs followed them in the treetops, swinging from branch to branch, shrieking. The carcass of the leopard was tied to the front grille of the jeep. The poor animal's mouth hung open, and its big head bobbed sickeningly as the vehicle bumped up the rutted road. Laborers whooped and hollered, and the whole procession came to a halt as the coolie women broke into a writhing snakelike dance, their hands looped around each other's waists. Forgetting all protocol, the whole crowd rushed inside the bungalow gate to get a closer look at the leopard.

"Layla!" Manik yelled, galloping up the stairs. He was filthy, sweat-stained with brown smudges of what could only be dried blood on his clothes. His face was animated and he walked with a new swagger. There was a primitive, wild-eyed look about him. Alasdair, by contrast, hardly looked as though he had spent the night up a tree. A little rumpled maybe, but still clean.

"Aye, that was a crack shot, Layla. Your man got him," Alasdair said.

"No, no, it was Alasdair," Manik said. "At such close proximity, this should have been child's play, but I hit it on the shoulder. The leopard would have bolted but for Alasdair, quick as a flash, shooting it on the side of its head and sending it crashing into the shrub." He pulled me by the hand. "Come see the leopard, darling. We brought it to the bungalow to show you."

"I...I've seen it," I said, feeling a wave of nausea.

"It won't bite, I promise," said Manik. He turned to Alasdair. "I think she's squeamish."

"I can understand that, Manik," said Alasdair. "A dead animal is not a pretty sight. Jamina is in tears every time I shoot something. But you must understand, Layla, this animal was dangerous. It had to be put down. It's already taken four lives."

"It's an aging male," Manik said. "We found two porcupine quills festering in its foot. No wonder it became a man-eater. It can no longer hunt."

The relief of seeing Manik alive and well was finally settling on me. "Of course it had to be put down," I agreed. "I am glad you got it. What are you going to do with the dead animal?"

"We will drop it off in the labor lines. The skin will be pegged with six-inch nails and treated with wood ash and alum before the hide is dry enough to send to the Calcutta taxidermist. The laborers eat the meat," said Alasdair. He smiled. "I've never tried it."

Manik turned to me. "I'm going to drop Alasdair off at Chulsa," he said. "I may be late for breakfast, so go ahead and eat, darling."

I was suddenly overwhelmed by fatigue. "I think I'll grab a quick nap," I said.

"I'll come back and nap with you," said Manik eagerly, giving me his new jungle-man look. "All through that long night, when I was up on the *machan*, all I could think of was...napping with my darling wife, right, Ally?"

"Aye," said Alasdair, and he looked away with a shy and secretive smile.

I have to admit my sudden and precipitous sexual awakening turned me into a bit of a moon head. I did things I am too embarrassed to repeat, things no sensible person would dream of doing. I gazed at the clouds, laughed at butterflies and floated around the garden feeling giddily and powerfully beautiful. If that was not bad enough, I went around without my brassiere. Abandoning my underwear had little to do with my newfound lustiness—although that would not be far from the truth—but because the hornet sting made wearing the undergarment quite unbearable.

A strange thing had happened. The wound healed, but the scar morphed, puckered and bloated around the edges, and to my utter astonishment shaped itself into a perfectly formed four-petaled rose centered deep in my cleavage.

"Damn," said Manik in wonderment, touching the "rose" lightly with his fingers, "it's a pure work of art. It reminds me of a tribal tattoo."

It felt strangely erotic when he kissed it. The skin was raised and exquisitely sensitive.

I peered down my neck, feeling a little worried. "I hope there's nothing wrong with it." The scar had changed drastically.

"Does it hurt?"

"Not really."

"I think Doctor Emmett should take a look at it."

"Who is Doctor Emmett?"

"The district medical practitioner. He is an English doctor and he'll be here on his hospital rounds tomorrow. I'll tell him to pop by the bungalow."

"No, no, please, Manik! I don't want him to see me naked!"

Manik stared at me incredulously. "Don't be ridiculous, Layla! He's a doctor, for God's sake."

"Still."

"Have you never been examined by a doctor before?"

"No, not like that."

"Well, get over it. Doctor Emmett will come and see you tomorrow. He will be here late morning."

"Maybe I can just describe the scar to him—that way I won't have to take my clothes off?"

Manik glared at me. "Absolutely not," he said sharply. "You will do as the doctor tells you. He needs to examine you. Do you understand?"

Doctor Emmett was an elderly man, with a thin, tired face, a receding hairline and kindly eyes behind half-moon glasses, which perched on the very edge of his nose. When he talked to me, he tilted his head back and squinted down his glasses with a faraway look, as if he was peering down a tunnel watching for a train.

One quick look at the bite and he told me I had nothing to worry about—it was only a keloid. A keloid, he explained, was a harmless skin scarification. It was the way certain types of skin tissue reacted and healed.

"Some tribes deliberately scar their bodies and rub in the juice of certain plants to form keloids. It is considered the ultimate beatification in tribal culture and marks the coming of age."

I smiled to myself. The keloid "rose" had definitely marked the coming of age for me.

"Is there something I should do about it?" I asked, as I hooked my blouse back on.

"I would just let it be," said Doctor Emmett, snapping shut his black leather satchel. "Unfortunately it is a permanent scar. A disfigurement or...enhancement, depends how you look at it." He smiled, suddenly appearing a lot younger.

"The coolie women have the most interesting tattoos," I said. "The designs must mean something."

Doctor Emmett peered over his glasses and gave a wan smile. "I see quite a few tattoos, as you can imagine. Some in rather unusual places. In my twenty-five years as a tea doctor, I've learned a few things about Adivasi culture. The wife of the village sorcerer, I believe, does the job. The tattoo ink is made by burning black sesame seeds and mixing in oil before it is injected under the skin. For antiseptic, they use, of all things, diluted cow dung!"

"*Cow dung!*" I exclaimed. "That would make an open wound even *more* septic, I would imagine!"

Doctor Emmett threw up his hands. "Beats me, but it seems to work," he said. "Most tea-gardens coolies are from the low-caste tribes in Orissa. Girls get their first tattoos as early as seven. Some designs are the special marking of their tribe. You may have seen the three dots on the chin or the V-shaped tattoos in the corners of the eyes—*chiriya*, bird tattoos those are called. Then there are also magic symbols that are supposed to protect you from a specific type of harm like drowning, fire, snakebites. I once saw a man suffer a cobra bite with no negative effect. He had a serpentine tattoo on his arm. Frankly, I don't know what to make of this hocus-pocus. As a man of science, it baffles me."

I wondered what a four-petaled "rose" tattoo would protect me from. This absurd thought made me smile.

"You're smiling," said Doctor Emmett, looking at me curiously.

"No, no," I said quickly, feeling my ears turn red. "Thank you for your visit, Doctor. I feel a lot more reassured now."

He left me some antiseptic ointment to help with the irritation and advised me not to wear tight undergarments until it healed fully. Because of the thinness of the skin tissue, the wound area would be ultrasensitive to touch, he said, probably for the rest of my life.

CHAPTER
21

Soon enough, my moon-head phase waned, thank God. I hooked on my brassiere once again, tied my hair back into my old ponytail and decided to take a good hard look around me.

Manik lived what I can only describe as a grandiose but ramshackle life. The household ran like a big creaky factory with lots of faulty parts. Besides the majordomos Halua, Kalua and Potloo, I counted thirteen servants in all. There was the *paniwalla*, or kitchen boy; not one but three *malis* to take care of the garden; a bent old lady who came to sweep the portico and cut the grass—by hand, using a curved scythe; a one-eyed janitor; a cowherd, which made no sense because we had no cows; a *bandookwalla*, whose job was to clean the guns and sometimes accompany Manik on shikar; a boiler boy, whose job was to attend to the coal-fed boiler room and make the hot water for our baths; and a young round-faced ayah, newly hired, who was supposed to be my personal attendant.

"What do I need an ayah for?" I asked Manik.

He shrugged. "All memsahibs have an ayah, so I got you one. She can help you put on your sari, comb your hair, massage your feet, tweak your toes—whatever you want."

"Don't be ridiculous," I said.

"Then sack her," he said.

"No, *you* sack her, since you got her in the first place."

"How can I sack her, if *you* are her boss?"

I sighed at Manik's facetiousness. It was impossible to talk sense to him sometimes.

On Wednesdays, the *dhobi* boy arrived with the clean laundry and took the dirty clothes to be washed. He was a rabbit-faced lad with big scared eyes and such an awful stutter that he could not speak a single sentence without collapsing into a babbling wreck. Halua's yelling and the occasional box in the ear did not help as he tallied up the items in a moth-eaten notebook. Our clothes arrived after being bashed on river rocks, boiled in rice starch and baked in the sun. The folds of my saris crackled and popped open like crispy wafers, and in just two washes the bright summer colors faded to a bleak, wintry sadness.

Manik was shockingly lackadaisical about his dress. For morning *kamjari*, he rushed off wearing the first shirt and Bombay bloomers off the top of the pile in his wardrobe. As a result the top six items on his shelf got worn over and over again—they were old and shabby, while the bottom ones remained spanking new. It did not cross his mind to flip the pile over. Some days Manik even rushed off with mismatched socks. Thankfully, slipshod dressing raised no eyebrows on a plantation. An assistant could report for *kamjari* mismatched, sockless or even footless as far as Mr. McIntyre was concerned, but if the job he was assigned to was not up to snuff, forget the feet, because the assistant's head was more likely to roll.

Manik had other appalling habits, as well. Most late afternoons when he came home from *kamjari*, he would leave his clothes strewn all over the house and expect Halua to pick up after him. Manik's muddy boots would be lying helter-skelter at the top of the stairs, his socks flung on the veranda and his limp bush shirt draped over the backrest of the sofa in the living room. If you followed the trail of dirty clothes it would lead you right to the sweaty animal himself, who would be lying flat on his stomach under the fan in the bedroom, recuperating from his prickly heat. Manik would bemoan his pitiful life and bribe me to scratch his back and act peevish and demanding.

"You are missing a spot, wife. Left, *left*, a little more. Stop! Scratch right there. Ahhhh!"

"Manik, did you know Kalua is charging us for two dozen eggs every second day?"

"Damn scoundrel," Manik mumbled dreamily into his pillow. "Scratch there...some more, darling, right there. Hmm..."

"He is robbing us blind. Don't you want to do anything about it?"

"Who? Who is robbing us?" Manik did not sound alarmed at being robbed blind.

"Halua or Kalua. Maybe both."

"I think YOU are robbing me. Hey, how many kisses are you charging me for this scratch? You are getting expensive."

"*Uf-hoh!* Please be serious. Are you listening to me or no?" I gave his back a smack.

"Oww! I am thinking about it. Deeply, as we speak."

"What do you want to do?"

"You are the memsahib. Stand them in a corner, shoot them. I don't care."

"Halua and Kalua have had a run of this place and here comes the new memsahib to curdle the milk," I complained.

Manik snorted. "Don't worry—the memsahib's job is to curdle the milk. It's time those two toed the line. I know what they are up to, but I am just too lazy to bother."

"What am *I* supposed to do, Manik, if you are not bothered?"

"Try thinking like the big boss. Ask yourself, what would Mr. McIntyre do?"

"Well, you have not exactly been acting like Mr. McIntyre yourself all this time, have you?"

"I plead guilty. I am a man of simple wants, darling. Love me, feed me and scratch my back in the right place. That's all I ask."

Aynakhal
12th March 1946
My dear Dadamoshai,
I hope you are keeping well.

I am writing to you drinking my tea here on the veranda. It is midmorning, beautiful with the flowers and new leaves on the trees. Earlier this morning there was a small flock of barking deer grazing on the lawn.

The hornet bite is healing nicely. The pain is under control and the doctor says I am fine, Dadamoshai. Please don't worry.

Manik left early for work this morning. On Wednesdays he has to attend what they call "Bichar" at the office. It's a sort of judicial proceeding, if you will. Once a week, managers have to listen to labor grievances and resolve disputes. Usually they are petty domestic issues—like someone running off with someone's daughter or stealing someone's cow. Alcohol and drug-related problems are common, too. Opium is a big problem here. There is a lot of illegal trafficking across the Burmese border. The coolies take opium, get sluggish and don't want to work, and then the management has a problem on its hands.

The coolies call the manager their Mai–Baap—*mother-father— and he is granted a godly status. The manager is seen as the giver, the taker, the protector and the savior. He is expected to be wise, and mete out fair justice. The childlike trust these simple people* have in their manager is naive and quite touching. Mr. McIntyre is superb in labor management. He is attentive to each and every case, no matter how minor, and is always firm and fair. Manik says he has a lot to learn by just watching Mr. McIntyre.

There are no rules. Most managers simply use common sense to solve disputes. This does call for an astute understanding of human behavior and the ability to come up with ingenious solutions. I must give you this one example, Dadamoshai, because being a judge, I think you will appreciate the cleverness of Mr. McIntyre's judgment in this case.

There was this coolie couple, husband and wife, who were seeking separation. There is nothing called "divorce" among coolie couples—they simply part ways—but in this case there was an acrimonious dispute over the distribution of pots and pans. Aside from cattle, pots and pans are the only asset these poor people have. This couple could not come to an amicable solution, and so they brought it up at the weekly Bichar.

And here is how Mr. McIntyre solved the dispute: he first asked the husband to divide up the utensils into two lots. Next, he told the wife she could choose the lot she wanted. So you can imagine the poor husband's anguish deciding which pot to put in which pile! When I heard the story, I told Manik that is exactly how my Dadamoshai would have solved the problem.

Our bungalow is large and comfortable but sadly in need of repair. We have quite a retinue of servants whom I have to learn to manage. I don't even know where to begin or what I am supposed to do. Every morning a small crowd gathers outside our bungalow gates. It is humbling to know they are there to see me. I am finally getting used to the idea of being on perpetual display. There is one curious woman I see every day in a green sari who lurks in the same spot. She dresses differently from the other coolie women, and I still have not figured out who she is.

I will send you some pictures soon. Manik has a Brownie camera that he will teach me to operate.

I miss you, Dadamoshai, and worry about you. Please keep well.

With my love to you,

Layla

Manik was a surprising lover. He could be intense and consuming and then with no warning at all turn into a rambunctious puppy. He was so curiously two-sided he reminded me of a beautiful heirloom shawl I had inherited from my grandmother. It was a rich black on the outside but woven with brilliant colors on the inside.

I came to understand and accept the decorum that was expected of us in public. There was no easy familiarity, no demonstration of affection and not even a tiny hint of the intimacy we shared in the bedroom. The stark contrast between our private and public life was titillating in a way and gave our very legitimate marriage the delicious intrigue of an illicit affair.

Not surprisingly, our meals got shorter, our siestas longer. Often we left our lunch barely touched and Kalua walked around with a glum face, worried perhaps his cooking was falling short. At other times we played childish pranks, buffeting poor Halua between us for our own amusement.

One day I acted as if I did not know Manik was home. Soon Halua came looking for me with a note.

Where is my Dundee cake? Manik wrote.

I frowned reading the note and said to Halua, "Tell *Chotasahib,* no Dundee cake today, only sandwich."

Halua went back with the message. Soon he was back with another note from Manik.

Let's make sandwich, the note read.

"Ask *Chotasahib*, what sandwich?" I said, sneaking a grin behind Halua's back as he scurried back to Manik.

Finally Halua returned looking very worried. The note read, *Do you want a PISH-PASH?*

I gave a noisy sigh and said, "All right, all right, tell *Chotasahib* I'm coming." Then I took my own sweet time before casually sauntering past the bedroom. I peeped in and feigned surprise to see Manik lying on the bed. "Oh, *there* you are, and I was looking all over the bungalow for you!"

"Like hell you were," Manik growled. "You are going to get a spanking for this."

Halua and Kalua always needed money. They lurked around shifty-eyed, fidgeting. As soon as my back was turned they whispered furtively into Manik's ear. Manik would absent-mindedly rummage in the bedside drawer and give them handfuls of cash. Nothing was kept under lock and key, and loose change lay in crumpled stacks and piles all over the house. The next time you looked it would be gone.

By the end of the month, after paying his club bills and the *Kiyah* bill for his groceries, Manik would be scraping the bottom of the drawer for small change. Kalua, I suspected, ran a thriving chicken and egg business in our own backyard to feed his poultry-hungry boss. With Manik's generous patronage it had undoubtedly grown into a cluckable fortune.

One thing became increasingly clear: Hal, Kal and Pots— as we now called them—were symbiotically linked to Manik, like the remora pilot fish to the shark. They stuck together and looked out for each other's interests. I, on the other hand, was the new parrot fish trying to swim along, pretending to be a part of this happy entourage. Most of the time they ganged up on me—even Manik, in his own crooked way.

It was a well-known fact that when a young tea planter enticed a wife to his jungle lair—a major feat in itself—there was much at stake to keep her there. Bungalow servants knew their boss would quickly forget the times when he had been a helpless babe at their mercy. After all, who cleaned him up and put him to bed when he staggered home on whiskey-sodden club nights? Who covered up for the seedy companions he sometimes dragged home? Who cajoled the young master awake on cold *kamjari* mornings with hot cups of tea to save him from the wrath of the tyrant *Burrasahib*?

Soon enough, the new memsahib would get a whiff of the nefarious activities and embark on a holy mission to reform her man. The first order of the day was to sack the existing servants, the ones who were in cahoots with her husband and knew more than they should. That way it blotted out all evidence of his bachelor past. A fresh batch of menials were installed and trained to higher standards. It was a memsahib prerogative.

Yet, when I complained about Hal, Kal or Pots to Manik, he grew increasingly tenderhearted and acted as if I was trying to drown a batch of helpless puppies. Manik was not too concerned about the *malis*, *paniwalla* and other riffraff, but for the three primary remoras, he made impassioned pleas.

Frankly, their inefficiency did not bother me as much as the blatant thievery. I had no aspirations to be the lady of the manor, if you could call our ramshackle bungalow that, but I was aware of certain expectations for a memsahib. I was the first Indian wife in a very colonial tea culture. I would be under intense scrutiny. If I acted gauche and incompetent, it would only confirm the suspicion that "natives" were not up to par. Someday Manik would be the General Manager or

Burrasahib, and I would be the *Burramemsahib.* I would have to learn the ropes of this new lifestyle.

Kalua appeared one morning with the pencil tucked behind his ear and a mangled *khata* notebook that looked as if it had been coughed up by a water buffalo. On the cover of the notebook was a faded sketch of Laxmi, the goddess of wealth, sitting atop a lotus and dispensing gold coins. Laxmi had indeed showered her fortune on Kalua. This notebook was where he wrote his shopping list for the *Kiyah* store. The *Kiyah,* I learned, was the local grocer, the only shop located inside the tea plantation that stocked basic supplies like rice, lentils, sugar and flour. mostly poor quality, weevil ridden items, exorbitantly priced. The *Kiyah* was also a moneylender of sorts for the laborers, who were often up to their ears in debt, having drunk away their Friday pay.

I found Kalua had charged us again for another two dozen eggs. Expensive eggs they were, too.

"Why are eggs so expensive?" I asked.

Kalua looked like a smacked puppy. A small twitch appeared in his left eye. "*Chotasahib* eating only best-quality egg."

"Does the *Kiyah* store have any vegetables?"

"No, memsahib, only potato and onion." Then he added brightly, "I buy vegetable from local *haat,* tomorrow, memsahib. Tuesday, local *haat* day."

"Why is the *mali* not growing any vegetables in the *malibari*?" I asked. There was a good-size kitchen garden at the back of the house. The soil was excellent. There was no reason why we should not be growing our own vegetables.

"*Mali* is lazy donkey, memsahib," Kalua said viciously. He obviously had a grudge against the fellow. "He not doing any work. Only smoking bidi under mango tree and going home."

Which *mali* was he talking about? I wondered. There were three of them. All three were monkey-faced and were seen puttering around the far reaches of the garden like gray ghosts in the early morning, but they vanished before the sun was fully up in the sky.

"I having a son, memsahib, making good *mali* boy..." Kalua said.

"I will speak to *Chotasahib* about the *mali*," I said quickly, not wanting to get into a conspiracy with Kalua without knowing what the issues were. "So what else is on the *Kiyah*'s list?"

Kalua's list for the day included a storage tin for sugar to keep out the *cheetis* (ants), potatoes, onions, kerosene, flour, cooking oil, rat poison and something that sounded like "figitin." He pointed to the page in his *khata* and said we owed the *Kiyah* a balance of three rupees and four annas from the last time. Everything he had written on the page looked like cauliflower florets floating in space. Kalua had circled the owed sum, and signed his initials in English—KP—with a dainty flourish.

I looked at him in surprise. "Three rupees for what?" I thought we gave him enough money each time he made a *Kiyah* trip, which was every other day.

Kalua frowned, studying the torn page. "For potatoes, onions, kerosene, flour, cooking oil, rat poison and 'figitin,'" he said.

I made him read the list for the week before. It was for kerosene, rice and "figitin." And before that for rope and "figitin."

"Figitin" seemed to be the most indispensable item on the list. What was even more puzzling was the price of "figitin" fluctuated wildly from week to week. One week it was three annas, another week one rupee and six annas.

"What is 'figitin'?" I asked finally.

"I...figitin," said Kalua, rolling his eyes dolefully.

"Flit?" I ventured. Maybe Kalua was talking about the mosquito spray. But as far as I knew, Flit spray was one of the items we picked up from Paul & Co., not the *Kiyah* store.

"I…figitin," Kalua repeated, looking more wretched than ever.

I sighed, feeling suddenly overwhelmed. Manik had appointed me as the financial controller. Manik's club bills were exorbitant, the *dhobi*'s charges made no sense, we always seemed to owe the *Kiyah* money for something or the other and now there was "figitin." Keeping track of Hal and Kal's slippery maneuvers was exhausting. It was impossible to verify any of their expenses. Their explanations were labyrinthine, meandering in circles and finally getting lost in a bog.

After some detailed questioning it turned out "I figitin" was Kalua's attempt at English: "I've forgotten," which was the balance left over after buying all the items on his list. It was Kalua's way of rounding up accounts. No wonder we never got any change back. "Figitin" took care of that.

The kitchen was a small independent building set a little ways from the house. On one side was the *malibari*, or kitchen garden, fenced in by barbed wire. On the other side of the kitchen were the servant quarters, a row of three small houses where Halua, Kalua and Potloo lived. They each had their independent accommodation where they lived with their families and domestic animals. From the pantry, only the top of the three thatched roofs could be seen, the rest covered by clumps of banana trees and other vegetation. Sometimes I caught a glimpse of a small child, or a chicken pecking in a corner of a dusty yard.

One early evening after tea, I decided to check out the kitchen garden. I opened the back door to the pantry and almost tripped over a small girl child sitting on the stairs playing with empty shotgun cartridges. She sang in a tuneless voice as she lined them up. Some were filled with pebbles, others with sticks and marbles. The child could not have been older than three. She was brown as a berry and dressed in a ragged pair of knickers with nothing on top. Her uncombed hair trailed a pink ribbon and fell over her eyes. She heard the pantry door swing open and turned around, staring at me with very big, very black eyes.

"Oye!" she greeted me happily.

She abandoned her playthings and followed me to the kitchen garden, touching my sari every now and then, but if I asked her anything she just sucked her dirty thumb and stared at me with her big, round eyes.

The kitchen garden was overgrown with weeds. A small hoe lay in one corner with a few rusted tin cans, an overturned bucket and a split rubber hose. There was not much growing in the garden except a small clump of sugarcane and a banana tree that had fallen on its side. There was, however, one neatly tended patch of healthy vegetation in one corner: a splayed leafy plant that I did not recognize. I broke off a leaf, and crushed it between my fingers. It smelled vaguely familiar, but I could not place it.

Weeds grew in profusion, proving the soil to be rich. We could easily grow our own vegetables, I determined. I imagined neat rows of tomato, eggplant, okra and green beans, and decided to speak to Manik about it.

Wanting to peek into the kitchen, I pushed open the netted spring door. Halua was sitting on a ratty cane ottoman in his undershirt smoking a bidi. Kalua was on the floor grasping the head of a skinned chicken with his feet. He had a butcher's knife poised in the air and was about to hack its head off. When they saw me, both Halua and Kalua sprang to their feet. Kalua's knife clattered noisily to the floor, and Halua threw the bidi butt to the side and flapped his arms madly to rid the air of smoke. They both looked horrified. They salaamed, then stood ramrod straight against the wall as though they were facing a firing squad.

Too late, I realized I had overstepped my boundaries. The kitchen was not the memsahib's territory—she was not expected to pop in. I was appalled at how filthy the kitchen was. It was sooty and dark with the smell of stale frying everywhere. There was a beat-up table in the center, but most of the pots and pans lay on the floor. The only window in the room looked out toward the servant quarters. It was grimy with grease, with dirty rags tucked into the broken windowpanes.

The child was peeping into the doorway from behind my sari. I saw Halua's eyes widen when he saw her. He made small angry gestures to shoo her away, but she just stood there stoutly behind me.

"What is this plant?" I asked, holding up the leaf.

Halua and Kalua looked like shifty-eyed twins. In their undershirts, without their uniforms, they looked astoundingly alike.

One of them scratched his oily head and cleared his throat. It was Kalua, I realized, because he had the twitch in his eye. "We are not knowing, memsahib. It is I thinking some *junglee* plant."

"No, no, these plants are not *junglee*. They are being grown by someone," I said.

"Memsahib, I am thinking it is the Potloo putting the plant," Halua said, fidgeting. Why would the night watchman be tending the kitchen garden? I wondered.

"Whose child is this?" I asked. The child clutched my sari and cowered behind me.

"Mine, memsahib," Halua said, giving her the stern eye.

"Budni, ghar jah!" he hissed sternly, pointing his finger and motioning her toward the servant quarters. He advanced menacingly, but little Budni clutched my sari tighter and whimpered.

"That's all right," I said, "please go back to your work." I closed the kitchen door. I walked around the side of the bungalow to the front of the house. The small girl skipped along.

I settled in the cane chair on the veranda and poured myself a cup of tea. The child sat on the front veranda steps and clapped her hands and sang a tuneless song. I gave her a tea biscuit, which she munched happily, feeding the crumbs to the ants. When Manik came home he almost tripped over her as he bounded up the stairs.

"Oh, Wendy!" he exclaimed.

"Salaam sahib," chirped the little one, saluting smartly, raggedy knickers and all.

I was curious. "What's her name? I thought it was Budni?"

Manik laughed. "Larry calls her Wendy. *Budni* means *Wednesday*, as you know, so she becomes Wendy. Right, Wendy?"

"Bhendi," lisped the little girl.

I told Manik about my kitchen visit. Manik had never visited the kitchen end of the house. The only time he had gone there was a year ago, when a herd of elephants had come and trampled the *malibari*. Not that there was much to trample there.

I showed him the leaf from the plant growing in the *malibari*. It was a little wilted now.

"Ganja," Manik said, sniffing it. "Marijuana. The one time I tried it, I missed *kamjari* and got hell. I suspect it's that scoundrel Potloo's doing. That fellow is always in la-la land. I used to think he was unusually dim. He can't even find the latch to the front gate some days."

A few days later when I looked back in the *malibari*, the plants had gone. The soil had been raked over and the surface was a barren moonscape.

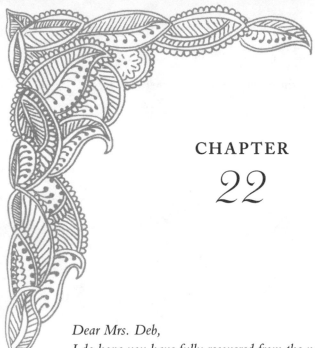

CHAPTER

22

Dear Mrs. Deb,
I do hope you have fully recovered from the nasty hornet bite.
    I have been wanting to invite you over for tea so we can get better
acquainted. Are you available tomorrow morning around 10:00 a.m.?
    Please send a word through Hussain, my driver, and I will
send the car to pick you up.
With warm wishes,
Audrey McIntyre

The invitation was handwritten on an ivory note card with
I. W. McIntyre, Esq. printed on the top. I showed the note to
Manik. "Why is there *Esquire* after his name?" I asked. "Is Ian
McIntyre some kind of nobility, like Alasdair?"

"*Conferred* nobility," said Manik. "General Managers of Sterling Tea Companies are entitled to add *Esquire* after their names.
I guess it goes back to the early days of tea when British companies had a hard time recruiting able managers to run the tea
plantations. After all, which fool would risk his life to work in
the jungles of Assam? And for what? The money is not great,
the weather horrible. So companies tried to entice them with

this English lord lifestyle with all its perks—massive bungalow, lots of servants, big-game hunting and a fancy title. Englishmen love titles. They hanker for social status. Make a man feel important enough and he will do anything. The tea companies understand this very well. But it's also true that General Managers have a free rein over their gardens. Full autonomy. They can run it any way they choose. The company does not interfere as long as the garden delivers profits."

"So when you become General Manager, you will be Manik Deb, Esquire?" I said.

"Correct. And you will be my *Esquiress*."

"What nonsense!"

"Anyway, you will meet the Esquiress of Aynakhal tomorrow. I think you'll like her. She's a lovely lady."

Audrey McIntyre was a tiny, birdlike woman with fluttering hands and an eager smile. She wore a rose floral-print summer dress gathered at the waist, with a white sailor's collar. Her brown hair was cut in a short bob. She came quickly down the steps of the veranda to the carport, followed by a very old cocker spaniel with sad milky eyes that greeted me with a tired but friendly *woof*.

"Layla!" she exclaimed, holding out her hands. Her voice had a musical chime. She wore a hint of pink lipstick and smelled pleasantly of lavender. "How lovely to meet you, finally." She kissed me lightly on both cheeks. Her blue-gray eyes crimped at the corners like miniature folding fans.

The cocker spaniel was licking my toe furiously.

"Shoo, Daisy!" Mrs. McIntyre said, giving the dog a pat on the fanny. "Oh, don't mind her, dear. She's rather old and completely blind, I'm afraid." She led me up to the veranda. "Oh, do have a seat."

She removed a copy of *Woman's Home and Garden* from the chair and placed it on the coffee table. "It's a shame Debbie can't join us. She was really looking forward to meeting you. Emma is running a fever. The child refuses to stay with her new ayah."

"Who is Debbie?" I asked.

"Debbie Ashton of Dega Tea Estate. She said Rob, her husband, met you in Silchar."

"Oh yes, I remember. He is a champion tennis player, isn't he?"

"Your husband, Manik, is not too far behind, you know. He won the Mariani runners-up trophy last year."

"Did he really?" I had no idea. Manik's letters had been full of his shikar exploits. He was modest about his other sporting abilities. I now remembered a few silver trophies wedged between books on the bookshelf. Manik never spoke about them.

I gazed at the garden in awe. The front garden was divided into flower beds in which tall gladiolas peeped over snapdragons, peonies and cosmos, planted in descending layers fringed by short rows of daisies and pansies in the foreground. The landscaping was impeccably planned and all the colors beautifully coordinated. Many segments were demarcated by midget hedges with multicolored confetti-like foliage. There was a circular rose garden with a birdbath and even a tree house tucked in the branches of a weeping willow.

"This is the most exquisite garden I have ever seen!" I said, thinking sadly of our bungalow's garden with its overgrown hedges, random flowers and disobedient bougainvillea. Compared to this pruned elegance, ours looked a juvenile delinquent running amok. "It must take a lot of work and upkeep."

"Oh, the *malis* do everything. I just instruct them on what to plant where. You need to closely supervise them, though.

Garden upkeep, as you know, is a memsahib job." Her eyes followed a fly on the coffee table. She picked up the magazine and swatted it, missing by a hair. Daisy the spaniel skittered to her feet and looked about in dazed panic, blinking her milky eyes. Mrs. McIntyre patted her head reassuringly till she settled down again.

Mrs. McIntyre rang a small, engraved brass bell. A tall bearer with a placid moon face and attentive eyes came through the doorway. He was dressed in a spotless two-piece white tunic with a burgundy cummerbund and wore a white turban. His feet were bare. Mrs. McIntyre spoke to him in heavily accented but clear Hindustani.

"Where did you learn to speak such good Hindustani?" I asked.

"Oh dear, I had no choice. I was forced to pick up the language trying to communicate with the servants."

I was thinking about what Manik had told me. The menfolk, especially young assistants, had an easier time picking up the native lingo, it seemed. They took private lessons from nubile "teachers" in more intimate settings. The company encouraged them to take a crash course, and this unconventional method was condoned because communication was crucial in labor management. Some of the vocabulary young assistants picked up was colorful, though superfluous for a planter's job.

"Would you like to take a walk around the garden, dear?" Mrs. McIntyre asked. "I can also show you our *malibari*. We have a fine crop of string beans and cauliflower this season. I was going to ask our *mali* to fix you a basket to take home."

We walked across the lawn. The freshly mowed grass was springy underfoot. Daisy followed, sniffing at anthills. A warbler sang from the low branches of a Semul tree.

"Are you interested in gardening, Layla?" Mrs. McIntyre asked.

"Oh, I am, but I have no idea what to do or even where to begin. Our bungalow garden is such a mess," I confessed. We passed through the arbor of trailing primroses, dense with fragrance.

"We are lucky—the soil is so rich here in Assam. All you do is throw the seeds down and nature takes care of the rest," said Mrs. McIntyre.

"Where do you get your seeds and cuttings from?" I noticed the flowers were show-quality specimens.

"I order most from the Sutton's Nursery catalog in Calcutta. The roses I crossbreed myself." She paused beside a patch of dazzling red poppies on long graceful stems and fingered a velvety petal tenderly. "These Oriental poppies I got from Mrs. Gilroy. She is a master gardener."

A Zebra Swallowtail butterfly, resplendent in black and white stripes with crimson and blue spots, quivered hesitantly on the petals of an orange cosmos, then flew off.

"It is amazing to think that Assam is home to sixty percent of the entire butterfly specimens of the world. We have some very rare and exotic varieties in the rain forests here," Mrs. McIntyre said.

That was surprising information. I had lived all my life in Assam and never known that!

The *malibari* occupied the entire back of the house and covered almost an acre. Sugarcane, papaya and banana plantations fringed the far edges. A small thatched hut in the corner housed bags of fertilizers, spades, shears, watering cans and hoses. Big clumps of green tomato hung heavily on stout hairy stems, snow peas and string beans curled tendrils around crosshatched bamboo trellises and juvenile carrots sprouted frilly stems from the ground. The cabbage and cauliflower planted in neat rows were big as footballs. In the centre of the *malibari* was a long netted enclosure running lengthwise, housing delicate strawberry plants nestled in straw.

Mrs. McIntyre made me feel wonderfully at ease. She was gracious and kind without a bone of pretension. I told her about Potloo growing marijuana in the kitchen garden, our two-dimensional egg and chicken diet, and my rather awkward kitchen visit.

"Oh dear, oh dear," Mrs. McIntyre tittered, clutching a hand to her chest, "so much to learn for a young bride in such a short time."

It seemed most bachelor assistants lived in the same abject condition as Manik. It was the memsahibs who made the servants toe the line. The servants were expected to dress neatly and behave with decorum. The company had provided all the uniforms, but if one did not keep an eye on them, servants would sell off uniforms to buy bidis or liquor and walk around looking like beggars. The memsahib's job was beginning to sound like a cross between a schoolmarm and a jailkeeper.

"Did you know all this before you became a tea planter's wife? How did you even know what to do?" I was beginning to feel a little panicked.

"I married Ian when he was a Junior Assistant, and his manager's wife, Mrs. Barter, was a very kind and lovely lady. She took me under her wing and taught me everything. She was like my surrogate mother, really. I was very lucky to have her."

"Will you...? Can you please teach me the things I need to know?" I asked hesitatingly.

"Of course, duckie," Mrs. McIntyre said, giving my hand

a little squeeze. "I will show you everything. You will make a fine memsahib for your man."

Tea had been served on the veranda. The bearer was laying out the food items on the glass coffee table. There was an iced chocolate cake, cheese straws and small rolled-up pastries with piped cream inside. He came around and placed a small plate with an organdy napkin and cake fork on the side table next to me.

Mrs. McIntyre poured a stream of strong, bright tea into the cups, gripping the handle of the teapot with a quilted parrot-shaped holder.

"That's a beautiful tea set," I said, admiring the old-fashioned bone china patterned with primroses.

"It's an old Alfred Meakin set belonging to my grandmother," said Mrs. McIntyre. "Oh, do try some of these." She held out the plate with the rolled pastries. "Brandy snap, our *borchee*'s specialty."

"Is your *borchee* a Mung cook?" I asked, taking a small bite of the brandy snap. It was light and gingery, with fresh whipped cream inside, and utterly delicious.

I knew Mungs were traditional tea-garden cooks. They were Buddhists from Chittagong in East Bengal and came from a proud culinary lineage and specialized in Anglo-Indian cuisine. Their recipes, closely guarded secrets, were handed down from father to son.

"Oh yes, he is a Mung. He worked in this bungalow since he was a boy. His father worked here before that."

Mrs. McIntyre said she knew little about Mung cooks back then. "The old *borchee* was a true culinary magician. He made the most exquisite wood-smoked *hilsa* fish with all those wonderful Indian spices and served it whole, after removing every tiny bone."

"I wonder how he did that," I said. *Hilsas* were delicious river fish, with a rich buttery taste, but a mesh of curved, sharp bones made it impossible for foreigners to enjoy it.

"I believe he used a muslin cloth to trap the bones like hair. It's a very ancient technique—only Mungs know how to do that. He taught our *borchee*, his son, every trick of the trade before he died. It was very strange how he died, too."

"What happened?"

"It's part of their tradition, I believe. They commit suicide because they don't want to be a burden on their family. The old *borchee* had become very old and feeble and one day he came to take our leave. He said he was going away. His son would now take over. The way he put it, we thought he was going back to his ancestral home in Chittagong."

"But he didn't?"

"No. The old man walked himself to death. He was found weeks later by the jungle road. Withered as a leaf. The calloused soles of his feet had fallen off and lay on the ground neatly like sandals. And his body was covered with thousands of butterflies."

"Butterflies?"

"Yes. Ian said a certain species of jungle butterfly feed off the salt on corpses. Ian fought in Burma during the First World War. There were corpses everywhere in the jungle covered with butterflies. Since then, Ian has hated butterflies."

The ceiling fan ticked. Daisy sighed.

I sat there morbidly imagining a creeper-filled jungle full of corpses covered with butterflies and the calloused skin of their feet fallen off like old sandals. How many miles would it take for a man to walk to his death? I wondered. Ian McIntyre hated butterflies for the same reason I hated lilies—because of their association with death.

★ ★ ★

The factory siren wailed. It was four-thirty and Manik was home early. He played tennis with Rob on Mondays. It was also social night at the Mariani Planters Club.

"Debbie is waiting to meet you," said Manik. He was sprawled on our bed in his underwear, his Bombay bloomers and sweaty workday shirt lumped on the floor. "I can drop you off at the Ashtons on my way to tennis and you can meet us at the club later together. What do you say?"

I was rifling through the hangers in my cupboard, pulling out saris, wondering what to wear. Yards of silk lay crumpled over the bed like a stormy sea.

Manik rolled up on his elbows, flipped a swath of silk over a shoulder and sighed breathily. "Look, I am Cleopatra!"

I ignored him.

"Wife, you are the big buzz in tea circles—the first Indian memsahib," said Manik. "News travels quickly by the Jungle Telegraph in these parts."

The Jungle Telegraph was an efficient conduit for local gossip. News traveled from garden to garden when memsahibs bumped into one another at the club store, cooks gathered at the local *haat* or ayahs chatted together at some child's birthday party. No information was sacrosanct in tea circles. I had little doubt my arrival had been noted.

"I hate this," I grumbled. I sat down on the bed feeling irritable and nervous. "I don't know what to wear. All I want to be is a fly on the wall."

I dreaded being the center of attention. I was a curiosity. I dressed and looked different. I knew I would be scrutinized. Manik, on the other hand, fitted in with hardly a ripple. Half the time the Brits even forgot that he was Indian. Nobody changed the topic around him. There were anti-British protests all over the country. It made foreigners uneasy around Indians. They were beginning to feel unwanted. And here I was, a lonely goat standing on the wrong side of the fence.

"What should I wear?" I asked, looking helplessly at all the saris strewn on the bed.

Asking Manik for his opinion was a mistake. I held up one sari after the other. He said "this one," then "no, that one" and then, "hmm, maybe...oh well, they are all very nice," which was no help at all.

"Do you really want my serious, honest opinion?" he asked.

"Yes." I waited while he pondered.

English ladies dressed conservatively, from what I could gather: muted colors navy blues, creams and grays. Evening dresses were tailored and understated, jewelry minimal—a string of pearls or a brooch, at the most. What they spent a lot of time on was their hair. I was the opposite. My hair was usually just looped into a casual hand bun. My saris, on the other hand, were gorgeous and unseemly flamboyant. I wished I had a more sober sari in a beige or cream. That way I would blend in better. But Mima would say that was dressing like a widow.

Manik flopped down on his back and pillowed his head on his crossed hands. "Here's what I think," he said. "How about the Goldilocks apron?"

"*Uuff!*" I said, flinging a pillow at him. I wished Manik would not joke when I asked him a serious question. Sometimes communicating with him was like sticking the tail of the donkey on its head.

I finally settled for a blue silk with aqua undertones and a thin vermilion-and-gold border. Even that, when paired with a matching vermilion blouse, made me look embarrassingly queenly.

The sari needed ironing. I wondered if I could trust Halua with the flattop iron he warmed over the kitchen coals. He would most definitely burn a hole in the delicate silk, I decided.

"Move over, Manik. You are crushing my sari," I said, giving him a little push.

Manik ran his finger along my midriff. "Your skin is so soft," he murmured, "just like silk." One arm threaded around my waist, while the other fumbled clumsily with the hooks of my sari blouse.

I tried to wriggle out of his grasp. "I can't do *this* right now, Manik. Please, don't you understand? I am all rattled about this club evening."

"I can derattle you, my darling," Manik murmured, worming his fingers inside my blouse.

I sighed—it was no use. We had reached the point of no return.

Don't ask me why, but I had expected Debbie to be a pukka English memsahib, a younger Mrs. McIntyre perhaps, but I was in for a real surprise. As usual, Manik had left out all the details when he talked about her: "Lovely girl, Debbie" was all he ever said.

Debbie had "gone native," as they say. She was a free spirit who had little interest in housekeeping and saw no glamour in playing the memsahib. The daughter of a famous English playwright and a London stage actress, she was beautiful in a careless way, with a sweet dimpled face, big brown eyes and her hair cut in a short bob. Debbie wore faded blue shorts and an old *kamjari* shirt of Rob's and walked around barefoot, as did her three-year-old, Emma, who had streaky blond hair that badly needed combing and the startling blue eyes of her father. Emma was dressed like an Indian servant child, in a cotton bordered skirt and cheap plastic bangles. There was a big mosquito bite on her cheek.

The Ashtons had just got a puppy that went by the name of Pekoe, like the tea. It was a brown mongrel with dopey eyes and a big splotch on its head, like a milk drop. Emma clutched the struggling puppy to her chest with its legs dangling. The puppy finally broke free of her clammy grasp and crawled under the coffee table, where it chewed on a naked doll with hair as blond and wild as Emma's.

The Ashtons' bungalow was a mess. The hedges were overgrown, the grass scuffed and patchy with outcrops of dandelion. There was a sandbox in the middle of the lawn with half-buried tin cans, spoons, old tennis balls and other mishmash of a child's world.

"Did you have an arranged marriage?" Debbie asked. She sat cross-legged on the sofa like a yogi, holding her teacup with both hands.

"Not exactly," I said. I watched little Emma push small pieces of a cucumber sandwich through the holes in the wicker on the back of her mother's chair. Emma stared back at me with bold, defiant eyes.

I told Debbie how Manik and I had met.

"Beautiful," she said dreamily, "so romantic."

Debbie had met Rob Ashton on board the *Eastern Saga* when she was sailing home from her first vacation in India. Rob was headed to Dublin on home furlough. Everything about India had charmed Debbie—the colors, the beautiful, warmhearted people. Even the heat and the mosquitoes were no bother. She hated going back to dreary old England. Then there was Rob, with his tanned good looks, his blazing blue eyes and his blond hair whipping in the sea breeze. He had seduced her with card tricks and his stories of Assam. At the end of the journey, Debbie didn't know if she had fallen in love with Rob or India. She wanted them both.

I asked Debbie how she spent her time. Not surprisingly, I learned she played tennis, hunted and fished with the boys. She was also an aspiring writer working on her first novel—a sizzling romance set in Assam, she said, between a *chokri* girl and a young assistant.

"You never get to know the real India if you live in the tea gardens. It is a cloistered existence. The English are very tight about socializing." Debbie brushed the crumbs off her shorts. "They don't mix with Indians. That's why I was excited to meet you. You are different, though. I thought you'd be more traditional." She smiled her dimpled smile. "Oh, don't get me wrong, Layla. You are wonderful. You are very easy to be friends with."

"Everybody thought Manik would come home with a village bride. They don't expect me to speak English, which is surprising, because most Indians speak English anyway," I said.

"They don't speak as well as you do. You have almost no accent. Your English is excellent."

She pivoted around suddenly. "*Emmi!* Give me that!" She pried the sandwich from the child's fist and flung it over the balcony rails.

The puppy scampered out from under the coffee table, bright-eyed, thinking perhaps she had thrown a ball, and little Emma quickly pounced on him and dragged him off to read him the story of "Jack and the Beanstalk."

"Look, Pekoe, it's Uncle Jimmy," she said, pointing to the red-haired giant in the storybook.

Debbie laughed. "That giant looks exactly like our manager, Jimmy O'Connor. He is such a gruff man but he has a big soft spot for our Emma."

Emma stuck a finger up her nose and looked at Debbie defiantly.

"No, Emmi, that's very rude. Please stop that!" Debbie wagged her finger sternly. She turned to me. "Uncle Jimmy has certain talents that Emmi admires. He has a missing forefinger and amuses Emma by sticking the stub up his nose. It looks like his finger has gone right into his brain!" Debbie pinched Emma's cheek playfully and laughed. "You love your uncle Jimmy, don't you, my pet?"

"I am going to marry him," said Emma coyly.

"Well, that's an interesting thought!" Debbie gave me a wink. "I am sure your daddy will be very happy having his tyrant boss as his own son-in-law—imagine that?"

I may have fretted less about what to wear had I known I'd be arriving at the Mariani Club in a battered, topless army jeep driven by Debbie Ashton. The floorboards had tennis-ball-size holes through which gusts of air rushed up my legs, causing my silk sari to billow out like a parachute. I did not know whether to hang on to my hair, my sari or my life.

The jeep, I learned, was Rob's anniversary present to Debbie, bought off an American GI. It was a ferocious thing with an awful growl. Debbie was often seen belting across bumpy tea-garden roads in her khaki shorts and oversize shirt, her wild hair flying. Sometimes little Emma rode along clinging like a burr. Thanks to her, I arrived on my first day at the Mariani Club looking like a storm-wrecked sailboat. Debbie in her faded summer shift and open-toed sandals looked no different from when we started out.

The Mariani Planters Club was no posh English country club but a beat-up homely establishment designed for camaraderie and sport. There were two scuffed grass tennis courts, a decent-size swimming pool, a large dance floor and a Ping-Pong table. This was the place where planters played, hung out and got hopelessly drunk. If anything made the isolation and loneliness bearable for tea planters, it was the Mariani Planters Club.

There was something about the very smell of the place, a mixture of beer and tobacco, muddled with the wet, whooshing blast from the air conditioner, that made the toils of the work-week slip away. The Mariani Planters Club was the only place where a Junior Assistant could share a round at the bar with his bristling, formidable seniors. If the whiskey-emboldened young-ster leaked out a pet peeve or two about his tyrant manager, his audacity was graciously pardoned. These incidents were rarely hashed over. Such was the unspoken rule. Loosening a valve or two was what the club was for. It was the only way to survive.

But despite the bonhomie, an invisible thread of hierarchy prevailed. The standing joke among young assistants was that the size of peg of whiskey varied by rank and it was measured by the matchbox. Junior Assistants were entitled to a peg the height of a matchbox sitting on its flat side. The manager's peg measured the matchbox on its striking edge, and as for the superintendents, company directors and other bigwigs, their pegs equaled the matchbox tall side up.

Debbie was greeted with cries of joy from the lads at the bar. She slipped easily into male company, I could tell, and stayed clear of the other wives. She slugged beer, shot darts and en-gaged in silly competitive sport like picking a matchbox off the bar with her teeth or laying bets with young assistants on who could shimmy up the veranda pole the fastest.

After his tennis game, Manik appeared all showered and fresh in his white slacks and open-necked shirt. He did not seem to notice my disheveled appearance. After a perfunctory round of introductions, he hit the bridge tables. Mrs. McIntyre led me over to the senior managers' wives gathered in the cushioned seating area adjoining the bar. They were dignified, coiffured ladies, each trailing a perfumed cloud of rose, lavender or patchouli.

"Oh my, isn't she the perfect little princess!" cried Mrs. Gilroy, flashing me a gold-toothed smile. "Look at that gorgeous sari, will you!"

As usual, the ladies were surprised to learn I spoke perfect English and did not have an arranged marriage. Most foreigners, I discovered, had a morbid fascination with arranged marriages.

"So how did you meet Manik Deb, dear?" asked a matronly lady with a doughy face and high bosom that crept up to her chin. She was introduced as Mrs. Howard. "We hear young men and women don't have much opportunity to meet together alone in your society."

I wondered how to answer that question. "We were introduced by a family friend," I said finally and smiled, thinking of Boris Ivanov. Technically speaking, it was true.

A pretty woman had just entered the bar. She had a round country-milkmaid face and was girlishly dressed in a gingham pinafore with her hair tied in a high swinging ponytail.

"Oh, there's Laurie Wood," said Mrs. Howard. She turned to the other ladies. "Wouldn't it be lovely for Layla to meet some of the younger ladies? Laurie! Laurie, dear!" she called, waving her hanky edged with tatting lace. The girl waved back, signed the bar chit, picked up her orange squash and walked over to the group.

"How do you do, Mrs. Howard," she said politely. She shot

me an awkward glance and nodded at the ladies. "Good evening."

Mrs. Howard tugged her arm, "Laurie, dear, have you met Layla? Manik Deb's wife, of Aynakhal?"

"Pleased to meet you," said Laurie. She extended her hand then pulled it back, as though worried perhaps of some hidden protocol in our culture. She fanned her face instead. "Gracious, it's hot in here!" she said, tossing back her ponytail.

"It would be lovely, dear, if you could introduce Layla to some of your friends," said Mrs. Howard. She turned to the other ladies. "Don't you remember how lonely it was at the beginning? I must have cried for a whole month!"

"My goodness, the endless surprises!" laughed Mrs. Gilroy, flashing her bullion teeth. "I'll never forget finding the six-foot python behind our rosewood Georgian sideboard. It had climbed up the mulberry tree and dropped into our dining room through the open window—can you imagine? I was laid up for weeks from shock."

"My biggest challenge was communicating with the servants," said a frail-looking lady in cat's-eye glasses. "One winter I took to bed with a chill. I asked the bearer to bring me some hot milk and a hot water bottle. He brought the hot water bottle but not the milk. When I asked him about it, I found he had put the hot milk *inside* the hot water bottle. My Hindustani has improved greatly since."

All the ladies laughed and Laurie Wood shifted her feet. Every now and then her eyes darted toward the door leading out to the hall.

"Are your friends here today, Laurie? Be a dear and introduce Layla around, will you?" said Mrs. Howard.

"Certainly," said Laurie in a bored voice. From her diffident manner, I suspected Mrs. Howard must be their manager's wife—in other words, Laurie's husband's boss. I was beginning to feel like an unwanted wart foisted on Laurie's arm.

"We're out by the Ping-Pong table," Laurie said to me, nodding toward the door.

We walked past the bridge tables where Manik was intensely absorbed in his game with three other assistants: Larry Baker, Alasdair and a mongoose-looking fellow with a sorrowful face he had introduced as Flint. Manik's eyes were narrowed and one finger absently tapped his whiskey glass. He looked over the top of his glasses and caught my eye. *Everything okay?* he seemed to ask. I nodded and pointed at the door and followed Laurie Wood out into the hall.

The group of young women stood at the far end of the hall by a Ping-Pong table. They turned their heads to watch as we navigated the length of the dance floor. Laurie walked with exaggerated slowness by my side, taking tiny steps.

"Blimey, how do you even walk in that...?" she said, sweeping a hand toward my sari.

"I'm used to it," I said. "Besides, I walk faster than this, you know. I don't really have bound feet."

"I beg your pardon?"

"You know, like the Chinese?"

Laurie gave me a blank look and shrugged. She turned to wave girlishly at her friends. The veiled look she exchanged with them seemed to say *listen, this was not my idea.*

"This is..." She turned to me, already forgetting my name.

"Layla Deb," I said.

There was an awkward silence. The ladies regarded me like an exotic but potentially dangerous animal. After a few stilted introductions, they concluded I did not speak sufficient English and resumed their conversation as though I wasn't there. Listening to them, I gathered they were an unsure lot, still struggling to come to grips with the oddities of Assam, the intricacies and challenges of playing the memsahib. They spent a great deal of time complaining about the "natives" or gossiping about who was having an affair with whom. It seemed a fair amount of bed swapping took place with or without tacit permission.

It was hard to imagine what it must have felt like landing in Assam from some distant, foggy shore, halfway around the world. It must have hit new brides with the impact of a sledgehammer. Assam, in many ways, was like being trapped in a swamp, where everything clawed and bit, and cries for help were swallowed by the screech of monkeys. The very delicate ones would take it the hardest, I imagined. The extreme humidity made hair collapse like a ruined soufflé. Lipsticks melted, nails chipped trying to open bloated drawers and high-heeled shoes took a nasty beating they did not deserve. Even a short walk from the parking lot to the club could risk a twisted ankle or a miserable step in the mud. I gathered when the young tea wives returned home on vacation, they were light years behind fashion with their bad haircuts, homemade dresses styled from Butterick paper patterns and Indian Bata sandals. The men were feathered warriors, whereas the women had turned into dowdy sparrows. In every way it was grossly unfair.

Betsy Lamont was newly married and in her early twenties. She was the wife of Danny Lamont, the Assistant Manager of Chulsa Tea Estate, and a high-strung beauty, groomed tight like a neatly clipped hedge. The other wives did not have the heart to tell her she was fighting a losing battle. Betsy sported an ugly purple bruise over her left eye. I was wondering if Danny Lamont was a wife beater, when I learned otherwise.

Hullock apes were the bane of Chulsa Tea Estate. The assistant's bungalow was in a deeply forested area, right in the middle of the monkeys' den. Not only did the Lamonts have to contend with howls and shrieks at the crack of dawn, but the rascals peeped into their bedroom and wandered in at any given opportunity. Betsy found a monkey smashing her lipsticks on the dressing table. The brazen creature bared its awful teeth and flung a hairbrush, narrowly missing her eye, before jumping out of the window and crashing into the mulberry tree.

"How dreadful," said Molly Dodd. She was a big-boned, flat-chested English girl with doleful eyes and terrible posture. "S'pose you have to keep the windows closed now all the time."

"I hate those filthy monkeys," said Laurie Wood, twirling the end of her ponytail with her finger. "Why don't you get Danny to shoot the bloody creatures."

"What, and have the servants blame us for killing their monkey god?" Betsy threw up her hands. "You can't kill monkeys, you can't kill cows and you can't kill...God knows what else. Danny says it can start a labor riot. Anything can start a damn labor riot. Bollocks! They're just damn coolies, for Pete's sake. Take away their jobs. Make them starve to death. It'll teach them who's the boss."

If we had no coolies we'd have no tea garden, I thought to myself. All our husbands would be out of jobs, boss or no. Labor management was a delicate balance of give and take. One side did not have more leverage than the other.

"Our jeep hit a white owl once." Molly blinked her bovine eyes. She leaned against the table, round-shouldered and pigeon-toed. "'Twas still stuck on the fender when we got home. The coolies blamed the low profits of the garden that year on that owl's death. The owl is the goddess of wealth or something."

Laxmi was the goddess of wealth. The owl was her mascot.

"So backward, these natives," said Betsy bitterly. "I feel like giving them a good rattling sometimes. Even the educated ones are no better."

There was an uncomfortable silence and they all looked at me. I pretended not to hear but I wondered what these ladies would make of someone like Dadamoshai.

"I see Jimmy O'Connor is here," said Laurie, changing the subject. "What happened to his neck, I wonder?"

Jimmy O'Connor. The name rang a bell. Then I remembered Emma's giant in "Jack and the Beanstalk." Now I could see why Emma thought so: the man leaning against the bar was massive, with flaming red hair. Jimmy O'Connor certainly looked as if he had fallen off the beanstalk, because his neck was in a brace.

"Danny said he got hit by a goose," Betsy said.

"A *goose*? What on earth!" Molly cried, breaking into a honking laugh, sounding rather like a goose herself. "*Bit* by a goose, you mean. Oh, for heavens sake!"

"No, darling, he was *hit* by a goose when he was out on shikar with that Alasdair Carruthers, from our garden." Betsy shot a sly look at the group. "Y'know, the one who has that *chokri* girl. He's s'posed to be an earl and all. I don't believe a word of it—"

"That Jimmy O'Connor also has, you know, one of those..." Molly whispered in a gossipy voice.

"OPs. Yes, yes." Laurie waved her hands impatiently. "Her name is Miss Shulai, if you must know. She's a Khasi whore. She speaks decent English at least. G'on, tell us about the goose, Betsy. What happened?"

"Well, anyway, they were out hunting and Jimmy O'Connor shoots a goose on the wing tip like he always does—"

"Why does he shoot them on the wing tip?" asked Molly, blinking.

"So that he can clip off their wings and keep them as pets. He always does that. Very odd man, that Jimmy O'Connor. He has big flocks of Himalayan geese wandering in his lawn. They are aggressive as any guard dogs and chase off intruders entering his bungalow. He is very antisocial and wants to be left alone, but he keeps getting bothered by that dodgy Indian Forest Officer from Mariani. Animals enter Dega from Kaziranga all the time and that man—"

Laurie threw up her hands. "Betsy, you are not getting to the point, darling. For God's sake, what happened to Jimmy O'Connor's *neck*?"

"Oh. He shot this goose and it came crashing down and landed on his head. They are huge. It almost broke his neck, so they say."

"How terrible," Molly said, shaking her head.

Laurie snorted. "Bloody funny, if you ask me. Anyway, I don't care about his neck. I wish he would give me some of his heirloom-tomato cuttings."

"Why don't you ask him for some?" said Betsy.

Laurie looked at her scornfully. "Who even *talks* to Jimmy O'Connor? The only people he's friendly with are the Ashtons and Alasdair Carruthers—that Carruthers is a dark horse, if you ask me."

"Have you seen his *chokri*? Ugly hag she is, short and dumpy," said Betsy. "I don't know what Alasdair sees in her. Danny says he's very faithful, though."

"She must be a hot chutney in bed," said Laurie.

I was thinking about Jimmy O'Connor's heirloom tomatoes. "What is special about the tomatoes?" I asked suddenly. They all stared at me, taken aback. I realized this was the first time I had spoken. All this while the conversation had flowed easily around me, like water around a river rock.

"Jimmy O'Connor grows the best heirloom tomatoes in the district. They are unlike anything you have ever seen," said Laurie. "He got the seeds from a gardener in some English castle. Jimmy O'Connor won't share the seeds with anybody."

"Has anybody asked him for some? Those tomatoes would take the blue ribbon at the flower show, for sure," Betsy said.

"*You* try asking him," said Laurie. "He's a real unfriendly sort. I believe he got that way after his wife died."

"She was trampled by a rogue elephant. I heard that awful story," Molly said.

"Danny says he is an excellent tea planter but has a drinking problem," Betsy said. "So talking about drinking, who is coming to my shandy brunch? Fiona Clayton is back and she'll be there. Oh, Laurie, darling, you must bring your homemade mulberry wine for tasting." Betsy looked around the group. Her eyes skimmed over me. There was an awkward pause. I guess I had not been invited.

I looked for an excuse to get away. "I heard they have a library here?" I asked Molly.

"Yes, through that small equipment office, toward the back," she said. "There's not much of a selection, though, I'm afraid."

I was grateful for an excuse to get away from those dreadful, gossipy women. I walked across the main hall still thinking about Jimmy O'Connor: his geese, his heirloom tomatoes, his missing finger and his wife trampled by a rogue elephant. What a strange man.

The equipment office smelled of carbon paper. There was a typewriter, piles of foolscap and a small shelf containing sport supplies: Ping-Pong rackets, a box of balls, some darts and billiard chalk. In the neatly ordered library beyond, I found a young Bengali man behind the desk, poring over a ledger. He had a serious, handsome face and wore glasses. He reminded me of a very young Manik.

The man looked up when I entered, capped his fountain pen and came around the desk.

"Good evening, madam," he said, smiling warmly. He walked with a polio limp. "You must be Mrs. Deb of Aynakhal. Can I help you find a particular book?"

He introduced himself as Raja. His father was the caretaker of the Mariani Club, and his family lived in the quarters behind the clubhouse. Raja was a medical student, home on vacation, volunteering his time reorganizing the library, cataloging the books and creating a checkout system. Most times club members helped themselves to books, and left them piled up on the desk when they were returned. The club typist then stacked them randomly in the shelves. As a result it was impossible to find anything.

"How do you like it here, madam?" Raja asked. "Mr. Deb always stops by the library. He's an avid reader. My brother Dinesh and I visited Aynakhal last summer. Mr. Deb showed us his guns and drove us around the plantation and explained how tea is grown. We will never forget his kindness."

I asked him about his brother and a shadow crossed Raja's face. He said his brother had dropped out of school to become a political activist. Dinesh hated the British and mocked his father for working as a mere clerk in a Planters Club, kowtowing to a drunken white population. Raja's father and brother no longer spoke to each other.

"Dinesh has cut ties with the family," Raja explained.

Before I could answer, Manik popped his head around the door.

"Oh, there you are. I was looking all over for you," he said.

"I see you have both got acquainted. Fine young man, our Raja is. He's going to be a brilliant doctor."

Raja flushed. He clearly hero-worshipped Manik.

"Raja's uncle is Bimal Babu," said Manik, then, seeing my blank look, he added, "Bimal Babu, our head clerk at Aynakhal. He's been there longer than Mr. McIntyre."

Babus were the Bengali clerks at the garden office, I learned. They were diligent paper pushers: townsfolk who maintained their townsfolk ways and had little involvement in other aspects of tea-garden business. It was fascinating how different classes of people lived together in a tea plantation yet maintained their compartmentalized lifestyles. I was reminded of multitiered tiffin carriers: people in separate containers but banded together tightly at the top by the General Manager.

"Raja here is interested in shikar," Manik said.

"Better I stick to my malaria research." Raja wagged his bad leg. "I couldn't run very far if a leopard chased me."

"I have to get back to my bridge," Manik said, turning to me. "Alasdair wants to speak to you."

"All right," I said. "Raja, you must come by and visit me the next time you are in Aynakhal."

"Most certainly, madam." Raja beamed. "And if there is any book you are looking for, please leave me a note and I will set it aside for you."

"No scratch marks?" Manik said as we walked back to the bar. "I saw you cozying up with the cat gang by the Ping-Pong table."

"Not sure I have anything in common with them," I confessed.

Manik gave me a warm appraising look. "They are jealous, that's what. You are too damn beautiful. Makes them feel dowdy."

"Rubbish," I said, but I felt a flutter in my stomach when he looked at me that way.

We walked back to the bar area and found the club bearer mopping the card table with a cheesecloth *jharan*. Alasdair looked ruefully at Manik.

"That was your whiskey, old chap." He flipped his finger to indicate he had tipped the glass over. "I just ordered you another one."

Larry shook his soggy matchbox. "*Cheesh*, Ally! Look what you did to my *deshloye*, you bugger." He skimmed his matchbox across the room, and landed it neatly inside a dustbin by the wall. He whistled softly. "Something tells me I am going to hear little Miss Debbie at darts tonight! Hey, Deb!" he yelled across at the bar. "C'mon, darling, let's have a game."

Alasdair smiled his deep, warm smile. "It's good to see you, Layla. Is Manik behaving himself?"

"No complaints so far," I said.

"I've been waiting to talk to you," said Alasdair. "To thank you."

"To thank me for what?"

"For being a friend to Jamina. She is very shy and does not talk to anyone, y'ken. Your friendship means a lot."

I wondered what Alasdair was talking about. I had never set eyes on Jamina.

"Jamina is really lonely," Alasdair continued. "She can't come to the club.... Nobody invites her anywhere. People act like OPs don't exist. But Jamina is more than that to me. In all these years, you, Layla, are the only person who has befriended her. Thank you for that."

I did not say anything, but I was beginning to connect the dots. The lady in the green sari came to my mind. She watched me from behind the hibiscus hedge outside our bungalow gate every morning. Was that Jamina? Why did she lie to Alasdair and tell him we were friends when we had not exchanged a single word? I once tried to approach her, but she turned and scuttled off as fast as her short legs could carry her as though she was being chased by a leopard. But now that I knew who she was, I had a plan.

CHAPTER

23

She was there again the next morning. The green of her sari blended perfectly with the color of the hedge. Betsy Lamont had described Alasdair's *chokri* as short and dumpy. The hibiscus hedge was barely five feet tall: the woman in the green sari was shorter.

I walked up to the railing and called out. "Jamina!"

The woman jerked her head and ducked behind the bush. I beckoned but she started to hurry away.

I ran down the stairs. "Jamina, wait!" I shouted. "Alasdair told me about you."

She turned around. I had expected Jamina to be a dusky nymphet, a hot chutney who had bewitched Alasdair and kept him faithful, but this was a homely girl with sad, drooping eyes.

"Come have some tea with me," I invited, but she stood there, her eyes downcast, fingering the free end of her sari.

"Please," I insisted.

Still there was no reaction. I gave up and started walking back to the bungalow when I heard the click of the gate latch open. She was following me. I waited in the veranda but Jamina never came up the stairs. The next thing I knew she was walking back toward the gate. She opened it and was gone.

The second day I called her again. This time she climbed the stairs, squatted on the veranda floor but did not touch the cup of tea I put on the peg table beside her.

The third day, Halua, on his own initiative, brought her a cup of salted tea in a chipped cup like the servants drank. Jamina drank the tea in noisy slurps and left without saying a word. I noticed if I paid her any attention she shied away, but if I ignored her, she lingered. Her behavior reminded me of a furtive jungle animal.

I was almost convinced she was a mute when on the fourth day Jamina began to talk. I could hardly believe my ears. Her whole story came tumbling out in a voice as high and thin as a mosquito, yards and yards of it in one whiny monologue.

She said her mother died when she was six and her stepfather, a poor Muslim fisherman, sold her to Auntie, where she worked as a servant girl while she awaited puberty. Auntie had big plans to auction off Jamina's virginity. She had heard of the "English King" who had become a tea planter and imagined Alasdair Carruthers to be very wealthy. Jamina was dressed up like an Indian bride and presented to Alasdair. Auntie had instructed her to let her sari slip off her shoulders so Alasdair could see her budding breasts. But the English King had looked shocked and walked out. Auntie slapped Jamina because she thought she had displeased him. But Alasdair returned the following week and offered to buy Jamina with the money he collected from selling two "purdah" guns to a colonel in Calcutta. The offer was so generous that Auntie had thrown a farewell feast.

"Purdah guns," I learned from Manik, were not religious Muslim firearms like I imagined but a pair of Purdys—heirloom hunting rifles worth a fortune that Alasdair had inherited from his grandfather. Manik commented that Alasdair must have cared a lot for Jamina, because no man in his right senses parted with a pair of Purdys.

"Alibaba is a good man," Jamina said. She called Alasdair "Alibaba" after his nickname "Ally," which Jamina mistook for "Ali," a Muslim name. They had not been intimate till she turned sixteen, Jamina said. Ever since she had been trying to conceive a child.

"I go to the Fertility Hill but Ali think I come to see you, *didi*." She addressed me easily as an older sister. "But you must not tell him where I go. He will be angry. He does not want me to go to the Fertility Hill."

The Fertility Hill was a popular place of pilgrimage with a dubious reputation. It was located inside the Negriting Tea Estate, between Chulsa and Aynakhal. Whether the name of the garden had anything to do with a slave girl is not known, but there was a hillock with a pagan shrine that had existed there for centuries. When Negriting was first established, the Fertility Hill was included as part of the property under the tacit agreement that the public would be allowed free access to it. This created serious problems for the Negriting management as all kinds of people traipsed through the garden to the Fertility Hill: barren brides, opium dealers and tantric ascetics with ash-covered bodies and matted hair, carrying trident spears. It attracted a criminal element and troublemakers who looked for an opportunity to "fertilize" any hopeful bride who came down the hill and often this led to brawls and bloodshed. There was an illegal shortcut through Aynakhal to Negriting that the fertility crowd trespassed through. Every now and then, Aynakhal management had to contend with a theft or some other misdemeanor, and it was always the Fertility Hill people behind it all.

"But I will tell you a secret, *didi*," said Jamina, loosening her sari petticoat string. "Feel my stomach. I think I am expecting a child."

Jamina's stomach was protruding to one side. It felt hard like a grapefruit.

"It is the baby's head," she said.

"Does Alasdair know?" I asked, feeling a little alarmed. Jamina's stomach did not look normal. "How long has this been…have you been pregnant?"

Jamina counted wordlessly on her fingers. "Eleven months," she said happily.

"*Eleven* months! You must see a doctor, Jamina. Tell Alasdair to call Doctor Emmett."

"Oh no," said Jamina, quickly covering up. "I cannot let an English doctor look at me without clothes."

She sounded like I used to.

"Jamina, you must see a doctor."

"I want to wait, *didi*. I am going to the village. I will find out from the midwife if it is a boy or girl. Then I will tell Ali."

I knew very little about pregnancy or childbirth but Jamina appeared to be completely clueless. She was naive and unworldly, and it was easy to see why. Alasdair had rescued her from the brink of low life when she was still very young and shielded her from the realities of the world. He was very protective and took full responsibility for her welfare. That, in my opinion, made Alasdair a very extraordinary and decent human being.

"Jamina, listen to me," I said. "Whatever the village midwife says, promise me you will see a doctor as soon as you return. This is important."

"There is no need, *didi*," said Jamina haughtily. "Village

midwife is very good. She is birthing babies all the time. Even bringing my own mother into the world. Then my brothers and me. All my aunties and uncles. No problem."

I was losing my patience. I had no choice but to resort to blackmail.

I looked her in the eye. "Are you saying you are not going to see a doctor, Jamina? All right, then I am going to tell Alasdair you have been lying to him all these weeks and going to the Fertility Hill instead of coming to see me. How about that? You have a choice."

Jamina stared at me as if I was the biggest traitor in the world.

"I am doing this for your own good," I added lamely.

She got up and walked off in a huff

Fearing I had jeopardized our friendship, I called out after her. "Jamina, please come again tomorrow." And I was relieved when the back of her head gave a little nod.

Aynakhal
27th March 1946
Moon, dear sister,
Letters are my lifeline in Aynakhal—my window to the real world. You have no idea how I wait for them. Our mail comes twice a week (Tuesdays and Thursdays), and Manik brings my letters home in the evening. I wait for him at the bottom of our hill and watch him carefully as he walks toward me. I can tell by his exaggerated casualness when there is something for me tucked inside his shirt. He makes me chase him up the hill and extracts as many "favors" as he can before he parts with my letters, the rascal!

I miss you, dear sister. I would give anything to share a cup of tea with you! Not that I am lonely here, mind you. Manik is wonderful company and Jamina comes every day. She is a simple girl and talks nonstop! Debbie Ashton is probably the closest I have to a friend. Debbie is writing a romance novel—"chutney fiction," she calls it.

Emma and Budni have become best friends. I made them saris by cutting up one of mine. The garden dhobi *burned a big hole in the saffron paisley one you liked so much. Never will I give my expensive saris to the* dhobi *again. I even stitched the girls tiny matching blouses and petticoats. You should just see those two playing house! They chatter nonstop in Hindustani and English with a lot of gibberish and head shaking thrown in. It just makes me realize language is never a barrier when there is a genuine desire to communicate.*

The younger wives at the club have no such desire where I am concerned. I will always be a misfit in their circle. The older ladies (Mrs. McIntyre and her friends) are gracious and very kind but there is an unspoken rule—I am expected to socialize with the Junior Assistants' wives.

You were curious about the "fishing fleet." Let me explain. The First World War, as you know, had wiped out a big section of the male population in Europe. The remaining men drifted to the colonies in search of jobs. India, as you can imagine, is the prime hunting ground for young girls and war widows. The "fishing fleet" are women who come to India every winter on the pretext of visiting a relative but more blatantly to hook a catch. I was surprised to learn the British government actually pays single women to travel overseas to find husbands. It's one way to make sure the whites marry into their own, I suppose. The ladies come in droves every winter and make a beeline for hill stations like Shillong and Simla, where most of the romancing takes place. I am told there is close to a stampede from young bachelors to seek their favor. The top pick of fleet ladies are the men in civil-service jobs living in big cities (look what Manik missed!). Next come the military lads and at the very bottom of the barrel are our poor tea planters.

Tea planters don't encounter much feminine company, as you can imagine—at least not the eligible kind. It takes a special kind of woman to make a good planter's wife. Debbie Ashton is a good example. She is independent, free-spirited and revels in adventure. Other wives adapt best as they can. Some suffer and survive, some run away.

Larry Baker is going to Silchar tomorrow and will post this letter. He will also pick up our order from Paul & Co. I am hoping the cake tin I ordered from Calcutta has arrived. Mrs. McIntyre has shared with me a wonderful recipe for Scottish Whiskey Dundee cake. The cake has to be "fed" four tablespoons of Scotch after baking. This makes it exceptionally rich and moist. Manik says if he got fed Scotch, he'd be rich and moist, too!

I am delighted to hear little Aesha knows so many words already. I think this one will be a chatterbox. As for Anik, I am glad he has a new favorite color, although I am not sure black makes his mother any happier.

I must end here, dear sister. I am writing to Mima next. Mima's letter to me is a long list of questions. It will take me three pages just to answer them all.
My love to you, Jojo and Anik & Aesha.
Layla

Manik ambled around to the back of the house looking for me. I was in the *malibari* instructing the *malis* to take down the trellis for the green beans they had spent all morning putting up in the wrong bed for the carrots.

"What? Is it lunchtime already?" I exclaimed.

"I'm home early," he said. "What's this bamboo crisscross thing?"

"For the green beans."

Manik made a face. When I turned around he plucked a sprig of fox grass and tickled the nape of my neck.

"Oooh!" I jumped, swiping my neck, thinking it was a caterpillar. The *malis* stopped in their work to stare at me.

Manik turned his bespectacled face, full of fake concern. "Is something wrong?"

"Behave yourself, will you," I laughed.

He flung the fox grass away, stuck his hands in his pockets and rocked on his heels. "Jimmy O'Connor was at the office. He came to see Mr. McIntyre."

"What about?"

"He shot a leopard in Dega and wanted to know about the one we killed. He didn't even bother getting a permit from the Forest Department."

"Won't he get into trouble? Won't that Mr. Sircar come after him?"

"Nobody comes after Jimmy O'Connor. That man is a law unto himself. Jimmy O'Connor says Sircar is a far bigger menace than the animals. He'd shoot Sircar on the wing tip, if he could. If Sircar shows his face at his bungalow, Jimmy sends his wild geese and dogs to chase him out."

It sounded as though the Forest Department had enough reasons, legitimate or otherwise, to concern themselves with Jimmy O'Connor. Kaziranga, the neighboring wildlife sanctuary, bordered three tea gardens: Aynakhal, Chulsa and Dega, but the major portion fell on the Dega side. It was common to have large animals wander into the tea plantations—water buffalo, elephants or deer, mostly. They were easily chased out. Leopards were a bigger menace, especially if they became man-eaters and started prowling the labor lines.

"Is it true Jimmy O'Connor killed a rogue elephant?"

"Not one—goodness, he has killed several! He's an excellent shikari. Jimmy is the only planter in Assam who can take down a rogue with a single shot. He never misses."

Rogue elephants were a tricky target, Manik explained. A shikari had only one chance to kill it by aiming at a spot precisely between the eye and earlobe. If he missed, most likely he was mashed meat. The demented fury of a rogue elephant is legend. Bloodcurdling stories abound in shikar lore. Typically a double-barrel .375 Magnum rifle is used with a four-inch bullet: powerful enough to stop a train. Not many tea planters owned such a weapon. Jimmy O'Connor owned not just one, but two Magnum rifles.

"Is that story about his wife true?" I asked.

"Yes, although the elephant did not kill her directly. Jimmy's wife got chased by a rogue and drowned in a river. Alasdair knew Jimmy's wife. They were just newly married, back then. He and Marie—I think that was her name—were fishing in Upper Assam when they encountered a rogue on the riverbank. The elephant backed Marie into the river and she was swept away by the current and drowned. The rogue came back to chase Jimmy up a tree. He spent a whole day with the beast trumpeting and shaking the tree. He escaped with his life but it became his obsession to kill this rogue. He spent months tracking it down. During this period, it was rumored he stayed with the Naga headhunters in a tree house, ate monkey meat and drank goat's blood. Finally he shot the elephant deep in Naga foothills. Alasdair says Jimmy was unrecognizable when he returned with his matted hair and tattered clothes. He brought back the massive tusk and had it capped in silver. He keeps Marie's ashes inside it, I believe."

I could just picture Jimmy O'Connor holding aloft the bloody tusk of the slain elephant. There was a primitive caveman quality about the man.

"I don't understand how he can pull the trigger of a gun, let alone kill a rogue with a single shot, if he is missing his forefinger," I said. "How did he lose his finger, anyway?"

"I have no idea. Some say he lost it in the war. Larry thinks it was bitten off by a rabid dog. Jimmy O'Connor is not the kind you can ask such questions. Coming to think of it, I am not sure how he fires a gun, but he is a crack shot, and I don't believe he is left-handed because Alasdair borrows guns from him all the time."

"Such a curious man, with his geese and tomatoes."

"The geese, I know about, but what tomatoes?"

"The ladies at the club were saying that he grows some kind of heirloom tomato and won't share the seeds with anyone."

Manik laughed. "That sounds like Jimmy, all right. That man's a genius. He is undoubtedly one of the best tea planters in Assam. He invented a cloning method for tea bushes that yields a premium leaf grade, and he won't share that secret with anyone, either. Dega Tea Estate has always had an edge over other gardens because of him. But he is a bit unpredictable with his drinking problem."

"That's because his wife died so tragically," I said, feeling sorry for the poor man.

Manik snorted. "A nice story to butter up the ladies, if you ask me. Jimmy O'Connor is Irish—alcohol is in his blood. He was a tippler long before his wife died."

"So, how did he know it was the same elephant—the one he shot—that killed his wife?"

"It had a bifurcated tail—"

"A what?"

"A tail split in its extremity. Tea-garden coolies believe an elephant with a bifurcated tail will one day take human life. Coolies are very superstitious. I think that's nonsense, really.

Rupali, our garden elephant, has a split tail, but she is gentle as a lamb and *saves* human lives."

"She's female, though. They are more docile than males, aren't they? Rogues are the male elephants in heat, right?"

"'In *musth*,' they call the condition. You can tell when a male elephant is in *musth* by a dark secretion that oozes just above their eye. In that condition they are extremely dangerous and will destroy anything."

"So how do they deal with domesticated male elephants when they are in *musth*?"

"The *mahuts*, their trainers, know how to handle them. They mix small amounts of opium in their diet and stand the elephant in a river for several hours a day to calm it down. The *musth* only lasts for a few days, but sometimes rogues get permanently deranged. When that happens, they have to be killed. The one that killed Jimmy O'Connor's wife was a permanently deranged one, I believe." Manik looked at me seriously. "I can show you a domesticated elephant in *musth*, if you like. They are not dangerous or anything."

I swiveled around. "Really? Where?"

"We have one here in Aynakhal. Now if you will kindly follow me to the bedroom…"

"*Ufff!*" I said, slapping his arm.

I suppressed a smile. Lately I noticed my ears no longer turned red when Manik teased me. His innuendos titillated, but they no longer embarrassed me like they did before.

Aynakhal
7th April 1946
Dear Dadamoshai,
I am sending this letter through Jamina, who is going to her
village. I am also sending you some fresh cauliflower from my

garden and a bottle of homemade marmalade. This is an old Scottish recipe shared by Mrs. McIntyre. She is a wonderful mentor and has been helping me to plan my garden. I was a little late with the flowers this year, but I am redesigning the flower beds to get them ready for next season. I have three new malis. The old mali was a hopeless opium addict and his two helpers complete duffers.

Kalua and Halua are so set in their bad habits. I have to do periodic kitchen inspections to make sure it stays clean. Kalua still can't cut a chicken without gripping it with his dirty toe and using some kind of hatchet. It is an uphill battle with those two. That goes, too, for their master, who views anything remotely green on his plate with suspicion. I finally got sick of our poultry diet and asked Kalua to buy mutton at the local haat. The next day I heard a loud commotion and here comes Kalua pulling a young, knock-kneed goat right into the living room to show me. The goat dropped pellets all over the house and almost made lunch out of my curtains.

But I must admit Kalua is picking up some nice recipes from the Mung borchee at the burrabungalow. The borchee is not happy about sharing his secrets but Mrs. McIntyre has ordered him to give cooking lessons to Kalua every Wednesday, so he has no choice. The borchee tries to slyly leave out some crucial ingredient or the other to throw Kalua off track, but Kalua, being a canny fellow, catches on or improvises. The other day, to our delight, he turned out a chicken Kiev fit for a king.

Among my other accomplishments: I have learned to drive the jeep and shoot a gun! Manik insists they are both basic requirements. When I asked him why, he said for the same reason one needs to know how to swim if one lives on a boat. Imagine my surprise when I shot a jungle fowl! I think the poor creature died of a heart attack, because we could not find a single bullet wound.

I hope you can visit us in Aynakhal soon, Dadamoshai.
There is so much I want to show you. Please give my best wishes
to Boris Ivanov. How long will he be staying with you?
With my love,
Layla

The topless Willys jeep careened to a halt and out jumped
a windblown and dusty Debbie Ashton.

"Who was that short girl in the green sari?" she said, nodding toward the gate.

"That's Jamina," I replied. When Debbie looked blank I
added, "Alasdair's…"

Debbie's eyes widened. "You know Alasdair's OP?"

"Well, yes."

Debbie gave a little jump. "Oh, I'd love to meet her. Can
I?" she cried. "Do you think she'll talk to me?"

"I don't know," I said doubtfully. "Jamina's awfully shy."

I told her briefly about Jamina's life.

"Fantastic fiction material," Debbie said meditatively. "Will
you introduce us?"

"Of course," I replied, "but don't be surprised if she clams
up."

"I'll wear a sari, if that helps. Every time I see Emmi in her
sari, I want to wear one."

I laughed. "I'll put one on for you."

"When do you suppose I can meet her?"

"Jamina is going to her village tomorrow. She'll be back
after two weeks. Usually she's here every day around nine. She
sits and drinks her salt tea on the floor—don't ask me why.
Maybe she is more comfortable that way."

"I will wear a sari, sit on the floor and drink salt tea, as well.
Also, can I go home wearing the sari? Imagine Robby's surprise

when he sees Emma and me waiting for him like maharanis on the veranda! Talking about that rascal, is she here?"

"She's out in the back playing with Wendy."

"Goodness, I have been all over the place looking for her. First to Jimmy O'Connor's, where I got nipped by a damn goose." She twisted her ankle to show me a cut above her shin. "Those geese bite everyone except Emma. She orders the dogs, the geese and even Uncle Jimmy around, bossy little thing that she is."

"Do you want some Dettol for that cut?"

"Nah, it's nothing," said Debbie. "I better go and get Emmi. I forgot today is her best friend Shirley's birthday. They adore each other. We better not forget to take our present. It's in the bathtub."

"What is it, a fish?" I asked.

Debbie laughed. "No, a guinea pig. Emmi wanted to give her best friend a brown-and-white guinea pig exactly like her Chico. So she goes crying to Uncle Jimmy, and Uncle Jimmy sends someone scooting off God only knows where to get a brown-and-white guinea pig. What that man won't do for Emma Ashton, I tell you. No wonder she wants to marry him."

"Why is the guinea pig in the bathtub?"

"I tried to put it in the cage with Chico but they're both males and almost killed each other. Who knew guinea pigs can be so aggressive."

We walked around to the back of the bungalow, where I found, to my chagrin, Emma and Budni feeding nubs of carrots, picked from my *malibari*, to the goat. The goat wore Budni's pink ribbon around its neck, and from the spoiled look on its face, I had my doubts we would see goat curry on our table soon.

"Emmi, c'mon darling. It's Shirley's birthday. Don't you want to go to her party?"

Emma stared back at her mother, a big mud streak on her cheek. She played absently with the goat's ear. It flicked her fingers away. "Can we go tomorrow?"

"Don't be silly, darling. Her birthday is today. Hurry up now. We have to put the guinea pig in a box and get ourselves cleaned up, don't we?"

"Can Wendy come to the birthday party?"

Debbie sighed. "Why are you being so difficult, darling?"

"*Please*, Mummy!" Emma pleaded, stamping her foot.

Debbie turned to me. "Actually, I don't see why Wendy can't come along to Shirley's party. I'll make her wear one of Emma's dresses. Where is Halua? Let me ask him."

"Are you sure?" I said. The children of servants never played with bungalow children, let alone went to their birthday parties.

"Oh, absolutely," laughed Debbie. "I don't suppose you've met Jill Melling of Tarajuli Tea Estate, have you? Shirley's mother? Jill is wonderful. All the servant children are invited for Shirley's birthday party. They are given pretty new clothes to wear and share Shirley's birthday gifts. None of this elitist baba-bibi nonsense with Jill, thank God."

Halua appeared at the pantry door.

"Halua!" Debbie said. "I am taking Wendy to a baba's birthday party in Tarajuli, all right?"

Halua's eyes widened. He looked at me uncertainly.

"It's all right," I said.

Debbie clapped her hands. "Girls, get in the jeep, quick. No, Emma Ashton, we are not taking the goat."

"But, Mummy—"

"Do you want me to get really cross with you? Come on,

who wants to have a race? We are going to run to the jeep. On your mark, get set—GO!" She galloped after the girls. "Ta, Layla, I'll see you Monday at the club."

CHAPTER
24

Jamina was inconsolable. The village midwife told her she was having a white man's devil child, a curse that would bring bad luck to her family, maybe even her whole village. The shaman gave her a *tabiz* to wear—a magic amulet inscribed with a spell to ward off evil.

"That's nonsense," I said. "You have to see Doctor Emmett. You must, Jamina—this could be serious."

"But, *didi*, how can I allow English doctor to see me?" she howled. "What if he is taking advantage of me?"

"He is a doctor, Jamina. He won't do that. He needs to examine you."

"Where?"

"*There.*"

Jamina let out a shriek. "*Why?* Midwife only look at fingernail and say if it boy, girl or devil child. Nobody seeing me *there*, *didi*, nobody."

"Listen to me, Jamina," I said a little sternly. "What you have growing inside may not be a baby. It could be a medical problem. You have to see a doctor because you may need treatment."

Jamina sighed noisily and a fat tear rolled down her cheek
and wobbled on her chin.

I tried to mollify her. "Doctor Emmett is an elderly man,
Jamina. He's very nice. He examined me. I will stay with you,
during the examination, if you like."

Jamina blew her nose into her sari and looked at me balefully through puffy eyes. "I am letting English doctor see me,
didi, only if you are staying in same room. I am coming to
your house and English doctor see me in *your* house. I am not
wanting Ali's servants see I alone inside bedroom with English man and door close."

Doctor Emmett came to see Jamina on his next round to
Aynakhal. Jamina clutched me with crablike claws, covered her
face with her sari and shrieked through the entire examination.

Doctor Emmett stared at her in exasperation. "I'll never understand why these *chokri* girls make such a holy racket. This
procedure is not supposed to hurt at all. They fight like wild-
cats and have to be held down the entire time. And all for a
routine exam. It makes absolutely no sense to me."

He washed his hands in a basin of water and reached for the
hand towel I was holding. "I don't know if this is good news
or bad news, but she is not pregnant. What she has looks suspiciously like a tumor. Carruthers must know she needs to see
a specialist. He should not delay." Doctor Emmett glanced at
his watch. "I will go by Chulsa and tell him myself. I can give
his girl a lift home, if she likes."

I translated for Jamina but she stared at me as if I was sending her home with her rapist.

"I think she'd rather walk," I told Doctor Emmett.

McNeil & Smith, the parent company of Chulsa Tea Estate,
refused to pay for Jamina's medical expenses.

"It's such a shame, really," Manik said. "Jamina is not Alasdair's legal wife, so she is not entitled to medical benefits. And because she is not employed by the tea garden, she can't even get the basic medical care the coolie women receive. It's terrible, really."

"So what will happen to her now?" I asked.

"Ally wants to marry her. That way Jamina will at least get the medical attention she deserves."

"Doctor Emmett said it could be serious."

"Ally is aware of that. Jamina will need to see a specialist in Calcutta. Ally wants to get married this weekend. I said you'd organize the wedding."

"Organize a wedding this weekend!" I gasped. I wished Manik would consult me before making such sweeping offers. "I don't know the first thing about weddings, Manik! Besides, what *kind* of wedding? Alasdair is Scottish. Jamina is Muslim...."

"Ally just wanted a simple court registration, but Jamina says she wants to dress up like an Indian bride. I don't think the religious part matters too much. Just throw something together, will you, darling? I told them not to worry—you'd take care of everything."

The wedding was a scramble. Alasdair and Jamina went to Silchar, where Dadamoshai got their marriage registered in the courthouse. Later that evening we had a small Indian celebration in our bungalow. I dressed up Jamina in my gold *Benarasi* sari and put flowers in her hair and painted red *alta* on her feet.

Jamina's father and brother had driven back with them from the fishing village to attend the ceremony. Her father was a foxy man with cunning eyes. I saw his gaze wander greedily around our bungalow, sizing up our meager possessions. Jamina's brother was a towering hulk of a man with tattooed arms and a prominent sickle-shaped scar running across his cheek. He lurked in the corners and looked so thuggish, he was almost a caricature.

Budni and Emma, dressed in their tiny saris, showered marigold petals on the bride. Debbie made a pineapple upside-down wedding cake and Kalua served his famous egg and chicken banquet, with a mutton curry thrown in. The goat was finally sacrificed for a good cause. The mishmash evening ended with the men getting hopelessly drunk. Irish, Scottish and Indian tea planters joined Muslim fishermen to sing ribald songs and do coolie dances around the veranda with their arms around each other's waists.

Debbie Ashton sat cross-legged on the floor of our veranda with a notebook on her lap, tapping a pencil on her teeth.

"Where's that Jamina today?" She frowned.

I glanced at the clock in the living room. "Goodness, quarter to eleven! That's not like her at all!"

Most mornings Debbie came to our bungalow to chat with Jamina. They would sit on the floor, drink salt tea while Debbie took copious notes. Sometimes I was called to act as interpreter, but mostly they managed without me, having devised their own creative ways of communicating that reminded me of Emma and Budni. Today I had invited them to stay for lunch. I was so busy in the pantry showing Kalua how to make Bengali fish croquettes, the kind Chaya made in Dadamoshai's house, that I lost track of time.

The latch of the front gate clicked open. It was the office peon on his bicycle. He had a note from Manik.

Alasdair lost his job today. I am going with him to Dega to talk to Jimmy O'Connor.
M.

"That is unbelievable!" cried Debbie. "Alasdair is one of the best tea planters. I bet this has nothing to do with his job performance. I get the feeling it's because he married Jamina. Tea companies have a very low tolerance for this kind of thing."

"Surely they can't sack him for marrying someone," I said.

"Oh, you bet they can," said Debbie with a trace of bitterness in her voice. "And they make no bones about it. As long as planters toe the line, tea companies are good to them. Step out of line and you're buggered."

"I am sure Alasdair will find another job. There are other tea companies," I said.

Debbie shot me a skeptical look. "I don't know about that, Layla. British companies are very clannish. They can boycott you. I've seen it happen. Once blacklisted, especially for this kind of thing, Alasdair can be out in the cold. What is so ironic—a planter can be unethical, steal from the company, even run the tea garden into the ground, but some desperate company will still hire him because he knows all about making tea. But marrying an OP—" she wagged her pencil " that's crossing a dangerous line." She sighed. "I wish my jeep was not in the workshop today. We could have gone to Chulsa to see Jamina. The poor thing must be so upset."

Rob Ashton came to pick up Debbie that evening. Manik was back home, and the four of us were drinking tea on the veranda. Alasdair's news had shaken us all. As I listened to Manik talk, one thing became increasingly clear: tea planters were misfits in any other job but tea. No other profession demanded the same acumen, the grueling on-the-job training and adherence to a unique lifestyle, like tea. Where would Manik go if he did not have his tea job? He had drifted too far from the mainstream to fit elsewhere. He gave up everything for tea, yet the company could terminate his job for no fault of his. It was a scary thought.

"McNeil & Smith's official reason for sacking Ally is he broke the company rule and got married without giving his thirty-day notice," said Manik. "That hogwash! The real reason is they don't approve of Jamina. She is not considered appropriate."

"They were never happy about Ally's association with Jamina to begin with," Debbie said. "She was not just another *chokri* girl. He was too committed. He even visited her family in their village."

"Putting it crudely, Ally's pecker went too deep," Rob added.

"*Chokris* are meant to be dispensable. You are not supposed to get too attached," added Manik.

"I find the hypocrisy shocking," said Debbie. "Tea companies encourage planters to get involved with local women, use them as sleeping dictionaries, even father illegitimate children, but when it comes to marrying them, it's a taboo."

"They are paranoid about who you marry," said Manik. "You should have seen the way I got grilled about Layla, and she's educated, English speaking, and her grandfather a Cambridge lawyer who personally knows James Lovelace."

"Otherwise they could have refused permission?" I asked a little incredulously.

Manik looked at me. "Without a doubt. Kona wouldn't have made the cut, for sure. So you see, either way, I would have got out of that arranged marriage."

"Who's Kona? What arranged marriage?" asked Debbie.

"Kona's the girl I was engaged to before Layla begged me to marry her."

"Rubbish!" I laughed.

"Now, if Layla was a white girl," Manik continued, "even if she was of dubious character, there would be no scrutiny at all. That is how two-faced tea companies are."

"So what is Ally going to do now?" I said.

"He will have to look for another job," said Rob. "I doubt if he will find one with a British tea company, but things are changing in Assam. Jimmy O'Connor was saying many Sterling tea gardens are being sold to Indian businessmen. They're looking for experienced tea planters to run them because Indians don't have a clue about growing tea or plantation management."

"Any tea garden will be lucky to have Ally," said Manik. "He's an excellent planter. But the management style under Indian ownership is bound to be different. It will be interesting to see how the labor reacts to Indian owners. They are used to an all-white management."

Debbie gave Manik a poke in the ribs. "So how come you pass off as a *peelywally*, old chap?"

"I hide my spots well, darling," Manik said with a grin.

"If the owners are Indian, maybe Jamina won't feel so ostracized. She may even make a friend or two," said Debbie.

"I am not so sure," I said. "In some ways Indians are more prejudiced about religion, caste and social status than white people. A blue-blooded Scot married to a Muslim prostitute is a tough fit anywhere."

"How long do you think it will be before Ally finds a job?" Debbie asked.

"It's hard to tell," said Manik. "Jimmy O'Connor is making some inquiries. Ally has been given a week to vacate his bungalow. The company is coming down hard on him." He turned to me. "I offered them our guest room, darling. They may stay with us for a while. Jimmy also offered his bungalow but Jamina says she wants to stay here."

"They can also stay with us," said Debbie quickly. "Such a damn shame. Ally rakes in big profits for McNeil & Smith every year. All he wants to do is take care of the woman he loves. And what does the company do? Kick him out. Why? Because he's a threat to the status quo. If planters start marrying their OPs the whole pukka tea culture would unravel, wouldn't it? This is the kind of dishonesty that almost makes me ashamed to be British."

A silvery dusk was falling, and we fell into quiet introspection. The soft gray of the distant trees pulsed with the pinpricks of fireflies. They floated into the veranda and alighted on everyday objects to paint them with the strokes of a dream. We never saw their wings; all we ever saw was their light.

Jimmy O'Connor did indeed have connections. He made some inquiries and got Alasdair a job in a tea garden in the Dooars district of West Bengal, three hundred miles away. The tea garden had just changed hands to Indian ownership.

Alasdair took Jamina to Calcutta for her treatment. Just as she had dreaded, her stomach had to be cut open and the tumor removed. It was a benign growth but unfortunately during the operation they had to remove her uterus, as well. The implications of that were lost on her.

Jamina clung to me and wept. "There is no Fertility Hill where I am going, *didi*. How to have a child now? How to live so far from my Abba? He so old—what if he die? How to live so far from *you*?"

There was little I could say to console her. Jamina would be unmoored and set adrift in an unfamiliar world. I knew that feeling only too well. But I also know this: even though water chooses the path of least resistance, it ultimately defines its own course. Rivers divide and merge, they braid and weave, they form complex wholes. They move apart only to rejoin at a different point. The geography of our lives would reconnect us again.

CHAPTER
25

In the spring of 1946, Percival Edwards Williams joined Chulsa Tea Estate as the new Junior Assistant. The pomposity of his name belied his tiny stature, so he was quickly nicknamed Peewee. Peewee looked not a day over twelve, though his official records claimed he was nineteen. He was a baby-faced lad, slightly built like a jockey, with a romp of golden curls and an enviable set of lashes. Peewee spent his first week recuperating from his mosquito bites and a terrible attack of diarrhea. Jimmy O'Connor's eyes almost popped when he saw tiny Peewee tiptoe into his office. According to Rob Ashton, who was present, Jimmy O'Connor wagged the stub of his missing finger to intimidate Peewee and acted as if he would eat the poor fellow with a toothpick.

Larry Baker took up the manly challenge of hand-rearing Peewee Williams. Barely had his mosquito bites subsided when Peewee, doused with whiskey, was marched off to Auntie's for his primary education. Larry played with Peewee for his own amusement. He made sure Peewee got his vernacular nicely jumbled: he confused *chokri* (girl) with *tokri* (basket) and *pisab* (piss) with *hisab* (accounts) and unwittingly said the most hilarious things. He turned crimson when the coolie women shrieked with laughter. But he was a good sport overall and had a sweet milk-fed charm that endeared him easily to women.

I was bottling my second batch of gooseberry jam in the pantry when I heard the wheezy honk of the Aston Martin coming up our driveway. Larry was at the wheel with Flint, the Kotalgoorie assistant, riding alongside while tiny Peewee bounced like a marble in the backseat.

"Yo, Manny!" yelled Larry, as the engine spluttered down.

He bounded up the stairs followed by Flint. Manik was in the living room reading peacefully on the sofa.

"Oh, Man-ny boy," sang Larry from the veranda. "The pi-pes the pi-pes are ca-all ing. Where are you, old chap. Where's Layla."

"She's in the pantry," Manik said, stirring from the sofa. "What's up, fellows?"

"Are you up for some bridge?" Flint asked. "Your old comrades eagerly await thee. We are playing at my bungalow and we need a fourth hand."

Manik shook his head. "I don't think so. I'm really…"

Flint held up his hand. His face wore a pious expression. "Spare us the excuses, old man. Just so that you know, you are getting awfully antisocial these days. I understand you have domestic duties, being married and all, but forgetting your old friends is a real shame—that's all I'm saying."

"Exactly!" agreed Larry. "Come on, Manny, just a few rubbers and we will drop you right back. Peewee here is keen to learn bridge. I told him you are a champion player."

"Is Manny coming?" called Peewee from the bottom of the stairs.

"Not a chance," Flint called back peevishly. "Manny is stuck to his wet nurse these days. What a crying shame."

"Wait, fellows," said Manik. "Let me see what Layla is doing. Maybe I can play for a little while. But I have to be home for dinner, though."

Flint snapped his fingers. "Attaboy. Go ask the old lady, will you?"

Manik sauntered into the pantry, hands in his pockets. Of course I had heard the whole conversation.

"Go," I said, waving him off, before he could open his mouth. "I don't want to be called your wet nurse."

"They are only joking, darling."

"I know, but please go. I have things to do here."

Manik kissed my neck and grinned happily. "Only for a few hours. I'll be home for dinner." He hurried out of the pantry. "Boys, I'm coming!" he yelled.

"Brilliant! No need to take your jeep, Manny," said Flint. "We'll drop you back. Oh, got a dram to spare, old chap? I am running low."

"Only some cheap whiskey."

"That'll do."

Larry poked his head into the pantry. "You're a brick, darling. We'll make sure your old man is back home for dinner. Boy, that jam looks awfully good."

It was past dinnertime, past bedtime, and there was no sign of Manik. The generator powered down, the lights went off, Halua and Kalua went home and Potloo reported for duty. In the distance the jackals howled, but still no sign of Manik. I must have fallen asleep on the sofa because when I woke the clock in the living room was striking twelve. *Midnight!* I sat up in panic. *Where was Manik?* Something terrible must have happened. Did Larry's old jalopy break down in the jungle? Was there an animal attack? Kotalgoorie was only seven miles away. I could possibly drive Manik's jeep, very slowly. I decided to take Potloo along and carry Manik's gun.

I banged on the door to Potloo's hut, but it was like trying to raise the dead. He finally emerged bleary-eyed, wrapped in his scratchy old blanket.

"I have to get *Chotasahib*," I said hurriedly. "Get in the jeep and bring your torch."

The jeep growled to life, coughed and died. I tried again and the engine throbbed and held. The gears engaged with a terrible squeal and the vehicle lurched forward. I sat at the very edge of the seat and inched out of the driveway, my hands white-knuckled on the steering wheel. Potloo sat behind, gripping the back of the passenger seat as we bumped down the hill and into the pitch-black night.

The night was thick, and eyes of furtive animals gleamed in the headlights. I drove the entire way in first gear and instructed Potloo to check the sides of the jungle road with the flashlight for signs of an accident—an upturned vehicle or, God forbid, bloodied human remains. But there was none, thank God. We entered the Kotalgoorie Tea Estate gate and drove past the factory to Flint's bungalow. All the lights were blazing. Flint had the luxury of a small kerosene generator in his bungalow. His manager was easygoing, so his bungalow was pretty much the party house for young assistants.

It was close to one o'clock when I arrived. There was a big racket going on and nobody heard me pull up on the driveway. I killed the engine and paused, listening. Somebody was twanging a guitar; there were shouts, drunken voices singing rowdy Irish songs and shrieks of female laughter.

I got out of the car. My head was thundering as I marched up the stairs. The living room was in shambles. Beer, whiskey bottles, glasses and plates strewn everywhere. Flint was flat on his back, his head cradled in the bosom of a dusky female, her sari falling off her shoulders. She was feeding him bits of what looked like omelet from a plate on the floor. Larry was shirtless, perched on the sideboard with his ankles locked around a slant-eyed girl, singing lustily. Peewee had passed out, like a baby bird on the sofa, and Manik and another fellow whom I did not recognize were attempting to build a house of playing cards on the coffee table. Manik swayed like a leaf in the breeze, trying vainly to tent two cards together. His glasses were hanging off the tip of his nose. He was hopelessly and completely drunk.

"Manik!" My voice slashed through the room like a whip. There was an instant chill in the air. Larry's hand froze on the guitar. The omelet froze halfway to Flint's mouth; the girls froze in their tittering and Manik glanced at me, then quickly down at the two cards on the table, which were now miraculously tented together.

"I believe that is my wife," he told the other fellow. He looked confused, not knowing whether to be dismayed at seeing me or triumphant at the tented cards. "I have to be home for dinner. I am a married man, you know."

All eyes were riveted on me. Suddenly I was mortified to think how I must have appeared: in my crushed sari and disheveled hair, I was the very caricature of the irate wife chasing down her faithless husband. I was the killjoy and a laughingstock. A hot wave of humiliation washed over me as I stood there blinking back the sting of my tears.

The awful silence woke up Peewee. He looked around fearfully. "What's going on, fellows?"

What followed was a confused babble, everybody talking at once.

I looked at Manik. "Let's go," I said acidly.

"Oh boy," said Larry, glancing at the others nervously.

I turned around and marched down the stairs.

Flint ran out to the veranda and peered over the railing. "Bloody hell, she drove here by herself. I didn't even know she could drive."

"Where is my shoe? Has anybody seen my shoe?" I heard Manik shout.

"Forget the shoe, old chap," said Flint. "You better go." He said to the others, "She'll make mutton chop out of him."

Manik tumbled down the stairs, wearing one shoe.

"Goodbye, fellows, have to be home for dinner. I am a married man, you know."

Blinded by tears and fury, I drove back to Aynakhal. Manik lolled around in the passenger seat and slept soundly. I left him in the jeep, went upstairs and locked the bedroom door. Potloo must have put him to bed that night, because in the morning Manik was asleep on the living-room couch, covered with Potloo's scratchy old blanket. How he made it to *kamjari* on time is anybody's guess.

Assam lies on a seismic fault that is wide and disastrous. Mild tremors are common. Once in a while, the earth gives an involuntary shudder as if imagining something frightful. The old bungalow creaks, lightbulbs sway and people forget what they were saying. One time we were halfway through dinner when it felt as though someone gave a violent jolt to the dining table. The walls weaved a little, the silverware clattered and the water glasses formed shuddering whirlpools. Then, just as abruptly, it all settled down.

The earthquake that hit Assam the first summer I was in Aynakhal measured 6.5 on the Richter scale. When I look back, I recall there was something different in the air that evening—a rigid stillness almost, like a clamped throat. The dusk did not linger as it normally does in Assam and night fell swiftly. There was not a single sound, not a single firefly.

Manik and I did not speak the whole next day after I pulled him out of Flint's. There was icy silence, and Manik crept about like a thief, coughing nervously. He looked awful and I'm certain he felt worse. I was still giving him the royal snub.

"The lads are very impressed with your driving," Manik offered, trying to be friendly.

I gave him a frosty look. "I don't care what the lads are impressed with, and I am certainly not impressed with *you*."

He took his evening tea alone in the veranda while I stayed in the bedroom. When he came into the bedroom for his bath, I went out to the living room. I sat at the writing desk and tried to compose a letter to Moon. Through tear-blurred eyes, I wondered how to tell her of my tragically flawed marriage. Each word took so long to write, the ink kept drying on the nib of my fountain pen until I ran out of ink altogether. I was filling my pen with the dropper from the inkwell when a movement against the wall caught my eye. It was about a foot long, thin like a snake but without the writhing serpentine motion, rather it bobbed up and down in a straight line. I moved a little closer to take a look and found to my utter astonishment a long line of very tiny mice. They were holding one another's tails and scurrying rapidly along the edge of the wall in a single file. The tiny convoy then turned the corner of the living room and disappeared into the darkness of the veranda. It was the most bizarre thing I had ever encountered, and I had no idea what to make of it.

Three minutes later, the inkwell flew off the desk and smashed against the wall. Books tumbled off the shelves, and the ground began to move in a violent sideways motion like a giant sieve. The desk tipped and jammed the bookshelf into the wall. I lost my balance and grabbed the sofa, watching in horror as it slid toward the dining table, dragging me along.

Manik ran out from the bathroom covered in soapsuds and wrapped in a towel.

"Get out!" he screamed. "NOW!"

The floor was tipping in the opposite direction now. He yanked me to my feet. We bolted down the stairs and ran to the far reaches of the garden. Halua, Kalua, Potloo and their families were already gathered outside, shouting, screaming and crying. When I turned around the bungalow was a sight to behold. The massive structure was shaking violently. The lightbulbs swung in giant arcs, there were rattles and thuds and then, like a giant freight train slamming on its brakes, it all came to a sudden and shuddering stop.

A split second of dead silence was followed by pandemonium. Thousand of voices broke out in the night, mixed with the braying of petrified cattle and the barking of dogs.

The crowd on our lawn began to ungroup. A quick head count revealed everybody was safe. The biggest wonder of all was that Manik's bath towel was still in place. In the midst of the chaos he had quietly slipped his arms around my waist. He held on to me like a drowning man, and I could feel his heart thudding through his bare chest.

"Please don't leave me, Layla," he whispered in a tortured voice.

I was so relieved we had both escaped unharmed, I could only cover his hand with mine and squeeze as Manik tightened his arms around me.

I believe sometimes the heavens move in curious ways to solve human dilemmas. A hornet was dispatched to solve our sex problem, but it took an earthquake to mend our squabble.

* * *

There was no sleep for anyone that night. No lights, no fan, either. The power lines were down and it was swelteringly hot. Without bothering to rinse off the soap from his body, Manik pulled on his trousers and ran to check the state of the factory. Damage to the structure and equipment would mean a major blow with the second flush plucking season just around the corner. But miraculously Aynakhal had been spared. Other than clearing the debris and straightening up the mess, there appeared to be no major damage.

Just when we thought the worst was over, the next day there was another calamity. Manik had gone to Mariani after breakfast, and I was reading on the veranda when I heard a sudden rumbling followed by what I can best describe as a wet slapping sound, like a loud *phlaat*, that came from the master bedroom. The sound was so loud that even the floor shook a little. I ran to the bedroom to find a large portion of the thatched roof had fallen in and entirely covered my grandmother's dressing table. Clumps of moldy straw, splinters of bamboo and rattan were strewn in massive heaps all over the bedroom, and a four-foot square patch of blue sky peeped overhead. What was more alarming was the bedroom was crawling with *snakes*! Several dozen baby banded kraits that had been nesting in the thatch descended with the debris. There they were all tangled up in a fat, writhing knot. I stood on the bed and screamed for help. Halua, Kalua and the *malis* ran to get sticks, brooms and shovels. By the time they returned all the snakes had vanished. The whole lot. The babies sought refuge in every nook and crevice they could find. They crawled inside our clothes cupboard and the laundry basket in the bathroom, and when we looked in Manik's shoes, each one had an angry baby krait hissing inside. Some even managed to slink off into the living room and veranda.

Mrs. McIntyre got news of our roof collapse and sent us sandwiches through her driver. Manik returned from Mariani at lunchtime to find the house pell-mell. That day the servants killed twenty nine baby kraits and days later they were still showing up in odd places. We even found one quietly curled on top of a record jacket right on Frank Sinatra's face, looking exactly like a mustache.

Since we had no roof over our heads, Manik and I moved into the guest room—the one with the hole in the floor. Halua, Kalua and Potloo spent the better part of the night clearing out Manik's hunting junk so that we could sleep. It was well after midnight when we finally went to bed.

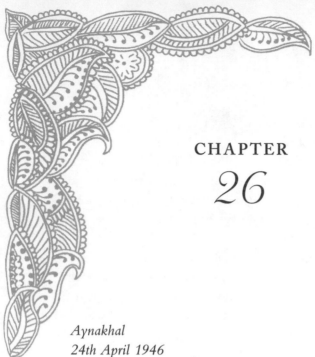

CHAPTER

26

Aynakhal
24th April 1946
Dear Dadamoshai,

I know you must be worried hearing about the earthquake. The epicenter was thirty miles from Aynakhal. But we are all safe. Our Chung bungalow withstood the tremors fairly well, considering how old it is. The only damage was that a part of the roof in our bedroom caved in. Huge mounds of moldy thatch everywhere! The roofs of these old-style bungalows are very heavily thatched to keep out all the rain we get here and sometimes the beams rot and give way. This is common. Oh, and the biggest dilemma of all! Our bungalow was crawling with snakes—banded kraits! They are extremely venomous. Halua and Potloo have killed more than two dozen so far.

The Jardine Henley director flew in today from Calcutta to do garden inspection. You will never guess who it is? James Lovelace! Charlie, the Jardine's pilot, flew the small yellow Cessna low over our bungalow so Mr. Lovelace could see the damage to our roof. I was in the bedroom at the time and waved at them through the hole in the thatch. It was very surreal. The McIntyres are throwing a cocktail party for James Lovelace this evening, so I will get to meet him finally.

Several other Jardine Henley gardens in the Mariani district have been badly damaged. The Dega factory has collapsed, damaging all the machinery. In other tea gardens, labor lines have been flattened and there is a substantial loss of life and livestock. The aftermath is even more horrific, because a deadly outbreak of cholera has crippled the workforce in many gardens.

I must get ready for the party now, Dadamoshai. I will give this letter to Charlie to post from Calcutta. It seems like letters take a shorter time to reach Silchar from Calcutta than they do from the gardens.

My love to you,

Layla

James Lovelace was a tall, bony man with a Van Dyke beard. He looked like an old-fashioned count. He was the brother of Estelle Lovelace, Dadamoshai's English sweetheart from his Cambridge days, and had known my grandfather as a young man.

"What was my grandfather like when he was young?" I asked him.

We were chatting in the smoking room of the McIntyres' bungalow, a large study-cum-library with teak paneling and a stone fireplace. Long shelves of books lined the walls. A tiger skin complete with a monstrous head and glassy yellow eyes was spread across the wooden floor. On one wall was a large framed photograph of a group of Scottish highlanders in their tartan kilts standing stiffly, their guns by their sides. *Gordon Highlanders, 1932* was inscribed at the bottom. A military sporran with long hairy, tasseled tails and a crested metal insignia hung on a hook to one side of the photograph. Everything about the room was warm, woodsy and manly.

"Ah, Biren Roy," James Lovelace reminisced, swirling the brandy in his snifter.

Biren Roy. I sometimes forgot my grandfather even had a real name. Everybody just called him the Rai Bahadur. "He was quite a firecracker even back in those days. An excellent debater. You could tell Biren Roy was destined for great things."

James Lovelace remarked he was surprised Estelle and Dadamoshai never married. They had exchanged letters for several years after Dadamoshai returned to India. It was Estelle who told him about Dadamoshai's educational work in Silchar. "She was very excited to hear I reconnected with Biren."

"Perhaps you could persuade her to visit India," I suggested.

"Well, it's certainly a possibility." James Lovelace smiled, stroking his beard. "My daughter Bridgette is doing her doctorate in Colonial History, and she plans to visit India next spring. I'll ask Estelle if she wants to come along."

I smiled at the thought of Dadamoshai reunited with his old flame. I was sure he still harbored tender feelings because when I once asked him about Estelle, Dadamoshai had acted surprisingly boyish and shy.

Ian McIntyre joined us. He was a stocky man in his late fifties, brusque and bushy-eyed, dressed in a tweed jacket with leather elbow patches over a white shirt with no tie. He was unmistakably an army man.

"Hello, Layla," he said, removing the curved Dunhill pipe from his mouth. "I hope you are doing a good job keeping our man Deb in check."

"Oh, I thought that was your job, Mr. McIntyre," I quipped.

"Ho! Ho! Ho!" guffawed Mr. McIntyre. "Been complaining about me, has he? Hey, Deb!" he called across the room.

Manik, who was leaning against the mantel chatting with Larry, sidled up, meek and respectful.

"You've been complaining about me to your wife, I hear?"

Manik looked discomfited, as if he had swallowed a marble. "S-sir?" His eyes darted at me nervously. It obviously didn't take much from Mr. McIntyre to turn my husband into a babbling wreck.

"Oh, never mind." Mr. McIntyre laughed amiably, giving Manik a thump on the back, causing him to teeter forward a little. "Let's just both keep him on a tight leash, shall we, Layla?"

Larry was talking to a dark-haired man wearing a fashionable dinner jacket. I recognized him as the stranger at Flint's house the night I dragged Manik home. The man had the slink of an alley cat. An unlit cigarette dangled from the corner of his mouth. Larry, as usual, looked slightly disheveled, with his dark curly hair and sleepy blue eyes. He waved us over.

"I don't know if you've met Charlie," he said, introducing us.

Charlie threw up his hands. "Please don't shoot me—I am only the pilot!" he cried in mock terror.

Manik grinned. "Charlie has the most enviable job in the world. He flies around in his little yellow Cessna…"

"And gets cozy with dishy air hostesses in Calcutta," added Larry.

Charlie gave a crooked smile. "What are you whinging about, mate? Give me a *chowkri* with a *tokri* any day." He looked at me with a straight, hard gaze that made me slightly self-conscious. "Pleased to finally make your acquaintance, Layla. The last time I saw you, you were hauling off our Cinderella without his shoe. I hope he got the lashing he deserved."

"Lashing for what?" cried Manik, indignantly. "I am innocent."

"I'll vouch for Manny," said Larry. "Charlie tried every trick to tempt Manny, but the fellow held on to his chastity for dear life."

"You know how I hate losing," drawled Charlie, "so I've kept your shoe as a trophy, old chap. I think I'll hang it off the tail of the Cessna for good luck. Indian style."

"You bugger!" Manik aimed a mock punch at him, but Charlie nimbly skipped out of the way.

"I'll give your shoe back," Charlie whispered huskily in Manik's ear, "if you find me a bedfellow like your one." He said it just loud enough for me to overhear.

Manik laughed, a happy boyish laugh. His gaze lingered on my mouth and I saw the heat rise in his eyes. Charlie's flirting fueled my husband's ardor, it seemed.

Charlie cleared his throat. "Easy now," he murmured. The man did not miss much.

A turbaned bearer was holding out a tray with triangular pieces of toast topped with spiced chicken.

"Nowhere in Calcutta will you find tasty *sikkins* like here in the tea gardens," said Larry.

"*Tasty sikkins?*" Charlie quirked an eyebrow and gave him a naughty look. "Am I missing something, old chap?"

"You dirty-minded bastard." Larry pointed at him with his toast. "*Sikkins* are appetizers—that's what they call them in tea lingo. A *borchee-khana* specialty."

"Ah," said Charlie, looking disappointed.

"Try these shammi kebabs with the mint chutney," said Manik, as the second tray came around. "They are my favorite."

"My favorite *sikkins* is not here," said Larry, looking around. "Where is Debbie Ashton?"

"The Ashtons may not come today," said Manik. "Both Ash and Jimmy O'Connor have their hands full with the rhino case."

"What rhino case?" asked Charlie, taking a bite of the kebab. "God almighty, this *is* spicy!"

"I'm surprised you have not heard about it, old chap, considering you land right on the Dega airstrip," said Larry.

"We flew in late this afternoon," said Charlie. "Mr. Lovelace drove straight to the Gilroys and dropped me off at Flint's on the way. So no, I've not heard about the rhino. Did Jimmy O'Connor shoot one?"

"It's not that simple," said Larry, wiping a greasy finger on his dinner jacket. "There's a big male rhino creating havoc in Dega. You know the earthquake we just had? It's common for wild animals to get disoriented and wander into tea plantations after one of those. We just chase them out when that happens."

"Dega borders the Kaziranga game sanctuary, doesn't it?" asked Charlie. "I know Kaziranga is famous for its one-horned rhino. They are an endangered species, I believe."

"That's right. Anyway, this rhino wandered into the tea plantation and instead of chasing it out, the laborers unwittingly drove the rhino deeper. Now it's wedged between the tea bushes, causing serious damage to that section. It's a belligerent animal and charges at the slightest provocation."

"Maybe I should offer to fly over it with the Cessna and shoo it out? That should be interesting."

"It won't work," said Manik. "Chances are the rhino will panic and injure itself and cause more damage to the tea bushes. It is in too deep and it can't get out by itself. This is a very serious problem. Thanks to this mess, tea plucking in Dega has come to a near standstill."

"So what is going to happen now?" asked Charlie.

"The easiest solution is of course to shoot the animal," said Larry. "Jimmy, as you know, would have wasted no time to do this. But Sircar the Forest Officer meanwhile got wind of the situation and sent him an official notice warning him that killing a one-horned rhino, an endangered species, is a criminal violation. So now the only option Jimmy has is to trap the animal and relocate it back to Kaziranga. But instead of dealing with Sircar he used his company connections to get the trapping permit directly from the Central Forest Department in Calcutta, bypassing Sircar's authority altogether—giving him the royal snub, so to say."

"That worries me," said Manik, thoughtfully. "I would be very careful dealing with Sircar. He's a snake in the grass, if there ever was one. Sircar is a petty man with a king-size ego, and he can make endless trouble."

Larry shrugged. "There's not much he can do, can he? Jimmy has his permit. He's following the law."

"So how are they going to trap the rhino?" I asked. All three men turned to look at me in surprise. As usual I had been listening quietly, unobserved.

"The same way you'd trap any creature, I'd imagine," purred Charlie, giving me a loaded look. "Stealth and cunning."

Larry, oblivious to the undercurrents, piped up earnestly, "Not just stealth and cunning, old chap—there's a fair amount of planning and logistics involved. You have to dig a pit, camouflage the top and drive the rhino toward it and make sure it falls in. The pit has to be measured and carefully constructed. It can't be too deep because then rhino might get injured. Also getting it out will be difficult."

"So how do you get it out, anyway? The damn thing probably weighs as much as the Cessna," said Charlie.

"We use trained elephants," said Manik. "Once the rhino is in the pit, we let down a bamboo ramp and use ropes and elephants to guide it out. It's a complicated and tricky procedure, but it has been done before. Rupali, our Aynakhal elephant, is very experienced in this kind of thing. She will lead the whole operation."

"It sounds bloody complicated, if you ask me," said Charlie.

"Put it that way...it's not simple," said Manik. "Things can go wrong."

Who knew *how* complicated it would be? You can plan an operation down to the minutest detail, get all the manpower, permits, tractors and elephants you need, but all it takes is a tiny shift in the universe to make things go wrong. Very, very wrong, as we would soon find out.

Three weeks passed. It was close to midnight when we got home from the Mariani Club. The full moon cast a waxy glow in the bedroom through the translucent sari curtains. We were still sleeping in the spare room. It would take another week for the roof repair in the master bedroom to be complete.

For some reason, I slept uneasily in that guest room. There was that dreadful hole in the floorboard, for one, temporarily patched up with a thin piece of plywood with the white chalk square clearly visible in the dark. Sometimes at night I imagined I heard dull thudding sounds coming from below. There was also the cloying smell of some oily chemical Manik used to clean his guns that bothered me. The bed was smaller, too: cozy to make love in, but some nights I would wake to find Manik spread-eagled, hogging the entire bed, and me pushed to one skinny corner like a discarded chicken bone on a dinner plate. This was one of those nights. Once awake, I found I could not go back to sleep. The gossip I heard at the Mariani Club that evening kept going through my mind. The latest news about Jimmy O'Connor was very disturbing. From what I could gather, a chain of rather bizarre events had catapulted the rhino case into a full-blown catastrophe, and Jimmy O'Connor had inadvertently walked into his own trap.

At first everything was going nicely according to plan, it seems. The trapping permit procured, the rhino was temporarily barricaded and the pitfall trap measured and dug out. Tea bushes were cleared to create a straight path leading up to it. All three neighboring gardens—Chulsa, Aynakhal and Kotalgoorie—pitched in with tractors, manpower and elephants. Manik was over at Dega most days and kept me updated on the operation.

On the day before the trapping, a group of laborers led by the Headman of Dega Tea Estate approached Jimmy O'Connor and begged him to reschedule the operation. It was unlucky Tuesday, they said, and that portended a disaster. Jimmy, of course, had little time for cosmic portents and hocus-pocus. The planets had never stood in his way; he usually pushed past them. But it did not happen this time.

The main problem was the size of the pit: it had been miscalculated. It was three feet too short in length, so when the rhino fell in, it got stuck halfway. The sheer weight of its body broke the rhino's neck and it died. It was a gruesome sight. The Forest Department led by Sircar came to assess the case. By the time they got there, crows had pecked out the rhino's eyes. At long last, Sircar had his revenge. He immediately filed a report that Jimmy O'Connor had willfully shot and killed the rhino and stuck it in the pit to make it look like an accident. Sircar identified the rhino's empty eye sockets as bullet holes. The next thing we heard was the Mariani police had slapped criminal charges on Jimmy, who now had to appear in state court.

My thoughts were interrupted by a dull thudding from under the floorboard. I peered over the side of my bed, listening. Was it a snake? The plywood was nailed to the floor and I prayed it would not come loose. It was unnerving. Manik murmured in his sleep and folded over, leaving me room to stretch out. Pillowing my head on crossed arms, I returned to Jimmy's dilemma.

So even though it was unlucky Tuesday and things had gone terribly wrong, nobody imagined any sensible judge would believe Sircar's ridiculous report. The "bullet holes" were obviously eye sockets. The rhino had died as a result of an accident. There was no malicious intent or cover-up. The case should have been dismissed with a fine. But this is not what happened, thanks to Jimmy O'Connor, who decided to go on one of his legendary benders.

Jimmy appeared in court completely drunk. He yelled at the Indian judge using unpardonable language and was held in contempt of court, dismissed and asked to reappear. Meanwhile, the rhino carcass rotted in the plantation, creating an unholy stink. It was unlawful to remove the body because the case was now under criminal investigation. Meanwhile, Jimmy O'Connor simply disappeared. It was rumored he was holed up in some Khasi village, steeped to his gills in rice toddy. Work at Dega Tea Estate came to a crashing halt. Crowds descended from all over to see the rotting rhino. The Fertility Hill miscreants wandered around the tea garden and pilfered from the factory, and things began to get completely out of hand.

There were two more hearings, and both times Jimmy O'Connor appeared drunk and in worse shape. At the last hearing he showed up with his Magnum rifle and threatened to blow up the court. Things started to snowball and before we knew it the unthinkable happened: Jimmy O'Connor, the General Manager of Dega Tea Estate and one of the most respected and senior tea planters in Assam, was slapped with a ten-year sentence in an Indian jail—an unimaginable predicament for a white man. He had boxed himself in so tightly nobody could get him out. The rhino case typified the complexities of intercultural relations of our time. It was an indication of the subtle shift of power taking place in Indian politics. Tea companies no longer had the influence to bail their planters out.

I sat up in bed. I had an idea. I would write to Dadamoshai and tell him the facts of this case. Who knew, maybe he could help.

It must have been close to 1:00 a.m. when I finished my letter to Dadamoshai. I turned off the kerosene lantern and let my eyes adjust to the moonlight before groping my way back to the guest bedroom. I stood at the door and was about to enter when I felt every hair freeze on my scalp. There was a man standing by the window on my side of the bed. I could see him clearly. He was tall and thin, with a long sorrowful face and lank hair that fell over his eyes. He just stood there without moving, turned slightly toward the bathroom door to his left. I was not sure if he had noticed me as I stood in the shadows, clutching my nightie to my chest and choking back a scream. I don't know how long I stood there, but I remember Manik mumbling in his sleep and turning over. The man scarcely looked in his direction. He then turned and walked through the open door into the bathroom.

I ran inside the bedroom and threw myself on the bed.

"Manik! Manik!" I whispered hoarsely. I shook him violently. "Get up! GET UP! There's a man in the room!" I was trembling uncontrollably.

I shook him again. He sat up in bed, and I immediately clamped my hand over his mouth.

"There's a man in the room," I whispered in his ear. "He's in the bathroom."

Before I could stop him, Manik grabbed the flashlight from the bed table, swung his legs off the bed and with all the stupidity in the world, marched right into the bathroom wearing nothing but his underwear. *This is it*, I thought. *I have a dead husband.*

"There's nobody here, Layla," he called. I heard him open and close the laundry bin in the bathroom. "Are you sure?"

He came into the bedroom, swung the flashlight around, switched it off and sat on the bed rubbing his eyes. He put his arms around me and drooped with sleep on my shoulder. I could not believe his apathy.

"Manik! He must be somewhere in the room." I was almost crying.

"Come to bed, sweetheart. I will explain everything in the morning."

"Explain *what*? I saw this man. With my own eyes."

"It's only Clive Robertson," Manik said. "He's nothing to worry about. He won't harm you."

Manik lay down. In five minutes he was snoring and fast asleep.

CHAPTER
27

Assam is no place for pretty boys. Planters are a scuffed, nicked lot, who live on the edge and survive by grit and guns. Tea jobs attract a certain kind of personality. You have to be drawn to it, rather like being an explorer.

It's a grueling existence any way you look at it. Every summer planters bemoan their lot in life and question what they are doing in Assam. It's only the memory of Assam's winter playground that makes it all worthwhile. Winter in Assam is like the mild and pleasant spring in the British Isles. There is plenty of game hunting and adventure fishing for the avid outdoorsman. That's the main reason why Brits were drawn to Assam in the first place. That and the chance to run away from the stoic, ordered world to which they are doomed.

When young tea-garden assistants return to the foggy shores of their homeland on furlough, they have become real men. They tell stories of Assam—so colorful, so outrageous, so exotic and wild that it leaves their fellow men gasping. Of course life in Assam is not quite so rosy. They don't speak about the isolation, the uncertainty, the backbreaking work, the tyrant boss. The watertight contract companies make planters sign makes defecting from the job near impossible. It's sink or swim. Only planters who survive Assam go on to become the legendary iron men in wooden ships.

What Clive Robertson was doing in Assam as a tea planter is anyone's guess. He was a pale, sickly young man who aspired to become the curator of an art museum. Clive Robertson had no taste for blood sport, abhorred guns and preferred instead to sketch scenery and listen to Bach. Assam was not what he had expected. He had imagined an idyllic life of simple pleasures with fine dining, cerebral conversation and some light plantation-management duties thrown in. Instead, he found himself in a brutal environment, hobnobbing with a bunch of ruffians who rattled around in their dirty jeeps and shot every creature in sight. Planters poked fun at his tidy clothes and the effeminate way he waved his hands. His manager, Mr. Peterson, picked on him constantly. He felt hounded and humiliated. Yet Clive Robertson could not be sacked. He had important connections that guaranteed him sanctity. His uncle, John Robertson, was the Director of Jardines in London.

On the third of June, 1932, Clive Robertson, the twenty-six-year-old assistant of Aynakhal Tea Estate, came home at midnight from the Planters Club. It was the cusp of the monsoons, and dark clouds covered the sky, breaking occasionally to unveil a full and brilliant moon. He drank four pegs of Chivas Regal, sitting on his veranda in the dark surrounded by the sounds of the night. He then went to his bedroom, secured the door by pushing a heavy dresser against it, loaded his 12-bore shotgun, put the muzzle in his mouth and blew a bullet through his brain.

The *chowkidar* later said he had heard a sound, but thought it was thunder. That night the worst monsoon of the decade broke, bringing torrential rain that slashed through the open

window of Clive Robertson's bedroom as he lay dead in rivu-
lets of blood. Nobody knew why Clive Robertson had taken
his own life but many understood. The loneliness and desperation that many planters faced in those early days was legendary. Maybe he had nothing to live for and nowhere to
go. This was not uncommon for young men of his time who
came to Assam to become tea planters. Assam had a way of
digging her creepers into a man's soul. Many would become
strangers unto themselves, and be doomed to wander forever
the forgotten wastelands of their minds. Maybe Clive Robertson was one of them.

Clive Robertson chose to die on the rainiest day of the
year. Giving him a proper burial posed the biggest headache
of all. Even in fine weather, organizing a Christian burial in
Assam had its challenges. The body had to be buried the same
day, usually by afternoon, because the warm, humid weather
caused it to decompose quickly. Telephones were nonexistent
at the time, so a boy on a bicycle was sent to the neighboring
gardens with a message imprinted on his wrist with indelible
ink. Quite often, planters got the news too late because of bad
roads and mishaps on the way.

So tea-garden folks just took care of their dead the best way
they could. The factory carpenter was ordered to build a coffin of green teak, still oozing sap, which made it atrociously
heavy. The Factory Assistant supervised the digging of the
grave, usually in some remote corner of the plantation, and a
few planters stood around with bowed heads with their *sola
topees* in their hands as the body was lowered to the ground.
There were no prayers, no priests, no eulogies, and barely a
tear shed for the departed.

Hundreds of scattered graves dot tea plantations in Assam. Most
of the dead were abysmally young, in their twenties and thir-

ties, killed by disease, drowning, wild animals or self-inflicted wounds. The company then followed official procedures and sent a telegram to the family notifying them of the person's death. A few months later all the belongings would be stuffed into tea chests and shipped back home.

The week Clive Robertson died the rains did not abate for a single minute. It poured in torrents and turned Aynakhal into a rolling, lurching river. Where and how could one begin to even *think* of digging a grave? Finally, four laborers held a tarp, while another four dug and scooped out buckets of muddy water that kept rapidly filling the grave. When Clive Robertson's teak coffin was lowered, it looked as if he was being lowered into a bathtub of muddy water. Several weeks later when the rains let up, Clive Robertson's coffin had floated up from the ground. It was found by a woodcutter, a quarter mile out in the jungle and bumped up against a log. The coffin was open and the body was missing.

Manik had never encountered Clive Robertson. Potloo saw him all the time and said the ghost knocked on his watchman's hut calling out *"Koi hai?"*—*who's there?*—in a gruff terrifying voice on moonlit nights. This was Potloo's legitimate excuse for staying stoned. Halua and Kalua had encountered him, as well, and I had most definitely seen him with my own two eyes.

"Ignore him, darling," said Manik. He was lacing up his canvas boots, sitting on the bed of the guest room. "Just treat him like a useless servant who hangs around and won't go away."

Ghosts were no joking matter, as far as I was concerned. I told Manik that.

"Well, what do you want me to do? I can't shoot him. I can't sack him. Every tea-garden bungalow has a resident ghost, if you must know. The Dega *burrabungalow* has a violent ghost that tried to strangle the VA one time. Jimmy O'Connor got an awful garden report that year, because of that."

It sounded as if Jimmy O'Connor could shoot rogue elephants with his powerful Magnum rifle but he was no match for a bungalow ghost.

"Ask Larry about the one at his bungalow. That ghost is a troublesome one. It steals whiskey and harasses the women. That's the other reason why his wife, Janice, ran off. It seems the men have no problems cohabiting with ghosts, but the women fuss a lot."

"The ghost has something to do with this room," I said, looking around.

"Well, if you have to know, this is the room where Clive Robertson shot himself," Manik said. He pointed his boot at the hole on the floor. "Maybe he comes up through that hole at night. You better watch out because he'll grab your feet when you step down from the bed!"

"That's not funny, Manik. I want to move back into our old bedroom."

"Just wait another week, darling, and the roof work should be done. I will send the factory carpenter to do a better job patching up this hole in the meantime. Now that you have Clive Robertson in your head, you are going to start imagining all sorts of things. Can you get the sweeper to clear out the hole today? I want to make sure we are not boarding up any snakes. There will be a big stink otherwise."

"There is something down there," I said. "I told you I sometimes hear noises at night."

"Well, make sure the sweeper fishes it out, whatever it is. I'll send the carpenter first thing in the afternoon."

That morning, the sweeper was prodding under the floorboards with a long stick when he hit upon a solid object. He pulled out a scuffed brown leather suitcase with rusty clasps. Inside was a brown leather diary, the pages filled with tiny writing, and several unopened letters addressed to a Miss Edith Blount in Sussex, England. They were all stamped Return to Sender. Wrapped in a powder-blue silk scarf were two photographs: a studio portrait of a young, dark-haired woman and another of a couple standing on a rocky beach. The woman was laughing as she clutched a flyaway scarf. Her other hand rested on Clive Robertson's arm.

I opened the last page of the diary and read:

The sky is waiting to open.
Edith my love, I leave you now
I was born with no purpose. I leave with no regret.
In these jungles do memories perish.
In these jungles I will remain.

The question was what to do with the suitcase. Manik thought it should be shipped off to Calcutta Head Office, but chances were, he added, it would just languish there because too many years had passed since Clive Robertson's death and nobody had the time to dig up old records and ship it back to England. Nobody cared. I felt the suitcase contained secrets that Clive Robertson did not want to share. It bothered me to think of strangers prying into the life of this very private and sensitive man.

"I will have to report finding the suitcase to Mr. McIntyre," Manik concluded.

"You don't have to do that. Nobody really needs to know we found it," I said.

Manik threw up his hands. "So what do you propose we do with it?"

"Bury it or burn it," I suggested.

Manik contemplated that for a moment. "Well, it would certainly save Mr. McIntyre a lot of headache. To document the suitcase he will need to fill out paperwork, list its contents, get it shipped, maybe even make a police report. A big waste of time, if you ask me, all probably for nothing. There is nothing of monetary value inside that suitcase anyway."

"Didn't you tell me there was a grave site in the woods marked with his name? Maybe we could bury the suitcase there. Where is this grave?" I asked.

"On the way down to the Aynakhal Lake. We can take a walk down there, if you like. It's a good three-mile trek through the forest. Let's have a picnic. I've been wanting to take you to the lake. It's a very pretty spot."

The picnic turned out to be a family outing. It looked as though Halua, the *paniwalla* and the *mali* were going to accompany us. A lunch basket was packed; a large thermos, rolled-up mats, camping stools and an inordinate amount of paraphernalia piled up on the veranda.

The way to the lake was through the back gate in the *malibari*, past the servant quarters behind the bungalow. The *mali* led the way carrying a shovel over his shoulder and a long curved *Khoorpi* knife with which he whacked the undergrowth to clear our path. The *paniwalla* boy came next, piled to capacity, like a beast of burden, which made him even more cross-eyed. Halua had put the entire load on his skinny shoulders, including Clive Robertson's suitcase, which nobody wanted to touch because it belonged to a ghost. Halua followed next, holding the picnic basket daintily over his arm like an old granny. Manik and I rounded up the party.

Manik whistled "It's a Long Way to Tipperary," and carried his rifle slung over his shoulder. Seeing our approach, a troop of golden langur set up a deadly din. They shrieked and followed us, crashing from branch to branch. We walked past a large pile of elephant dung, fibrous and disintegrating. A week old, Manik said.

"Look at that butterfly, Manik!" It was the most enormous butterfly I had ever seen. It circled the treetop, flying on powerful wings.

Manik shielded his eyes, looking up. "That's not a butterfly," he said. "That's a cardinal bat. It's a magnificent creature and very rare. You don't usually see them this time of the day."

We found Clive Robertson's grave overgrown with creepers. I sat on a log as the *mali* dug a hole beside the grave marker and we lowered the suitcase into the ground. I thought sadly of the mysterious young man who had died such a lonely death so far away from home. I said a quick prayer for him and we continued on our way.

The forest cleared and suddenly the lake was before us, full of lilies and shimmering with dragonflies on radiant wings. But a cold hand clamped over my heart. It was surreal. I looked at the lilies and the tall waving reeds and there was no mistaking it: this was the lily pond of my dreams. Visions of Manik, the fireflies and the floating face of my dead mother came into my mind. I gave an involuntary shudder.

"I know, it's very creepy," Manik said. He thought I was reacting to an engorged leech on his calf. He plucked it off. "Here, watch this," he said, as he tossed the leech into the water. There was a silver flash as a giant fish jumped up to gobble it up.

"Ooh, it's hot," said Manik, peeling off his shirt.

The servants had already set up camp. A tarp was strung across the low tree branches, mats laid down, two pillows, two towels, a thermos of chilled water. Yet the three men were nowhere to be seen.

"Where did they go?" I asked, looking around.

"Oh, they're somewhere around, having their own picnic, I suppose. They keep out of sight but they are within earshot." Manik was pulling off his pants.

"What are you doing?"

"Going for a swim, of course." Manik was down to his underwear. "Aren't you coming?"

"No, Manik!" I waved my hands in panic at the reeds. "Not here." The visions of him being dragged down by the lily stems flashed through my mind. "No, Manik, please no." I clutched at his arm.

Manik looked at me curiously. "What's wrong with you?"

"I had a bad dream, about this lake—"

"Layla, please don't be ridiculous. I swim here all the time."

"Isn't it...dangerous?"

"There's nothing in there. Lots of fish and maybe a few water snakes. They don't bite."

"I don't know," I said fearfully. I realized I must sound ridiculous.

"You are coming in, too. I can teach you how to swim." He stripped off his underwear, threw down his glasses, then, without a thread on, he dived like a knife into the water and disappeared with barely a splash. I held my breath for what seemed like forever. Finally he popped up and flicked his hair, sending the water flying in a graceful arc. He looked at me with wet shining eyes. "Are you coming in or not?"

"I didn't bring a change of clothes," I said.

"You don't need one. Take off your clothes, use that towel to cover up, if you like, then get in."

"What about…?" I nodded toward the forest, indicating the men. "I don't want them to see me—"

"Layla, the servants don't pry where they are not supposed to. You are missing out. The water is wonderful."

I inched up to the water's edge and stuck my toe in. The cool water did feel good. Throwing modesty to the winds, I disrobed quickly and waded in, checking over my shoulder to make sure Halua wasn't lurking behind a tree.

Soon I forgot my fears and became accustomed to the unfamiliar sensation of the water on my naked body. I began to enjoy the soft ripples caressing my skin, the silken mud yielding between my toes. It was deliciously arousing. After a while we toweled ourselves dry, lay on the grass mat and made love, our bodies still damp. I marveled at how ingeniously the tarp had been angled for our privacy. All I could see before me was the flat shining mirror of the lake reflecting a fathomless sky. *Aynakhal. Mirror Lake.*

A crimson dragonfly hovered and settled on the end piece of Manik's glasses lying on the grass mat.

"Never in a hundred years did I ever imagine making love under an open sky," I murmured.

"I did," said Manik drowsily. He looked me full in the eyes and traced the four-petaled rose between my breasts lightly with his finger. "I dreamed about making love to you right here by this lake. Just like this."

"I dreamed about this lake, too, but it was a bad dream," I said, waiting for that dark foreboding to envelop me, but it never came.

"Maybe I can change that for you," Manik said, and kissed me deeply. "Maybe you will remember this dream instead."

Halua and the *paniwalla* miraculously appeared around lunchtime to serve us boiled eggs, cold cutlets, bread and butter, followed by hot tea. Later, Manik dozed on his stomach while I occupied myself with stamping tiny leaf patterns all over his bronze back with small ferns I found with a white powdery underside. It reminded me of my childhood days with Moon. We were always decorating each other's skin with powdery ferns.

"Manik!" I shook him awake. "Look, elephants!"

A whole herd had come down to the lake on the opposite bank. They were so close we could hear them snorting and harrumphing. We counted nine in all, a dominant male tusker, five females, two youngsters and a tiny baby walking right between its mother's legs. The elephants played and rolled in the shallows for half an hour. Then they all lumbered back into the forest, as silently as they had appeared. All the time I was watching them, I could hardly breathe.

Manik burrowed his head into my armpit and went peacefully back to his nap. I loved the feeling of his arm across my chest, the easy weight of his leg draped over my body.

I breathed the deep aroma of his skin and felt suddenly overwhelmed with tenderness for the man I had married. A deep comfort settled on my sun-warmed body. I watched a puffy cloud elongate into a swan before sailing off over the ragged treetops and thought to myself, if Clive Robertson's ghost could be laid to rest, maybe so could mine.

CHAPTER
28

1th May 1946

Maiyya,

I am glad I could be of help. The Jimmy O'Connor issue, as I understand, is a political one. I am sorry that this has caused so many problems at Dega Tea Estate. As you know, when two elephants fight it is the grass underfoot that suffers.

Sunandan Bakshi, the high court judge who is in charge of this case, turns out to be my junior. I know him well. He is an astute judge and a reasonable man. O'Connor will have to sign some papers that will be mailed to him. The case will be dismissed. The testimonies from other planters and his garden staff are greatly in his favor.

I received a surprising letter from Estelle Lovelace, my lady friend from my old Cambridge days. She is a writer of some repute and lives in Cornwall. Her niece Bridgette Olson (James Lovelace's middle daughter) is planning a visit to India next spring, and Estelle says she may accompany her. Estelle is very keen to visit the tea gardens. She mentioned a certain Ginny Gilroy, a cousin of hers, who is married to a tea planter in the Mariani district. I wonder if you know of them?

I take great joy hearing about your life in Aynakhal, maiyya.
I can tell you are happy.
My love to you and your dear Manik. May all good things be
yours.
Your Dadamoshai

The packets of seeds I had ordered from the Sutton's catalog
arrived by mail. I turned each one over and read the growing instructions. Mrs. McIntyre had advised me what to plant
and the planting order. Cauliflower, cabbage and lettuce first.
Carrots and tomatoes next, chilies, parsley and cilantro last.
The *malis* had tilled the ground in the *malibari* and created long
rows. We were ready for the planting season.

A mud-splattered jeep honked at the gate. It roared up our
driveway and a large man heaved himself out. It was Jimmy
O'Connor. Two magnificent German shepherds leaped out
behind him. The dogs shook their shaggy coats and scampered
at the feet of their master. He snapped his fingers and pointed
at the ground and they flopped down obediently at the bottom of the stairs.

Jimmy clomped up to the veranda. He was an impressive
man with powerful shoulders and big corded arms. His mane
of flaming red hair was covered with dust from the open jeep
ride. His face was tanned a deep copper and his eyes a flecked
and faceted emerald-green. He towered over me.

"Hello, Layla," he said, extending a hand, big as a tennis
racket. "I came by to thank ye."

He said he had given up hope and had resigned himself
to serving jail time when to his surprise the rhino case was
abruptly dismissed. He had no idea why. At first he suspected
foul play—a trap of some sort, so he called up the judge to
find out. The judge said somebody called the Rai Bahadur had
vouched for his innocence. The Rai Bahadur, it seemed, was a

man of great integrity and the judge took his word seriously. Jimmy did not know who this man was and it had taken him a long time to trace it all back to me.

"I had me a narrow escape," he said. "I am not sure I would have made it out of the Indian clink alive."

"My grandfather says you got caught in dirty politics," I said.

"That, plus I got me a sewer mouth, lass. I shouldn't have brassed off the judge."

"Well, I am glad it worked out."

"Aye, thanks to ye," he said quietly, his voice husky with emotion. "Dear Mother o' God, I don't know what I did to deserve a second chance."

There was an awkward silence. He leaned forward and picked up the packet of tomato seeds from the coffee table and turned it over to read the back, tapping the edge of the packet with the stub of his missing finger.

"I am trying to get my *malibari* started," I explained.

"My Marie—" He paused and a shadow crossed his face. "My wife used to love gardening," he said quietly, putting the packet down. I saw the tug of memory in his eyes.

"I'm told your heirloom tomatoes are very famous."

He gave me a crinkled smile. "Are they, now? Why don't y'come to my bungalow and pick some, lass? Y'can have all ye want. What do y'say we stop by your man's office and tell him I am kidnapping you for an hour, aye?"

"What—now?"

"Why, y'busy, then?"

"Well, no…"

"So what're we waiting for, then? Christmas?"

Jimmy O'Connor lived in a *Chung* bungalow on top of a steep wooded hill. The winding road was lined with a tall plant with large red flowers that looked like a cross between a poppy and a dahlia. I had never seen anything like them. They grew thickly and blazed a fiery red trail all the way from the bottom of the hill up to the bungalow gates.

A convoy of enormous geese chased the jeep as it pulled up to the portico. Jimmy O'Connor shooed them away. His two German shepherds jumped out and trailed behind him, pointed and sleuth-eyed. I never once heard them bark, but they were sharply keen and watchful.

We walked to the *malibari*. The geese paddled around Jimmy's feet, honking affectionately. How he walked without tripping over them is a mystery. They nibbled at his calves, looked eagerly up at his face, bobbed and ducked, and stepped all over his big boots. They seemed to have forgotten that he had shot them down in the first place. The dogs followed at a watchful distance. Every now and then a possessive goose stuck its neck out and charged off after one of them like a torpedo, and they cringed back, ears flattened. German shepherds, for all their intelligence and might, were no match for the aggression of a Himalayan goose.

A wooden stile to keep out the geese led into the *malibari*. We stepped over it and the whole gaggle set up deafening honks of protest on the other side. The dogs jumped easily over the stile fanning their tails, looking happy at last to be rid of the nuisance.

There was not much growing in the *malibari* besides chilies and tomatoes. But what tomatoes! I had never seen anything like them. They were a deep reddish-purple like clotted blood, monstrously clumped and falling off the vine. Simply magnificent.

"Here, I'll let ye pick," Jimmy said, handing me an old pillowcase. "Take all ye want. I'll ask my *mali* to put some seeds aside for ye."

"Oh, thank you! I did not dare to ask you for them."

"Hush, lass, why not? Y'saved my life, didn't ye? Just don't share them with anybody unless they save yours."

"I have never seen tomatoes like this," I said.

"Aye, it's a rare variety," Jimmy said. "They have a dense flavor and low water content." A black-and-red-spotted ladybug was crawling up his shirtsleeve. He let it crawl on the stub of his missing forefinger and watched it fly away. "I got the seeds from Alan Hanks, the royal gardener at the Sudeley Castle. I give him Assam tea and he gives me seeds and cuttings. Did y'see the red flowers when we were driving up to the bungalow? He gave me those, too."

"What are they? Some kind of poppy?"

"It's a hybrid he's developed from the Helen Elizabeth poppy variety. They grow only at the Sudeley Castle. But they seem to like it here in Assam. They've taken over the hill as y'see."

"They are spectacular." The pillowcase was getting heavy. "I think that's all the tomatoes I need." I set the pillowcase down on an upturned wheelbarrow.

He winked at me. "I know a secret spell to grow plants, lassie, that nobody knows."

I was intrigued. "What do you mean? What kind of spell?"

He leaned forward conspiratorially. "It's an old Celtic spell. What do y'know, my grandmother was a famous Irish witch. I can teach ye the charm, aye, if ye promise never to write it down."

I laughed. "I promise I won't."

"Plant the tomato cuttings in early October and remember to water them with diluted milk and…"

"Diluted milk!"

"Aye, one cup to a pail of water. Say the spell over the young plants, lassie, when they are taking root and your tomatoes will overrun yer garden and grow plump as a milkmaid's rump."

"What do you do with so many tomatoes?"

"Oh, I give them to the servants, feed the cows—after I am done making my chutney, of course."

"You make chutney, too?"

He winked. "Does that surprise ye, lassie? I'm not called Chutney Jim for nothing, y'know."

I looked at Jimmy O'Connor, this great big wall of a man with his fiery hair and kaleidoscopic eyes. He did not look like a Chutney Jim to me. The man was surprising in more ways than one.

"Let's get to my pantry and get ye a bottle. I'm making more next week. Ye'll want my chutney recipe now, as well, won't ye?"

Aynakhal
16th May 1946
My dear Dadamoshai,
My pantry is full of chutney! The chutney is Jimmy O'Connor's special recipe. The man is a genius if there ever was one. His bottle-khanna *has been turned into a laboratory where all sorts of things brew, bubble, hatch and grow. There are jars of Kambucha mushrooms growing in tea solution; a homemade incubator with several dozen goose eggs hatching, and winemaking, and I don't know what all. Jimmy has even invented his own pressure cooker—a rather untrustworthy device that sometimes shoots its contents up into the ceiling.*

This man has opened his heart and home to me, thanks to you, Dadamoshai. He is not considered the friendly sort and is generally misunderstood by people. I wish you could meet him. He is the most interesting man, and you should see his mag-

nificent library of scientific books and his antique gun collection. Best of all, he tells the most exciting shikar stories—all true.

Jimmy recently visited Alasdair in Dooars. Alasdair's garden is in bad shape, he said. The new Indian owners have cut the tea pluckers' pay and want to cut down one-third of the work-force. As you can imagine, the coolies have nowhere to go. They have been estranged from their old Adivasi way of life for several generations and tea plucking is all they know. So Alasdair is facing a lot of labor trouble in his garden.

Things are changing in tea, Dadamoshai. Many British planters are leaving Assam. I think the Dega rhino case was a wake-up call. Tea companies can't do much to protect their planters anymore.

I was delighted to know you are in touch with Estelle Lovelace. Thank you for sending me a copy of her book. I will read it with great interest. Yes, I am well acquainted with Ginny Gil-roy. She is a good friend of Mrs. McIntyre's. Mrs. Gilroy is another avid gardener. But nobody can grow heirloom tomatoes like Jimmy O'Connor.

With my love,
Layla

Jimmy O'Connor's famous chutney recipe called for a unique blend of spices: dry roasted chilies, coriander and mustard seeds, ground in a mortar-pestle with malt vinegar and sea salt and cooked with tomatoes in that unreliable pressure cooker of his. The day we made the chutney, the pressure cooker hissed and spluttered and my sari was soiled.

Manik came to pick me up from Jimmy O'Connor's bungalow. I wanted to make a quick stop at the club store on our way home to pick up some baking powder. It was only minutes before the store's closing time and I did not expect to find anybody there, but sure enough I had to bump into Laurie Wood. She looked curiously at my tomato-stained sari.

"Oh, I was just making chutney with Jimmy O'Connor," I blurted out.

I immediately realized how it sounded, but it was too late.

A sly look crept into her eyes. "Making chutney with Jimmy O'Connor, eh?"

There was not much I could do. The cat ladies would have a good chinwag over that one, I could tell.

That year I took the blue ribbon at the flower show for both the heirloom tomatoes and the tomato chutney. Jimmy O'Connor, who was rather drunk, cheered noisily when I went up to collect my ribbon. In my little acceptance speech, I tried to give him credit, but just to embarrass me he yelled it was all hogwash and claimed not to know what I was talking about.

Later, I overhead Betsy Lamont in the ladies' room saying, "I can only imagine what Layla Deb gave Jimmy O'Connor in exchange for those tomatoes. These native women are so desperate. They won't stop at anything to get what they want."

I pitied the cat ladies. They would never know the joy of true friendship between a man and woman. Jimmy O'Connor's trust was a rare and precious gift, and it made me feel very special.

CHAPTER

29

The rainbird, the harbinger of the monsoons, started calling toward the end of May. Its plaintive cry—*"make-more-pekoe, make-more-pekoe"*—looped and twirled through the forest branches. The sky grew heavy and small drizzles fell, innocent and faltering at first, then in a steady drum of hoofbeats. Hundreds of miles to the south, the monsoon churned and roiled up the Bay of Bengal. The purple-black clouds swooped over the Assam Valley, the sky crashed open and a hard rain fell in flat, gray sheets, like steel.

The Koilapani River, which cut through both Aynakhal and Dega tea estates, swelled to four times its size. The floodwater uprooted trees and carried huge mounds of debris and vegetation swirling and bumping in its tide.

June limped into July. The air grew thick, and Assam turned into the abject armpit of the nation: the most dreaded and undesirable place on earth. By noon, the sun had been swallowed by a white-hot sky and humidity weighed down like wet burlap on all the miserable creatures below. The nights were even worse, sticky and rancid, with no respite.

For planters it was the busiest time of the year. If the monsoons arrived on time and the pruning, fertilizing and pest control had been attended to during the year, tea bushes flushed at an hysterical rate, and the succulent tips were ready for plucking every five to seven days. If a single cycle was missed, the leaf became coarse and useless. This meant double work and wasted manpower because the outgrown leaf still had to be broken off by hand so that the bush could regenerate new growth. Keeping track of the sections to be plucked and managing the labor was the assistant's job.

The season was short and every productive minute meant profit, and profit promised bonuses for both labor and management. Pluckers worked in the rain with woven bamboo rain covers over their heads and baskets. Soggy leaves could weigh down and rot, so the baskets had to be emptied frequently. Every batch of leaves had to be monitored for quality. If assistants were not watchful, lazy pluckers would throw in coarse leaves and stalk and this would lower the grade of tea. The Jemindars, haggard and red-eyed, yelled at the pluckers, assistants yelled at the Jemindars and Mr. McIntyre yelled at anything that moved or breathed.

Every able hand was put to work. Children plucked weeds and gathered broken leaf tips off the ground. Toddlers minded newborn infants in thatched shelters. If the baby cried it was taken to the mother to be breastfed while she continued plucking. Tractors putted up and down to the factory. The plucking schedule was ramped up to four shifts. It sometimes began as early as 3:00 a.m., the pluckers working by kerosene lamps. The last shift ended at 10:00 p.m. But the factory rumbled on all night.

This was the life of a tea garden blessed by a rainbow. Not many other gardens in the Mariani district were so lucky that year. The tea gardens to the east of Aynakhal suffered a freak hailstorm that sliced off the tops of every tea bush, cleanly as if with a razor. Within a few hours the entire year's profit lay wilting on the ground. Other tea gardens were still recovering from the earthquake or embroiled in labor problems. But for Aynakhal it was a year of abundance.

Tea wives fled during summer months, retreating to cooler climes, to get away from the foul weather, and to escape their even fouler husbands. Summer was no time to be around a tea planter.

I could see why. It was difficult to be around Manik. He chain-smoked, stank of stale whiskey, and was red-eyed, uncommunicative and inconsolable. He was rarely home for meals, ate sandwiches and cold cutlets at odd hours and, if he came home in the afternoon, fell asleep on the veranda with his boots on. Most nights he passed out like a wounded beast only to be woken up at odd hours to be summoned to the factory to troubleshoot some dilemma or another. It could be a machinery breakdown, a brawl or some other foul-up. Manik was on call twenty-four hours a day. He was like a man with a toothache: he could think of nothing else. Everything had ceased to exist in his world, including me. My presence made him feel guilty. He was unable to give of himself, and he hated for me to see him this way.

I suggested I go visit Dadamoshai for a while.

"Excellent idea." Manik was visibly relieved. "Stay for a month. Spend some time with the old man. I will come and get you as soon as the workload lightens. Hopefully we will have exceeded our production targets this year and there will be a good bonus. We'll celebrate when you get back."

There might be another reason to celebrate, as well, I thought. I had missed my first period, but I wanted to be sure before I told Manik I was pregnant.

Dadamoshai was scheduled to meet with a publisher for a book on which he had collaborated with Boris Ivanov, and had to leave for Calcutta the day after I arrived. He was so rushed and distracted I hardly got time to speak to him. That evening he had a long meeting with a group of people inside his study. They were all unfamiliar faces and the only person I recognized was Amrat Singh, the Police Chief. By the time they left it was well past our dinnertime.

"There is this matter of Prasad Sen's daughter," Dadamoshai said to me at the dinner table. "She has returned to her father's house. There may be a court case."

I stopped eating to stare at him in surprise. "Kona? My goodness, what has happened?"

"Her husband died and her in-laws abandoned her. It's a pathetic story, *maiyya*. Moon will give you the details. She will be here on Thursday with the children. In the meantime, if there is a crisis and Kona comes to this house seeking help, Chaya knows what to do. Bithi Mondol, the social worker— she was the elderly lady who was here today—will need to be contacted immediately. Kona may need police protection. Amrat Singh knows about this. I don't expect anything to happen during the two weeks I am gone, but I am telling you all this just in case."

I barely had time to absorb what he was saying when Dadamoshai pushed back his chair and got up from the table. His dinner was almost untouched.

"You must excuse me, *maiyya*, but if I don't get my papers in order I will miss the train. I have to be at the station at dawn. Please finish eating properly and get some rest. We will have plenty of time to talk when I get back."

I thought about Kona a great deal the next day. Dadamoshai's cryptic words kept playing in my mind. *Kona involved in a court case. Why would she need police protection?* I wondered. I walked past the Sens' house on my way to the river, hoping to catch a glimpse of her. From the high river embankment I could look over the walls of the pink house and see a slice of the courtyard. The first thing that caught my eye were two white borderless saris—the kind worn by Hindu widows— fluttering on a clothesline. The windows of the house were tightly shuttered. A moldy-looking female peacock walked by pecking in the yard but not a single soul stirred in that heavily fortressed, strawberry-pink mansion.

Aynakhal
24th July 1946
My darling,
It's agony here without you. The lack of sleep plus not having you next to me doubles my misery. I have moved into the guest room just so I don't miss you so much.

Production is at a feverish pitch. This is one of our best years. As an incentive Mr. McIntyre has promised the pluckers an additional bonus so work goes on nonstop. Our new tractor broke down and the spare part is taking forever to arrive. This has backed up production and caused some problems but we are managing.

Yesterday I ran over a twelve-foot python (a monster!) in Section 3 with the jeep. The laborers cut open its stomach and found a baby goat inside. I have taken a photo to show you.

Wendy has been hospitalized with typhoid fever. She is out of danger now, but it was a close call.

I have some sad news but I might as well tell you. Mr. McIntyre has announced his early retirement. He is leaving Aynakhal end of this year and going back to his hometown of Grantown in Scotland to take over the family distillery. On a

happier note: it looks like Aynakhal will hit a production re-
cord this year and there will be a BIG bonus for us all. We will
be rich, darling wife, and you can have anything you want in
the world.
All I ever want now and forever is you.
M.

One day I noticed a slim lavender envelope, postmarked
Cornwall, England, for Dadamoshai in the mail. It was from
Estelle Lovelace. I placed the letter prominently on top of his
desk and hoped I would be there to watch his face when he
picked it up upon his return. Perhaps I would detect a glim-
mer of excitement in his eye, but with Dadamoshai it was always hard to tell because he hid his feelings well.

Moon finally arrived with the children. Anik was now
a serious young man of five—a self-conscious, unhuggable
age—who walked around with the aloof air of a preoccupied
professor. He had been soundly chastised by his rascal sister,
Aesha, a tiny hellfire not quite two. Aesha had coal-black eyes
in a small pixie face and deep dimples like her mother. Moon
said if Anik had aged her by ten years, Aesha had aged her by
another twenty.

It was early afternoon and the children were asleep. Moon
and I sat on the porch steps of Dadamoshai's house eating green
mangoes sprinkled with chili and salt. Sharing this tangy deli-
cacy brought back memories of our childhood summers. Now
pregnant, I craved sour mangoes all the time.

"Moon, what happened to Kona?" I asked.

Moon looked at me levelly. "Dadamoshai didn't tell you
the whole story, did he? Kona's husband died. He had a sudden attack of meningitis. He was dead within days. It's very
sad because Kona has two small children."

"What is this about a court case?"

"Yes. It may come to that. You see, Kona's in-laws are very conservative and very superstitious. After her husband died, they packed Kona off to the widow's ashram in Vrindavan. It's a terrible place, Layla. Widows are forced to shave off their hair, dress in white rags and beg for alms outside the temple. It was heartbreaking to see her."

I could hardly believe what I was hearing. Dadamoshai had told me about the infamous widows' ashram in Vrindavan, one of India's holiest cities. The inhumane treatment of Hindu widows was a social disgrace, he said.

"You saw Kona? Begging in Vrindavan?" I said, aghast.

"No, no, not me. Spinster Aunt did."

"What was Spinster Aunt doing in Vrindavan?"

"That old bat has a religious streak, as you know. She goes to holy places to pray for wicked souls like me. Spinster Aunt went to Vrindavan on a pilgrimage. She saw the widows lined up outside the temples, banging their begging bowls on the ground, making a terrible din, she said. They are mostly toothless hags but some young ones, too, abandoned by their families. Spinster Aunt was coming out of the main temple when this young widow grabbed her sari with scabby hands and cried in a shrill voice, 'You know me. *You know me.* I am Kona. Please, help me!' The girl was wearing a torn, dirty sari, and there were all these mangy dogs, her pets, sniffing around her. Spinster Aunt said she was thin and bony and looked just like a beggar."

I found it hard to imagine Kona, the pampered daughter of the richest man in town with her fine saris, delicate hands and gold bangles, now a beggar! What a tragic reversal of fortune.

"Kona wept and told Spinster Aunt her in-laws had taken her children away," Moon continued. "They drugged her unconscious and abandoned her in Vrindavan. Kona's mother-in-law thinks she brought bad luck to the family because their only son, Kona's husband, died so young. They don't want her around anymore because they now believe that even her shadow falling on someone will bring bad luck."

"Does Dadamoshai know all this?"

"Oh yes! Ma wrote to Dadamoshai about it. Dadamoshai confronted Kona's father and threatened to take him to court," Moon said.

"But can he do that?" I asked. Domestic disputes were rarely addressed in court, as far as I knew. The court dealt mostly with criminal cases. There were thousands of widows in Vrindavan. Many put there by their families. Nobody went to jail for it.

"Things are changing, Layla," Moon said. "Now, with the women's reform movement, there are new laws. Any unjust treatment of a woman is a crime. Widow discrimination, rape, dowry—they're all coming to light. Of course, the woman has to testify in court against her family or in-laws and not many are willing to do that."

Kona, least of all, I imagined. She was so docile. She probably had never made a single decision of her own her entire life. But what Moon said next surprised me.

"The good thing is Kona has agreed to testify in a court case against her in-laws."

"That's very brave of her," I conceded. "I can't imagine what kind of courage it would take for someone like Kona to go against her family! But tell me, Moon, what will happen if she wins the case? Where will she go? Will her parents take her back?"

"That is the sad part, Layla. Nobody wants the poor girl. She is a social outcast. Her father says his daughter seen as a holy widow in Vrindavan is better for his political image than a single woman trying to remake her life."

That did not surprise me.

Moon laughed. "He is such a donkey! You should have seen Dadamoshai's face. I watched the whole drama on this veranda from your room. Ma and Dadamoshai tried to persuade Mr. Sen to take Kona back, rehabilitate her, give her an education and all that. At first, Mr. Sen got nasty. He said, 'Rai Bahadur, sir, please keep your nose out of our personal family business. Kona is my daughter, and we will do what we think is best for her.' This sent Dadamoshai's blood pressure skyrocketing! He told Mr. Sen Kona was going to testify in court and that would put him and her in-laws in jail. Then guess what that sly mongoose says?

"He started to whine and says he is a true patriot and only trying to uphold traditional Indian values for the purity of our society. Then he made the fatal mistake of slipping in a snide remark—he said he would never for one minute think of harboring a Muslim's whore in his house—he was talking about Chaya, of course. Dadamoshai's eyebrows bristled so much I thought they would fall off his head!"

I could well imagine that.

"Dadamoshai!" Moon laughed and clapped her hands. "You should have just seen Dadamoshai. I was squirming for poor Mr. Sen. Dadamoshai gets dangerously quiet, as you know, when he is very, very angry. Dadamoshai said, 'Mr. Sen, it was your traditional and patriotic Hindu brothers who threw acid on a sixteen-year-old girl's face in the name of preserving the purity of our society. Muslim's whore or not, I beg you, sir, please explain to me how is that under *any* circumstances acceptable human behavior.' Mr. Sen changed tactics and started to grovel. 'Please, Rai Bahadur, sir,' he begged, 'I beg you, this will be the death of my political career. I am only trying to do what is good for the country.' Dadamoshai said, 'I'll tell you what is good for the country, Mr. Sen. You take your daughter back, get her back on her feet, otherwise I will make sure your political career is cow dung.'"

I cheered inwardly for Dadamoshai but felt a twinge of apprehension. "Won't Kona's father mistreat her, if he is forced to take her back?"

Moon shook her head. "He can't do a thing, Layla, because by law Dadamoshai can send a social worker to check on Kona, and if there is even a single complaint, Mr. Sen will have to answer in court."

A twanging sound came from down the road, and a bearded man with long flowing hair and a saffron robe appeared outside our gate. He picked at an *ektara*—a one-stringed instrument made of a hollow gourd covered in goatskin. His bare feet jingled with ankle cuffs of tiny bells.

"Joi guru hari bol!" the man called in greeting. His voice was clear and ringed with overtones.

Moon and I exchanged smiles. "Nimai Baul!" we both said in unison.

Nimai Baul was one of the many wandering minstrels of rural Bengal. We had known him since we were children. The *bauls* were spiritual freethinkers, without caste or religion, welcomed by both Hindus and Muslims as they wandered from village to village singing their devotional songs of life and love. They were songbirds, Dadamoshai said, pure of heart; their only quest was to seek personal salvation.

Nimai Baul plucked his *ektara* meditatively, tapped his jingled feet before breaking into a song. His powerful voice soared to the sky, where the note held and trembled for what seemed like an eternity before plummeting to earth. This was followed by a lilting, joyful refrain. He sang a folk ditty about man's ceaseless quest for inner peace. His simple words of wisdom were like a balm to my soul, and I was reminded of the essential human goodness that still existed in our broken, prejudiced world.

As I listened I could not help but wonder about the irony of it all. *Bauls* had no possessions except the clothes on their backs and their *ektaras*. They had nothing to offer but their wisdom in a song, yet people opened their doors gladly and gave them food and shelter. They were welcomed in every home. But who would take Kona in? The only person I could think of was Dadamoshai, but it would be socially awkward for him, now that Manik was his grandson-in-law. Surely there was someone else? Aha, I thought. Yes, there was.

Martha, Miss Thompson's housekeeper, was going senile. She forgot to use a strainer for the tea and the cups and saucers were all mismatched.

"I don't know what to do about her," Miss Thompson whispered. "She is really getting on. I wish she would retire and go back to her family in Goa, but I think she worries about me living alone. She has always been that way, since Daddy died. Not that I can't manage without her, mind you. I have a part-time maid who does all the cooking and cleaning anyway. Martha is really more a companion."

I asked Miss Thompson if she had heard the news about Kona.

"Yes, the poor child lost her husband, I heard. And so young. What a tragedy," she said sadly, handing me a cup of tea.

It sounded as though she did not know the whole story, so I told her.

Miss Thompson sat at the edge of her seat, her tea growing cold, her eyes wide with disbelief. "What a terrible, terrible thing," she said. "To think her in-laws would treat her so poorly. As for her own father not wanting to take her back... my goodness, she is their only child!"

"If Kona leaves her family she will need a place to stay," I said tentatively. "Would you, by any chance, consider taking her in as a boarder?"

"Oh of course, dear, without a question," cried Miss Thompson. "I will do anything I can to help the poor girl. In fact, I will speak to Rai Bahadur myself as soon as he returns from Calcutta. Konica is welcome to stay with me at no cost. She does the most exquisite hand embroidery, did you know? I have seen some of her beautiful tablecloths. She can easily find work at the Sacred Heart Convent, if she likes. The nuns are always shorthanded in their sewing department and could use some help."

Martha hobbled in to clear the tea tray.

Miss Thompson glanced at Martha's retreating back. "Who knows, this may even be a blessing in disguise. If Martha is reassured I am not alone, she may be convinced to retire."

Suddenly I felt lighthearted and joyful. "I am happy to know at least Kona has a choice." I mulled over the word. "Isn't that the most wonderful word, Miss Thompson? *Choice?*"

"Yes, my dear," Miss Thompson said, leaning forward to pat my hand. "It is the best gift a parent can give a child. It is what your grandfather gave you."

CHAPTER
30

It was the end of July, and one pearly dawn, just like that, he was there. Manik crept into Dadamoshai's house through the unlocked kitchen door, entered my room and crawled into bed with me. The sun was a smudge in the sky and the birds still had not woken. It was barely four o'clock.

Suspended between dreams and wakefulness, I felt his body mold into mine. He kissed the nape of my neck. Manik had day-old stubble, and his hair smelled of dust from the road. He stroked my face gently. "Why did you go away?" he whispered. "Last night I missed you so much, I could not bear it a minute longer. I had to come and get you."

He kissed my throat and ran his hand softly over the curve of my belly.

"Manik," I said, covering his hand with mine. "Please wait…I have something to tell you. I'm pregnant."

I felt his sharp intake of breath followed by a rigid stillness.

In the dim light, his face hovered over mine and I saw the question in his eyes. I nodded and his eyes filled with child-like wonderment and joy. He buried his face in my breast. I felt his breath through the thin material of my nightdress.

"Oh, Layla," he said, his voice cracked with emotion. "This is wonderful news."

"I don't know how it happened.... We were so careful," I murmured, running my fingers through the tangles of his hair.

"We are having a baby," Manik said softly.

"Yes," I said, suddenly thrilling at the thought, "our baby."

The sparrows were beginning to stir on the jasmine trellis, and the first slat of sunshine slipped through the curtain and fell diagonally across the bed, lighting the parrot print on my bedcover. Manik made love to me with a deep tenderness, a reverence almost. We were both acutely aware of the precious life inside me. The world seemed so much larger that day, expansive and fuller somehow. It had stretched beyond its normal boundaries, and it would never be the same.

Back in our bungalow in Aynakhal, Manik had a surprise waiting for me. The "surprise" was five weeks old and had just had a small accident on the veranda. Jimmy O'Connor had offered Manik the pick of the litter, and this little pup had attacked his shoelaces and would not let go, so of course he had to be the one. The puppy cocked his head from side to side as Manik talked about him. He was coal-black with a caramel smudge on his chest and caramel stockinged feet. His eyes were bright and curious and his ears pricked at the slightest sound.

"Purebred, pedigree Alsatian. Prime stock," Manik said proudly, tickling the puppy, who rolled over on his back and tried to chew his hand with tiny pointy teeth. "They make the best guard dogs in the world."

A mynah cackled loudly on the lawn and the puppy gave a panicked look and crawled under the coffee table. "Of course he will need some confidence building before that," Manik said.

"What will we call him?" I tried to entice the puppy out,

but he gave a tiny growl and looked fierce. He was so droll I had to laugh.

"I was thinking of naming him Marshal. But you can choose a name. He arrived only four days ago."

Hearing his name, the puppy pricked up his ears, gave a tiny woof and ran out from under the coffee table, wagging his tail.

"I think he has decided for himself," I said. Marshal sounded too serious for this tiny ball of fun, but hopefully he would grow into his name.

The puppy tugged the bottom of my sari and ran around my legs, almost tripping me. Then he went off to fetch an old tennis ball from under the hat stand. It was too big for his mouth so he pushed it along with his nose, growling menacingly

"Alsatians are intelligent and fearless guard dogs. They protect you with their life." Manik gave Marshal a little prod with his toe. "I'd feel better with him around, especially now with the baby. You'll take care of Layla and the baby, won't you, Marshal?"

Marshal gave a small woof, which quickly turned into a sneeze. He rubbed a paw over his wet nose. Then he sneezed again and looked at us, bewildered.

"I could watch him all day," I laughed.

"Someday he will watch you," Manik said. "We have to be strict with him from the beginning. Alsatians need discipline and training. I got some tips from Jimmy O'Connor. Marshal must be kept in check and never allowed into the living room or bedroom. The veranda is his limit. If he tries to enter any other room, give him a smack on the nose and say 'NO' very loudly."

As I walked toward the bedroom, the puppy followed on clumsy feet, wagging his tail. He hesitated at the doorway; his ears drooped as he turned to look up questioningly at Manik, cocking his head slightly. Manik wagged a finger and barely mouthed the word. The puppy gave a plaintive whimper and flopped down outside the door. I guess in four days Marshal had already received his fair share of "nos" and nose smacks.

Given Manik's penchant for shikar, I was curious why he had chosen an Alsatian, a guard dog, over a hunting breed like a Lab or Retriever. Manik became thoughtful when I asked him. He pushed his glasses up on his forehead and rubbed his eyes. When he looked at me, a shadow quickly crossed his face.

"Times are uncertain, Layla," he said soberly. "There has been trouble in several gardens."

"What kind of trouble?"

"Labor trouble. Local politicians are infiltrating the gardens, waving communist flags and pushing the labor to get unionized. Bribing them with money and opium."

"Why aren't the companies doing anything about it?"

"British companies are changing hands to Indian ownership. This is a period of transition. Nobody quite knows what will happen." Manik's eyes were serious. A small muscle twitched in his jaw. "There may come a time when we tea planters have to protect ourselves. Guns and dogs are all we have."

The puppy scratched on the bedroom door and whimpered.

Manik smiled. "But now with our trusty mastiff, we don't have to worry, do we?"

Alsatians are one-man dogs, they say, and Marshal considered Manik his alpha leader. Marshal eventually grew to be eighty pounds of muscle and stealth. He had powerful sloping shoulders and long pointed canines. He was unmistakably a guard dog. Within the next few weeks he lost his puppy playfulness and became self-assured, razor sharp and quick as an arrow. His ears were always pointed, his brown almond-shaped eyes watchful. Any suspicious sound and the muscles in his body pulled back like a slingshot.

With the arrival of Marshal, one more servant got added to our retinue: the *Kutta-walla*, or dog caretaker. Servants in bungalows had very specific and regimented roles. One person's work never overlapped the other. The bearer would not care for dogs, and the cook would not cook for the animal. Animal care was deemed below their status.

The *Kutta-walla* was a man called Montu. He was a morose-looking fellow with a long face and sad eyes. Montu's job was to boil the beef for Marshal's meal and pluck the burrs and ticks from his shaggy coat and hose him down if he got muddy.

Marshal was a true aristocrat. There was a certain aloofness about him: no fawning, begging or greedy gobbling. When Montu dished out his food, Marshal cocked an ear and waited awhile before he sidled up to his dish. He never wolfed down his meal but ate always alert and watchful. The only attention Marshal sought was from Manik. It was not petting or a treat that he wanted but validation. If Manik said, "Good dog," Marshal fanned his long sweeping tail slowly from side to side. His jaw hung open and he smiled, his brown intelligent eyes acknowledging the tribute. He was modest, never humble.

22nd September 1946
Layla-ma,
Are you eating properly, ma? You must take your egg in the morning and eat plenty of curds and drink milk twice a day. Good nutrition is most essential. This is not the time to think of yourself, but what is good for your baby. You have very poor eating habits since a child. I blame your Dadamoshai for this. He got you too much interested in books and should have never allowed reading at the dining table.

As you can see from the newspaper article, your uncle Robi received a prestigious award from the Assam University for his Bacteriological research. But what can I tell you, maiyya! *He is so absentminded he forgot to attend his own award ceremony! What a shame. He did not mention a single word about this to me, otherwise I would have made sure we attended the function.*

I am just back from Silchar. The Sacred Heart Convent had its annual fundraising fete and I saw some lovely hand-embroidered tablecloths in a stall and wanted to buy one for you. I was so busy choosing the tablecloth, I did not notice a girl smiling at me. When I went to pay her, I could not believe my eyes—it was Kona! You will never recognize her now with her skirt and her short curly hair. She looks exactly like an Anglo-Indian, but I must say she is looking very well.

You may have heard Moon and Jojo are leaving for Uganda? Jojo has a 3-year contract with the petrochemical company. I have mixed feelings about this. I will miss the children, especially my little Aesha, but I think it is best for them to have their own life separate from Jojo's parents. Jojo is too much a mama's boy, if you ask me. My only complaint is, did they have to move so far away?

You must be careful now, ma. There is no need for you to engage in rough activities like driving the jeep and shooting the guns. Manik should have had more sense than to teach you all this.

With my love,
Mima

25th September 1946
Dear didi,
I now real memsahib in burrabungalow. *Bungalow too big. Many servant keel-meel everywhere. Nobody listen. I tell*

borchee *make chili omelet but he make fry egg with raw top like English eat. For Ali birthday I make Dondy cake like you teach, but it come out too hard like brick. I think I forget the bake powder. All tap in bathroom new. All room having fan. But I cry,* didi. *Silchar too far for Ali to take me to see my Abba. Also Ali busy. Mr. Botra, Indian owner, want to make too much tea. Not English quality, he say, but big amount for India people. India people not understand English tea. They boil too much and take strong. Mr. Lohia giving no bonus to coolie. So there is coolie trouble.*

No good shikar here for Ali. Ali go all day with gun and come home with only one hedgehog. Who kill hedgehog, I laugh. Didi, I dream you have girl. I make green sweater for baby, knitting with hedgehog needle. Green is lucky color. I make sweater little big, so baby can wear long time. You tell baby when she is understand Jamina Auntie who make her sweater with hedgehog needle. Didi, you must eat two-spoon ghee every day. It make passage slippery. Baby come out easy like magur fish. No problem.

Alibaba want to take me to Scotland but I afraid of plane. But Alibaba say it safe like motorcar only going in air. But, didi, *how to go to bathroom so high?*

My respects to your good husband.

From your sister,

Jamina

15th October 1946

Didi,

My heart is burst, I come to see you. Every minute knitting knitting. Sometime not sleeping at night. I want to make two more sock, two more sweater and one blanket for baby. I already buy wool in Gauhati. Now I think I buy too many green. Inshal-

*lah, I finish everything in two more week. Ali say, "You make
Layla baby look like green sheep." I happy you having baby
in cold season, sister, that way Jamina can make baby sweater.
My finger fat like banana no good for embroidery but knitting
no problem.*

*Ali happy he going shikar with your good husband. He clean-
ing gun all day and talk about duck. Let me do knitting now
so I finish.*

*I happy I am Auntie soon. Your baby my baby. Same-same.
My respects to your good husband.*
From your sister,
Jamina.

The autumn air crisped and the hills turned a foggy blue.
Duck-hunting season arrived and Aynakhal was a shikari's paradise. The giant marshland called the *bheel*—where Aynakhal
bordered Kaziranga—was prime bird-hunting ground. Duck,
geese and snipe migrated in large flocks all winter long.

Jimmy O'Connor organized a duck-hunting camp and invited Alasdair and three other shikaris from Dooars. Together
with Manik, Larry Baker, Rob Ashton and Peewee Williams
there would be eight shikaris in all. Peewee Williams, to everyone's surprise, turned out to be a crack shot, earning him
Jimmy's grudging respect.

Duck camps were elaborate affairs. It took weeks of planning. The jungles were cleared, makeshift huts and an out-
house constructed. Shikaris took manpower, supplies and dogs,
and camped out for days. Decoys—duck-shaped cutouts made
from old tea chests—were floated in the *bheel* to attract the
flock to land. When the ducks landed, the Beaters, who were
hired help, whacked together bamboo slats to create a mighty
racket and direct the birds to fly over the heads of shikaris

camouflaged in the brush. Then it was a matter of skill and marksmanship as to how many birds you could down with a scattershot.

Alasdair and Jamina were staying with us. Jamina arrived with three pillowcases full of knitted baby clothes. All in various shades of green. She was so emotional to see me that she cried nonstop the first day. Then she was back to her chatty old self.

"English people make too much *hoi-choi* to shoot few ducks." Jamina clicked her tongue disdainfully seeing all the paraphernalia strewn over the portico. Two vehicles were parked on the gravel driveway and several men scurried about, loading up supplies, guns and camping gear. "What's there to catch ducks? My brother catch more ducks, with only goat bladder. No guns. No problem."

"What do you mean?" I asked.

"They throw goat bladder in *bheel*. Ducks gobble-gobble. Next morning come and find duck nicely tie up like koi fish. Just pick and take home. No problem."

It was the old village method, Jamina explained. Villagers caught ducks simply by throwing a goat's empty intestine into the marsh where the ducks flocked. The ducks mistook the pink gut for a giant worm and gobbled it, but it was too long and stringy and came out of the other end. Then, disgustingly enough, the second duck gobbled it up and the same thing happened. Soon there were three or more ducks all threaded together from beak to tail, flapping around, tied up in a bunch. One had to simply pick them up and bring them home. No fuss: no guns, no decoys, no Beaters, no problem.

Manik grinned, hearing Jamina. He was sorting through a pile of cartridges on the veranda coffee table, putting the orange ones to one side. Marshal lay with his nose on Manik's shoe, looking wretched and miserable. He knew he was not being taken to the duck camp. The other planters were bringing their dogs, mostly Labradors. Labradors were the perfect hunting breed: they were excellent swimmers and had soft jaws that never crushed a bird. Marshal's jaws crushed everything.

"That can't be true, can it?" I asked Manik. "Catching ducks with a goat bladder. Sounds too fantastic."

"Actually, I've heard about it," said Manik, tying up the sack with the orange cartridges. He turned to Alasdair, who had just come out of the living room. "What do you say, Ally, we forget about the duck shoot and just throw some goat bladder into the *bheel*?"

Alasdair laughed. "Aye, just think how brilliant that is. We make such a fuss about hunting and marksmanship when all you really want is a bird for dinner. We should learn from the natives, y'ken. They outsmart us in more ways than one."

"The Assamese have an ingenious way of panning for gold, as well," said Manik. "Ever notice how much gold they wear? Even the poor farmers? All the villagers do is float sheep wool in running streams to trap the gold flakes. They leave it there for days. Once during shikar I came across the wool in a stream. I thought some animal had died or something, then the tracker showed me how the wool was anchored through a stick in the mud and explained the whole gold-panning method."

"How do they get the gold out of the wool?" I asked.

"Oh, they just burn the wool and collect a neat little nugget. It's that simple." Manik thumped the bag of cartridges on the coffee table. "So, Ally, old chap, all you really need in life is a few goats and sheep. No need to budge from your hut. Sit inside and drink your rice wine. Everything in life will come to you."

"Aye, that sounds wonderful," said Alasdair. "My heart yearns for the *lahe-lahe* life."

Jamina whispered furtively in my ear. "When I go to Scotland, Ali's mother give me *not even one* thin gold bangle. Just imagine, *didi*, and I am new bride." She rolled her eyes theatrically. "Indian people not so stingy like Scottish people. Everybody know Scottish people most stingy people in the world. Wait till our husbands go then I tell you whole story of what happen in Carrots Castle."

She put her finger on her lips and gave me a loaded look, as if it was all a big secret she could only share with me in private. Just imagining Jamina in the prim-and-proper "Carrots Castle" was enough to make me smile.

"Carrots" Castle was the Carruthers' ancestral home—a gigantic turreted structure, with dusty rooms and cold drafty staircases. Jamina's in-laws lived in one solitary wing. The rest of the castle was occupied by Sir Malcolm Edward Carruthers, the notorious family ghost.

Jamina's mother-in-law, Alasdair's formidable mother, was in her eighties, with papery hands and the complexion of a dead fish. Strangest of all, Jamina never saw the woman blink even once.

On her arrival, Jamina had mistaken the butler for an old uncle and bent down to touch his feet to receive her blessing as a new Indian bride. The man jumped as though Jamina was going to bite his toe. "No more feet touching," Alasdair had told her after that. Just shake hands or kiss. The kissing business confounded Jamina. She did not know which cheek to offer first, and there was always the danger of noses banging or the kiss landing in the wrong place. Also, was one supposed to actually kiss or only make the kissing noise while pressing cheekbone to cheekbone?

As for the food, it was completely ghastly. The meat was pink and uncooked, the potatoes boiled with no spices. They had curry and rice in her honor. The curry was a sickly yellow stew. Completely inedible.

"So what did you eat?" I asked, hiding my smile. Jamina was still her plump little self, from what I could tell.

"Only cake," said Jamina, "and pudding. And *toosth* with jam. Strawberry jam is very fine but *mamalaid* little bitter because lazy cook leave orange peel inside."

Most days Alasdair would go off hunting with the lads, leaving Jamina stuck with the mother-in-law in the musty parlor. Conversation was minimal, since Jamina did not speak English. Out of boredom she had counted the stone slabs in the fireplace a hundred times and knew every crack by heart.

There was a banquet held in her honor with about fifty guests, all very fine and rich people. The mother-in-law wanted Jamina to wear a long dress with some kind of hard basket contraption inside. The maid had pulled the laces tight and Jamina's breasts had almost fallen out. It also made going to the bathroom impossible. Jamina's bladder had nearly burst.

Then with much fanfare she was presented with a blue velvet box. Inside was a glass pendant, which the mother-in-law clasped around Jamina's neck. Then everybody clapped and made a bread, Jamina said.

"Made a bread?" I wondered what she was talking about.

"You know when the English people raise their glass and say 'to your good health' they are making a bread to you."

"Oh! A toast," I said.

"Bread. *Toosth.* I bring glass pendant to give your baby to play. But only give baby when big, otherwise he swallow and choke."

Jamina undid the end of her sari and handed me the necklace. It was a glittering heirloom diamond the size of an almond. I was utterly speechless.

"Do you know what this is, Jamina?" I gasped, carefully holding up the chain. The diamond swayed, catching dazzling arrays of light. "This is a very, very expensive diamond. I don't even know what it's worth, but it's more than what you and I can imagine."

Jamina snorted. She thought I was pulling her leg.

"Listen to me, Jamina. Don't carry this around tied to your sari, understand? Where is the box it came in?"

"The box is very fine. I am keeping the hedgehog needle inside."

"Put this necklace back in the box and keep it safe. Don't tell anybody about this. Someday you will be lucky you have this."

"If only they giving me few gold bangles, *didi*. Even one or two."

"This is worth a lot of gold, Jamina. A whole boatload of bangles."

Jamina gave me a tired, disbelieving look and rolled her eyes.

"Didn't Alasdair tell you anything? He should know better."

"Ali does not care," Jamina snorted. "If it does not shoot, he is not interested."

CHAPTER
31

One mild November day, the prophecy came true: Rupali, the lumbering, sweet-natured Aynakhal elephant, in an act of goaded frenzy, killed her *mahut*—the same *mahut* who had lovingly hand-reared her from the time she was a month-old calf. For forty-one years, Rupali had lived outside his hut. The *mahut*'s babies crawled in the dust under her belly and played with her trunk; as toddlers they leaned against her enormous tree-trunk legs to take their first faltering steps into the world. Rupali was a part of the *mahut*'s family, and the mindless ferocity with which she murdered him came as such a shock to us all.

As the story goes, the three *mahuts* were bathing the elephants at the Aynakhal Lake. The gigantic beasts lolled in the shallows like miniature islands while the men traipsed up and down their backs, giving them a good rubdown with coconut husks, which they enjoyed greatly. Suddenly, without any warning, Rupali heaved herself to her feet, sending her *mahut* sliding into the water. The other two *mahuts* watched in horror as she grabbed the man by one leg and dragged him over the river rocks and into the jungle. There she killed him with one deadly blow against a tree trunk, with such brute force it was rumored his brains had to be scraped off the tree bark. Rupali then proceeded to trample the *mahut*'s body before crashing off into the forest, trumpeting with demented fury.

Manik had gone to the lake where the incident happened. The sight of the *mahut*'s mutilated body was so ghastly he was sick to his stomach. He had been unable to eat lunch that day.

It made me sick to even hear about it. "Surely, there must be a reason why it happened," I insisted.

Still shattered, Manik only shook his head dumbly.

I later wondered if it was something to do with the way young elephants are domesticated in captivity. The animals are captured and chained by their feet during their taming period and forced into servitude by being deprived of food and water. When they are broken and become submissive the heavy metal chain is removed from their feet and replaced by a rope. The elephant can easily break free of the rope, but by then they are psychologically conditioned to believe they are powerless. Rupali had reclaimed her power and freedom. She fled into the forest, never to be seen again.

This was not the first time an elephant had gone on a rampage and killed its *mahut*. Often there was no explanation as to why a domesticated elephant turned rogue. Some conjectured the *mahut* may have abused Rupali in fits of drunken rage, but this was soon dismissed. The only illogical conclusion one could come to was Rupali was a marked animal with a bifurcated tail and violence was inherent in her nature.

News traveled quickly in tea circles. Holly Watson's notoriety preceded him like the stink from a rotting carcass. It was rumored he was a corrupt manager who left every tea garden bankrupt or embroiled in labor problems, that he took bribes from equipment suppliers and sold timber and bricks from the garden for personal profit. Jardine & Henley could not sack him because he had connections in the higher ranks. When things got tight they simply transferred him. And now the bad news was Holly Watson would be taking over from Ian Mc-Intyre as Manager of Aynakhal Tea Estate.

"I heard about that bastard," said Larry. "I am not going to survive a single day working under him." They were at the Mariani Club. Manik had been playing tennis with Rob Ashton, Larry and Peewee. Debbie and I sat on the shaded club veranda, drinking fresh lime soda while little Emma ran around picking dandelions, which she piled on my stomach, "for the baby."

"Is this the same Watson who beat a coolie and started a labor riot?" Rob Ashton wiped his face with a white towel. Emma was pushing dandelions into her daddy's socks.

"That's right," said Larry, scribbling his order on a club chit. "Gin and tonic. Finger chips," he said to the bearer, handing the pad back. "That incident happened in Baghpara Tea Estate when Watson was Manager. The coolie went into a coma and died. He was kicked to death, I believe."

"Have you had something to eat, darling?" Manik asked me.

"I'm fine," I said, still trying to digest the disturbing news about Manik's future boss. Manik did not appear to be bothered, for some reason. I turned to Larry. "Do you know anyone who's actually worked under Holly Watson?"

"As a matter of fact, I do," said Larry. "Do you fellows remember that tall drummer fellow who played with the band on New Year's Eve? Lovely chap. I forget his name."

"Are you talking about Mike Leonard?" said Rob. "Folks call him Lonnie."

"That's right. That's the chap. Lonnie," said Larry. "Lonnie was assistant at Baghpara during that riot. He said Watson's a mean bastard. His wife's a raving alcoholic—a closet gin drinker."

"Aren't you worried, Manik?" I said. "Watson is going to be your new boss."

Manik shrugged, sprinkling salt and pepper over his finger chips. "I don't know, darling. I haven't met Watson and I wouldn't jump to conclusions. Sometimes rumors are just that. Rumors."

Larry shot him an exasperated glance. "Oh for God's sake, get a grip, Manny. This guy is notorious. Ask anyone in Dooars. I'm not hanging around to find out, that's for sure. I've applied for a transfer."

"You are leaving Aynakhal?" I asked incredulously.

"I've put in my application. Whether I get the transfer is a different matter," said Larry. "But I know for sure I don't want to work under Watson. I have heard enough bad things." He turned to Debbie and looked mournful. "Besides, my girlfriend Debbie is following her worthless husband to Papua New Guinea. How can I live without her?"

That made me even more depressed. Debbie had told me they were thinking of moving to Papua New Guinea. A new tea industry was opening up there and British companies were looking for experienced planters to run the plantations. Many Assam planters had opted to move there. The pay was great; so were the perks.

"When are you leaving for Papua New Guinea?" I asked Debbie.

"We don't know yet, but Robby's papers should arrive second or third week of January. It's such a shame to be moving in January. It's party season in Assam and raining cats and dogs in Papua New Guinea."

"I wish you didn't have to go," I said. The very thought of the Ashtons leaving filled me with sadness.

"Oh, we don't want to go, either," Debbie said, giving my arm a little squeeze. "I will really miss you, Layla. But we have to think of Emma's education. The company will pay for her boarding school in England. And Emmi will learn to speak with a la-di-da accent and marry a Greek millionaire, won't you, my darling?" She winked at Emma. "Then she can take care of her mummy and daddy in their old age."

"I am not going to Pappy Ginny. I am going to marry Uncle Jimmy and stay in Dega," announced Emma.

"Say, Emma, that's not fair!" cried Peewee petulantly. "You said you'd marry *me*?"

Emma looked a little guilty-eyed as she pulled apart a dandelion. She had indeed publicly announced her betrothal to Uncle Peewee.

"Then I'll marry *both* of you," she said brightly.

"That's even better," said Rob. "I can't think of a more charming pair of sons-in-law."

Everybody laughed but me. I was beginning to get a bad feeling in the pit of my stomach. All the familiar faces would be gone: Larry had applied for a transfer, the Ashtons and McIntyres were leaving. And then there was Holly Watson....

"I'm going to the library to return my books," I said to Manik, struggling out of my chair. I was getting big with the baby.

I stepped gingerly across the main hall, where two men were polishing the wooden dance floor with rags and Mason's polish. Molly Dodd waved to me from the doorway to the bar. She and another lady were putting up the decorations for the children's Christmas party. A massive piñata was strung across the length of the dance floor and colorful crepe streamers hung from the ceiling fans.

In the library I was surprised to find Raja shelving books. He gave me a big smile.

"I didn't expect to find you here," I exclaimed.

"I'm only here for a day, madam. I came to take my sisters back to Silchar," Raja said. "When is the baby due, may I ask?"

"In another seven weeks or so."

"You will return to Silchar, I suppose, for the delivery?"

"That's the plan."

"I see," said Raja. He thoughtfully stacked one book on top of the other. When he looked back at me, his eyes were serious. "You may want to consider leaving early, madam," he said quietly. "My brother Dinesh has sent word there is going to be a big political rally in Mariani. He fears there will be violence and bloodshed. Which is why I came to take my sisters back to Silchar."

"When is this rally?" I asked, feeling slightly alarmed. "And what is it about?"

"I believe it is next month. The Communist party is staging a demonstration to unite and unionize the labor in the tea gardens. They are planning a big uprising. Many activists are arriving by train from other parts of Assam. Mariani is going to be the hub."

"Is your mother leaving for Silchar, as well?" I asked.

"Ma does not want to leave Baba here by himself. She will stay with him as long as she can."

"Is your brother Dinesh a member of the Communist party?"

"Yes. He is one of the group leaders under Prasad Sen."

"*Prasad Sen!* Prasad Sen of Silchar?"

"Yes, madam. He is the main Communist party leader in Assam."

Kona's father!

"Thank you, Raja, for telling me this," I said, feeling bewildered at the news. "I will tell Manik and we will make a decision."

Manik insisted I leave immediately for Silchar with Raja and his sisters.

"We should not take a risk with the baby, Layla. Things can turn ugly very quickly in situations like this. I have to take over as Acting Manager after Mr. McIntyre leaves, and I won't be able to leave Aynakhal until Holly Watson arrives. He is supposed to be here the first week of January. What if something happens in the meantime?"

"There is no point in me going to Silchar six weeks early, Manik," I said. "Raja said if he hears any further news he will pass it on to us through his uncle Bimal Babu at Aynakhal. If things get really bad, Raja's mother is going to leave. I can leave with her."

"So Prasad Sen is behind it all!" Manik exclaimed. "This is the same Communist party that is creating all the problems at the Fertility Hill. I didn't know he was the party leader. I really think he is out to take personal revenge on me."

"Or on Dadamoshai. He is not happy because Dadamoshai forced him to take Kona back."

"Well, he can't do much to rile up Aynakhal labor for sure," said Manik. "We have a very loyal labor force here. They got a big bonus this year, and they are not interested in getting unionized. Besides, they fully trust their managers to take care of them."

I was suddenly not so sure. I knew the quality of tea-garden management began at the top. The General Manager was the head—the mind and brains of a tea plantation; the assistants were his arms, and the Jemindars in charge of the *chokri challans* were the legs that moved the entire labor force. Good labor management was at the heart of all successful tea gardens. More than knowledge or expertise, it took integrity, sound judgment and excellent people skills to be a good *Mai-Baap*. The *Mai-Baap* had to be firm, fair and above reproach. Holly Watson had misused his power and kicked a coolie to death. I wondered if violence was inherent in his nature—like an elephant with a bifurcated tail?

I believe from that day onward, everything began to change in Aynakhal.

Work in the tea plantation slowed during the cold season. There was no plucking, only pruning, fertilizing and maintenance work in the growing areas. The machinery in the factory was overhauled and new roads and labor lines built. Our bungalow was undergoing structural repairs.

There were many changes in the weeks that followed. Manik was appointed Acting Manager and expected to "hold the fort" in the interim till Holly Watson arrived in the third week of December to replace Ian McIntyre. Larry Baker got his transfer and moved to another Jardines garden in Dooars, leaving Aynakhal to find a new Junior Assistant. Meanwhile, we moved temporarily into the McIntyre's old *burrabungalow*.

It felt strange living there. Audrey McIntyre's well-ordered household and beautiful garden seemed to belong to somebody else: it was like stepping into another person's perfectly tailored but ill-fitting clothes.

I noticed a change in the *borchee* the very first day I arrived. He looked sullen and discontented and had an insolent air about him. No matter what menu I specified for the day, he cooked what he pleased, mostly bland and unimaginative food, hurriedly thrown together. One time we got mulligatawny soup three days in a row. When I questioned him, he gave me airs and acted as though it was beneath his dignity to take orders from an Indian memsahib. I also found out he hardly came into the kitchen anymore and the *paniwalla* was doing all the cooking. I finally had enough of him.

I told him to take extended leave. "Report back for duty when the new memsahib arrives. I don't need you in this bungalow any longer." I made it clear he understood that he was taking leave without pay. The *borchee* was not one bit happy about it.

The bearer was slipping up, as well. His uniform was dirty. The tea tray was left lying on the veranda long after it should have been cleared. When I rang the bell he took his own sweet time to answer it, and sometimes he did not come at all. I was heavily pregnant and often laid up in bed. One time he asked to take the day off, claiming he was sick. Later that day on my way to the Ashtons, I saw him at a political rally in an open field just outside Mariani. I gave him the "extended leave" ticket, as well. Halua and Kalua were temporarily assigned in the *burrabungalow*. It was much easier managing with the known devils. I did not want to bother Manik with my domestic issues. He had enough on his hands as it was.

The Fertility Hill was causing serious problems. The devotees trespassed through Aynakhal using an illegal shortcut and created a nuisance. There were reports of petty theft, vandalism and opium trading. When Manik tried to block the shortcut, the Communist party landed up in Aynakhal and staged a protest outside his office. They were mostly hoodlums, and having entered the garden they tried to incite the Aynakhal labor. They declared India would soon be a free country, and there was no need to grovel and slave under foreign masters. Those servile days were over. Workers now had rights and could set their own demands.

The coolies were confused. They were a simple, tribal people; all they wanted was to be fed and taken care of by the *Mai-Baap*. Many were second- or third-generation tea pluckers: tea-plantation life was the only life they had ever known. They could not envision breaking free of the imaginary chain that bound them.

The evenings grew shorter, and night fell quickly after a brief and fleeting dusk. I missed our old *Chung* bungalow. I used to feel so much safer there somehow: it was like a fortress elevated off the ground, with only two entrances accessible by flights of stairs. You could see who was coming and going and observe animals at a close proximity from a safe place. In contrast, the Aynakhal *burrabungalow* was built on ground level and had several doors and tall French windows. At night the jungles seemed to creep inside. Most evenings I was alone in the big bungalow. Halua and Kalua left before it got too dark to get back to their own quarters in our old bungalow and Manik was often held up at the office dealing with various problems.

One evening—it must have been around six-thirty or seven—I looked out of the living-room window and saw a civet cat wander casually into the veranda. It scratched its whiskers on the edge of the cane sofa, lifted its tail and sprayed the legs of the coffee table, and then just as quietly wandered out.

I told Manik about it when he came home.

His face tightened. "From tomorrow, Marshal will stay here with you," he said.

★ ★ ★

I woke up to go to the bathroom and saw Manik's side of the bed was empty. I found him smoking on the veranda, wearing his old hunting jacket over his pajamas, his gun resting on his lap. Marshal was crouched beside him, looking keenly alert.

"What's wrong, Manik?" I said.

Manik looked startled. "Why are you up, darling? Please go back to sleep."

"Is it an animal? Why are you sitting here with your gun?"

Manik was silent. The tip of his cigarette glowed as he drew deeply. "I thought I heard something," he said softly.

I did not say anything but I knew it was not an animal he suspected. Marshal had a sharp, excited bark to warn us of prowling animals but a distinct throaty growl when it was a human—the suspicious kind.

I watched Manik's profile in the dim light of the veranda. A muscle twitched in his jaw. Lately he had been remote and preoccupied. He did not discuss Aynakhal's problems at home. Perhaps it was to keep me from getting worried, but this created an uncomfortable distance between us.

"You must leave Aynakhal after the Christmas party," he said finally. "Raja's mother and Bimal Babu's wife are going to Silchar on Monday. I want you to go with them. We got news today that the situation in Mariani is unstable. Riots have broken out around the railway station. Mariani has a big Muslim population, as you know, but now the Communist party is holding their rallies and touting Hinduism and this has the Muslims up in arms. Then to add to it all there is the Fertility Hill issue."

"I heard the Fertility Hill shrine is not even a Hindu shrine," I said. "I don't even know what it is. Jamina used to go there, and she is a Muslim."

"It's a very ancient pagan shrine that's been there for hundreds of years. The Communist party is claiming it as a sacred Hindu shrine. They are using this as an excuse to enter Aynakhal, only to stir up trouble." Manik leaned forward to stub out his cigarette and rose to his feet. "Let's go to bed, darling. Whatever was out here is gone." He held out a hand to help me up. "Goodness! We are going to need a crane to haul you up soon."

We made our way back into the bedroom. Manik did not bother to take off his hunting jacket. He lay in bed with one arm flung over his eyes, his gun on the floor beside him. His breathing was short and sharp, the muscles in his body tense. Every now and then his eyes flickered open and I saw the whites move in the dark.

Torn by nerves and concern, I just lay quietly beside him. How very different he was, I thought, from the Manik I once knew who slept blissfully spread-eagled on our bed and woke in the morning, his eyes clear and calm from sleep. The Manik who whispered in a teasing way and loosened my hair to feel it fall over his face. I hardly recognized this stranger with his flat, unseeing eyes, his fingers constantly twitching for cigarettes.

In just another ten days, I would have to leave Aynakhal. I wished Holly Watson would hurry up and take over the garden. Manik was only the Acting Manager, and Aynakhal's problems were ultimately the General Manager's responsibility. I hated to leave Manik alone, but I had no choice. There was our unborn child to think of. As if on cue, the baby turned over and kicked in my stomach.

CHAPTER
32

The next day, Flint, the Kootalgoorie assistant, went missing. The company jeep he was driving was found abandoned on a deserted forest road close to Mariani. Three days passed and a wave of panic swept through the tea gardens. Just when people started fearing the worst, Flint showed up in Kootalgoorie riding a bullock cart and wearing women's slippers. He described how hoodlums had ambushed his jeep on his way to Mariani and seized his gun. Luckily, it was an old blunderbuss, complicated to use, and Flint—being the street-smart fellow he was—always carried a small extra firearm in the glove compartment. He shot his way out, commando-style, hid in a *bamboobari*, crawled across rice paddies and landed up at Auntie's, where the Sisters of Mercy took him in. He remained in hiding for two days, his head covered in a sari, before he could make it back to Kootalgoorie.

Flint was hailed as a hero at the Mariani Club. The young assistants wolf-whistled, called him "sister," threw a bar towel over his head and danced with him on their shoulders. Flint joked he had so much fun eating fish and rice and hanging out with the Sisters of Mercy that he seriously contemplated giving up his planter's job to join Auntie's establishment, in any capacity, he didn't care what. The *lahe-lahe* life suited him just fine.

But despite the jocularity, the grim reality of the situation was not lost on anyone. One thing became clear: the roads had become unsafe, and planters could no longer travel alone. Every trip had to be reconnoitered. Now the garden truck was sent ahead to check out the road situation, and sometimes coolies were posted along the way. But the disturbing news was that bungalow servants were often in cahoots with thugs, who bribed them with opium to pass the word when the sahib was headed out of the tea garden.

The attendance that Monday Club night was spotty. Nobody played bridge or shot darts. Nobody got rip-roaring drunk. The men talked quietly around the bar to share the latest updates. There had been rumors of kidnappings and ransom demands in other parts of Assam. Now that the war was over, many planters were sending their wives and children back home to England. The risks were too high. Not even the ayahs and servants could be trusted any longer.

"It's our guns they are after," Flint said. "Everybody knows planters own guns."

"Who are the 'they'?" asked Peewee.

"From what I gathered at Auntie's, they are Communist hoodlums," Flint replied. "Some are members of small guerrilla groups, others part of larger organizations. They are trying to collect arms in any way possible. Tea planters are easy targets because we travel alone on open jungle roads. Many of these hoodlums want to enter the gardens to incite labor to rise up against management. They call themselves union leaders but they're just thugs."

"Just as well you have a high ranking with the sisters," Larry laughed. "I must say your loyal patronage paid off this time."

"I have lots of insider tidbits to share, fellows. You won't believe," said Flint with a mischievous wink.

"What?" said Peewee Williams, leaning forward eagerly. "Oh, Flinty, do tell!"

Flint glanced slyly at Debbie and me. "Ladies, you may want to close your ears. This is strictly for the lads."

"Not a chance," Debbie shot back. "I want to hear every bit. G'on, tell us, Sister Flinty. Pretend I'm a barstool or something."

"Larry, old chap, remember how you wondered about the ladies' rosy derrieres? The sisters actually *color* them," Flint said. "They sit in tubs of tinted water to make their bottoms *pink*. I am not joking, fellows. It's a daily ritual with the sisters. They use some kind of red foot paste to color the water."

Alta, I thought to myself. *How very curious I had never heard of this.* The whole business sounded completely ridiculous. I did not say anything. The subject matter was too personal for my comfort.

"And here I thought it was au naturel," said Larry, feigning disappointment.

"They must look like monkeys with their pink bottoms." Debbie nudged me and giggled.

"But I can tell you it's *very* attractive," said Flint. I got the feeling he was about to launch into seamy details. Mrs. Gilroy waved to me from across the room and I beat a hasty retreat.

Mrs. Gilroy was sitting alone in the cushioned area. She patted the seat next to her and flashed a toothy smile.

"Have a seat, dear. My, my, we are carrying quite a load, aren't we! I am sure your feet could do with some rest. So, when is the little one expected?"

"In another six weeks, Mrs. Gilroy," I replied, thankful to

be sitting down. The three-legged barstools were certainly not designed with pregnant ladies in mind.

"I must say you are looking very well. Oh, I must tell you, I received a letter from Stella, a cousin of mine. She is a writer and lives in Cornwall. She said she knows your grandfather. He is also a writer, I believe. Now, isn't that a small world?"

"Stella? Estelle Lovelace?"

"That's right. Stella was the brilliant one in the family. She went on to study in Cambridge and I married Nathan and moved to India. But we have kept in touch. I invited her to visit us in Assam, although this may not be the best time with all the political problems going on. I think you would really enjoy meeting her, Layla."

"I know I will," I said. "I've heard wonderful things about Estelle Lovelace."

Mrs. Gilroy left and I, reluctant to abandon the comfort of the sofa, sat and waited while Manik finished his drink at the bar. The usual clique of ladies had gathered next to the empty card tables. Betsy Lamont was wearing a tight red dress that made her bottom stick out like a tom-tom. Laurie Wood, in stark contrast, was dressed like an English schoolgirl in a plaid skirt, black stockings and a turtleneck sweater. Then there was Fiona Clayton, a horsey-looking woman with enormous teeth, and finally Molly Dodd, the dreadful slouch. The four of them looked like mismatched cousins at a family reunion.

"D'you s'pose the Christmas party will be canceled this year?" asked Molly, lank-haired and doleful. She had a terrible pigeon-toed way of standing.

"Who cares," said Betty. "I'm off to Manchester. Assam gives me the shudders. Danny sacked the *chowkidar* because he thinks he's conspiring against us. Danny is getting more and more paranoid these days. Now he's up all night thinking somebody is going to attack the bungalow, and he is miserable to be around in the daytime. I've just had it with this place."

The others averted their eyes. Everybody knew—courtesy of the Jungle Telegraph—why Betty Lamont had "had it" with Assam. The Hullock apes must have reported her, because Danny Lamont came home one day and found his wife making hot chutney with Charlie the pilot.

"I don't think I could leave my husband and just go off with a clear conscience," said Molly virtuously. "After all, he needs me the most right now. It would not be the right thing to do." She looked to the others for reaffirmation.

"Well, stay here, then," Betsy snapped back heartlessly, "and good luck. India has obviously rubbed off on you. No doubt you will go down as the most devout wife in history. Next you'll be covering your head and walking ten paces behind your husband. I have no such aspirations, thank you."

"Well, *I never!*" cried Molly with an indignant squeak. "That was jolly unfair, Betsy. I just don't think it's—"

"Oh, stop your damn bickering, you two," Laurie interjected, tossing her ponytail impatiently. "As far as I know, the Christmas party is still on, but I don't think there will be many people attending it. Gemma and I are going back home. Johnny is making me nervous. He tells me to keep an eye on Gemma even if she is playing in the garden. I am so used to just leaving her with the ayah. It is quite nerve-racking, really."

"Is Johnny still applying for a transfer to Dooars?" asked Fiona. Her eyes kept flitting to the bar, where her husband, Greg, was steadily knocking back his *burra* pegs. He was a notorious drunk, famous for falling off the three-legged barstools.

"No, we decided against it. We hear the trouble in Dooars is worse than Assam. We may move to Papua New Guinea or

Kenya eventually. Gemma will enjoy the animals in Kenya, but she will soon be five and schooling is a problem."

"That Alasdair Carruthers transferred to Dooars, didn't he? And married his ugly *chokri*, did you hear?" Betsy said.

"*And* got kicked out by the company for it. Serves him right. He's with some third-rate Indian tea garden now," said Laurie. "Well, what did he expect? Why did he have to go and *marry* the *chokri*, for God's sake. It makes no sense."

"Maybe he got her preggers," said Fiona.

Laurie snorted. "Oh c'mon, like that's something new. *Chokris* get knocked up all the time. Nobody *marries* them. The half-breed runts are just packed off to Doctor Graham's orphanage in Kalimpong. At least the little bastards get a decent education."

"Maybe Alasdair Carruthers wants a legal heir," said Molly, who seemed to have recovered from Betsy's jab.

"Oh, I could have given him that, easy," said Betsy. "I'd gladly give him an heir for a few heirloom diamonds. No problem."

Fiona gave a neighing laugh.

"He's a bit of an oddball, but a rather nice-looking chap, really," said Laurie. "He seems to be only interested in his *chokri*, though. I don't know what he sees in that ugly midget. She must be a witch."

I was so enraged, hearing their spiteful talk, I wanted to heave myself out of the sofa, barge in with my big stomach and tell them a thing or two. But Manik was gesturing me over from the bar, indicating we should leave. As I got to my feet, I thought sadly about Jamina and wondered what the ladies would say if they heard about her heirloom diamond, how meaningless it was to her and how gladly she would have given it for a baby. Jamina didn't care if the child was a legal heir or not. All she wanted was something soft to love and to hold.

The Christmas party was a nostalgic affair. For many planters it would be their last Christmas in Mariani, and for some, their last in India. The Ashtons, McIntyres and Larry Baker were all leaving. Despite the constraints, Mariani old-timers were determined to make it a Christmas to remember.

Father Christmas was late for the children's party. He finally made his appearance wafting whiskey fumes with every "Ho, ho, ho," and perched on top of a decrepit old elephant with a white star painted on its forehead. Emma Ashton stared at Father Christmas with angry blue eyes, punched him solidly on the arm and said loudly, "Uncle Jimmy, what have you done with Father Christmas?"

Father Christmas "Ho, ho, ho"ed in denial.

"Then take off your hand socks and show me your fingers at once," Emma demanded sternly, pointing at his white-gloved hand where one finger hung empty. Father Christmas insisted a reindeer had bitten off his finger, but Emma remained unconvinced.

A big sausage-shaped piñata—a Mariani Club Christmas tradition—was filled with puffed rice, hard candy, copper *naya paisas*—*new coins*—and tiny toys. Father Christmas took a number of badly aimed swipes before the piñata broke open and the goodies rained down. Young folk engaged in the traditional puffed rice fights, shrieking and stuffing handfuls down each other's clothes. They skidded and slid all over the floor pretending it was snow.

By late evening the tots were packed off with their ayahs and the real party began. No club party was ever complete without live music. The Mudguards, a rookie band made of young assistants with their homemade electric guitars and noisy drums, arrived just in the nick of time. Their microphones screeched terribly, but they belted out a hard beat and made the dance floor thunder. There had been doubts whether the Mudguards would make it this year, but Jimmy O'Connor drove the several hundred miles to Dooars, piled them up in his open jeep and brought them to Mariani. Little wonder Father Christmas was late for the children's party.

A group of merry RAF fellows showed up, Flint's cousin, Eddie, among them. The war now over for real, they had survived Burma and were finally heading home. Charlie the pilot swaggered in with three gorgeous air hostesses on his arm— Shireen, Maureen and Candy. There was something close to a stampede among young stags to bag dances and soon a brawl broke out amongst them. Somebody got hit on the head with the microphone. Lonnie the drummer cowered behind his drum set while the two guitarists dived under the Ping-Pong table. It all ended amicably with free rounds for all. To everybody's surprise, Candy, the dark-eyed, pretty air hostess, got moon-eyed over, of all people, Peewee Williams. *Peewee Williams*—that baby face! I took a closer look at him. To my surprise, I realized in just six months Peewee had transformed dramatically into a tanned and strikingly handsome young man with windswept hair and all the debonair airs of a French Riviera lover boy.

After midnight the Mudguards packed up and the music was turned over to the club's gramophone. The lights dimmed and Perry Como's "Till the End of Time" swept over us in soft sentimental waves. Manik held me close, a little awkwardly, my big belly between us. A deep sadness like a desolate river fog was creeping over me. *I will be gone in two days*, I thought miserably, choking back a lump. *Manik will be alone.* The world felt precarious and close to a tipping point. I could see nothing beyond, but I got the feeling there was a deep, dark abyss, looming somewhere, waiting to swallow me whole.

Leaving Manik on that foggy December morning was by far the hardest, most painful thing I have ever done. I was traveling to Silchar with Raja's mother and two other ladies in a private taxi. During our last days together, the thought of going away had consumed my every waking moment and tormented my dreams. The pain was almost physical. At night the tears came and would not stop.

"Don't cry, my love." Manik's eyes were soft with sadness. "I'll come as soon as I can get away. I'll be with you when the baby is born. It won't be too long now."

On the morning of my departure, we waited silently on the cold veranda, me huddled in my shawl, my tea untouched. The taxi arrived and my suitcase was loaded. I covered my face to hide my tears. Manik held me wordlessly for a few moments. "Don't worry," he whispered, kissing the top of my head before I got into the car. I turned back to look at him one last time as he stood in the middle of that big circular driveway. He looked so utterly alone: a tall, thin man in a brown suede hunting jacket, hunched in the cold, his dog by his side. The trees behind him loomed pale and gray, and I watched through tear-blurred eyes as he disappeared from my view, swallowed by the morning fog.

We drove out of Aynakhal just as the fog was lifting and passed through Mariani, still shuttered with sleep. A black, sticky haze hung over the town, and there was the acrid smell of burning rubber in the air. The roadside tea stalls had not yet opened, and a few huddled beggars stirred at the railway crossing. The plywood factory appeared to be abandoned: piles of

logs lay haphazardly in the yard and graffiti defaced the factory boundary walls. A few miles outside Mariani, the Assam-
Bengal goods train looked as though it had been halted in its
tracks. The hinged side door of a trolley car hung open and
piles of coal lay strewn over the tracks. The rust-colored bogies had been scratched over with political slogans. As we drove
through the main section of town, we saw that several shops
had been gutted and burned. It was a relief to finally get out of
Mariani into the peaceful Assam countryside. Here the world
was unchanged. The mist trailed like a delicate chiffon scarf
over the rice fields, and the frail winter sun was inching over
the bamboo groves.

It was only in hindsight I realized how lucky we were to pass
through Mariani unarmed that day. We got the news that violence had erupted only hours after we had driven through; the
bloodshed and mayhem that followed carried on unabated for
days. The local police had not been able to control the mobs,
and several people were killed in the clashes. When I heard
the news, all I could think of was there was only one road in
and out of Aynakhal and it was through Mariani. Mariani was
now a minefield and Manik was on the other side.

There was no news from Manik for the next ten days. Then
James Lovelace sent a telegram from Calcutta to say that the situation in Aynakhal was still tense, but that Manik was safe. The
only news of Aynakhal the head office received came through
Charlie the pilot, who flew in and out of the Dega airstrip.

A few days later Bimal Babu, the head clerk of Aynakhal,
arrived with a letter from Manik. He was a thin, earnest man
with a receding hairline. The situation in Mariani was temporarily under control, he reported, but each day fresh hordes
of political hoodlums arrived by train, and there were rumors

of further clashes in the days to come. Manik had ordered the Aynakhal office staff to vacate the garden. Only Baruah, the Compounder Babu in charge of the hospital, had chosen to stay back to take care of the critically ill.

"I am sorry, madam," Bimal Babu said, wiping his forehead with a white handkerchief. "I would not have left Aynakhal. But Sir insisted. Some of us have our missus and small children to think of, you see?"

"How bad is the situation in Aynakhal?" I asked. I found it difficult to breathe. I fingered Manik's letter, dreading the contents, but I needed to get firsthand news from a reliable source. I knew Manik would paint a softer picture in his letter.

"The union has *gheraoed* the office," said Bimal Babu. His eyes darted nervously. "They want to shut down the factory. The coolies are getting harassed if they report to work."

"Have the coolies joined the union?"

"No, madam. The coolies have no such interest. These are just outside people who want to make trouble. They are calling themselves union leaders. Many are just the *goondas* from the Fertility Hill, madam. Troublemakers. They just want money. What can I say?"

"Is there any news when Mr. Watson will arrive?"

"No, madam. He is still on furlough. There is no definite word when he is joining Aynakhal."

I was silent. I wondered if Holly Watson had heard of the trouble and was deliberately delaying his arrival.

"I think Sir is relieved that you are here in Silchar, madam. In your advanced condition, it was not safe to remain in Aynakhal. When is the little one due, may I ask?"

"In about three weeks. Do you think Mr. Deb will be able to come to attend the birth?"

"It difficult to say, madam. Sir may reach some settlement

with the union soon. This *gherao* cannot go on forever. Also, Mr. Watson is expected any day. I don't think Sir will leave Aynakhal unattended unless somebody takes charge. The *goonda* elements are looking for a chance to take control over the garden. I think the Jardines company people are trying to get the Mariani police involved. But the situation in Mariani is hopeless."

"What is the latest in Mariani?" I asked.

"Oh, madam, I cannot even begin to tell you!" Bimal Babu was silent for a few moments. "It was with great risk we drove through Mariani. Several times we feared we were going to be attacked. All the shops were burning, madam. Near the plywood factory *goondas* threw kerosene on a man and burned him alive. I had to cover my children's eyes, madam. There were dead bodies lying on the road." He looked away. "In some respects, Mr. Deb is safer in Aynakhal than Mariani. At least the trouble in the garden is not Hindu-Muslim related. Union problems can be solved peacefully by negotiation."

"But, Bimal Babu, you say the *goondas* from the Fertility Hill are the ones creating trouble. They have a religious agenda, do they not?"

"Yes, so they say," said Bimal Babu, "but they are only troublemakers, madam. They are using the Fertility Hill as an excuse to enter Aynakhal. Sir carries his gun to the office and the dog is there at all times. Nobody dares to come near the dog."

I thought gratefully of Marshal. Marshal would not let anybody get within ten feet of Manik; that much I knew. He would guard Manik with his life.

"I must take my leave, madam," said Bimal Babu, getting to his feet. "I regret to bring you all this bad news, but I am hoping the trouble will be over soon, and then we can go back to our normal lives. I wish you a safe delivery, madam. May

I come and visit you in the hospital? I expect you will be at the Welsh Mission?"

"Yes," I said. "Thank you, Bimal Babu. I needed to get first-hand news of Mr. Deb. I feel better knowing what is going on than getting no news at all."

CHAPTER
33

Aynakhal
2nd January 1947
Dearest wife,
I think of you and our baby all the time. I hope you are both doing well. I am thankful you left when you did because the situation in Aynakhal has deteriorated. The company has given me the choice to evacuate. This puts me in a dilemma because this is exactly what the union goondas are looking for. Our laborers are still on the side of management but they are powerless and cowed down. If we abandon them now they will feel betrayed and we will lose Aynakhal. But don't worry, darling. It is now simply a matter of time before the union backs down. They have to because they are getting no support from our laborers. I just have to hold firm till this deadlock breaks.

This brings me to the sad news. I may not be there for the birth of our child. This grieves me more than I can say. Even if the union relents, I cannot leave Aynakhal without someone in charge. It's uncertain when Holly Watson will join us. He is still in England, as far as I know. I am relieved Mima will

*be with you soon, darling. Silchar is still very safe from what I
hear. Maybe it is because of the presence of the military there.*

*I don't think we discussed names for the baby, did we? If it
is a girl, will you please consider naming her Jonaki? The name
came to me one evening as I watched the fireflies. It has a pretty
sound, don't you think? This child is a spot of brightness in
my darkest hour. She is my firefly. On the other hand, if it's
a boy, please choose a name, darling. But something tells me I
will have a daughter.*

*I end with my love to you, dearest wife. Please be well for
our sake.*

M.

The Welsh Mission Hospital in Silchar was built for expatriates. It had a residential feel to it and looked more like
a Governor's mansion, with its finely manicured lawns and
sweeping marble stairway. From the windows of my room on
the second floor, I could see the tall front gates and past the
curved driveway that opened out on a busy street. The gates
were locked and manned by armed military guards. I caught
fleeting glimpses of passing cars, people and rickshaws. Once
in a while a procession of people marched by, shouting slogans
and carrying flags and banners.

Maria, the Anglo-Indian nurse, breezed into my room. Her
starched uniform looked as though it had been ironed onto her
flat-chested body, and a white cap resembling a small paper
boat sailed gaily in her black, wavy hair.

"Oh, you are wakie-wakie, love," she said. "Your grandfather and auntie came to see you but you were sleeping. Auntie
came straight from the railway station."

"Why didn't someone wake me up?" I asked.

"They were talking to Doctor Hughes. Your auntie has gone home to change. She will come back in an hour, she said."

I felt a small stab of worry. "Nurse, is something wrong? I have not felt the baby move since my water broke."

"Hush, dear. Baby is ready to come out. Doctor Hughes will be here in a few minutes to talk to you."

Just then Doctor Hughes walked in, snapping on a pair of rubber gloves. He was a tall, handsome English doctor, who looked like a faded movie star. "Well, well," he said. "Let's see what's going on here. So, how do you feel, Mrs. Deb?"

"The same," I said.

He examined me and said something to Nurse Maria. She looked at her watch and scribbled on a clipboard.

"I am afraid we will have to pull this little monkey out," said Doctor Hughes. "I have to do a Cesarean, Mrs. Deb. The good thing is you won't feel a thing. The bad thing is you will take a little longer to heal."

"Can we please wait for my aunt to arrive?"

"I am afraid I can't risk that," said Doctor Hughes, pulling off his gloves. "Your aunt will be upset, and I am going to get the short end of the stick from her. She wanted to stay, but I told her we still had time. But looking at you now, I don't think we should delay the operation any further."

He turned to Nurse Maria. "Prepare OT. Doctor Harrison to assist."

He patted my arm. "Try and relax now. When you wake up, you will have a brand-new baby."

"Layla, Layla, wake up, *maiyya*." Mima shook me gently. "Don't you want to see your baby girl?"

"A perfect little angel, she is," said Nurse Maria as she propped up my pillows and helped me sit up. I felt dull and heavy but there was no pain. It must be the medication, I thought.

A tiny bundle was placed in my arms. The baby's face was a fiery red. A plume of black hair shot out from the top of her head like the tail of a comet. Her eyes were squeezed shut and the tiny pink fingers of one hand opened and closed like a delicate sea anemone.

"I wonder what color her eyes are," I said, feeling a little strange holding the minuscule creature.

"They are dark brown, like Manik's," said Mima. She gently tickled the baby's cheek. The baby turned her face toward the finger and opened a pink gummy mouth. "Little Jonaki is hungry."

"Do you like the name Jonaki, Mima?"

"Of course I do. After all, I chose it, didn't I?"

"I thought it was Manik…"

"Stop! That man is always trying to take credit for everything. Little Jonaki knows it was her Boro-mima who named her."

"Has Manik got the news?"

"Yes, Calcutta Head Office sent word."

"I wonder what his reaction was. He always wanted a daughter."

"He said, 'So what, who cares,'" quipped Dadamoshai, coming into the room. "Layla, what do you think of the name Jonaki for the baby?"

Mima looked at him sternly. "Dada, I came up with that name a long time ago."

"Why," said Dadamoshai, round-eyed with surprise, "I was the one who thought of the name. In fact, when we were talking on our way home from the station—"

"I suggested Jonaki—" said Mima fiercely.

I caught the twinkle in Dadamoshai's eyes. He was teasing

Mima of course. I had told him about Manik's letter, and he liked the name. Between the time Mima got off the train and arrived at the hospital she was firmly convinced, the baby's name was her idea. Who dared to argue with that?

I smiled at them and said softly to little Jonaki, "It is your daddy who named you, baby. You are every bit his little girl."

Jonaki. *Firefly.*

The baby gave a tiny little shudder and opened her eyes. She gazed at me peacefully with the fathomless wisdom of an old soul. The whites of her eyes were a silvery-blue, the pupils dilated and shining. How I wished her father could touch those tiny dimpled fingers and feel the velvet of her cheek against his own. She was the tiniest, brightest little thing in the universe, only my heart cried out silently because Manik was not there.

A week passed and there was still no word from Manik. This was getting worrying. Dadamoshai used the courthouse to make a trunk call to the Jardines Head Office in Calcutta. He came home with some disturbing news. I was giving Jonaki an oil massage before her bath when he walked into my room.

"The new manager is not going to join Aynakhal," he said abruptly.

"Holly Watson? What do you mean?"

"The company found some serious corruption charges against him. He has been fired."

My heart was pounding. This was extremely bad news. "So who is going to take over Aynakhal?"

"They don't know yet, *maiyya*. The company is trying to sort that out."

Dadamoshai said it sounded as if Manik was expected to stay on as Acting Manager until Jardines figured out a new game plan. The new assistant, Desmond Williams, who was going to replace Larry, had arrived from England only to land in Calcutta in the middle of a deadly political riot. He was holed up in his hotel room, and Charlie was unable to fly him out to Aynakhal until the situation calmed down.

It was just as well, I thought. A new assistant would be more of a headache than help to Manik, given the current situation in Aynakhal. New assistants took a while to adjust to a tea job. They had to be spoon-fed and mentored. Who was there now to show him the ropes? Manik had his hands full. Aynakhal at that moment was a headless entity, with one barely functioning arm and paralyzed feet. This was a very bad situation indeed.

There was also news that the trouble in Mariani had escalated. The police station was attacked and several policemen lynched by the mob. The army had been called out, but was unable to get to Mariani because the Dargakona Bridge had been damaged by a pipe bomb.

I looked away. The deep fear that was filling my body erupted in a silent howl. I looked down at Jonaki as she lay there, a tiny seashell curled on the white sheet. A tear rolled down my cheek and plopped on her little brown belly, where it trembled like a dewdrop. Jonaki looked up at me with her sweet, peaceful eyes, so bright and clear that I saw the sky from the open window reflected in them. They were Manik's eyes looking back at me.

The next day Hindu-Muslim riots broke out in the Muslim village across the river. We were in the middle of dinner when the first flames licked up into the night sky. Soon long rows of houses lit up like a string of firecrackers and the entire village blistered and burned in a bloodred sky.

None of us slept that night. A feathery dawn had broken over the river. Tattered smoke spiraled over the treetops from the still-burning village. Panic now swept through the Hindu section of the town on our side of the river. Everybody feared a deadly retaliation. Shop owners barricaded their doors, the fish market did not open and not even a pariah dog ventured out into the deserted streets.

"Hai bhogoban!" Mima cried. *"Such madness!"* "Why did they have to attack the peaceful village? They were such simple fisherfolk who never troubled anybody. Now the Muslims will want an eye for an eye. Didn't Gandhi say, if Hindus and Muslims each took an eye for an eye, the whole country would be blind?"

I sat on the old plantation chair on our veranda as a fine silvery ash settled on the wooden armrests like a silent ghost. I was not thinking about what Gandhi said or the splintered politics of our country. I was thinking only of Manik. Suddenly he seemed so far away, so impossibly out of reach.

The turgid silence of the ashen dawn was broken by the lonesome sound of a *baul* plucking his *ektara* as he traversed between two hate-torn worlds divided by a river with no bridge across it. He sang of man's betrayal and sorrow. Only a *baul* could rise above this madness, without judgment, powerless but unafraid.

Then the boats started coming across the river filled with half-dead, broken people; men with beaten bodies; women with vacant eyes; children with voiceless cries. They crawled across the rice fields, begged from door to door, sometimes with not even a rice bowl to beg with. One morning we found a small group huddled on our doorstep: an old man and a young mother with her two infant children.

"Save us!" the old man cried, falling at Dadamoshai's feet. "Oh, save us! Our house is burned, everything gone. All gone!" He raised his upturned hands to the sky. "Hai Allah have mercy!" he implored. I gasped when I recognized the ravaged face: the old man was none other than Jamina's father!

The woman covered the lower half of her face with the torn end of her sari. She stared straight ahead with unseeing eyes. A newborn infant, hardly a few months old, drooped listlessly on her shoulder and a small toddler clung to her legs. The woman's name was Reza, we learned. She was Jamina's brother's wife. I recalled the menacing tattooed man with the sickle-shaped scar from Jamina's wedding. Jamina's brother had stormed out of the village vowing revenge on the Hindus. They feared he would never return.

Dadamoshai gave them shelter. It was risky harboring Muslims at that time, but who in his or her right mind ever dared to tell Dadamoshai what to do? After all, he harbored all kinds of people in full daylight: fallen Hindu women like Chaya, Russian communists like Boris Ivanov and even a bad-luck child like me. This confused people because nobody quite knew what he was about or whose side he was on.

"Why should these people hide like thieves? What have they done?" Dadamoshai tapped his umbrella furiously on the floor. "Let me see who dares to come after them. They will have to cross this threshold over my dead body."

Jamina's family slept on our veranda. I could hear them outside my bedroom window: the soft sucking sounds of a nursing child, the prattle of a toddler and sometimes late at night the muffled sounds of a woman crying.

Late one night I woke up and lay in bed listening: there was another man's voice on the veranda. I parted the curtains and saw the shadowed back of a stranger. Reza's husband had secretly come to visit her. At daybreak, when I looked out again he was already gone.

★ ★ ★

The next day the postman arrived with a telegram.

"It's for you," said Dadamoshai, handing it to me.

Telegrams were either good news or bad news. I had a sinking feeling about this one. I opened the pink sheet with trembling hands.

MANIK DEB INJURED STOP *CONDITION SERIOUS* STOP *DETAILS TO FOLLOW*
STOP
JAMES LOVELACE

I passed the telegram to Mima, left the veranda silently and went to my room. I lay facedown on my bed and everything started shaking violently all around me. I finally broke and my tears came in great hacking waves. Through the dense wall of my sorrow, I heard a thin, monotonous wail—persistent and forlorn. It was the sound of my baby crying.

Nothing could have stopped me that day. No riot, no earthquake, no flood—not even my five-week-old baby daughter. I had to get to Manik somehow.

The situation in Silchar had turned ugly. The violence had spread from the village to the town. There were reports of looting and killing. Very few vehicles plied the roads and gangs of young hoodlums had taken to the streets brandishing *khurpis* and sticks. There were rumors of mosques and temples being burned, women raped.

I lay in bed thinking. The only way I could get to Manik was to take the passenger train from Silchar to Mariani. From Mariani I would have to figure out a way to get to Aynakhal. I would just have to take it one step at a time.

I knew Jonaki would be safe with Mima and Dadamoshai, safer here than any other place I could think of. I would ask Reza to be her wet nurse. How ironic, I thought, a Muslim woman breast-feeding a Hindu child when all around us Muslims and Hindus were killing each other.

I told Dadamoshai and Mima my plans.

"But *how*, Layla-ma?" Mima cried. "Please have some sense. This is complete madness. Do you have any idea how risky it is? Nobody is going by train anywhere. They are full of *goondas*. I don't even know if the trains are running properly. God only knows how long it will take you to get to Mariani, if you get there at all. You will get killed, Layla. You will get raped. A young woman like you, on a train alone. Please have sense, *maiyya*. You are a mother now…you have a child to think of." She turned to Dadamoshai in panic. "Dada, stop her. We can't let her go like this!"

Dadamoshai was silent.

"Manik is seriously hurt, Mima. How can I sit here and do nothing?" I said quietly. "All I ask is you take care of Jonaki. Reza will breast-feed her while I am gone. I have already spoken to her."

"Layla-ma, I know you are upset, but please try to *think* clearly," Mima pleaded. "The situation in Mariani is terrible. *Terrible*. Even if you reach Mariani, how will you get to Aynakhal from there? It is what—fifteen miles?"

"I have not thought that far, Mima."

"Dada, how can you remain quiet? Why are you not saying anything?" Mima wailed.

"When do you plan to go, *maiyya*?" asked Dadamoshai.

"I want to leave immediately. On the next train, if possible. I know there is one that leaves tonight at seven-fifteen from Silchar station."

"I am going with Layla," Dadamoshai announced.

"No, Dadamoshai!" I said sharply. "I am doing this alone. You must stay here. I know people in this house will be safe only if you are here."

Mima ignored me. "Layla-ma, please, listen to me," she said. "You just had a Cesarean operation and your body has not even healed. If you ask any doctor, they will forbid you to travel. You are seriously risking your health, *maiyya*."

"She will go whether you like it or not, Mima," said Dadamoshai. "There is no point trying to talk her out of it. I know Layla. Once she has made up her mind, you can't change it."

"*Hai bhogoban!*" Mima wailed. She covered her face with both her hands and howled like a child. I stared at her in shock, I had never seen Mima cry. Mima could be angry, belligerent, outraged, upset and indignant, but *Mima crying*! I could hardly bear to look at her. After a while she dried her eyes with the end of her sari. "You must take chili powder in your purse, Layla-ma," she said, "and by God, you are going to need it this time."

Amrat Singh, the Police Chief, offered to drive us to the station in his jeep with armed guards. On the way he tried to talk me out of what he called my "suicide mission."

"Layla, please think about this carefully," he said. "I want you to fully understand the gravity of the Mariani situation. The CRP was sent there. You know what the CRP is, don't you? It's the special paramilitary police force used for dire insurgencies. We heard even the CRP could not enter Mariani. There is complete anarchy there. Now there is talk about the army being deployed. *The army!* Do you see how serious the situation is? As yet, we have no count of the total number of people killed."

I did not say anything.

"The mobs have infiltrated several tea gardens near Mariani," Amrat Singh continued. "Most planters have left with their families. The unmanned tea plantations have fallen into the hands of *goondas*. Only a few planters remain. The Irishman involved in that rhino case is one of them who has stayed back. The crowds are afraid of a white man with a gun. What I don't understand is why Manik did not leave the tea garden when he had the chance."

Manik did indeed have the opportunity to leave Aynakhal, but it was not something he would ever do. The responsibilities of a *Mai-Baap* had been deeply ingrained in him by his ex-boss, Mr. McIntyre. Manik would argue Mr. McIntyre would never abandon the tea garden during a crisis, nor would someone like Jimmy O'Connor. If a manager gave up control of a garden, chaos would reign and the damage would be irreparable. The delicate politics of labor management in a tea garden was not easily explainable to an outsider so I did not even try.

The Assam-Bengal passenger train pulled into the platform at Silchar station. The station was deserted except for the policemen and Dadamoshai. The train was running empty.

Dadamoshai stood forlornly on the platform holding his umbrella, unable to speak a word.

"Please leave, Dadamoshai," I said softly. "I don't want anybody to see me getting on this train." I lightly touched his fingers and slipped quickly inside a bogie. It was filthy. A number of bluebottle flies had entered through the open window and buzzed over the dirty leaf plates with remnants of rotting food under the seats. All I carried with me was a small cloth bag, with some dry food packed by Chaya and a water bottle. I was dressed in an old sari; I covered my head and did not wear a single piece of jewelry or carry a purse. I switched off all the lights and huddled in a corner of the seat. The compartments had no doors. If anybody glanced inside, hopefully they would not see me and go away. I kept window shades pulled down, but left a four-inch gap at the bottom through which I could see a slice of the platform. It was stale and stuffy inside the train, making it difficult to breathe.

The train gave a series of metallic squeaks as it pulled forward. I saw the moving concrete and occasionally a pair of feet, sometimes a bundle lying on the platform. Then it gathered speed—the silver rails snaked together and parted, growing farther and farther apart. Soon we were in the open country-side speeding through purple-green rice fields deepened by the fading twilight.

The rhythmic rocking of the carriage invited sleep, but I was sharply and acutely alert. A few small stations rattled by, washes of concrete with amber pools of light. They looked deserted. Then the dark night swallowed us as the train steamed toward Mariani.

Small bits of gray ash floated in through the crack in the window. I could smell burning. We passed by a crowd of ragged villagers holding burning torches. They ran alongside the speeding train trying to clamber aboard. I caught a glimpse of a blood-soaked child in a woman's arms. Then everything washed away into the night.

Suddenly, I realized I was not alone. I heard the twang of the one-stringed *ektara* and a nasal voice singing a folk ditty. It was a *baul*. I saw the flash of his orange garb as it passed by my doorway. How I envied him! If only I was a *baul*. Only a *baul* could travel anywhere unharmed. No Hindu or Muslim would think of lifting a finger against him.

I felt an enormous sadness when I thought of little Jonaki. I wondered if I would ever see my little baby again. She was my little fallen star. I yearned to touch her honey skin and feel her tiny fingers curl tightly around my thumb like the tendrils of a fern. How thrilling it was to see that beautiful mouth open in a perfect heart-shaped yawn and see that dimpled smile as she chased her dreams. How I wished Manik could see his little daughter. Would Jonaki ever know the funny, handsome man who was her father? What if I never returned? She would grow up an orphan. I had chosen to undertake the most dangerous journey of my life and anything could happen. But one thing I was sure of—Jonaki was safe and would be well cared for. Who I worried about was Manik. *Injuries serious*, the cryptic telegram read. Would I reach Aynakhal to find him *dead*? Would I reach Aynakhal at all? I felt sick with worry. But now there was no turning back.

The train was slowing as it pulled into what looked like a major junction. I looked at my watch; it was midnight. Judging by the distance we had traveled, that would be the town of Lumding, halfway to Mariani. We passed several open trailers of an idling freight train. Then the brakes squealed and groaned before the train came to a shuddering stop. I heard the sound of running feet on the platform. Shouts. I peered through the gap in my window and my heart froze: there was a mob beating a man. The man howled like an animal, covering his face with his hands as the men rained down blows on his head and body with thick, stout sticks.

"Kill the Hindu dog!" one of them yelled.

The man went down and the hoodlums kicked his lifeless body, which was unresisting, soft and pulpy, his limbs flung at odd angles. Finally he just lay there in a broken heap, a dark pool forming around his head.

I felt the bile rush to my throat. The gang loped down

the platform, whooping and catcalling to one another. They banged on the doors of the train and ran their sticks along the metallic walls of the compartments, making a staccato noise like a machine gun. The sound grew louder and louder and then stopped outside my compartment. A stick poked through the window as someone tried to pry the window open from the outside.

I could see the bottom half of a man's face, his teeth stained red from chewing *paan*. "Motherfucker," he muttered before giving up.

Somebody wolf-whistled from the front end of the train. The man banged the window angrily and then took off running down the platform. The train was beginning to pull forward slowly. The platform was empty. This meant one thing only. The men had boarded the train.

We must have been traveling for about half an hour when all of a sudden the wheels screeched, sparks flew on the tracks and I was thrown violently from my seat onto the floor. My compartment rattled and shook as the train came to a shuddering stop. Somebody had pulled the emergency chain. We were in the middle of nowhere. It was pitch-dark outside. Shouts broke out. A flashlight swung, lighting up a steep embankment, and dark shadows clambered down. I counted about twenty men. They carried sticks and I saw the flash of curved *khurpi* knives tucked into their waistbands. The men took off into the dark night, calling out to one another. I could tell they were running across a paddy field because their flashlights bounced up and down as they navigated the narrow dividers. One of them howled like a jackal and the others took up the chorus. Somewhere in the distance, dogs started barking, first one followed by the others. I saw the outline of palm trees and huts against the night sky—a village—the men were headed in that direction. I thought of the poor villagers peacefully asleep in their mud huts. Little children curled beside their sleeping mothers. What would they wake up to?

The engine panted like a sullen beast as it idled on the tracks. Suddenly a loud whistle shrilled followed by a shuddering intake of steam. The compartment squeaked and jerked, then haltingly moved forward as the train started down the tracks.

I sat back in my seat and closed my eyes. The tautness in my chest slowly subsided. At least the men had got off the train. I had not even taken a sip of water all this time, fearing I would need to use the bathroom. I took out my water flask and had a drink, stood up and stretched my legs for the first time in four hours. Then I decided to sneak a trip to the bathroom. I passed a long row of compartments. There were no other occupants in the carriage besides me. Most of the compartments were full of trash: rags, bundles, bottles and rotting garbage.

Back in my compartment, I figured I should have something to eat. In my cloth bag I found an apple and in the small zippered pocket a tiny pocketknife. I smiled, thinking of the day I got the pocketknife. It was a gift from Dadamoshai.

We were eight years old, Moon and I, when Dadamoshai returned from one of his trips to England. He had been invited to give a talk at a college in the small town of Sheffield and brought back two tiny gifts for us. Next morning we found them under our pillow: exquisite blue velvet boxes with some kind of kingly crest stamped in gold. They looked unbearably precious. We wondered what was inside.

"I think it's crown jewels," said Moon. "Maybe Dadamoshai stole them from the castle."

The inside of the case was lined in velvet, and snugly nestled in the indent was a curious item the size of my little finger, covered in a shimmering mother-of-pearl. Mine was cream-colored and Moon's slightly pinkish. We turned them over in our hands, completely bedazzled.

"What is this thing?" I asked.

Moon snapped awake and sat up in bed. There was a big pillow crease on her cheek. "It's a crown jewel," she said decisively. She put her gift carefully back in the case, shut the lid and fastened the tiny scalloped clasp. Then she closed her eyes and inhaled the box deeply. "It's very expensive. Maximum expensive."

"What is a crown jewel? What do you do with it?"

"You put it inside your crown," said Moon, vaguely.

"Why?"

"Because it is very expensive and you can get robbed. So you keep it inside your crown. There is a bowl inside the crown to keep maximum expensive things. Rubies and diamonds and...and crown jewels."

That somehow did not sound right. "I am going to ask Dadamoshai," I said, clambering off the bed. Moon followed me, kissing her case. Dadamoshai was in the veranda reading the papers.

"Ah, so you found your gifts, I see. Here, let me show you," he said. He opened my box and took out the object. The morning sun captured tiny gold glints in the mother-of-pearl, making it look even more bejeweled and precious. Dadamoshai pushed his glasses over his forehead, gripped a tiny notch on the side and pulled. A shiny blade opened with a lethal click. Moon and I gasped with disbelief. It was a miniature pocketknife!

Mima floated onto the veranda in a tent-shaped African caftan with fierce rhino prints.

"Ma, look what Dadamoshai gave us," Moon cried, bouncing up and down on the sofa cushion. "A knife. A real knife."

Mima's eyes popped. "Good heavens, what is this? Dada, you should know better!" she cried in horror. "Why are you giving the children knives, of all things? They will hurt themselves."

"Not if they are responsible human beings," said Dadamoshai, giving us a sly look, "which I believe they are. Only sensible, mature people should rightfully own knives. Not hooligans."

"I would not be so sure," said Mima apprehensively. "But why give them knives?"

"What better way is there to teach them responsibility?" He looked at us. "The girls know if I ever see them use the knives to destroy things, to harm or intimidate anybody, I will not only take them away but I will be very, very disappointed. Now, somebody get me a potato from the kitchen. I want you both to learn the proper way to open and close the knife. You should also know how sharp the blade is, and if you are not careful, you can very easily slice off your finger."

Moon and I spent the rest of that day, and probably the better part of our summer, gazing at our pocketknives, taking them in and out of the cases and opening and closing the blades very carefully as Dadamoshai had taught us to. We whittled wood and cut tiny pieces of green mango and eventually got over our fear of the knife's potential to do harm. Whatever nefarious activities we may have been up to that summer, we never once misused our pocketknives. Nobody got attacked or had a finger cut off. We were not willing to jeopardize Dadamoshai's trust for anything in the world.

CHAPTER

34

I had barely sliced into my apple when I heard voices. My heart almost stopped. Men. There were several of them. They sounded as if they were near the toilet end of the carriage, about four compartments down. I quickly switched off my flashlight and squeezed myself into the corner of the seat, covering my head with my sari. I heard footsteps come down the passage, banging each compartment door. They stopped at the compartment before mine. I could see one of them lean against the window in the passage. He cracked a match and lit a bidi. The sharp flame illuminated his face momentarily. The man had a broad, pockmarked face, with narrow slitted eyes. He waved the match out, and the tip of his bidi pulsed in the dark.

"You are stoned, you fucker," another man said. "You damn nearly fell off the train. Don't grab me next time. I almost went down with you."

"I am so fucking tired," said another. "Don't think I have slept in three days."

"I have not fucked in three days. That last Hindu bitch was a good one. What was she—around twelve?"

"You animal, I could not do it. She reminded me of my kid sister."

"You are an asshole, Salim. Who is looking at the face?"

The men stood there smoking silently.

"Here, give me a drag," said the guy called Salim.

The cigarette passed hands, pulsed twice in the dark and got passed back.

My heart must have stopped. I sat there with the apple and pocketknife frozen in my hands.

A flashlight switched on and beamed down at the floor. Then it flashed inside the compartment next to mine.

"This one is a pigsty," the man said.

He walked over to my compartment, stood in my doorway and swiftly skimmed the inside. The beam grazed over me. He did not see me huddled in the corner.

He leaned against the doorway and yelled, "This one looks okay."

Other footsteps came down the corridor. The men entered my compartment. There were four of them. The beam swept the overhead bunks and around the compartment, passed over me, then jerked quickly back. The flashlight dropped with a loud clatter on the floor and rolled under the seat where it rocked from side to side, the long beam lighting up my feet. The man staggered, pushing back on the others.

"What the...? *Fuck!*" he yelled. "There's someone in here!"

"What!" Another flashlight clicked on. The beams pointed directly at me as I sat there with my face covered.

"I don't believe this," one of them said softly. "It's a woman."

He reached out with his stick and lifted the end of the sari covering my head, shining the flashlight directly at my face. He whistled softly.

"By God, look at those eyes? Is she real?"

"She's real, all right," said the man with the flashlight. He spoke softly. He tilted my chin up with the end of his stick.

He glanced down and saw the apple and the pocketknife on my lap.

"I am going to enjoy this. Maybe she'll share her delicious apple with me," he purred, tapping the fruit softly with his stick.

What was happening to me was so grotesque and terrifying that I experienced what I can only describe as an out-of-body experience. Suddenly I was not in the train compartment anymore. I soared high above and watched almost dispassionately at the scene unfolding before my eyes. Every drop of blood in my body had congealed. Every nerve, every muscle, every fiber was pulled taut to the breaking point. I even wondered if my heart had stopped beating.

Things started happening almost in slow motion: it was like watching a scene underwater. I was a marionette; my movements were slow and very precise. Somebody was pulling the strings, making me do things I had no control over. I saw myself lift the hand holding the apple. Then the other hand holding the pocketknife also lifted as if pulled by an invisible string. All this while I never once took my eyes off the man's face. I don't think I even blinked. I made two angled incisions in the apple and pulled out a tiny and perfect slice with the very pointed tip of the pocketknife and put the piece slowly and deliberately in my mouth. I chewed slowly all the while pointing the blade of the pocketknife toward the men. Then I repeated my actions. I have no idea how long I continued to cut tiny pieces of apple and eat it. Time had ceased to exist.

I remember observing dispassionately the men had their mouths hanging open. What I saw on their faces that day is something I will never forget: it was pure and abject terror.

Then the man with the flashlight turned abruptly and ran out of the compartment.

"It's a ghost!" he cried.

"Ghost! Ghost!" echoed the others.

Then one of them said, "You guys are assholes. She is just a woman trying to act tough. Did you see the size of that pocket-knife? What the fuck can she do with that?"

"If you were so sure, why didn't you jump her?"

"Just get Karim. He'll fix her."

"Guard that door. See that she doesn't get away."

"There's something wrong with that woman, I swear," said one of the guys stationed outside. "Why was she staring at us like that with those funny-colored eyes?"

Meanwhile, I had descended back into my body. Great spasms shook me violently. I could not stop my teeth from chattering. I looked down at the apple and noticed that I had cut a beautiful crisscross pattern into it. I had turned the apple into an exquisite work of art.

But my fear was now jagged and open. I was collapsed inside and filled with terror. Could I kill myself? I wondered. Jump from the running train? The men were blocking the door. I looked at the pocketknife. Suddenly the pip-squeak blade was laughable. I just had to await my fate. This was the end, I thought. The men would rape me and throw my body from the train. Nobody would ever find me. I would become just another nameless body decomposing in the rice fields. I thought of Manik lying wounded. I had tried my best to get to him, but failed. I was just grateful he was not there to see me die this way.

The voices got louder down the corridor. The men were shouting. I could hear another voice, deep and rumbling.

"The woman scared you assholes with a *two-inch pocketknife?*"

"And an apple. You should have seen the apple. I don't know which was more frightening, the apple or the woman."

"Her eyes. Her eyes are white, like a ghost."

"You fellows are fucking jokers," said the man in the gruff voice. "Move out of the way. Let me see this ghost."

A big bulk framed the doorway. The man carrying a powerful flashlight walked up to me. I smelled stale rice liquor on his breath and the acrid sweat of an unwashed animal wafting off his skin. He stood there breathing heavily. Blinded by the light, I could not see his face, but could make out the big bulk of his body and the dark tattoos on his arms. A thin gold chain glinted around his neck. I was completely drained. I felt life less, as though something in me had just drifted away. Only the shell of my body remained. I did not look at the man. I stared right through him.

The man abruptly switched off the flashlight. He turned and shoved the others crowding the doorway.

"Move!" he yelled. "Don't any one of you motherfuckers touch this woman. Do you hear?" There was a surprised silence.

"So you want to enjoy her all to yourself, is it, Karim?" one of them leered softly. "Come on, brother, share the goods. Let us have a piece of the action."

Karim turned around and slapped the man hard on the side of the head. He staggered under the blow.

"Did you not hear me, asshole?" he hissed viciously. "I will fucking kill any son of a bitch who touches this woman. You do not speak to her. Leave her alone, do you understand?"

The train rattled past a small station. The light from the platform fell on Karim's face. I covered my mouth and choked back a cry. The man had a sickle-shaped scar on his cheek.

★ ★ ★

How I got to Aynakhal that day defies all probability. Small moments stand out in my memory. There was a lorry waiting for the men at Mariani station. I rode in the front seat of the cab, sandwiched between the driver and Jamina's brother, Karim. I remember seeing a small idol of Ganesha, the Hindu elephant god, on the dashboard. How ironic, I thought. Ganesha, the lord of new beginnings and the powerful remover of obstacles, in a lorry piled with Muslim hoodlums out to kill Hindus. Later I heard it was a stolen lorry from the plywood factory in Mariani.

Mariani had been reduced to a pile of rubble. The streets were empty, most of the shops cindered. There were piles of rotting garbage everywhere. A mangy pariah bitch with sagging teats crossed the railway tracks, tripping over her newborn cubs.

It was 5:00 a.m. when we reached Aynakhal. There were disturbing signs everywhere. The boom gate was yawning open, the guardhouse unmanned. We drove past the factory. There was a sense of eerie quiet. A pile of broken tea chests blocked the factory gate. A tractor with a twisted trailer stood abandoned in the middle of the road. The doors to the office were locked, but the long veranda was littered with garbage. It looked as though people had been camping out there at night.

"Which way from here, sister?" asked Karim. We had not spoken a single word the entire way. Something told me Manik would be at our old bungalow. As I directed the lorry driver, I was filled with a terrible dread. Was Manik even alive? All I knew was that he had been seriously injured. I had no idea what to expect.

The lorry roared up the hill. The monkeys were nowhere in sight. The bungalow roof came into view. We were just a short distance from the front gate when Karim shouted to the driver to stop.

"It is not safe for us to take the lorry any farther, sister," he said. "Somebody may hear us and shoot. We have to leave you here."

"Thank you," I said, clambering down.

"No mention, sister," said Karim in English. "*Inshallah*, this madness will end soon."

With that, the truck turned around and rattled back down the hill.

I walked to the gate. It was wide-open on its hinges. The marigold pots were cracked and broken. Manik's jeep was parked haphazardly outside the portico. I lifted my sari and started to run toward the house.

"Manik!" I screamed. "Manik, please, God."

I heard barking. A black streak bounded down the stairs. It was Marshal. He galloped toward me. He had a crooked limp and his thick fur was caked and matted with blood. His eyes were wild and he was foaming at the mouth. Seeing me, he whined and collapsed at my feet and rolled over.

Then I heard Manik's voice. "Who is there? Stop! Or I will shoot!"

"It's me, oh, Manik!"

I ran up the stairs, and there he was slouched over his gun in torn and bloody clothes. Manik looked up briefly. His glasses were missing; his left eye was closed and misshapen. When he saw me, his gun clattered to the floor.

"Layla," he said, stunned. "How did you come here? Where is the baby?"

Manik had an open wound on the side of his head, his hair was clotted with blood and his arm hung at a funny angle, but he was alive.

Tears streamed down my face and he collapsed into my arms.

The servants had fled the bungalow. The pantry and kitchen were deserted. I filled Marshal's water bowl and found some stale bread, which I broke into pieces for him. All Manik

wanted was a cigarette and a stiff shot of whiskey. I heated a
kettle of water to give Manik a sponge bath. He had not bathed
in two days and had not budged from the veranda in the past
twenty-four hours, nor had he eaten. My stomach turned when
I saw his wounds. Manik's back was striped black-and-blue
with stick beatings. He had trouble breathing. And when he
coughed, there was blood.

"I feel your tears on my back, Layla," he said softly. "Please
don't cry, darling. I will live, I promise. I will not die without
seeing my daughter."

Just hearing him say that made me feel better. I mixed Dettol with water in the basin and washed his wounds. I found
one of my sari petticoats in the cupboard, cut it into long strips
and bandaged his wounds as best as I could.

"They are still around—the men," said Manik. "They will
try to get into the bungalow to kill me. But Marshal is there.
He saved my life, Layla."

Bit by bit he related what had happened. For the past three
weeks, the union leaders had held protests outside Manik's
office. The crowds were getting harder to control. Every day
the tea pluckers were harassed on their way to the plantation
and the factory workers threatened. The union leaders hi-
jacked the tractor bringing in the leaves from the plantation.
They beat up the driver and overturned the trailer, throwing
the leaves on the road. Despite everything Aynakhal was still
managing to function.

One day a young coolie reported that there was elephant
trouble in the plantation. It was only in hindsight Manik realized that this man was a well-known troublemaker who had
been recently suspended from work.

Manik drove to the section where the trouble was reported.
He found a tree felled across the road. He assumed that it was

the elephant's doing. Had he been a little observant, he might have noticed that the tree had been chopped down. He got out of the jeep to investigate, leaving his gun in the car, when five or six men hiding in the tea bushes jumped on him. Marshal ran to his rescue and savagely attacked the men, ripping flesh from their bones as they tried to fend him off with sticks. Finally Manik fell into a culvert and Marshal stood guard over him so ferociously the men did not dare to come near. Most of them had suffered Marshal's bites in one way or the other. Some of them had serious injuries: one had his face bitten terribly and another had his arm in shreds. They had no choice but to leave. That was when Manik crawled out of the culvert, got into the jeep and drove home with Marshal. They had been holed up in the bungalow ever since.

Later that day, the men returned to break into the servant quarters and chase the servants away. At night they tried to enter the bungalow, but Marshal was always on guard and Manik fired several rounds from the veranda.

Then Manik stopped talking abruptly and looked at me through his wounded eye. "How did you get here, Layla?" he asked. "Who brought you from Silchar?"

I sighed. Given the state he was in, I didn't think Manik could stomach the details of my grisly journey. "It's a long story," I said finally. "I'll tell you about it sometime."

Manik would not stay in the bedroom. He rested on the veranda, but refused to sleep while I kept a lookout with the gun. He ate six boiled eggs and drank half a bottle of whiskey, but managed to stay alert and sober.

Around 2:00 p.m. Jimmy O'Connor's jeep drove up. Peewee was sitting in the back, brandishing two guns, one in each hand. There was another man on the passenger seat: he turned out to be a doctor who had flown in from Calcutta with Charlie. His name was Doctor Watson and he was from the Woodlands Hospital.

Jimmy said the army had finally reached Mariani and the violence was now under control. A contingent was on its way to Aynakhal. The miscreants had heard of the army approach and fled.

The doctor checked over Manik, administered first aid and gave him a morphine injection. "Mr. Lovelace has told me to bring you back to Calcutta," he said. "We will be leaving in a couple of hours."

"Who will take charge of Aynakhal when I am gone?" Manik asked.

"I would let the company worry about that," said the doctor. "Right now you need medical attention."

"And Marshal—"

"Marshal will stay with me," Jimmy said.

Manik looked at him. "You are not leaving Dega?"

"Hell, no," Jimmy said. "That's out of the question. Williams here has volunteered to stay, as well. We have the coolies to take care of."

Manik was silent. "Are my injuries life threatening, Doctor?" he asked quietly.

"They are serious," the doctor replied. "I suspect you have multiple breaks in your arm, broken ribs and a head injury. My worry is you may be hemorrhaging internally."

"But are my injuries *life threatening*?" Manik repeated.

"Well, depends what you mean—"

"I am not leaving Aynakhal," said Manik abruptly. "I cannot leave things the way they are."

"Manik, you have to," I insisted. "You need medical attention."

"Your wife is right, Mr. Deb. You may have a concussion, or serious internal injuries," the doctor added.

"I am willing to risk that, Doctor, but I cannot leave the garden. The Compounder Babu in the hospital, he's still here, isn't he? He can attend to my medical needs. We get plenty of broken bones down here, leopard attacks, factory accidents and whatnot. The Compounder Babu takes care of everything. I am in good hands, Doctor. Layla can go back with Charlie."

"I am not going back without you," I said, then unaware I was parroting Jimmy O'Connor, I added, "Hell, no. That's out of the question."

Manik bolted upright and pinned me with his bad eye. He looked alarmingly thuggish.

"What do you mean 'hell, no,' Layla!" he yelled. "I am shocked at your irresponsible behavior. You had no business to leave the baby and come here. I order you to go back with Charlie, do you hear?"

Order, did he just say *order*? The thunder went shooting straight up to my head. I had not survived a death-defying train ride, held off a gang of hoodlums and ridden in a truck to arrive at Aynakhal only to be bossed around by a patched-up Manik Deb or whatever broken bits remained of him.

"You can yell all you want," I said firmly, "but I am not going back."

There was an uncomfortable silence as we both glared at each other. The doctor looked at his shoes, and Jimmy O'Connor cleared his throat.

"I guess yer lass is staying put, Deb," he said with a grin. "Not much ye can do about it, aye?"

"I will have to report to Mr. Lovelace that your injuries are serious but you are choosing to stay back. He will want an explanation. What do you want me to tell him?" said Doctor Watson.

Before Manik could answer, Peewee shouted from the railings of the veranda.

"Manny, look! There's a big crowd gathering outside your gate!"

Hundreds and hundreds of coolies had collected outside our gate, some of them carrying baskets, bundles and marigold garlands. It looked as if the entire population of Aynakhal had descended on our bungalow.

"I should go and talk to them. They must be worried," said Manik, struggling to his feet. I offered him my arm, which he accepted. He turned to the doctor. "Thank you, Doctor. Please tell Mr. Lovelace that I will be all right. There is no need to worry. The Aynakhal hospital staff will attend to my immediate medical needs." He paused to catch his breath at the head of the stairs. "But if there is one favor I could ask of Mr. Lovelace, it is this. Can you ask him, as soon as it's safe, if he could please fly my baby down from Silchar in our company plane? My daughter is six weeks old and I still have not seen my baby's face. I want to see her more than anything else in the world."

With that, he limped slowly down the stairs, one painful step at a time. A loud cheer went up from the crowd as they surged through the open bungalow gate toward him.

Epilogue

Two years have passed. Cruel, relentless years, they were. India's hard-won independence was marred by the bloodbath of partition. The orgy of violence that followed the division of India and Pakistan would mark indelibly the generation to come.

Aynakhal remained remote and insulated. The peaceful Mirror Lake reflected nothing but the forest and sky. We heard the distant thunder and saw the war-torn clouds on the horizon, but the waters stayed calm, the lilies bright and full. Only the air became dense and charged and we became watchful.

Manik was appointed General Manager of Aynakhal the year following the riots. It was a hard-earned promotion—paid for in blood. We have both changed. We are still the same clay but remolded on the inside, and in some ways reinforced and stronger. Manik wears his leadership quietly, like a sabre: it's sheathed, but there. I see the flat steel in his eyes and the involuntary flex of his shoulder blades and, much as I try to, I can't read him anymore.

Jonaki is Manik's lightness, his release. He teaches her to

fly. He lifts her up on my grandmother's dressing table, steps back and swings like a catcher in a cricket field. "Jump, Jonaki!" he shouts. Jonaki flails her tiny wings and throws herself right into his arms. I hear Manik's easy laugh and see his eyes limpid with love, and I recognize the man I used to know.

Aynakhal tea prices continue to climb. The garden runs like clockwork, and Manik's reputation with the company is riding high. Manik managed to negotiate additional capital-expenditure funds from the company this year. It will pay for better labor housing, a new elementary school and rebuilding our old bungalow. Sadly, our old bungalow will be demolished soon. The roof suffered another collapse and white ants have eaten through the floorboards in every room. It looks as though rebuilding the entire bungalow will be cheaper than the repairs. The new bungalow will have a solid tin roof, modern plumbing, an attached kitchen and even a *jalikamra*. Netting off the veranda section will mean no more teatime with the fireflies. When you shut yourself in, you sometimes shut out the good with the bad.

I miss our old bungalow so much sometimes. I remember the blazing bougainvillea that tumbled over the veranda like a magenta waterfall, the soft wink of the lake through the trees. I wonder if my rose garden is still alive. Jimmy O'Connor was just teaching me how to graft roses before we moved to this bungalow. My regret is I did not stay there long enough to see anything bloom.

How I loved the sound of Manik whistling "Tipperary," his boots thundering up and down those wooden stairs. I never felt isolated in the old bungalow. The outside world was always within reach. If I looked out from the veranda, I would see little coolie children playing in the dirt outside our gate and women sitting around on their haunches, their baskets on the ground. The gates of the manager's bungalow where we live now is at the end of a long winding driveway and nothing is visible except trees from where I sit drinking my tea on the veranda.

I am suddenly filled with a longing to see our old bungalow again. Just one more time. A glance at the clock tells me it's three-thirty. Manik left for the office just a little while ago. It's a short five-minute walk from this bungalow. Jonaki is still asleep and her ayah, Lachmi, is there if she wakes up.

The jeep is parked in the circular driveway. I start up the engine and ease it out of the front gates and down the main road. A small choko boy runs alongside, spinning a bicycle rim at the end of a hooked metal rod. He stops to watch me and lifts his hand in a salaam. I drive through the tea-growing sections and past the factory wafting a heady smell of fresh tea tumbling through the dryers. When I reach the *bamboobari* I take the fork toward our old bungalow. The jeep groans up the hill, surprising the golden langurs that scatter from the middle of the road. The big male, the one with the lame foot, bares his teeth and chases behind the jeep. I honk outside our bungalow gate, but Potloo is nowhere to be seen. I open the gates, drive in and park.

All around me is a sense of unkempt desolation. The flower beds are overgrown and clogged with weeds. Waves of papery bougainvillea surge and roll in the wind tunnel under the porch. The wooden stairs groan as I climb up to the veranda, and my footsteps echo on the teak floors. Dust covers the coffee table. A wolf spider has fashioned an impressive web on the antlers of the mounted deer head, and the elephant-foot umbrella stand is stuffed full of old newspapers.

Overcome with nostalgia, I wander from room to room. A portion of the roof has collapsed in the living room right where our bookshelves used to be. In our bedroom the sari curtains are sun-bleached and sad, and the discolored mattress, folded in half over the bed, looks lumpy. In the bathroom I find a dead bat in the tub shriveled to a leaf. I open and close the drawers of the bedside tables. Something rattles and rolls inside. An old torch battery, I think. I pull the drawer open, and at the far back, it's our old butter knife! I sit on the metal frame of the bed, hold the cool blade against my cheek and smile, remembering. It seems like a lifetime ago.

Carrying the butter knife, I walk through the dining room, past the pantry and down the steps leading toward the back of the house. The kitchen door is barred with bricks. A pair of pigeons escapes in a sharp clatter of wings through the broken window. I notice they've built a nest on the old stovetop.

I wander out to the *malibari*. There is nothing there but a pumpkin patch with one distended pumpkin turned to seed. And in the far corner, what do I spy? A lovingly tended patch of marijuana! The cheerful leaves wave back at me like happy hands.

The rose garden is struggling. There are no blooms—no, I see there is one. It is a red rose. I turn its face toward me. It is a curiously shaped blossom with magnificent curly petals. Using the butter knife, I score the stem and break it off. The rose smells deep and sweet, and I fill my lungs with its heady aroma as I walk back to the jeep just as the four-thirty factory siren shrills through the air.

I must hurry. Estelle Lovelace is coming for high tea. She is here in Assam staying with the Gilroys. Such a lovely woman she is, with her husky voice and gentle manners. I was so taken by her, as is Dadamoshai. I had to manipulate Dada-moshai's visit to coincide with hers. Estelle and Dadamoshai don't know they are meeting each other today, but something tells me they won't be disappointed. It's a lovely time of the year, the air calm and dusk falls softly. The rest, I think, I can leave to the fireflies.

★ ★ ★ ★ ★

Author's Note

I often am asked if *Teatime for the Firefly* is the real story of my parents. The answer is no. My characters Layla and Manik are very different from the people my parents were, and some of the things I have made the characters say or do would earn me a nice finger-wagging from my mother, were she still alive—bless her soul! Having said that, I will admit some incidents are true—my father's injury in the riots, for one, as well as my mother's horrific train journey, although the two incidents were unconnected. My parents were a rare and spirited couple, and nothing that I could fictionalize would ever fully capture the courage and integrity with which they lived. They are still fondly remembered and respected in tea circles all these years later.

Several books were helpful in my research for creating the cultural and historical backdrop for my novel, among them John Griffiths's *Tea, The Drink That Changed the World;* Jim Corbett's *The Man-Eating Leopard of Rudraprayag; The Wildlife of India* by E. P. Gee, and *Tea Tales of Assam* by W. Kenneth Warren. I also have drawn inspiration from photographs and planters' stories at *www.Koi-hai.com.*

Although this book contains actual historical facts and references to real places, it must be read as a work of fiction. The small towns of Silchar and Mariani, for example, have been reimagined, and the names of some of the tea gardens are real, but have no geographic relevance to the story. What I have tried to do, diligently, is to capture the authentic flavor of Assam and tea-plantation life. The story of the discovery of Assam tea and Sir Bruce tramping through the jungles has been colored by my overactive imagination. The same goes for the history of Assam and the riots in Mariani. My intent here was not to trivialize or distort facts, but to create a rich and layered backdrop for my story.

Shona Patel
Fountain Hills, Arizona
February 2013

Acknowledgments

Several people were instrumental in bringing *Teatime for the Firefly* to fruition. To them I owe my sincere gratitude:

The lively community of retired tea planters, who shared with me photographs and stories and answered my pesky, random and often irrelevant questions with humor and love. Davey Lamont, Larry Brown, Ali Zaman, Alan Leonard, Alan Lane, Ravi Lai, Roy Church and David Air, I owe it all to you.

Doctor Prithvish Nag, for being an invaluable sounding board for my research.

Kiran Grover, Maya Deb and Baruna Dey, for sharing stories of my parents' early life in tea.

Sarah Sharma, for human-friendly legal advice.

Rob Hall, my first writing teacher.

My early readers Anne Coe, Roxane Wellman, Elizabeth Boisson and Diana Kempton, for their insightful feedback. And WRC, my Wednesday writers group, for keeping me grounded.

My sister Mithoo Wadia, for excavating stories and being the kind of sounding board only a sister can be.

Mimi Dutt, my friend and tough-love critic, whose critique I value and trust.

Chet Ross, my mentor and secret ally.

April Eberhardt, for being all that I could ask for in an agent. Your wise counsel and unfailing support made me trust myself as a writer.

Susan Swinwood, my gifted and diligent editor, who felt the pulse of the story. *Teatime* is a fuller and richer novel, thanks to you.

The talented team at Mira Books, for their efforts in putting this novel together.

And finally with love: Vinoo, who built me the best writer's desk, who listens to my heart and always says WDGJ. Thank you.